Fly by Night

ALSO BY WARD LARSEN

The Perfect Assassin
Stealing Trinity
Fly by Wire
Thrillers: 100 Must-Reads
(contributing essayist)

Fly by Night

A Novel

Ward Larsen

Oceanview Publishing
LONGBOAT KEY, FLORIDA

ISBN: 978-1-60809-066-2

Published in the United States of America by Oceanview Publishing,
Longboat Key, Florida
www.oceanviewpub.com

2 4 6 8 10 9 7 5 3 1

PRINTED IN THE UNITED STATES OF AMERICA

To Mom

Fly by Night

PROLOGUE

BURCO, SOMALIA
HORN OF AFRICA

The young boy trudged up yet another dune and was breathing hard when he reached the crest. Squinting against the fading light, he scanned the next wadi for his wayward beast. Nothing. His grandfather's words came to him. *Never give yourself completely to either hope or despair. A wise man lives between the two.*

It was a regular thing for lambs to wander off at this time of day, but finding them was usually easier. The boy had been searching for a full twenty minutes, and if he didn't find the lamb soon he would be forced by the new moon to wait until morning. When he considered that the rest of his flock was roaming untended, the boy picked up his pace. With darkness gathering, the jackals would soon begin their rounds.

He kept moving, angling for the highest ground on the next rise. As he walked, his sandals kicked up tiny clouds of dust with each step, fine powder from the Sahara that had migrated a thousand miles east. It hadn't always been this way. The boy was only twelve years old, but even he could remember when the Golis Mountains had been awash with vegetation, before the soil had begun to dry up and blow away. Now he was forced to go farther each month, deeper into the plains of Togdheer to find sustenance for his flock. The other young boys did the same, trekking great distances to keep their families' tenuous prospects afloat until things got better. Things had to get better.

The next dune was unusually steep, and the boy felt sweat beading on his forehead, mocking the cool evening air. On reaching the top, he paused, and that was when he saw it. His spirits fell. The wretched creature was twenty paces ahead, clearly dead, its hooves sticking up at awkward angles, the head bent unnaturally to one side. As he moved closer, the boy's first thought was for himself—his father was going to give him a terrible lashing. His second thought was for his younger sisters, who would see their prospects of a prosperous marriage dim that much further. His family's wealth had been decimated in recent years, and here was another setback. Small, to be sure, but the most recent of a thousand cuts. The drought had taken their cattle and two goats, the warlords their modest home. The sheep were all they had left.

The boy stopped next to the carcass of his wayward lamb, and in the fading light he was struck by two curious things. First was the lack of blood. When the jackals worked there was always blood, staining the sand and trailing off into the desert as flesh was torn from bone and dragged away. And that was the second problem. No flesh was missing. None at all. He saw only a broken, misshapen corpse, like the poor creature had been hit by a truck. Yet there were no trucks here. The boy reached down with his hand and felt the body. Still warm. He stood straight and looked around cautiously. Whatever had happened, it had nothing to do with jackals.

It was then that he noticed the trench. Fifty feet away, a deep groove plowed through the sand, disappeared, then carried on again all the way to the top of the next rise. It reminded the boy of a vehicle track, although much deeper. And what kind of vehicle left only a single rut? A motorcycle? No, he decided. No motorcycle would ever cleave a path a full meter in depth.

The boy went to the trench, and as he closed in he began to see other marks in the sand, smaller and intermittent, but parallel to the first. It was definitely something man-made. He searched the area guardedly, listened for any sound. In this part of the world, anything having to do with man was trouble. Smugglers, soldiers, bandits. That was the norm. The few remaining nomad families led an increasingly anxious existence. The desert here was a lawless place, and the boy knew the wicked truth of this new desert order—a few sheep and a half loaf of bread weren't much of a prize. *He*, on the other hand, was of great value. Another reluctant conscript for someone's wandering army.

The boy hesitated, knowing he should just go back. Knowing that nothing good could come from whatever was beyond the next ridge. He stood still for a very long time, until his curiosity got the better of him. He began to climb carefully, quietly. At the top of the dune he peered over and saw—something. The boy tried to make sense of the dim image. It was very big, the size of a truck. But the shape was unearthly, a great wedge of angled metal, the color as dull and dark as a starless night sky. He looked around carefully, yet saw no one. He was still alone. The boy edged closer, not pausing until he was an arm's length away. There were wisps of smoke at the back of the wedge, wafting up slowly, almost delicately in the cool evening air. This made him abandon any thought of touching the thing. It seemed almost alien, like something from another world. Then he recognized the emblem on one side, an image that made the object seem very worldly indeed. The boy was not educated, could neither read nor write, but he had heard enough stories, seen enough Hollywood movies. He might not know how it had made its way here, but he knew what it was.

He tried to subdue his excitement. Carefully, just as his grandfather had taught him, he took his bearings using the stars. Then the boy ran. He bypassed the carcass of his lamb, and five minutes later went right past his flock. Twenty minutes on, he was completely out of breath when he reached his father's tent.

CHAPTER ONE

Jammer Davis was running hard. So were the other twenty-nine players on the pitch.

The deluge that had begun at halftime had slackened to a cold drizzle, but plots of standing water held fast on the rutted pitch. Not that anyone cared—this was, after all, the championship game of the Virginia Rugby Union Fall Classic. Over-30 Division.

Deep into the second half, the score was tied at twenty. Both sides chased the oblong white ball as it careened haphazardly over a mud-strewn field. Grass ripped out by the roots and players went sprawling into ankle-deep muck, all amid a muffled chorus of grunts and slapping skin.

The moment of truth came out of nowhere. It often did. A squat back from Davis' side scooped up the ball and, in the instant before he was flattened, slung a lateral to a teammate. The receiver was immediately corralled, but not before off-loading a long square pass that Davis caught in dead stride. He was the biggest man on his team, a prop forward with the traditional number eight on his back. And Davis was quick for his size. He beat the first tackler with a stiff arm. The second got hold of his thick legs, but couldn't hold on. Free of that challenge, Davis made a hard diagonal cut that left two defenders grasping air. When he picked up his eyes, he saw open field. Lots of it.

He had a head of steam now, legs pumping and arms churning. His left ankle hurt like hell. With twenty yards to go for the try, Davis had one man to beat. It was the biggest guy on the other team, an off-duty cop who had to go six-six and was as big in the shoulders as Davis. He was the cop you wanted to see walk through the door when there was a bar fight to be broken up. Not the prop forward you wanted to beat at the goal line with the game in the balance.

The guy took a good angle and made the cutoff, set his feet square, and waited. Davis had plenty of room. He could go left or right. The big cop knew it and waited for the move. Ten yards from victory, Davis stuttered a half step and saw what he wanted. The cop lightened on his feet for an instant, ready to react to Davis' change of direction. There wasn't one. In that critical moment, Jammer Davis dropped his shoulder and went full steam ahead.

Half a lifetime ago, in an even more miserable plot of mud, a drill instructor had taught Marine recruit Frank Davis an important lesson—size meant little without balance. Now that lesson was replayed. The impact lifted the cop off his feet and propelled him over the goal line. He landed flat on his back. Davis fell right beside him, bounced once on the ball, and came to rest in a heap.

"God dammit, Jammer!" The cop rolled up to a sitting position and put an exploratory finger in his mouth. It came out bloody. "That's the same tooth I had fixed last month. My wife's gonna be pissed."

"You cops have good insurance," Davis said. "And besides, your wife is a dentist. That's money in your pocket, Tom."

The cop spit out a mouthful of blood, then smiled big enough for Davis to see not one, but two misaligned teeth.

The referee blew the final whistle and muted cheers came from the sidelines. The teams began to mingle like two colonies of insects, one red with black stripes, the other royal blue on white. There wasn't much in the way of either celebration or agony. Just tired handshakes with hands on hips, a few predictions on how things would or wouldn't be different next year. Everyone gravitated to the sidelines where energy drinks in plastic bottles were snapped open. Damp towels stained with mud, sweat, and blood got draped over shoulders.

The captain of the opposing team came over. He was limping and holding a hand to his back in a way that would put dollar signs in a chiropractor's eyes. He handed Davis a beer, and said, "I guess the first round's on us, Jammer."

"Thanks, Mike." Davis took the bottle and tipped it back for a long draw. When the bottle came down, he froze.

It was a strange thing, trouble. Strange how you knew it was coming. Davis had always wondered if there really was a sixth sense, some aura or electrical impulse that shot out bolts of bad vibes. Or maybe it was based on smell, a hormonal aerosol that rode on the wind. But then, he'd never been good at biology or chemistry. All Jammer Davis knew was that his old boss, Larry Green, was standing on the far side of the field staring at him.

And he wasn't here to watch bad rugby.

Green met him halfway, his brisk runner's stride countering Davis' limping gate—his ankle still hurt like hell. They merged at the far sideline.

"Hello, Jammer."

"Larry."

"You look like a kid who just came in off the playground," Green said. "Well, times four, maybe."

Green looked like he always did. He wore dark pants and a sober gray sweater under an unbuttoned raincoat. Green was small and compact, with a lean, angular face. The haircut was strict regulation, high and tight, unlike Davis' own ragged mess. He'd been needing a trim for weeks, which somehow made him oddly uncomfortable in front of his old commander. Davis had worked for Green twice, first in the Air Force, and later with the National Transportation Safety Board. Their transition to civilian life had been concurrent, Green retiring from a two-star pentagon billet to take a high-level job at the NTSB. He was the kind of guy who always rose to the top. The cream. Davis had retired as a major with a résumé that was a lot shakier. More curdled.

"Did you catch the match?" Davis asked.

"A little at the end. You looked pretty good out there. Not that I would know. Rugby was never my sport—don't have the size."

"You'd be surprised. Some of those little guys can hit hard."

"Thanks, but I'll stick to my marathons." He pointed to Davis' ankle, and said, "That's going to be sore tomorrow. You know, Jammer, there are certain sports you can play forever. Golf, tennis, swimming. Rugby's not one of them."

"I'll give it up one day."

"Yeah. I've got a friend who says that all the time. He's an alcoholic."

Davis said nothing.

"So how is Jen?" Green asked. "Is that semester in Norway working out?"

Davis' eyes narrowed. He hadn't seen Larry in months, and couldn't remember if he'd mentioned the exchange program. "I talked to her yesterday. She's doing great. When she comes back in two months I'm sure she'll be all European. You know, converting prices to euros, putting bars through her handwritten zeds."

Green said, "I'm surprised you let her go, Jammer. You've always been a little heavy-handed with Jen. Especially since Diane died."

Davis' wife had been killed in a car crash, the kind of tragedy that strikes out of the blue. The kind of tragedy that only strikes other people. A friend of a friend, a distant relative. When it happened to Jammer Davis and his daughter it was like a hurricane, and ever since he'd made it his job to act as Jen's foundation, to hold things together. It didn't help that she was at that maddening age when kids start to separate anyway, start loosening their genetic tethers.

"She was getting restless," Davis said. "That's how teenagers are supposed to be, or so everyone tells me. I thought it was time to give her a little freedom."

"Norway is a long way from home."

"I know. But she's with Nordo and his family."

Davis saw instant understanding in Green's expression. Nordo was Sven Nordstrom, a Norwegian F-16 pilot who'd done an exchange tour with the squadron back when Larry was in charge. Nordo was a great guy with a terrific family, and he was the only reason Davis had let his teenage daughter fly off to Scandinavia for three months.

"So what's this all about, Larry?"

"That's what I like about you, Jammer. You think like I run—no wasted effort."

They began strolling the sideline.

"I've got a job for you," Green said.

"The kind where I fly an airplane or the kind where I pick up the pieces?"

"A crash."

"Where?"

"Sudan."

"Sudan? Africa?" Davis shook his head. "Don't airplanes ever crash in Tahiti?"

"Not lately. But if it happens, I'll take care of that one myself."

Davis still had his beer. He took a long pull.

"You know, that's not a good way to hydrate," Green admonished.

"Want one?"

"Honestly, it looks pretty darn good. But how about I buy you a cup of coffee instead?"

"That's not a good way to hydrate either."

Green waited impassively.

"You're serious."

No reply.

Davis sighed. "All right, coffee it is."

CHAPTER TWO

They found a coffeehouse two blocks south. It was a toney place, the very air inside seemingly brewed in rich aromas taken from exotic mountains—Sumatra or Colombia or Java—and flown halfway around the world. There was furniture the color of well-steeped tea on dark wood floors. The coffee was four bucks for a *venti*, which was Italian for big. Even at that price they had to stand in line, so Davis figured it had to be good stuff. He watched the lady in front of them pay eight bucks for what looked like a milkshake. When it was their turn he ordered a large coffee, plain and black. Green got a bottle of water along with the tab.

Davis was still wearing cleats with his warm-up gear, so when he followed Green across the room to a table his steps clacked over the hardwood floor. The shoes made him an inch taller than he already was, and the bulky clothing made him wider. He was limping on a sore ankle, and his wet hair was matted with sweat and grass, and probably traces of blood. In what had to be some sort of statement on contemporary society, nobody gave him a second look.

Green led to a pair of wide chairs in one corner that were covered in a supple, leathery material. Dark and smooth. Just like the coffee. Davis settled in and took a long sip from his cup. It really was good.

Green began his pitch. "What do you know about unmanned aerial vehicles, Jammer?"

"UAVs? They've become big business. As an ex-fighter pilot it breaks my heart, but the reality is that thirty years from now the Air Force won't have pilots flying tactical missions. It'll all be drones."

"I fear you may be right, that's where things are going. And I'm sure you know it's not just the military flying them. The CIA operates a big fleet. Intelligence, surveillance, even strike missions. Most of the airframes they use are common to Air Force versions, but the CIA has also undertaken a handful of black projects. One of the most recent is a vehicle known as Blackstar."

"Never heard of it," Davis said.

"That's good, because it's classified. They've been operating a handful of these airframes for about a year, based out of airfields in Saudi Arabia and Afghanistan."

"Okay. Good for them. Why are we talking about it?"

Green looked around the room. Davis noticed that the seats Green had chosen were as far as possible from the rest of the quietly chattering patrons. It broke a lot of rules to talk about classified information in a public place, and Larry Green was typically a by-the-book guy. But with a little discretion and a dash of common sense—it happened every day.

"I got a call from Darlene Graham yesterday."

This got Davis' attention. Darlene Graham was the director of national intelligence, a sharp woman who'd taken over a post that had been little more than symbolic for many years, and turned it into a powerful overseer of the old-school intelligence agencies. And while the NTSB didn't typically overlap with the D.C. intelligence community, a year earlier Davis had blurred the lines between the two when a crash investigation he'd been working on had blossomed into a full-blown global crisis. Working with Graham and the CIA, Davis had averted a disaster. Since then, he'd been on leave of absence to concentrate on his daughter.

Green continued, "The CIA had a Blackstar go Magellan on them last winter, just wandered off and started exploring after the uplinks and data feed stopped. Eventually, they lost it."

"Serves them right for not having a pilot on board."

Green smiled.

Davis asked, "Could it have been shot down?"

"Doubtful. The operators would have seen something. A fighter in the area, radar activity from a surface-to-air missile site. And it was flying too high to be hit by small arms fire. Since Blackstar is a brand-new design, the odds are it was just a technical glitch."

"But what does that have to do with us?" Davis asked. "We've never been in the UAV business. Those are exclusively military toys, including collecting the smithereens when one hits the dirt. If the CIA needs help investigating this crash, they should talk to the Air Force."

"It's not that simple. Blackstar was operating in the Horn of Africa, right on the border of Somalia and Ethiopia. After contact was lost, there was an intense search. Every imaging device we have scoured the area, but couldn't find a thing. In the end, the CIA decided it must have gone ballistic, ended up in the Red Sea or maybe the Indian Ocean."

"That sounds a little hopeful."

"You and I see it that way. We investigate stuff like this. But the CIA is just getting their feet wet when it comes to aircraft. They decided to write the whole thing off—that is, until last week."

"What? Did some fisherman pull up a piece of Blackstar in his net?"

"Worse. The CIA got an intel report that an advanced UAV of some kind was squirreled away in a hangar at the new airport outside Khartoum."

"But you said it went down east of there, in Somalia."

"Khartoum isn't that far away from the crash box. Certainly plausible. And when you consider the number of places you could stash aircraft wreckage in that part of the world—well, you get the idea."

"What was the source of this information?"

"Darlene Graham would only tell me that it was a reliable human source."

"Reliable," Davis repeated.

Green shrugged.

"So is this a government-owned hangar?" Davis asked.

"That's the funny thing. It's owned by a private party, an outfit called FBN Aviation."

"What do they do?"

"On paper they fly cargo, but in reality it looks like your standard shell company. It was set up in the Bahamas by a law firm that does that kind of work exclusively—Franklin, Banks, and Noble."

"FBN," Davis said.

Green nodded. "The company directors are three lawyers who probably couldn't tell a DC-3 from a salad shooter."

"DC-3s? People still fly those?"

"Apparently this company does. They work about a half dozen airplanes around Africa and the Middle East."

Davis had seen companies like it before. The corporate office in a place with loose regulatory oversight, the operations end set up in a dark corner of the world. From a distance, FBN Aviation would look a lot like UPS, a company designed to move air cargo. But up close it would look very different. There would be legitimate shipments, but mixed in you'd find arms and drugs and diamonds. You'd find record-keeping that looked like it was done in a mirror.

Green said, "The guy in charge is named Rafiq Khoury. He's some kind of cleric. Other than that, we don't know much about him."

"A cleric needs a cargo airline?"

"I didn't like the sound of that either."

Davis heaved a sigh. "Okay. So Darlene Graham lost one of her toys. And it might be sitting in a hangar owned by some kind of arms merchant. That doesn't explain why a cheapskate like you just bought me a cup of coffee. You said you had work for me, Larry, a crash. Are we talking about something besides this drone?"

"We are," Green said. "A DC-3 went down two weeks ago off the coast of Sudan, in the Red Sea. The exact location is a little fuzzy, but the crash site is clearly inside their territorial waters. Sudan has juris-diction."

"Let me guess—FBN Aviation."

Green nodded.

"Doesn't Sudan have people who can run an investigation?"

"There's a Sudanese Civil Aviation Authority, and on paper they have a guy in charge of flight safety. But he's just somebody's cousin, no formal training. Remember, we're talking about a country where over seventy percent of the national budget goes to the military."

"But if Sudan needed outside help, we'd be the last ones they'd ask. We were bombing them back in the nineties."

"True, but Sudan is in a tight spot right now. As you know, air carriers aren't allowed to fly international routes without ICAO's seal of approval."

Davis did know this. The International Civil Aviation Organization was the U.N. agency tasked to set worldwide standards for aviation. For developing countries, the bar wasn't set particularly high, but they had to go through the motions. Otherwise, they risked losing their certification and could find themselves without air service.

Green continued, "Sudan is in the middle of an ICAO safety audit. It's an inspection that comes around every five years or so. Teams go in and check out airline operations, air traffic control, safety programs."

"And suddenly they have a hull loss right in the middle of their paperwork party."

"Exactly. Sudan has to play this by the book, and the book says that when a nation doesn't have the expertise for full-up crash investigation, it has to bring in help."

"And the NTSB is their helper of record?"

"No, they actually use France. But the French are a little short-handed right now, and they suggested we might be able to help."

"How convenient," Davis said.

"Yeah, I thought so too."

"You think Director Graham had a hand in that?"

"Probably," said Green.

Davis surmised, "She thinks the crash of this jalopy DC-3 will give her a ticket to look inside that hangar. Or should I say, gives *me* a ticket."

Green nodded.

It was all starting to make sense. But Davis still wasn't satisfied.

"Larry, you have a lot of investigators. How did I draw the short straw?"

Green paused for a hit on his water bottle. He said, "You're the best guy for the job, Jammer. This is going to be a solo effort. No tech help from contractors or lab teams. Nobody in my office is as good on their own as you are. Sudan will make a show of going through the paces, but the truth is, they probably don't give a damn why this DC–3 went down. They might even not want to know—it could be that one of their air traffic controllers was at fault, or maybe their maintenance oversight is lacking. For the Sudanese, nothing good can come from any findings. They'll want an investigator who will come in, ask a few easy questions, then shrug their shoulders and go home."

"And you think that's what I'll do?"

The general smiled. "It's only important that the Sudanese think that's what you'll do. All we want is one look at that hangar."

And there was the endgame, Davis thought. A game he didn't like for one big reason. "So nobody really cares why this airplane went down."

"I never thought I'd say it, but in this case the cause of the crash is not an overriding concern."

"Unless you were the one who happened to be out flying that night."

Green grimaced. "Yeah—I had that coming. Tell you what, Jammer. Figure out why this sixty-year-old airplane went down, and next time I'll buy you a beer."

Davis reached for his coffee, took a long sip. He was nearing the bottom of his cup, which meant it was time for a decision.

"Larry, I appreciate your confidence in me, but there are a dozen people in your section who could handle this."

"Not like you would," Green argued.

Davis straightened up in his chair and stood. "Well, anyway, thanks for the offer. And the coffee."

Davis started to walk away.

Green said, "Bob Schmitt."

It hit Davis like an anvil.

CHAPTER THREE

Davis stopped in his tracks. Turned around and stared.

Green didn't say a word. He pulled a handful of papers from his pocket. They were folded in a military manner, neat hard creases that made them the size of a long envelope. Davis took a cautious step back and slowly held out his hand.

"Last page," Green said.

Davis began to unfold the pages, took his time and rifled through one by one. He was looking at a hastily thrown together briefing package, and definitely not the kind of thing the NTSB would assemble. It had to have come from Darlene Graham's office. He saw satellite photos of the hangar and airfield. A request for technical assistance from ICAO. And on the last page, amid the corporate profile of FBN Aviation, one name highlighted in yellow. Davis hadn't heard it in years. In truth, he'd never expected to hear it again. Bob Schmitt.

Davis settled back into the plush chair. "Was he one of the pilots in the crash?" he asked.

"No. There's not that much justice in the world."

Davis nodded, and the sorry Air Force career of Bob Schmitt came back like brown water over a failed levee.

The training process for military aviators is brutally efficient. Even so, a handful of misfits slip through, people who earn their wings yet have no place in the profession. Bob Schmitt was one of them. Technically, he was proficient enough. In truth, he'd been one of the best sticks in the squadron, always at the top of the bombing competitions, always a challenge in the air-to-air tangles. But what he lacked was far more critical. Integrity and trustworthiness. With Schmitt on your wing, you never knew what to expect. He regularly flew too low or too loose. Worst of all, he didn't see any problem with that. Davis had endured his share of terse debriefings with Bob Schmitt. After two tumultuous years, Schmitt had been transferred to a unit in South Carolina. Soon after, there was a crash, a midair collision. Schmitt was involved but ejected safely. His flight lead, Walt Deemer, hadn't been so lucky. Davis had known Deemer from the Academy. He was a good shit, which, in the parlance of the squadron, was the best you ever said about anybody.

Davis had seen his chance. He'd lobbied hard to be put on the investigation team and got his wish. The inquiry was short and quick, the evidence clear. Schmitt went to a Flying Evaluation Board and lost his wings. He was out of the Air Force a month later, lucky to have not ended up doing time in Leavenworth. That had been ten years ago; Davis hadn't heard the name since. Not until today.

"So Schmitthead is flying in Sudan."

"With a stain like he's got on his record—you can only fly the darker corners of the world. But it gets worse. Schmitt's not just a line pilot. He's the boss, FBN's chief pilot."

"You gotta be yankin' me. Bob Schmitt runs this circus?" Davis shook his head in disbelief.

"Jammer, when Walt went down . . ." Green hesitated, "I know you wanted to make sure Schmitt never flew again."

"And he didn't. At least not in the Air Force. That final report was rock solid. I nailed his ass to the wall, got everything I wanted except ten minutes in the alley behind the officer's club."

"So," Green said, "here's your ten minutes."

Davis eyed his old boss for a long moment, then turned his attention to the scene outside. Rain was falling again from a hard gray sky, and the coffeeshop window was peppered with mirror-like silver dots. People on the sidewalk were moving briskly against the foul weather, the typical leisurely pace of a Sunday accelerated by the elements. It was a day that should have kindled thoughts of fireplaces and cups of hot chocolate. But Davis had another picture in mind—Walt Deemer sitting in the living room of his military base house. They'd all gotten together for a Super Bowl or some equally vital event. It was funny how you remembered people when they were gone. No matter how vivid their personality, how encompassing the relationship, it all ended up as one or two snapshot visions. The exception for Davis was his wife, but he knew why—he had Jen, a living vestige, full of Diane's DNA-inspired mannerisms and features. But a buddy like Walt, he was forever a guy on a Barcalounger with a Budweiser, fist in the air as he cheered on his Packers. A good picture to remember.

Green read him perfectly. "Walt was my friend, too, Jammer. One of my guys, way back when."

"So you want me to take a look at FBN Aviation—as a pretext to see what's in the hangar."

"Something like that. And if Bob Schmitt gets caught in your crossfire—"

Jammer Davis nodded, completing that thought on his own.

"So are you in?" Green asked.

Davis sank lower in his chair. He twirled what was left in his cup, the dregs thick and silty and brown. He found himself wondering if they drank coffee in Sudan. Davis tried to divine a way out of it, some practical impediment. He couldn't think of one. Jen wouldn't be home until the end of the semester. He didn't have any other job right now. There wasn't even rugby practice for the next three weeks. No way out. But what really stuck in his mind was Bob Schmitt. The man had landed on his feet, even if it was in an African backwater. And now people's lives rested on his decisions. That was what clinched it.

"You know, Larry, you're a real piece of work."

"Coming from you, Jammer, I take that as a compliment."

"So whose payroll will I be on? NTSB or CIA?"

"Does it matter?"

"The way I see it, one makes me a consultant, the other a mercenary."

"I'll let you pick your job title. Meet me in my office tomorrow morning. I'll brief you on everything we've got. Then you can go to TMD and make your arrangements."

Davis was about to ask, *What the hell is TMD?* when it hit him. "Traffic Management Desk?"

"Yep. That's what they call the travel office now."

"Jesus, Larry. I'm beginning to think like the government."

Green chuckled. "Don't take it too hard. I'll see you in the morning." The general got up and walked off briskly, like he always did, and soon disappeared into the heavy gloom outside.

Davis tipped his cup and drained it. It might be his last good cuppa for some time. Which seemed like a really good excuse to go back to the counter and order a refill.

Davis woke early the next morning and started his day by scalding a cup of "Colombia's Best" in his three-cup maker. Soon after that he was standing over an open suitcase.

In the military they called it mobilization. The United States armed forces are a global fighting force, which means that any soldier can be ordered on a moment's notice to deploy anywhere in the world. The orders might be for a week, or they might be for a year, so the military has a hard-and-fast process to make sure everyone is prepared. You stand in line in a warehouse to be issued the necessities of your new life. Mobilization is not a happy process to begin with because you know you're heading far from home. Then you see what they're handing out. Gas masks, ammunition, Arctic sleeping bags, nerve agent antidotes, immunizations against rare infectious diseases. The JAG is there to make sure your will is up to date. The chaplain is there just in case you needed to talk. Davis had been mobilized many times, and he'd always thought it seemed like some large-scale, institutionalized omen. Bad things to come. Now that he was a civilian, the process was different. Davis was standing in his bedroom throwing clean socks into an old Samsonite roller bag with a broken wheel. He could have been going on a cruise. Even so, he was shadowed by that same ill feeling.

As he stood next to his bed wondering what he'd forgotten to pack, Davis picked up the cordless phone and dialed Jen's number for the third time this morning. He cradled the receiver between his ear and shoulder as he stuffed shaving gear into a pouch. On the fifth ring Jen's message came.

"Hey, it's Jen. You know the deal." A beep.

"It's Dad. I'm heading to Africa for an investigation. Call me."

He hung up and tossed the phone on the bed. That had been happening a lot lately, even before she'd gone off to Europe. He had two years left with his daughter, a tiny window that was shrinking every day. *And then what the hell will I do?* Davis grabbed a pair of work boots and threw them into the suitcase.

Probably what I'm doing right now.

Only after she'd gone had Davis realized how closely he was moored to his daughter. Jen had been away five weeks, and he was already starting to drift. He'd been lifting more iron at the gym, swimming a thousand laps in the pool, hitting harder in the rugby matches. But none of that was enough. When Larry Green had come calling yesterday, Davis hadn't been looking for crash work. He hadn't been looking for any kind of work. But here he was, throwing shirts in a suitcase, getting ready to fly off to one of the least developed countries in the world to look for a lost drone. Larry Green might say he was going because he had unfinished business with Bob Schmitt. But deep down, Davis knew the real reason he'd taken the job.

He'd realized it last year, in France, when an assassin had tried to gun him down. He needed the adrenaline rush, the thing that used to get satisfied when he flew an F-16 on the deck at six hundred miles an hour. Maybe Larry Green knew it. Maybe he had tried to make the job sound challenging, even impossible, just to lure Davis into it. A smart guy, the general.

Davis stood looking at the open suitcase, wondering if there was anything he'd forgottten. That, too, was something you learned in the military. No matter how well you prepared, there was always something missing, and you wouldn't realize what it was until you stepped off an airplane and into some godforsaken hellhole halfway around the world. But then, that was part of the challenge.

Davis zipped up his bag. Mobilization complete.

CHAPTER FOUR

Six thousand five hundred and fifty miles. That was the direct distance between Washington, D.C., and Khartoum. Davis had covered a lot more.

He noticed the pitch of the engine change as the Qatar Airways A-320 began its final descent into Khartoum International Airport. It was the final leg of an odyssey that would have given Homer pause. Altogether, four flights and two airport lounges, thirty-nine hours since leaving Larry Green's office. Adding the time zones, two calendar days. But Davis hadn't wasted the time. Much he'd dedicated to sleep, which was something he had a talent for. In his military days, Davis had spent two weeks in the desert sleeping under a poncho strung between a pair of cacti. He'd snoozed soundly in the crotch of a gumbo-limbo tree during jungle survival training. So a thirty-four-inch pitch seat in coach didn't bother him one bit, even if it was three inches shy of his own personal pitch.

He looked out the window and saw the city of Khartoum. Every shade of brown ever coined was there—taupe, tan, beige, coffee—all blended and fused, brewed into an angular urban landscape. In these last few minutes above the fray, Davis prepared himself. He mentally reviewed the information Larry Green had presented two mornings ago. It didn't take long. There had been almost nothing on Imam Rafiq Khoury, enigmatic cleric and head of FBN Aviation. Davis had seen one grainy photo of a slight man with an angular build, his limbs jutting out at awkward angles like he'd been snapped together using some kind of child's building set. The rest of him had been hidden behind a white turban, bird's nest beard, and dark glasses. Khoury's background held an even poorer resolution. He had appeared on the scene less than a year ago—nobody knew from where—to build FBN Aviation from scratch. That was all. Khoury and his company were like a holograph, something that changed its appearance depending on the angle from which it was viewed. Davis was not pleased. He liked to go into an investigation with knowledge, because knowledge begat clout. Ten minutes from now, and five thousand feet down, he was going to have precious little of either.

On final approach, the airplane rocked as it was buffeted by thermal turbulence, the same bumps you got anywhere in the world where the temperature changed by fifty degrees from day to night. The pilot handled it well, though, and brought the jet in to a nice touchdown. Davis appreciated a smooth landing. A gust of wind, turbulence from a departing heavy jet—it didn't take much to screw one up.

As the airplane taxied to the terminal, it struck Davis that there wasn't going to be anyone here to meet him. Nobody waving from a balcony or parked in a cell phone waiting lot. He didn't have a single friend in Khartoum, or for that matter, in all of North Africa. Possibly five hundred miles north, in a command post in Riyadh, Saudi Arabia. Davis might know somebody there, an old Academy classmate or a buddy from flight school. That was the best he could hope for. That was how alone he was.

Jammer Davis got off the airplane five minutes later. It felt like he was stepping into hell.

From the cool cabin of the A-320, the stairs delivered him to a blazing hot tarmac. It was a desert heat, languid air stirred by a choppy breeze. The sun was at its apex, pounding down from the dead center of a faultless blue sky.

Davis fell in with a crowd that was moving slowly toward the terminal, probably dazed by the heat. He was limping slightly from the weekend's rugby match. He had tried to ignore the injury, but it was undeniable, written in black and blue all over his ankle. The terminal was new, glistening concrete and polished metal shimmering in the sun. Attached to it were two new jetways sagging flaccidly to the

ground, clearly broken. That was what happened in places like this. The
Transportation Ministry had probably purchased the newest equipment, only to later discover that the airport authority didn't know
how to operate jetways with laser sensors. So the jet bridges were
abandoned, left there like a pair of dinosaurs with hangovers, and a
fifty-year-old set of rusted stairs was wheeled up to every arriving
flight. It served as a reminder to Davis of the world he was entering,
a sovereign moshpit of corrupt bureaucrats and tribal strongmen and
baseline incompetence.

When he entered the terminal, it felt like he'd stepped into a walk-
in cooler. It was the kind of massive carbon footprint only a net ex-
porter of oil could love. He saw too much space, saw too few
passengers. The brand-new marble floors were already dirty and
scuffed, and stacks of unclaimed luggage sat behind empty check-in
counters. Airports were showcase facilities, commissioned by governments, so when this terminal had been designed, the efficient trans-
port of passengers was likely a secondary concern to visual
impressiveness. It was only here to upstage whatever was in Addis
Ababa or Damascus. Bigger and better.

Davis made his way through customs and took a hard stare from
a pair of guards at the exit. He was traveling on his real passport. Larry
Green had forwarded an offer from the CIA to provide something
else, but that had only struck Davis as a get-into-jail-free card. He
retrieved his bag from a conveyor belt that worked, then went outside
to find a cab. Davis spotted a sign that said TAXI at the far end of the
terminal. He started walking.

"Hey mister!"

Davis turned.

"You need taxi?"

Davis saw a smiling man who had probably never seen a dentist in
his life. He was pointing to a cab parked on the curb behind him. The
car looked a lot like the guy's teeth, chipped and dinged. The front
right fender reminded Davis of a crumpled beer can. But he saw a
dozen other cabs coming and going, parked on other curbs, and they
all looked the same.

Davis said, "Sure."

He climbed in and threw his suitcase on the seat beside him. The cab had no meter, and since they were only going to the far side of the airfield, Davis negotiated his price in advance. The driver didn't haggle, which seemed strange. In Davis' previous forays to the Middle East, the art of negotiating prices for things like cab rides was a veritable art form.

They got under way, and the driver kept one hand on the steering wheel and the other on the horn as he weaved through a sea of cars, scooters, donkey carts, and darting pedestrians, all the while keeping up a commentary in choppy English. A tiny fan on the front dash oscillated back and forth, taking the place of an air conditioner. The windows were the old-fashioned kind with crank handles, and all were half open, allowing hot air to wash the interior in thick waves.

"You like our new airport?" the driver asked.

Davis had never seen the old one. He said, "It's great."

"You are U.N.? Relief agencies?"

"Yeah, that's me. I'm the U.N."

"If you want, I will take you into town while you are here. Our lovely city was designed one century ago by the British Lord Kitchener. The streets, they are very good, very wide. And if you look from above, they make the shape of the Union Jack."

Davis thought, *I can't imagine why they don't like Westerners*. He said, "How interesting."

The airport was surrounded by a ring road, and as they swung east to the far side, the bustle of the passenger terminal disappeared. Here Davis saw nothing but desert, although not desert in its purest form, not the massive sand swales of Saudi Arabia or southern Egypt. The earth was dry and cracked, baked into hard layers by a relentless sun. Stunted bushes grasped the rocky soil, their brown and green shades muted as if the pigment had been seared right out of them. The driver turned off the perimeter road and onto a side street. He had gone quiet, which was fine with Davis. The only sounds now came from the car, the low hum of the engine, groans from the undercarriage, and the little fan in front banging back and forth.

But something felt wrong.

Davis had always been blessed with a kind of internal compass. It was a thing he'd never really understood. Maybe it had to do with the way he sensed the sun and the stars, or how he saw the terrain. Maybe he was like a migratory bird or sea turtle, some deep part of his brain registering the earth's magnetic field. Whatever it was, it was working right now. They were heading east, away from the airport. Larry Green had shown him satellite photos that covered the whole complex, so Davis knew exactly where FBN Aviation was situated. It wasn't down this road.

Davis ran through possible explanations. The driver wasn't running up the meter because there was no meter. He wasn't padding time or mileage. He wasn't avoiding rush hour traffic because it was the wrong time of day and the wrong part of the planet. And he wasn't giving a trial version of his tour. There was nothing to see here. Only sand and dust and waves of heat.

"Is this the right way?" he asked.

The driver glanced at him in the rearview mirror. "There is much construction on the main road. This is only way to get where you are going. We will be there in two, perhaps three minutes."

Davis hadn't seen any construction. When the pace of the car slowed, more ideas came and went. The road wasn't in great shape, a marginal stretch of graded earth and crushed stone. Still, Davis had taken a lot of cabs, in cities all over the world, and they all had one thing in common—the drivers were always in a hurry. Eager to drop off their fare so they could get back to the queue. The car slowed further, no more than ten miles an hour. No faster than Larry Green could run one of his races. The only sound was the soft crush of sand and gravel under rubber, the mechanical gyration of the little fan in front. Back and forth.

Something was definitely wrong.

Davis studied the front dash. In any cab in the states there would have been a license or registration with a picture of the driver. He saw a spot where there *had* been something, a hardened blob of dried glue on the glove compartment, but whatever had been there was gone. The driver was completely silent now, eyeing him steadily in the rearview mirror. Davis looked outside, scanning ahead. The desert was taking over, thick scrub lining the margins of the road. He sensed the driver's foot easing further off the accelerator. A hundred feet ahead on the right, Davis spotted a dull black tube extending from behind a large bush. A gun barrel.

There wasn't time to think. Davis vaulted the seat.

The startled driver yelled something in Arabic, but it was cut off when Davis wheeled an elbow hard into the guy's head. Davis slid sideways until he was behind the wheel, actually sitting on the driver, his feet planted on the floorboard and pressing like he would on a squat rack in the gym. The stunned driver tried to move but was completely immobilized, frozen by Davis' weight and the power of his legs. With the steering wheel now in hand, Davis looked for his primary threat—the gun barrel. He saw it fifty feet ahead, attached now to a man wearing a long robe. Another guy appeared on the opposite side of the road with a machete in his hand. That made three.

The driver was crushed beneath him. The man with the machete was holding it out like a pirate ready for a sabre duel. The gunman was craning his neck, trying to see what was going on inside the car. That was Davis' tactical situation.

The taxi was barely moving now because the dazed driver's foot could no longer reach the accelerator. Davis changed that. He stomped on the gas and whipped the steering wheel hard right. The car lunged ahead, its spinning wheels spewing dirt and rock. The man holding the gun was suddenly faced with the most important decision of his life. Try to shoot? Or jump aside? He did both, which was like doing neither. He was half a step to his right, with the gun barrel rising through forty-five degrees, when the car hit him. The gun exploded a round into the front grill, and the gunman went sprawling across the hood, hit the windshield with a thump, and rolled off. The gun stayed on the hood.

Davis hit the brakes, glanced left just in time to see the machete coming through the half-open window. He rolled toward the passenger seat, pulling the driver with him as the blade came scything inside. With a thump, it lodged in the driver's-side headrest and stuck there.

An arm was still connected to the handle, struggling to pull the blade free. Davis grabbed it. Once he got a solid arm bar, he reached outside with his free hand, grabbed blindly, and was rewarded with a fistful of hair and part of a turban. He yanked it all in through the half-open window. With his head inside the car and his body outside, the man tried to push away. But he couldn't, not without losing half his scalp. He released the machete, and when he did, Davis let go of his arm. But not his hair. Davis reached down and cranked the window up, kept going until the guy's neck was pinned tight with his head inside the cab. Davis gave a vicious twist to break off the window handle and tossed it into the backseat.

He yanked the machete out of the headrest and paused to check the big picture. Three men. Gargling and choking noises on his left from the guy who'd lost his machete and now had his head trapped in a window. To Davis' right, the driver was still immobilized, stunned. Outside, the man who'd had the rifle was rolling in agony on the dirt shoulder. Davis grabbed the driver by the collar and shoved his head out the passenger-side window, cranked it up and broke off another handle, giving a mirror image of the other side—body in the cab but head jammed outside. He locked the passenger door, brought the machete down to sever the locking knob at its base, then gave the same treatment to the driver's side. Two down, one to go.

The car was still rolling, so Davis put it in park. He climbed into the backseat, grabbed his bag and, with the machete still in hand, got out. He took a good look at the surrounding desert, but didn't see anybody aside from the man who was already down. The one who had just shot a taxicab. Davis did see three looted suitcases in the brush, and some clothing and paper scattered in the nearby desert. Which meant that he wasn't their first victim. He was dealing with bandits, common thieves. The cab was almost certainly stolen. The suitcases in the brush looked like they'd been there a while, so Davis wasn't going to inquire about the owners. They had either made their police reports or were rotting in the desert. Nothing he could do either way. But it was a vivid welcome. Like the abandoned jetways, another reminder of what he was getting into.

Davis went to the car's hood and retrieved the gun, which turned out to be a baseline AK. Three minutes later, he had the third man standing outside the cab with his head secured in a rear window. Two outside, one in.

He put the car in gear, and watched as it began to idle ahead down the road. All three men were struggling to get free. The driver with the bad teeth, the one who was mostly inside, was trying to steer with his foot. The pair outside were walking fast to keep the pressure off their bruised windpipes. Trying not to fall and break their necks. The combination of rolling wheels and stumbling feet kicked up a hell of a cloud of dust. The picture reminded Davis of a clown car at the circus. He gave them five minutes like that. Sooner or later, somebody would realize that there was only one way to get out of the predicament—break a window. They'd have to use a fist or an elbow, not an easy thing to do against tempered safety glass on a hot day. The winner of that cranial challenge would rescue the others. Of course, everything would go faster if the guy steering changed direction, if he realized that the thick brush would bring them to a stop. But right now Davis wasn't seeing thoughtfulness and teamwork. He heard shouting and saw arms flailing—a lot of flailing—so he amended his original estimate. Ten minutes.

Davis studied the gun and wondered what to do with it. It had a carrying strap, so he could sling it over his shoulder. That would be one way to walk into the headquarters of FBN Aviation and start his investigation. He still had the machete too, which would fit nicely under his belt. In the end, Davis decided against it. Now wasn't the time for that trajectory. Not yet. He ejected the magazine from the gun, cleared the round in the chamber, and tossed everything into the bushes. Far and in different directions. He took a firm grip on the machete, pulled his arm back, and heaved the big blade fifty yards through the air, watched it twirl and spin like some kind of misguided javelin.

Davis then picked up his suitcase, turned toward the airfield, and began to walk.

CHAPTER FIVE

The helicopter, a Russian-made Mi-24 Hind-D, disappeared in a swirl of dust as it settled onto the uneven surface, a patchwork amalgam of broken concrete and sand. The wheels flexed as weight was transferred from rotor blades to earth, and the whine of the engines fell in both frequency and pitch, more and more until everything came still. There was nothing for a time, nothing except the faint crackle of cooling engines and a curtain of dust drifting on the indifferent breeze. The craft was emblazoned with the markings of the Sudanese Air Force, and a small flag bearing five stars was affixed to one cockpit window. Finally, the helicopter's side door opened, and two men clambered down to the broken earth.

They were an odd pair, the general and the imam. On physical appearance alone, as different as two men could be. The general was a strapping specimen, even if the straps had gone a bit loose—the circumference of his barrel chest was more than matched by that of his gut. He moved with a soldier's bravura, yet took five strides to reach full swagger. His stiffly pressed uniform was pinned with rows of shining brass, and the breast of his jacket was a veritable billboard of ribbons. The general's features were typically Nubian, the dark eyes wide-set and humorless. Any remains of his bristly hair had long ago been shaved away, and the ring of ebony skin at the base of his wheel hat gleamed in the midday sun. His shoulders carried the weight of five stars—he had once considered six, but not even Idi Amin Dada had taken things that far—and the general walked in front, as generals tended to do, with the firm purpose of a man in control.

The imam was the general's somatic counterpoint. He did not so much walk as drift, a long white robe floating on the breeze. His black beard, long and unkempt in the most pious tradition, fell to the top of his chest, and his eyes were obscured by wide wraparound sunglasses. He was small of stature and slightly built, a circumstance aggravated by the general's bulk. This contrast, a matter of mere chance at the outset of their association, had served both men well in the careful cultivation of their respective images. One commanding, one humble.

After twenty heavy paces, the general stopped in his tracks and put his hands on his hips. The imam drifted to his side. Both men scanned the horizon all around. There was nothing here to catch the eye. Nothing at all.

"This is the place?" the general remarked in his gruff baritone.

"Yes," the imam replied. "We are only a few miles from the Egyptian border. It is barren, of course, but that is to our advantage."

The general nodded.

There truly was little to take in. Sand dominated the horizon in every direction, an ocean of swales that no doubt shifted as freely as the Red Sea itself. Yet at this snapshot moment, the landscape looked as still as stone. They were situated at the center of a rubble field, perhaps ten acres of concrete falling to dust. Both the general and the imam knew the history of the place. A former airfield, it had been built by the Allies during the Second World War, then abandoned as the Germans were pushed northward. Thousands of such makeshift air bases had been constructed in haste all over the world, only to be orphaned with equal alacrity in the wake of frontal advances. For a time after the outbreak of peace, the government had made halfhearted attempts to revive the place, but inevitably it had fallen to disrepair, doomed to rot by forces more destructive than any military campaign—lack of funds, cronyism, bureaucratic indifference. Whatever strategic design had existed in 1944 to build this place had long ceased to be relevant. Without a populace, without backing from the Sudanese Air Force or commercial interests, all that remained was a triangle of beaten concrete waiting to be reclaimed by the desert—time taking man's work back from whence it came. But this very isolation, together with the geographic location, was what suited their needs so perfectly.

"Give it to me," the general ordered.

The imam reached into his robe and produced a handheld GPS navigation device. He handed it to the general. The big Nubian pressed buttons to register the waypoint in memory. Then, wanting no chance for error, he said, "Write down these numbers."

The imam produced a pen and paper, and scribbled the numbers recited by the general. Later, they would compare the coordinates to those on an aeronautical chart that displayed the airfield. The whole process was tedious, but a necessary step. Maps of this region were notoriously inaccurate, a nuisance born not of careless cartography but rather intent—such charts were, by definition, public domain, and the Arab countries of North Africa didn't want to make things easy should the Israelis or Americans come calling again.

When they were done, the two men stood in silence for a time.

The general looked down and turned over a loose chunk of concrete with the toe of his gleaming boot. "Is this surface adequate?"

After a pause, Imam Khoury said, "For what we have in mind, it is perfect."

The general stared at him. He was not a man given to humor, yet as Rafiq Khoury watched, the general's brutish, rough-hewn visage seemed to crack as little used muscles regained memory. The man, apparently, could smile after all.

Five minutes later, they were back in the helicopter and skimming across the desert toward Khartoum.

Davis had been in Sudan for an hour, and he already had three enemies.

He reached the perimeter road and walked straight across, kept going until he hit the tarmac. There, he turned left and skirted the edge of the flight line. For all Sudan's shortages, he could see that one thing was in abundant supply—concrete. The ramp and taxiways stretched for miles, a gray-white ocean of rock.

As he made his way, Davis studied the aircraft parked along the flight line. The fleets were segregated by utility. A flock of military helicopters sat idle, rotors tied down and plastic plugs stuffed into the engine intakes to keep sand out. Davis had spent a lot of time in the Middle East, and so he knew all about sand. It got into everything—your pockets, your food, your ears. And your aircraft. Sand was the enemy of machinery, so this handful of Russian-made choppers probably didn't get daily runs. More likely they were kept ready, clean and oiled, waiting for a crisis. Waiting until the government needed a show of either force or goodwill.

The next section of ramp held a cluster of aircraft with a wide mix of types and registrations. Russian, Chinese, Italian, United Nations. This was the humanitarian ramp, the place where boxes with red crosses and bulk food arrived, the frequency and size of the shipments correlating to the immediate state of the world's conscience.

Finally, at the far end of the concrete ocean, Davis saw what he was looking for. Two DC-3s sat baking on the ramp, doors and windows left ajar to keep the heat from building inside, their aluminum skin undulating in the radiant mirage that rose from the tarmac. By Larry Green's count, FBN Aviation had seven airplanes at its disposal after the recent mishap. Which meant five were likely in service right now, plowing through African sky to do the bidding of Rafiq Khoury. And beyond the DC-3s, connected by a long taxiway, Davis got his first look at his objective—the remote hangar run by FBN Aviation. It looked just like it had in the satellite photos, a massive block of corrugated metal surrounded by a low fence. He saw a squad of mismatched vehicles parked in front, including two small pickup trucks with guns mounted in their beds. And inside the hangar? A state-of-the-art CIA drone? Davis drew to a stop and wondered.

He'd always had reservations about the entire concept of unmanned aerial vehicles. Pilots were natural skeptics, but from any point of view, drones were part of a strange new world. They flew high and at night so that those being targeted had no way to see or hear them. No way to know what was coming.

For the most part, UAVs in the Middle East were operated by men and women sitting in bunkers in Nevada and California. Surveillance data from their sensors got uplinked to satellites, then downlinked. The information was studied by people sitting in soft armchairs in air-conditioned rooms. Tactical decision trees were run and authorizations to engage sought from uniformed lawyers. Once everything was approved, another uplink and downlink in reverse made things happen. Bright, loud things. That was the reality of air combat today.

It had to be a bizarre way of life for the drone operators, David thought. You wake up in a cozy house in Las Vegas, drop the kids off at school, go to work and sit in front of a world-class gaming console for eight hours. On a given day, you might bore circles in the sky for your entire shift, like some kind of remote-controlled Zamboni driver. Or you might launch a salvo of Hellfire missiles and kill a truckload of people, relying on intelligence assessments that the targets were indeed enemy combatants. Either way, when the day was done you clocked out and picked up the kids from soccer practice. Grilled a few burgers for dinner.

It really was weird.

In Davis' experience, there were moments in combat when you needed to see and feel and hear everything. Even smell it. Situations changed, and sometimes you had to react fast, almost instantaneously. That was his burn when it came to drones. No flexibility, too much time lag between seeing and acting. But there was an upside—drones carried little risk, which was why commanders liked them. You never had to worry about pilots getting shot down behind enemy lines. Never had to worry about risky search and rescue missions. All you could lose was the hardware.

Of course, even that carried risk, proven by the fact that Davis was here right now.

CHAPTER SIX

Whoever first called the earth's outer layer its crust had probably lived right here. The brown desert was baked into layers that had cracked for lack of moisture, and a high midday sun was vulcanizing everything in sight.

Davis set his bag on the tarmac in front of FBN Aviation. Standing on the groomed concrete, a searing wind snapping at the cuffs of his pants, he filled his lungs with the dry, musky air. This was his target box, and so, just like flying a combat mission, the first order of business was to get his bearings. The FBN Aviation building looked relatively new, a given really, since the whole airport complex had been nothing but scrubland seven years ago. The main building was big, two stories of concrete and burnt brick. It reminded him of any number of military facilities he'd seen. Brown, gray, tan—shades so dull Michelangelo couldn't have done anything positive with them. On the flat roof, two box-like swamp coolers were working hard. There was little in the way of architectural detail. Just square corners and a few token windows, institutional and cheap, a budgetary stepchild to the over-the-top passenger terminal a mile away. Behind the main office was a second building, three stories that reminded Davis of a college dormitory. And that was probably what it was. Finding homegrown pilots and mechanics in the Middle East was a challenge, so companies like FBN Aviation were usually operated by expatriates. And when foreign contractors were brought in, part of the bargain had to be housing. You gave the hired help a place to live, kept them fed, particularly important when the cultural differences between the host nation and employees were so stark. A little distance to keep everyone out of trouble.

Davis walked toward the entrance and passed a row of parking spaces. Back home, the spot closest to the door would have been reserved for the handicapped. Here a sign said: CHIEF PILOT. It was occupied by a relatively late-model Mercedes. The building's front door was glass, and opened automatically with a rubbery sticking noise as it rotated inward, like a refrigerator door opening—weather stripping still new enough to be doing its job. When Davis walked inside the temperature dropped forty degrees.

His first impression was that the place looked strangely familiar. There was an L-shaped counter, two young men seated behind it. They were clearly locals, clearly bored. Behind them, taking up an entire wall, was a dry erase board with lines corresponding to the days of the week. Flight numbers and routes and crews were all listed in colored marker, a half dozen of these strewn in a gutter at the base. The different colors were codes, maybe blue for a regularly scheduled flight, black for a special charter, red for a maintenance test flight. Also in the gutter was a collection of crumpled rags for making changes. There were always changes. Weather delays, broken airplanes, shipment foulups, sick pilots. The whole setup reminded Davis of the operations desk in a dozen squadrons he'd been assigned to.

The two men behind the counter straightened when they saw Davis. One stood and said something in Arabic. At least he thought it was Arabic.

Davis didn't respond, and soon the second guy got up. He was tall enough to look Davis in the eye, probably weighed a hundred pounds less.

"Can I help you with something?" The question came in English, but the tone said he didn't really want to help. It said, *Are you lost, or what?*

"I'm here to see Bob Schmitt."

"For what reason?"

Davis almost said, *I'm from the government and I'm here to help*, but he decided that in a place like Sudan the government might not be a laughing matter. He said, "It's official business."

The men eyed one another before the taller one picked up a phone.

"Name?" he asked.

Davis thought about that. He wondered if Schmitt knew he was coming. Larry Green had sent word that an investigator was en route, but Davis knew he hadn't given a name. Still, FBN Aviation had to have some connections to the government, and the government ran customs, which could check things like passenger manifests and passports. So Schmitt *might* know he was coming.

"The name's Davis," he said. It was common enough.

The tall man had a quick conversation on the phone in hushed English, then jabbed a thumb toward the hallway. "Second door on your right."

Davis said, "Thanks," and headed for the second door on the right.

There was a placard at the entrance: CHIEF PILOT. Just like the parking spot outside.

The door was open, and Davis turned the corner to find Bob Schmitt working at his desk. He had not seen the man in ten years, and he'd definitely changed. Schmitt had always been built like a bulldozer, squat and thick, but now he was overweight and his complexion had gone ruddy. He looked like he must have arteries as hard as copper pipes, a cholesterol count of a million. But some things were the same. His dark hair was still thick and coarse, like a black Brillo pad—if they made black Brillo pads. When Schmitt looked up and saw him, he shot to his feet like his chair had caught fire.

"What the hell are you doing here?"

From across the room Davis watched with inner satisfaction. The veins at Schmitt's temples bulged, and his face went from red to purple, like some kind of arterial kaleidoscope. Right there, Davis' first question was answered. Schmitt *hadn't* known he was coming.

A number of smart-ass replies came to mind, but Davis just said,

"I'm here to investigate your crash." He liked the sound of that. *Your* crash. One of the hits you had to take when you ran a flying unit. "The aviation authorities here in Sudan don't have a lot of experience with investigations like this, so they had to call in help. It fell to the NTSB."

Schmitt settled into the same angry look Davis had last seen, on the day when he'd been drummed out of the service. It was a look that said a lot—the man still hated him. For Davis, that alone made the trip to Sudan worthwhile. All thirty-nine hours.

Schmitt seemed to recover. If there was anything positive about the man, it was that he kept control. He was confident and couldn't be intimidated. Davis knew because he'd tried. Schmitt strode around the desk and puffed out his thick chest.

He said, "And you're with the NTSB now."

"Small world, huh?"

"No, not that small. Whose ass did you kiss to get this assignment?"

One minute, maybe less, and the interchange was already going down like a MiG in flames.

"Just another investigation to me," Davis said.

"Sure. And you want my complete cooperation."

Davis shrugged. "If you were to make things difficult for me, I'd have to put that in my report." Davis tried to say this in earnest, as if he was going to write a report.

Schmitt didn't respond.

"For starters," Davis said, "why don't you tell me about this outfit. Who controls FBN Aviation?"

Schmitt made him wait a moment before answering. "His name's Rafiq Khoury."

"What's he like?"

"He signs my paycheck."

"Is he a hands-on kind of owner?"

"In what way?"

"You know, does he tell you what to put on the airplanes, where to take them? That kind of thing."

"You know what kind of operation this is, Davis. Want to see load manifests and flight plans? I've got lots of them."

"Yeah, I'll bet you do. And I'm sure Khoury is a real stand-up guy. Not the kind of boss who'd throw a chief pilot under ICAO's bus if he needed a scapegoat."

Schmitt scowled, his squat forehead plowed with furrows. "I've been under the bus before. Fact is, I've still got your tire tracks on my ass."

Again, Davis smiled inwardly. Outside nothing changed. He said, "Look, let's cut the crap. You lost an airplane, and I'm here to find out why. Agree to put our background aside, and I'll call this crash like I see it."

"And if I don't?"

"Get in my way, and I'll make this crash an anchor. I'll tie it to your civilian license, and drop everything into the deep end of the ocean."

"Just like last time."

"Last time? I didn't bust you out of the Air Force, Schmitthead," Davis said, reverting to the old squadron nickname he hated, "you were always going to crash and burn. This time it might be different. Maybe you're clean."

Schmitt stood there thinking, calculating. Dealing with him was going to be tricky. When organizations got investigated, the people in charge were always cautious. But Davis and Schmitt had a past, and from it, a residue of mistrust that wasn't going to wash away under a beer or two.

"Okay," Schmitt said. "What do you want?"

"For starters, a few answers—since you *are* the chief pilot."

"Chief pilot?" Schmitt gestured toward the door. "Of that bunch? I'm more like a parole officer."

Davis thought, *He still has his people skills.* Yet there was a grain of truth in the comment. The pilots here would be journeymen, a global collection of the adventurous, furloughed, and malcontent.

Schmitt picked up, "I've got fourteen pilots to run seven airplanes. It's my job to keep them in line."

Davis couldn't resist. "It's your job to keep them operationally safe. Last month you had sixteen pilots and eight airplanes."

"Go to hell."

"Right. And now that we've settled that, tell me what you know about the crash."

"It was a maintenance check flight. They'd just rerigged the flight controls, done some work on the aileron mechanism. The airplane took off at nine o'clock that night. By ten thirty, we realized it was overdue. We tried to raise the flight on our company radio frequency, but there was no reply, so we reported it to the Sudanese aviation authorities. They couldn't find the airplane either. It was officially declared missing at around midnight. There were no reports of a landside crash, so we figured it went down off the coastline. According to the flight plan that's where they'd been headed for the checkout work."

"How far off the coastline?"

"I don't know. An air traffic controller said he remembered seeing the airplane over the water for a while, but then it just disappeared. He figured the crew had dropped down to screw around at low level."

"Your guys do that a lot?"

"Never to my knowledge."

Schmitt and Davis locked eyes again.

Davis asked, "Do the Sudanese authorities keep records of their radar data?"

Schmitt laughed. "In this country? They can't keep track of who's born and who dies. Sudan's Civil Aviation Authority isn't exactly the FAA. Sometimes you can't even raise the air traffic controllers on the radio. They just disappear, walk away to get a cup of tea or pray or whatever. We don't worry about stuff like that. We fly, with or without them."

"Should I put that in my report?"

"I don't care what you put in your damned report. That threat rings hollow with me, Davis. If the Sudanese government steps in and shuts down FBN Aviation, it'll be up and flying again inside a week. Same airplanes, same pilots, new name. You know what FBN stands for?"

"It's a Bahamian law firm. Franklin, Banks, and Noble."

Schmitt shook his head. "That's what's on the letterhead, but the pilots know the real name—Fly by Night Aviation." He chuckled. "A limited liability corporation."

Davis actually saw the humor in that. "Right. So tell me, when this airplane was discovered to be missing, was there a search?"

"According to the government there was. I saw a couple of the helicopters down the street launch. As far as I know they didn't find anything. That airplane just disappeared into a big, deep ocean. Things like that happen."

"Is that what you told the pilots' next of kin? 'Things like that happen.'"

Schmitt's eyes glazed over to his trademark glare.

"Was there any record of a mayday call?" Davis asked.

Schmitt shrugged. "Not that I ever heard about. If I was you, I'd call back to D.C. If there was any call for help on 121.5, the good old U.S. Navy probably has a record of it."

Schmitt actually had a point. The U.S. Navy was plowing continuously over the Red Sea and Persian Gulf, every day and night. If there had been any transmission on 121.5 MHz, the international distress frequency, they'd have it on record.

Davis asked, "What kind of voice and data recorders do your airplanes have?"

"You kidding me? These airplanes are Third World military surplus. We get them because places like Burkina Faso and Antigua figure they're past their useful lives. If they have any recording devices, we don't keep them up."

Davis was no expert when it came to equipment requirements for civil aircraft, but he was sure this was some kind of regulatory violation. He let it go for now.

Schmitt suggested, "If you really want to figure out why that airplane went down, you should start looking for the wreckage. Sooner or later, you're going to have to dredge it up."

Easy to say, Davis thought. *Not so easy to do.* "Tell me about the pilots. Who were they?"

"A couple of Ukrainian guys."

"Ukrainian?"

"I hire captains from all over the world. The only requirement is lots of DC-3 pilot-in-command time. No choice, really."

"Why is that?"

"Because the Sudanese government, as an informal condition of our operating certificate, has dictated that we hire local copilots."

"Sudanese pilots?"

"Unfortunately. It's basically an ab initio program. The government supplies candidates, usually some big shot's brat kid. They fly a few hours in light airplanes, then get sent to us to build time as first officers."

"Which means your captains are essentially flying solo."

"Like I said, I have to get experienced guys. I just had another of these damned Sudanese kids show up last week, which brings me to three."

"But the accident involved two expatriate pilots," Davis said, "Ukrainians. Neither of them was paired with one of these local copilots?"

"That crew was an exception. Neither spoke very good English, so I kept them together. I figured they could at least talk to each other."

Davis realized that Schmitt would likely regard this as a sound management decision. He asked, "You have any records on these guys?"

Schmitt got up and went to his filing cabinet.

As he began to dig, Davis said, "And while you're at it, check for the rest. The usual stuff—flight plan, logbook records, weather."

"This will probably surprise you," Schmitt said sarcastically, "but I've already collected all that. Damnedest thing—I actually like one of those stupid Cossacks."

CHAPTER SEVEN

While Schmitt was busy at his filing cabinet, Davis studied the room. From a practical standpoint, it was standard issue for a chief pilot. A big desk for sorting papers. A cheap carpet for tap dancing. Two chairs facing the boss's desk that looked uncomfortable, no arms to grip when you were getting your butt chewed. But if the furniture was conventional, the décor was something else.

Davis was no expert when it came to interior design, but it didn't take a professional to see that Schmitt's office was a testosterone-fueled calamity. There was a deer's head mounted on the wall over his desk—or, to be exact, something called a springbok. On the file cabinet was some kind of medium-sized creature, like a Tasmanian devil or something. It was presented standing on its hind legs, baring pointed teeth, and had stitch marks up the gut as if Dr. Frankenstein had done the taxidermy. A bandolier of 7.62-mm rounds was hanging from a hat rack. Altogether, it was like some kind of half-assed rod and gun club. What the room lacked was anything personal. There was the obligatory government-issue portrait of Sudan's glorious leader, but no awards or plaques of commendation, no family pictures. Davis remembered that Schmitt had been single with no kids, and he doubted that had changed. The closest thing to a personal touch was a hand-carved wooden nameplate, the same trinket every Air Force pilot who'd ever been stationed in Korea had planted on his desk.

Schmitt sent a manila folder spinning across the desk and sat down. "There," he said, "that's everything I've got. Take it if you want."

Davis did. But instead of opening it, he said, "Tell me about your maintenance program."

"I've got two mechanics, a Jordanian and an American."

"Are they good?"

"They have their licenses."

"Where do they work? Is there a hangar somewhere?"

"There's a remote hangar, but we don't use it."

"I think I saw it," Davis said. "Why would anybody build a hangar way out there in the scrub like that?"

"Around here? Probably because somebody's brother had the asphalt contract. And if you're thinking about taking a look, you can forget about it."

"Why's that?"

"The place is off-limits. Khoury and his bunch don't give tours."

"That seems a little secretive," Davis suggested. "Is that where Khoury hides the cargo he doesn't want people to see?"

"Damned if I know."

"And would you tell me if you *did* know?"

There was a long silence, until Schmitt crossed his thick forearms on the desk, and said, "You know what I think, Davis? I think you're going to make this whole thing personal. I don't think you even care about this accident."

"You're half right."

Schmitt sat there looking like a well-shaken beer, pressure building, just waiting to blow.

"I want two things," Davis said. "First, a place to stay. Second, I want a good look at the flight line. I need to see how things run around here."

"All right. I've got one empty room."

Davis wanted to make a crack that he likely had two empty rooms, but he held back.

"And as for the flight line tour," Schmitt said, "help yourself."

"I don't need any clearance? An ID or something?"

Schmitt fished into his drawer and pulled out a small plastic card. He tossed it over the desk and Davis caught it. It was Schmitt's FBN Aviation ID.

"Try that. Staple your own picture on if you want. I haven't used it since I got here."

Davis dropped it back on the desk.

Schmitt chuckled. "Welcome to Africa, Jammer."

Schmitt gave Davis directions and a key—not a plastic card with a magnetic strip, but the old-fashioned metal kind with teeth. Davis went to find his room, and as he walked through the operations building, people stopped what they were doing and stared at him. Maybe they'd been briefed that somebody was coming to perform an investigation. Maybe they'd been told to look professional or pretend to help. Rumors had to be swirling by now—Davis had been here all of twenty minutes, which was plenty of time. Whatever the case, the looks weren't much different than those he'd gotten in a hundred other places.

A short hallway ran from the operations building to the residence area, and Davis took the stairs to his third-floor room. When he walked in, the air conditioner was blowing at hurricane force, the room chilled to the level of a meat locker. The place stank of sweat and nicotine. Davis went to the thermostat and saw it had been turned full cold, probably by the cleaning staff. People did things like that when they weren't paying the electric bill. He turned it off and took stock of the place. It was a studio with an attached bathroom. There was one window, one chair, but no desk. A nightstand carried a cheap alarm clock. The bed was shoved against a wall that had to be common to the elevator shaft. Just then, the window began to rattle as a jet outside thundered to takeoff power. Davis figured Schmitt had given him the most uncomfortable room of those available, maybe hoping he wouldn't get any sleep. Truth was, the bed looked better than most to Davis. There was no headboard or footboard. For a guy his size, that was a home run.

Davis went to the window. The cheap curtains had clothespins clipped to the inner edges. He pulled them off, and bright light streamed in. He could see the runway in the distance, and one corner of the main passenger terminal. Closer in was a parking lot, half asphalt and half dirt, that would hold a hundred cars. There were three. Right under his nose was a recovering swimming pool, bone dry, two men slapping Spackle in the deep end. What wasn't there—and what he'd hoped to see from the third floor—was FBN's hangar. He knew from the satellite photos that it was roughly a mile east of here, but his internal compass kicked in and told him that east was at his back.

Davis retrieved the file Schmitt had given him. It seemed thin, weighed almost nothing. Even so, there might be something useful inside, one golden nugget that could be a pretext for gaining access to the hangar. He opened the folder, spread the contents on the bed, and started to read.

When the helicopter landed at Khartoum International Airport, Rafiq Khoury was collected by his ragtag security detail. The motorcade consisted of three vehicles—a well-worn Land Rover sandwiched between a pair of teknicals. The teknicals were both small Toyota pickups, one brown and the other probably white, though it was hard to tell through the shell of dust and grime. Armed with Soviet PK 7.62-mm machine guns, the two makeshift fighting vehicles were fast and mobile fixtures of warfare in North Africa.

The procession moved quickly—always preferred here—and snaked up the mile-long ribbon of asphalt that led from the main airfield to FBN Aviation's hangar. The pavement was unusually high quality, as it had been laid down not as a road but rather a taxiway, a logistical tributary that connected the remote hangar to the main airfield. The hangar was no different from ten others that dotted Khartoum International, if one could ignore the fence and the armed men stationed around the perimeter. Roughly a square, it was two hundred feet in each dimension and fronted by a wide asphalt pad that fed the main doors, two massive sliding panels designed to accept aircraft as large as a Boeing 737. As had been the case for some months, however, the doors remained closed.

Khoury undertook his usual inspection as they approached the hangar. Two months ago, the place had been busier. Trucks, equipment, and crates moving in a regular flow. Now things were quieter, the only

constant being his men. For the moment, he saw them positioned cor-
rectly and looking alert. But then, they had known their imam was
coming. He doubted they were so vigilant at other times, when his
signature parade was not bearing down. A few likely remained watch-
ful, held in line by the constancy of their faith, but they were the ex-
ceptions. It all mattered little to Khoury, because in his mind they
were guarding against a threat that could not possibly exist. The Americans might search from above with their spy satellites, or—he
mused—their high-tech drones, but there was no chance of enemy
agents infiltrating this place. Khoury had far greater worries.

The Land Rover slowed as they approached the hangar, and he
turned to his driver. Hassan had become a permanent fixture, at his
side for many months now. In truth, the relationship had been forced
on Khoury, yet he had quickly leveraged the circumstance to its fullest
use—the Nubian might not be his most trusted man, but he was certainly the largest. The Land Rover was not a small vehicle, yet Hassan
fit into the driver's seat like a walrus into a fish tank. His far shoulder
was wedged against the window and, on most of the local roads, his
melon-like head banged continuously against the roof, though this
seemed to have no effect to the detriment of either Hassan or the
vehicle. The top half of the steering wheel disappeared in his hands
and his knees were bent awkwardly underneath. To an even greater
degree than with the general, Khoury's slight stature was magnified by
the monstrous Hassan. The man had the added benefit of being an
experienced soldier, and as such, Khoury allowed him a free hand in
managing his followers.

"Have we found any new recruits?" Khoury asked, the Rover
nearing the gate.

Hassan nodded and pointed to a skinny young man who was trying, quite unsuccessfully, to look sharp with his Kalashnikov. "That
one, sheik."

Concern washed over Khoury's face. "You have already issued him
a weapon?"

Hassan smiled, an awkward undertaking where his massive jawline
came creased by furrows of flesh. "It is not loaded, my sheik."

"I see."

Khoury's little army was growing, steadily gaining strength, yet he had not crossed the threshold where legions offered themselves to do the bidding of God. Soon that would change, if all went as planned. But today Imam Khoury was still taking his followers one by one. Taking them as they came.

The Rover pulled to a stop, and four men, including the new lad, rushed to greet them. They formed a makeshift receiving line at the passenger door, spiking to attention as Khoury eased out of the truck. Each bowed to their leader in turn.

"Allah be with you, sheik," said the first.

Another, "Praise be to Allah."

Khoury said nothing. He simply raised an open palm to hip height, a minimalist acknowledgment of their good wishes. It seemed the clerical thing to do. Khoury made ten paces toward the hangar, moving slowly, his head cocked at a benevolent angle. Then, rather suddenly, he stopped. He turned and pulled up his gaze—this still obscured by his wide black sunglasses—and directed his attention to the new boy.

The skinny lad stiffened.

Khoury moved closer, and stopped directly in front of him. The youngster was no more than his own height, scrawny and malnourished.

"You are new here?" Khoury asked.

The boy nodded briskly. "Yes, my sheik. Yes."

After an appropriate pause, Khoury said, "And you will join us in our struggle?"

"If it is the will of Allah, my sheik."

Khoury very slowly reached up and pulled the sunglasses from his face. He locked his eyes to those of the boy. Watched him react. The boy was clearly struck.

In the first fifty-two years of his life, Rafiq Khoury had seen many reactions to his eyes. As a child he had often been teased that he was some kind of half-breed or bastard. Later, women often saw him as impure or tainted. Long into adulthood, Khoury had cursed his genetic quirk—one eye brown, the other bright green—as something to hide. Then, in the autumn of his existence, he had finally come to realize its leverage. Instead of hiding his affliction, he displayed it openly, if judiciously, to create a mystique. The Arab culture, as with many across the world, viewed the eyes as windows to the soul. There was a mysticism about them, in particular, when they were unusual, or even dysfunctional. How many blind clerics kept large, devoted followings? Once Khoury had understood this, it was a simple matter of adjustments to his carriage and demeanor. And here he was.

He stared with laser intensity and watched the young man closely. First he saw awe. Then something more permanent. Reverence.

Barely breathing, the young man bowed his head.

And Khoury knew he had another.

CHAPTER EIGHT

Davis started with meteorology, but found nothing remarkable. No thunderstorms or turbulence or weather fronts on the night in question. No dust storms, which could be a concern in this part of the world. All in all, the conditions on the night of the accident had been quiet, almost serene. Certainly nothing to make an airplane fall out of the sky. He studied the flight plan and aircraft history, and again came up empty.

This wasn't going to be easy. Davis was accustomed to going into an investigation with teams of experts from the NTSB, military, and industry. He was used to having people who specialized in tiny corners of knowledge: engines, structures, aircraft performance. He was used to having photographers to document wreckage. He was used to having wreckage. Davis felt like a homicide detective trying to solve a murder without a partner or a medical examiner or even a body.

He pulled out the crew profiles, and right away two pages jumped out at him—the personnel records on the two pilots. There were no photos, just two vibrant lives, each condensed to a single page of words and numbers. The captain's name was Gregor Anatolii, former Ukrainian Defense Forces. Born in Kiev. Nine thousand hours of flight time, including eighteen hundred in the DC-3. First officer Stanislav Shevchenko, former Air Belarus. Native of Sevastopol. Eighty-four hundred hours, nine hundred in the DC-3. There were dates of hire and contract terms regarding pay and housing. Copies of airman and medical certificates issued by the EASA, Europe's regulatory sister to the FAA. Then Davis' eyes went to the bottom of each page. Address of record, next of kin. Two wives and seven kids between them.

Christ.

Davis hunched forward on his chair, elbows on knees and chin cupped in his hands. He stared at the names. The information did nothing to help solve the crash. But it did a lot to complicate things. It always did. Davis had been brought here to find a missing drone, a mangled pile of high-tech hardware. Yet things were never so simple. Larry Green should have known better. *He* should have known better. An airplane had gone down and two pilots were dead. Nobody knew why. Not their boss, not their fellow pilots, not the mechanics who'd worked on the airplane. Worst of all, not their families.

It was a terrible thing to be in the dark about something like that. Davis had felt it when Diane had been killed. He'd wondered why. Her car had been T-boned by a delivery truck. On first glance, a straightforward tragedy, yet it had been all he could do to stand back and let the state police run their investigation. When he eventually got a look at the final report, Davis had to be restrained from taking the investigating officer's head off. The delivery truck had recently been in for brake maintenance, but nobody at the scene had bothered to check if the brakes were working. Nobody had checked phone records to see if the driver had been talking on his cell phone or texting at the time of the crash. Loose ends everywhere. The supervisor had tried to convince Davis that it had just been an accident, one driver missing a stop sign. The who and the when and the how were all right there, clear as day. But the why was left unanswered. Davis and Jen had been forced to live with that, and they had. But right now two families in Ukraine were asking that same agonizing question. *Why?* In a place like this, a dysfunctional corner of North Africa, Davis knew that if he didn't find the answers, nobody ever would.

And then there was the other part, the thing he'd mentioned tauntingly to Schmitt. Aviation really *was* a small world. A brotherhood, even. If Davis didn't get to the bottom of this crash, he would be haunted by questions. Could the same disaster happen to another crew? Possibly someone he knew? Would another pilot lose his or her life to the same faulty part or shoddy procedural screwup?

Not if Jammer Davis could help it.

He would find the CIA's drone—find it if it still existed. But at the same time, he was going to get to the bottom of this crash.

When he entered the familiar hangar, Khoury took off his sunglasses and paused to let his eyes adjust. The light inside was good, but no match for the brilliant desert sun. The place was cavernous inside, and while an attempt was made to cool—big fans overhead stirring and blowing—the system never quite kept up. Until eight months ago, Khoury had never been in an aircraft hangar in his life. Now he had come to appreciate their utility. It was a Spartan place, naked light and ventilation fixtures mounted openly to the walls and rafters, no effort made toward a tidy appearance. Benches and toolboxes and work stands encircled the perimeter, all of it bathed in the brazen fragrances of machine oil and rubber.

As he walked around the old airplane with the crazy antennae, he encountered Muhammed. The mechanic was tending to something underneath an engine, and when he saw Khoury he clambered to his feet and bowed respectfully. Khoury gave him the wave, but said nothing. The Jordanian recruit was at one end of Khoury's spectrum, the last man he would ever have to worry about. Raised in a strict madrassa, he was as devout an extremist as Khoury had ever seen. If Muhammed were not here, he would certainly be in Kandahar or Lahore being fitted for explosive underwear.

The hangar's second working area was well defined, separated by a high partition of plywood and cloth. Inside he found Fadi Jibril. By training, the man was an engineer, years spent in university learning things Khoury could never hope to understand. His freshly earned doctorate in aerospace engineering was taken from a top school in America, and while Khoury did not know Jibril's exact age, the man was young, certainly no more than thirty. Presently he was standing at a workbench, smoothing a long bundle of wire with his thin fingers. Everything about Jibril was delicate, almost feminine. There was no question about his sexuality—he was married to a thick, matronly woman who was, rather predictably, five months pregnant with their first child. Still, Fadi Jibril was not a man's man. His limbs seemed to swim in the loose-fitting shirts and trousers he preferred. His shoes looked too big, like those of a clown. Yet there was no doubting his intensity, the focus that encompassed everything he did. This was forever etched in his eyes, a thing Khoury appreciated, yet never quite understood. Religion was part of it—that was why he was here, indeed why any of them were here—yet for Jibril there was something more. Khoury sensed it at this very moment as he watched the engineer caress the insulated wire, watched his sharp black eyes critique his work. Khoury could not dismiss the idea that he was watching a man who was, at heart, more an artist than a scientist.

He cleared his throat and Jibril straightened.

"Sheik," he said, "I am honored."

This was what Jibril always said, each day when Khoury came to check his progress. He supposed Jibril was not being polite. He truly *was* honored. Khoury smiled inwardly.

"And how does our work progress?" the imam asked, the pronoun covering not only the two of them, but God as well.

Jibril sighed. "Certain parts have been difficult to work with. Our lathe is not the best. If we had a better machine—"

"Fadi, Fadi," Khoury interrupted, acquiring his most patient tone. "You know our troubles. We must make do with what we have. You have made great strides, no one can deny it." He swept an arm across a work area that was surrounded by tools, machinery, and electronics. "Six months you have been at that bench, hammering and turning screwdrivers. Time, however, is not our ally."

The young man relented. "Yes, sheik, I know. But things are always more difficult when one turns the screws clockwise."

Hand tools had never been a friend to Khoury, but the metaphor was clear enough. It is easier to take apart than to build. He committed this thought to memory, recognizing its potential for a future sermon.

"The schedule cannot be altered," Khoury insisted. "You must distinguish between what you would like, and what you must have."

Jibril's put his hands to his temples. He looked defeated, near exhaustion.

Khoury put a fatherly hand on his shoulder. "Fadi, look at me."

The engineer did, and Khoury asserted his most persuasive gaze.

"Always remember—you will be to Sudan what A. Q. Khan was to Pakistan. The father of a nation's technical might." Khoury watched the young man swell, his ego stoked by the bellows of his words. Khoury thought perhaps he might have struck upon it. What was different about Jibril? Scientist *and* artist—what combination could breed a more outsized ego?

"Now," Khoury suggested, "tell me where your troubles lie."

Jibril picked up his gaze and led Khoury to a bench where circuit boards and test equipment were strewn haphazardly. Khoury recognized a pungent electrical odor, burnt insulation or arcing wires. The engineer picked up a metal box the size of a bread pan. Three wires dangled freely, their loose ends stripped of insulation and scorched with solder.

"This is the telemetry interface module," Jibril said. "I told you yesterday it was giving me trouble. This unit is defective. I now suspect they are all defective."

Khoury sighed. "Yes, the Chinese do not have a reputation for reliability."

"Which is the very reason they paid us such a favorable price for the unit we removed."

"Indeed," Khoury said. He pointed to the electronic box. "Can you fix it?"

Jibril acquired a fresh air of enthusiasm. "I think it will not be necessary. I began to lose confidence in the Chinese equipment some weeks ago, so I went to the trouble of ordering a wholly different device from a German manufacturer. It should arrive today on the flight from Hamburg."

Khoury was impressed. For a young man, the engineer displayed an uncommon balance of patience and initiative. He was working twenty hours a day in this place, moving heaven and earth to bring success. Yet the purchase from Germany was a concern. Much of Jibril's hardware had already been acquired at considerable risk. Some clever, promotion-minded bureaucrat behind a customs desk might make uncomfortable connections.

"Hamburg?" Khoury said hesitantly. "Is this not dangerous ground, Fadi? The West watches certain exports very closely. This device you have ordered, might it be on someone's list of sensitive technology? Are you sure there will be no questions?"

The engineer shrugged to say no. Or perhaps to say that he hadn't really considered it.

Khoury let it go and moved to more familiar ground. He asked the question he always asked. "Will the deadline still be met?" The edge in his voice was clear.

"Yes, sheik. I will install the part as soon as it arrives. Yet . . ." Jibril hesitated, "I can only perform the most basic of bench tests. If there were more time—"

Khoury chopped his hand upward to cut the engineer off. There was a time for coddling and a time for discipline. He gave Jibril his most solemn gaze.

Jibril was duly inured. He bowed, and said, "It will be done, my sheik."

The bed was surrounded by paper as Davis studied the maintenance records for a second time. Every airplane has a logbook, a bound record of that airframe's flight and maintenance history. Since they always stay on board, the original logbook for the mishap aircraft was now resting on the bottom of the Red Sea. Fortunately, logbooks also have duplicate pages that are removed and kept as a permanent record. This was what Davis had in his hands.

The tear-out sheets were dry and brittle, like the paper had been baked in an oven. Arranged in chronological order, he was able to see where the airplane had been. Ten days prior to the crash, a hop from Dubai to Khartoum. The next day, an oil service and tire pressure check, then off to Lagos, Nigeria. On it went, bouncing around Africa and the Middle East. Two tires changed, a landing light replaced. A few gripes written up by pilots, subsequently addressed by maintenance.

Every write-up he saw was entered after a landing in Khartoum, so there had never been any contract maintenance performed at a far-away airport. In an outfit like this, Davis knew, 95 percent of pilot complaints regarding inoperative systems came after landing at the home field—not a function of where things broke, but a function of the five hundred U.S. dollars FBN Aviation would have to pay for a contract mechanic in Cape Town or Mombasa. Or the five hours the crew would have to wait for them to show up, if they showed up at all.

The logbook pages advanced chronologically until Davis reached the day before the crash. He saw a pilot-entered discrepancy: *Ailerons out of trim—five units right of neutral required for level flight*. Signed legibly at the bottom: *Captain Gregor Anatoli*. Then below, the corrective action: *Ailerons rerigged and centered to zero units in accordance with maintenance manual procedure 56–7. Test flight required*.

So there it was in black-and-white. The ailerons were long tabs that ran along the trailing edges of the wings, the surfaces that made an airplane roll and turn. A critical flight control. The pilot had reported that they were out of adjustment. The attending mechanic had certified that he'd realigned them to perfection. Everything in order. Everything by the book. Davis looked at the signoff block and checked to see if the time and date made sense. They did. Then he checked the signature, saw the mechanic's name, along with his Airframe and Powerplant certificate number. Muhammed al-Fahad. The Jordanian, no doubt.

Then something hit him.

Davis shuffled back to the crew profile sheet and compared it to the logbook write-up. *Gregor Anatoli*. The captain's signature was right there on the logbook page, clear and legible. Maybe a little too legible. *Anatoli*, with one "i." The captain had spelled his name wrong.

Davis looked closer. He was no expert in handwriting analysis—it wasn't the kind of thing that usually came up in aircraft accident investigations—but this one didn't look right. A pilot like Anatolii would have a signature that was smooth and quick, like he'd done it before fifty thousand times. Which he certainly had. A captain was always signing for something—a flight plan, cargo paperwork, crew accommodations, fuel slips. But the signature on this logbook page had perfect lettering, slow and deliberate. Not like any pilot Davis had ever known. He went back over some old pages in the logbook, and a week before the crash found another write-up by Captain Gregor Anatolii. Correct spelling, two i's, different signature. Completely different. Barely legible from the speed. Probably whipped out in a second, two at the most.

Davis leaned back in the tiny chair and rubbed his temples. The more he found, the less sense everything made. The write-up for the ailerons—the purported reason for the accident—was almost certainly bogus. Which meant that the corrective action by the Jordanian mechanic had to be equally bogus. But why? An excuse for the crash, inserted into the records after the fact?

The elevator rumbled past, and his little pile of papers vibrated. Frustrated, Davis stuffed them back in the folder, put the folder on the nightstand. He got up and stretched, thought about sleeping but knew he couldn't. He was restless. It was the same feeling he got when he took a spell on the bench in a rugby match. There was a lot you could learn from sitting back and watching a game flow. You could study and theorize. See who was fast and who was slow. Who held formation and who didn't. But after a time, sitting and watching was a pursuit of diminishing returns. There came a time to lace up, trot back out on the pitch, and start throwing yourself around.

So Davis switched to his work boots and laced them up. Grabbed his room key and headed for the flight line.

CHAPTER NINE

The heat was everywhere as Davis walked across the tarmac, as if the world had a fever. It radiated down from the sky, up from the earth, into everything. His shoes, his clothes, his lungs. And there was probably no worse place in all Sudan than right where he was standing—on a busy flight line. Superheated exhaust from big turboprops, jet engines at takeoff power, brake assemblies smoking after high-energy landings. It was all there, seared into the breeze.

He saw two FBN airplanes in the process of being unloaded, men pushing cargo out of the openings, stacking crates on the concrete ramp. Davis adjusted his vector in that direction. Just as Schmitt had said, there was no security in sight. Just two DC-3s parked on a broiling ramp, their cargo doors open wide like a pair of mouths straining for air.

It was for aircraft like the DC-3 that the word venerable had been created. Davis knew they'd been around since before the Second World War, and that tens of thousands had been built. Three quarters of a century later, hundreds were still in the air, plowing through equatorial thunderstorms and landing on Arctic tundra. Davis hadn't seen one in a long time, and he figured there were more in museums than in the air.

Different airplanes had different looks. Some, like the F-22, looked fast. Some were pretty, like the Boeing-757. The DC-3 in front of him wasn't any of those things. It was all business, functional and boring. From a distance, these two specimens looked in decent shape. They were dressed in a generic paint scheme, a coat of eggshell white that had been faded by dust from the Sahara and rain from the Amazon and

soot from China. There were no corporate marks or logos, no gaudy
fin flashes to establish ownership. For a company like FBN Aviation,
that was probably the idea—anonymity. From where Davis stood, the
only way to tell the two airplanes apart was by their registration numbers, this an unavoidable acquiescence to international law. X85BG
and NH33L. Big airlines often paid a little extra to get sequential registration numbers, which helped to keep a fleet organized. These two
numbers looked like they'd been chosen using Ping Pong balls from
a wire tumbler. As random as you could get. Once again, maybe by design.

When Davis got closer to the airplanes, he started to see differences. Dents on cargo doors and fuselages, hail damage on the wing
leading edges. The front aircraft's radome was pocked, and the paint
looked like it had been sandblasted off, probably from flying through
a sandstorm. Such minor damage was inevitable on two aircraft that
had over a hundred years of service between them. All the same, given
their far-flung histories, these DC-3s were about as much alike as any
two could be.

The airplane to the rear had already been unloaded, and a flatbed
truck parked next to it was piled high with boxes and shrink-wrapped
supplies. It looked like a legitimate load, some of the boxes having red
crosses, others bearing the caduceus emblem, two snakes around a
winged staff, to signify medical supplies. The loading crew was walking away, leaving two people near the truck, a teenage boy and a
woman. The woman was securing the load with tie-down straps while
the boy buttoned up the cargo door on the airplane.

Davis went the other way, toward the lead airplane, where a guy
was sitting on a forklift with his thick arms crossed over the steering
wheel. He was watching closely, giving a few directions, as a large
wooden crate was being eased out through the cargo door. The box's
length was longer than its width, and with a little tapering at the sides
might have passed for a coffin. It was obviously heavy, and the three
guys struggling to move it had one edge jutting out into the air. The
side panel was covered in Cyrillic writing, which was a mystery to
Davis. The translation could have been MEDICAL EQUIPMENT or MOS-

QUITO NETTING. More likely ROCKET PROPELLED GRENADES or SURFACE-TO-AIR MISSILES. He hoped they didn't drop it.

The three guys in the loading crew looked local. The forklift driver didn't. He was straight from central casting—burly, two-day growth of black beard, brown watch cap, cigar in his mouth—a longshoreman from the docks of Jersey.

Davis walked up to him, and said, "Need any help?"

The guy looked at him, up and down. "Don't worry yourself, buddy."

Davis thought, *Yep, definitely Jersey*. He pointed to the cigar, and said, "That thing's not lit, is it?" He jabbed a thumb toward a fuel truck parked fifty feet away. The side of the truck had a warning stenciled in bright red letters: NO SMOKING WITHIN 100 FEET.

The guy reached down and turned the key, and the machine went from a rattling diesel idle to silence. He took the cigar out of his mouth. It wasn't lit. He looked at Davis again, up and down.

"And who the hell are you?" he asked.

"Me? I'm an inspector." Davis left it at that, glancing at the big crate hanging two feet over the lip of the cargo door. The loading crew had stopped shoving and were looking back and forth between Davis and the driver.

"What the hell kind of inspector?" the man asked.

"You know—safety."

The guy crossed his thick forearms, chomped back down on his half-cut stogie. He was wondering why an American dressed for a round of golf was wandering around his cargo ramp. He probably had Davis pegged as being with the United Nations, or maybe an oil company. That would make sense.

"So are we?" the driver asked.

"Are you what?"

"Safe."

Davis said, "Well, you're cigar isn't actually lit, so that fuel truck over there won't explode. And you probably won't get lung cancer in twenty years. So, yeah, I'd say you're safe."

"Good. Then you won't bother us anymore."

Davis looked at him, then looked at the crate. The driver was sweating. Possibly because he was nervous. More likely because it was a hundred and eight degrees in the shade.

Davis lunged forward.

The driver stiffened, put up an arm to defend himself, but Davis went nowhere near him. Instead, he grabbed the crowbar he'd spotted under the seat. Two long strides later, he had it jammed into the crate and was prying off the lid.

"Hey!" the driver protested. "What the hell?"

But protest was all he did. He stayed where he was, because Davis was a lot bigger and had a crowbar in his hand. The loading crew pulled back as well, disappearing into the airplane's cargo bay. Whatever was happening, they wanted no part of it. Nails in the crate lid gave way, creaking like an old door hinge. Davis pulled the lid open.

He called over his shoulder, "Have you seen this?"

"Listen, buddy, I don't know what's in 'em," the driver stammered. "I just move 'em around."

Davis reached in and pulled out a sample. He said, "No, I mean— have you *seen* this?" He held up a packaged DVD. *Titanic*. It was one of a hundred different titles in the crate. "What about this one?" he asked, holding up *Star Wars: The Empire Strikes Back*. "Everybody's seen this one."

The driver looked at him like he was crazy. Then he looked at the crowbar and nodded.

"Did you like it?" Davis asked.

Another nod.

"Me too. Only—there was one thing that drove me crazy." Davis paused.

The driver didn't ask.

"Those damned Imperial Storm Troopers. How could anybody shoot that bad? I mean, as many rounds as they fired? Blind luck says they hit somebody, right? Or maybe a ricochet. Do laser weapons ricochet?" Davis turned around and smiled.

So did the driver. Sort of.

Davis put the movies, which were undoubtedly counterfeit, back into the crate. He pulled down the lid and, using the crowbar as a hammer, battered a half dozen nails back into place. When he was done, he tossed the crowbar to the driver. This clearly surprised him, but he made the catch. Davis then squatted low and, using his shoulders, pulled the crate through the cargo door, lifted it clear, and heaved it onto the prongs of the forklift. The big machine rocked forward under the weight, then settled.

Davis smiled again.

So did the driver, this time probably meaning it.

"What's your name?" Davis asked.

"Johnson."

"You work for FBN, Johnson?"

"Two year contract as an A and P."

A and P stood for Airframe and Powerplant, shorthand for his professional certificate. "You're an airplane mechanic?" Davis asked.

"That's right."

Davis checked his fingernails. They were dirty, which was good. It was his personal policy to never trust any mechanic who didn't have grease under his fingernails.

He said, "So how come you're driving a forklift? Don't they have loadmasters to do that?"

"It's a small company, so I do whatever. Get the job done, you know?"

"Yeah, I do know. That's a good attitude. You like your work?"

"Banging on sheet metal and hauling crates in a hundred and ten degree heat—what's not to love?"

"Right. So tell me, Johnson, how many mechanics does FBN have here?"

"I do most of the work, as far as taking care of the airplanes. There's another guy, Muhammed, but I only see him for big things I can't handle on my own. He spends most of his time on another job."

"What job is that?"

"He doesn't say much about it. Something out there." Johnson pointed toward the remote hangar.

Davis nodded. "What's his background?"

Johnson paused, like he was deciding how much to give. "He used to work at a big operation over in Riyadh. I think it was depot-level maintenance."

This got Davis' attention. Depot maintenance was heavy-duty stuff. Big airplanes taken out of service for months at a time to get stripped down and refurbished. New fittings and engines, corrosion addressed. If there was a spa for airplanes, depot checks were "the works."

"So your buddy, Muhammed," Davis suggested, "he must know how to take an airplane apart."

"Sure," Johnson said, "I'd guess he'd be pretty good at it." He then shot Davis a jaundiced look. "But you still haven't answered *my* question—who the hell are you?"

"Jammer's the name. I'm a pilot."

"You a replacement? For the ones that went down last month?"

"No, I'm not here to take anybody's place. I'm a crash investigator. I was brought in to find out what happened to that airplane."

The beefy mechanic climbed down off the forklift, put the crowbar back under his seat. "Well, I hope you figure it out. Those two pilots, they were good guys. Not assholes like most pilots."

Davis grinned. "So maybe you can help me out. What's the rumor on the ramp?"

Johnson's suspicion got the better of him. "I don't hear nothin'."

"They tell me it was a maintenance test flight, some kind of aileron rerig. Did you do the work?"

"No."

"So it must have been Muhammed."

Johnson thought about that, his thick brow creasing. "I don't know anything about it. That airplane came from—" he stopped cold. Davis followed his eyes and saw him staring at a spot near the airplane's cargo door.

"Came from where?" Davis prodded.

"Never mind," Johnson said. He hopped back onto his loader and started writing on a clipboard.

"From the remote hangar? Is that where they kept it?"

No response. Davis decided he'd pressed far enough. "All right. Thanks anyway."

Johnson nodded distractedly. The loading crew filed out of the DC-3, and gave Davis a wide berth. Johnson had a few quick words before sending them away. He cranked the forklift and it belched to life in a black cloud of diesel exhaust.

"Hey, Johnson," Davis said, loud enough to be heard over the rattling engine.

The driver looked up.

Davis jammed his thumb toward the open cargo door. "You mind if I have a look inside?"

Johnson gave him a suit-yourself shrug. "You're an investigator, right?"

Davis nodded.

"So investigate."

Davis climbed through the cargo door and made his way up front. He took the captain's seat and immediately felt right at home. Certain elements of the flight deck looked no different from an airplane that would come out of a factory today. There was a flap lever and landing gear handle, a set of rudder pedals. Yet for every part that cued familiar, Davis saw dozens that belonged in a black-and-white photograph.

The instruments were mechanical round dials, not the vibrant color displays that dominated contemporary aircraft. This particular collection of gauges had most likely been installed in a factory during World War Two, with a select few getting replaced and upgraded over the last seventy years. The end result was like some kind of aeronautical totem, a story of where the airplane had been and what kind of work it had performed. This cluttered presentation made Davis' search of the front panel a bit harder, but he knew the thing he was looking for had to be there.

Every airplane is required to have a registration number, the aviation equivalent of an automobile VIN number. Assigned by the International Civil Aviation Organization, a registration number is issued to every airplane that leaves a factory, and follows that airframe to its grave.

There are certain conventions involved, and one of the most vital involves the first character. Usually a letter in the Roman alphabet, it signifies the country of registry of the owner. N represents the United States, so the accident airplane, N2012L, had been originally registered there. Also by regulation, this identifier has to be displayed on the fuselage, near the tail, and thus is often referred to as a "tail number."

Davis, however, had sensed something wrong with the registration of this particular airplane. Outside, he'd seen Johnson staring at the aft fuselage, and there was only one thing there—X85BG in bold block lettering. So Davis decided to cross-check. He knew you could find the tail number of an airplane in any number of places. It would be printed on documents on the cockpit door, and sure enough, Davis confirmed that X85BG was printed on the registration certificate, neat and clean. But anybody could take a registration certificate from one airplane and switch it to another. There was, however, another spot that was easily overlooked, one that was more permanent. A tail number had to be placarded on the cockpit forward instrument panel. Davis found it in front of the captain's control yoke, below the artificial horizon. It wasn't any kind of embossed placard, but instead just scribbled on the framework with an indelible marker. The letters and numbers had faded over the years, but there was no mistaking what he saw. And what he saw was a problem.

He went back outside. Johnson was gone, but Davis saw the forklift parked near a small building with a roll-up metal door. Probably a mechanic's workshop, he guessed, a place to keep tools and cases of engine oil. He walked toward the tail section of the airplane, and stared again at the letters and numbers on the aft fuselage. It wasn't obvious—you'd have to *know* to look in the first place—but it was definitely there. X85BG in heavy block letters. New paint—bold, black, and undeniable. But underneath he could just make out a thin coat of white, and under that a ghostly image of the old characters. Numbers and letters the same as the ones he'd seen scribbled in Sharpie on the forward instrument panel. N2012L. The registration number of a DC-3 that was supposed to be at the bottom of the Red Sea.

Somebody was playing musical airplanes.

CHAPTER TEN

Davis needed help, needed shade. At the nearby mechanic's workshop he tried for both.

He walked through the roll-up door, but didn't see Johnson. A big floor fan was pushing hot air from one side of the place to the other, distributing the misery. Davis pulled out the phone Larry Green had given him. It was a satellite gadget that looked pretty much like any phone, maybe a little bigger, a little heavier. He was sure Green had gotten it from someone in Darlene Graham's orbit, probably the CIA. He'd been told to use it like any phone. Call, text. Davis figured the U.S. government had phones like it spread all over the Middle East. Military attaches, intelligence types, informants. Probably handed them out like candy, preloaded with contact numbers for anonymous tips and reward information.

When the phone powered up, it showed decent signal strength. He'd been told the thing was secure, and while Davis might have doubted that in certain corners of the world, here the promise likely held. Sudan's capability for signal intercepts and decryption, if there was any at all, had to be primitive. Davis figured the government in Khartoum was worried about the same things governments here had been worrying about for a thousand years. Food, water, rival warlords. The basics.

Davis checked for messages from Washington, but didn't see any. He did the math and figured it was midmorning in D.C., so Larry Green ought to be at work. He pecked out his message, which was a lot of typing because he had a lot of requests. That being the case, he didn't expect a reply anytime soon. Looking at the handset, his thoughts turned to Jen. She had probably returned his call from three days ago, but he'd been traveling constantly and his regular phone didn't work here. They hadn't talked in almost a week now, and Davis realized that their linkups had become increasingly less frequent since she'd gone to Norway. Jen was distancing herself, probably without even realizing it. Soon she'd be gone for good to college.

Davis typed Jen's number into his CIA sat-phone as a new contact. That gave him two. It was late afternoon in Norway, so he hit the call button, and once again got her message after five rings.

"Hey, it's Jen. You know the deal."

"It's Dad, I've got a new number." He gave it and said, "*You* know the deal. Call me." Frustrated, he ended the connection and shoved the phone in his pocket.

Davis looked over the workshop and saw just what he'd expected —screwdrivers hanging on a pegboard, racks of spare tires, a pile of spent oil cans. The wrench turners might work outside, but they had to have shelter for their tools and spare parts. Davis poked the toe of his boot into a completely bald airplane tire. It had good pressure, so he pegged it for a worn item that had been recently removed. Then again, it could be a dubious spare. Kept in stock to replace something worse.

Davis noted another portrait of Sudan's glorious leader, this one tacked to a support column. It looked a lot like the one he'd seen in Schmitt's office. Same pose, same artist, this particular article faded from the heat. The president was depicted in military garb, his jacket breast covered in medals and ribbons like some kind of war hero. His eyes were cast downward slightly. Watching. Which was probably the point.

Davis heard a sudden rush of mechanized noise, and he caught a glimpse of a military truck and a jeep speeding by the open workshop entrance. They were moving fast, like they had somewhere to go. Davis edged outside, looked to his right, and saw the little convoy pull to a hard stop in front of the second parked DC-3, the one where the young man and woman were preparing to drive away in their truck. The jeep blocked the truck's forward path, and the troop carrier blocked the rear. A squad of soldiers with rifles held across their chests spilled out and fanned into a circle.

Davis stepped out of the workshop but kept in its shadow.

The last guy to dismount was the jeep's passenger. He was thicker than the others, wore green fatigues with patches and brass bars and colorful insignia. He didn't need any of that. The way he moved, full of an airy swagger, was enough. Colonel, captain, whatever. This was the guy in charge. The officer put himself squarely in front of the delivery truck. The man and woman in the cab didn't move, so they all just stared at one another through a dust-encrusted windshield. Nothing happened for a time, not until the officer gave a hand signal. On that command, half the soldiers shouldered their weapons and began shifting the load of supplies from the delivery truck to their own carrier.

The officer stood watching like a patient headmaster, waiting to beat down any dissent. It was the woman who finally ended the stalemate. She bounded down from the driver's side of the cab, circled around back and began yelling at the enlisted men. Davis was fifty yards away, but he could hear enough to know she was speaking Arabic. The words meant nothing to him, but her tone was clear. Accusative, demanding. When she yanked one box out of a soldier's hands and threw it back on her truck, the men froze with stunned looks on their faces.

A line had been crossed.

Davis was impressed. It was a stupid move. Exactly the kind of move he might make. The soldiers were clearly not used to getting yelled at by a woman. Having stopped the flow, she stood defiantly with her hands on her hips. Davis couldn't help but notice that they were nice hips. Her work clothes were drab and loose, but cinched in the right places, certain seams challenged when she moved. Her hair was black and full and long. The woman began barking orders, gesturing for the supplies already unloaded to be put back. The soldiers didn't move.

Their commander did.

So did Davis.

Davis had only gone two steps when he felt a hand on his arm, pulling him back. It was Johnson.

"Easy, buddy," the burly mechanic said. "They might not act like it, but those are soldiers. They show up once or twice a week and take whatever they want, call it a tax."

"The government is raiding aid shipments?"

"Not exactly. The government looks the other way. They can't pay the soldiers much, so nobody cares if they take a little on the side."

"Who is she?"

"I don't know her name, but I've seen her before. She's an Italian doctor, I think. Works for one of the NGO's."

NGO. Non-governmental organization. Davis had heard the term before, but never seen one up close. He liked the sound of it. Anything nongovernmental had to be good. It was probably an organization that worked, one that wasn't bound by organizational charts and performance evaluations. Just a handful of committed individuals getting a job done. Which was what the lady on the ramp was trying to do right now.

The officer stopped a few paces in front of her. Just as he opened his mouth to speak, the woman unloaded. Both barrels. She began screaming, Arabic again, but if Davis wasn't mistaken with a few Roman expletives thrown in. He wondered what the officer could be thinking. Of all the reactions he might have expected from a female Italian doctor, a military-style ass chewing probably wasn't one of them. The woman's partner in the truck was staying out of it. Smart kid. Johnson's arm came down, and Davis held steady as he tried to calculate outcomes. There was a chance the soldiers would simply settle for what they had and leave. If so, the woman might stand down and watch as a few of her supplies were driven away. If that was how things progressed, Davis would stay put.

But the doctor didn't allow it. She worked herself into a lather, hands jabbing and hair flying. Davis wished she was in a hospital somewhere, setting a broken bone, giving an immunization, shining a light in somebody's yellow eyes. There, if she felt the need to come unglued, she could vent at a nurse or another doctor. Maybe a difficult patient. That was the kind of conflict doctors were used to dealing with. Not squads of armed soldiers.

"Shut up," Davis muttered.

The commander only stared at her, and Davis had a bad feeling. Every country has its indigenous equations of culture and morality. This woman was pressing hard against the local standard deviation. But there was another variable, something Davis had served long enough in uniform to understand. The dynamics of command. Discipline, particularly in a ragtag outfit like this, was a precarious thing. No officer could allow himself to be dressed down in front of his men by a civilian. Let alone a foreigner. Let alone a woman.

Davis had a very bad feeling.

Johnson must have sensed what he was thinking. "I'm telling you, don't get in the middle of that. The military here doesn't play by our rules. They don't worry about judges or court-appointed lawyers, and it won't matter if you're an American or a pilot—whatever. That bunch will make you disappear."

Davis didn't respond. He was watching the officer's hand. When he saw it edge toward his sidearm, Davis moved.

"Jammer!" Johnson whispered harshly.

Davis ignored it.

"That's enough!" Davis yelled. He said it at maximum volume. Intonation, command. He might have been calling a formation of Academy cadets to attention. Only these weren't cadets. Still, it had the desired effect.

Everyone looked.

Larry Green got Davis' message just before lunch. It came via secure courier, forwarded by the CIA after they'd done their magic—unscrambled, cleansed, filtered. The flow of communications was something Green didn't like, but he figured he had to choose his battles. The message read:

NEED ALL AVAILABLE BACKGROUND ON TWO DC-3S. TAIL NUMBERS N2012L AND X85BG. FULL BACKGROUND, INCIDENT REPORTS, OWNERSHIP HISTORY. ALSO NEED RADAR DATA AND 121.5 RECORDS FOR NIGHT OF CRASH. CHECK WITH U.S. NAVY/AIR FORCE.

Green read it again, and thought, *You don't ask for much, do you Jammer?*

He wondered about the tail numbers. N2012L was the accident aircraft, but the second registration number meant nothing to Green. He dialed Darlene Graham's number and was immediately put on hold. She had told him all requests were to go directly through her office. The director had been pleased when he'd told her that Davis had accepted the assignment. She had a lot of faith in the man, as did Green. The fact that there was nothing in the message about Blackstar meant Davis hadn't gotten into the hangar yet. But he'd find a way.

Green had been working with Davis for a long time. He had dressed him down more than once, and also put him up for commendations. There was a strange asymmetry to Jammer Davis. Investigating aircraft accidents could be delicate work. Intricate forensics, technical know-how, sensitive interviews with the next of kin. In that kind of environment, a blunderbuss like Davis would seem a surefire liability. Indeed, every time Green put Davis on an investigation he felt like he was pulling up a deck chair to a dangerous intersection, just waiting for the crash. On one occasion, Davis had blown up a mothballed airplane to see how a pressure bulkhead would fail. He hadn't gotten any kind of permission or permit—he'd just packed a jet with explosives and blown it up. Green had once seen Davis climb into a bulldozer and push around sections of wreckage until he found the defective engine fan blade he was after. Then there was the full-bird

colonel who had ended up in the hospital with a broken jaw because
he'd tried to order a lieutenant to fly a jet that Davis was convinced
wasn't safe. That had gotten Davis busted from lieutenant colonel to
major, the rank at which he'd retired. It had also saved the taxpayers
an F-16 and probably the lieutenant's life.

Wherever he went, Davis managed to piss somebody off. But he
got away with it, because he was right. At least, every time Green had
seen him in action. In some Neanderthal-savant way, Jammer Davis
knew where to stick his big nose. And once he had a scent, there was
no shaking him. You might as well light off an Atlas V rocket, then try
to keep it on the pad.

Green wished he was there to watch. Right now there was probably only one person in all Sudan who even knew Davis, and Bob
Schmitt hadn't known he was coming. So a little airline had readied
its books for inspection, stacked manuals on desks, and double-checked
logbooks. All the procedural ducks were lined up in a nice neat row,
everyone standing at attention with belt buckles polished. Ready for
the usual ICAO inspector, a button-down overseer of standards and
protocols. A stiff professional in a stiff suit. What they'd get was Jammer Davis.

With the phone still clenched between his ear and shoulder, Larry
Green smiled. *It'll be like a meteor strike on Walden Pond.*

His long strides gave Davis presence, a sense of purpose. It also gave
him no more than twenty seconds to figure out what the hell to do.

Option 1: Get in the commander's face, tell him to take his boys
and shove off. That might work. More likely he'd get arrested. Worst
case, shot. Davis kept up his pace as he struggled for Option 2. His
trajectory was taking him to the tiny gap between the officer and the
doctor. The soldiers were all frozen in place, watching Davis with the
same regard they might give to an oncoming steamroller.

He noticed that much of the cargo was stenciled with U.N.
logos. When he was two steps away, Davis yanked out his NTSB ID
and quickly fanned it in front of him. Nobody looked at the credentials because they were busy watching him. Jammer Davis knew how

to intimidate. He had the size and the stare. He also had the perfect voice, a bass reverberation that passed right through soft tissue and lodged in people's spines.

"Davis, with the U.N. Inspector General's office," he said. "Whatever the hell is going on here, it stops right now." He put out an arm and barged in between the two like a referee separating a pair of prizefighters. Once established, Davis made his choice. He half turned to face the doctor.

"*You*," he said stridently, "will back off and let these men finish their work!"

Her eyes went wide with surprise. She'd been expecting an ally, a knight in shining armor.

"Who are you to tell me this?" she responded in English.

Good, Davis thought, *she speaks English*.

He turned to the officer and got his first close look. A gaunt man, he was leering at Davis with reddened, dopey eyes. The eyes of an addict. There was no name over his breast pocket, no embroidered block letters or acetate tag. The boss-man did, however, have a distinguishing mark—a scar on one cheek. He seemed to hold his chin at an angle to put it on display, probably hoping Davis would think he'd gotten it in a knife fight or some kind of duel to the death. It might have been that. But more likely it was a vestige of something less dramatic. A car wreck or a drunken father.

If the man was worried about Davis being less than a yard away, it didn't show. He was confident. He was also stupid. Jammer Davis had joined the United States Marines right out of high school, had boxed at the Academy. He'd learned a lot about close-in combat from some of the most skilled practitioners in a very nasty business. Right now, Davis was close enough to render the man's sidearm useless. He figured he could break this doped-up loser's neck in about two seconds, and based on what he'd seen so far, tomorrow he wouldn't feel particularly bad about it. But there was more to consider. To be exact, seven considerations, all with rifles and machine pistols. The other men here might be soldiers in the loosest sense, but a disciplined fighting unit they were not. If Davis took out their leader, the guy with the quickest trigger finger would have the inside track to becoming the new alpha dog.

Having figured all that out, Davis addressed the woman again.

"You have no authority here," he said. Which implied that perhaps he did. "These men should finish their work. I'm sure the supplies will be put to good use."

Scarface appeared to contemplate this, which suggested that he too spoke at least some English. His hand was still near the handle of his revolver, but more relaxed now. Davis looked right at the guy, then rolled his eyes in the direction of the doctor and shook his head, the way guys did to say, *Women!* Two clouded eyes came alight, like searchlights out of a mist. The boss man smiled and said something to his men. It was probably an off-color joke, something sexist and demeaning. Scarface chuckled, and when he did, everyone seemed to lighten up.

Everyone except the doctor.

Davis saw her reaching a boil, so before her lid came off he reached out and grabbed her by the arm. Grabbed hard, his fingers clamping like a vise. The doctor winced, and again Davis thought, *Good.* She had gotten so wrapped up in her objective that she'd lost her situational awareness. Pilots simply referred to it as SA. Knowing what was going on all around you. In aerial combat, you had to do a lot more than just fly your own jet. You had to know where your adversaries were, where your wingman was, the height of the mountains below and the clouds above. Sometimes it was a lot of information, a big picture that had to be whittled down and prioritized. That was what this passionate Italian doctor had lost. The big picture. She'd been so incensed by the hijacking, all she'd wanted to do was challenge it, not study the odds. But now her arm hurt, and that made her forget about her precious truckload of supplies. Made her consider a lower level on Maslow's hierarchy of needs.

Davis leaned closer to her, and twisted his head so no one else could quite see. He whispered, "*Faites-confiancemoi. Laissez lui allez.*"

The doctor stared at him. She was certainly educated. And Italy was right next to France, so there was an excellent chance that she would understand the French phrase. *Trust me. Let it go.*

She did. Or at least she calmed down. Davis eased his grip on her arm. Let *her* go.

The soldiers switched the load from one truck to the other with quick efficiency, like they'd done it all before. Davis took note of what they were stealing. Blankets, medicine, bulk food. Most would probably still make its way to those in need. There was just another middleman now. That's what Davis told himself, again and again.

The doctor backed away, clearly not wanting to watch. She went to the driver's side of her truck, still seething, but quiet. She had her SA back. When the thieves were done with the transfer, the officer looked at Davis and gave him a knowing grin, along with a two-fingered salute. Davis returned it, rather subtly, with a one-fingered variant. The little convoy drove off at a more leisurely pace than it had arrived. Sitting in the passenger seat of the jeep, the commander looked smug. Davis wondered briefly if he had made the wrong choice, wondered if he should have broken the guy's neck after all. The other men might have cheered. Might even have made Davis the new squad leader. *Yeah*, he thought, *that's just what I need. My own private army.*

Once the trucks were out of sight, he turned to the doctor. She was at the running board going over a clipboard with a pencil, probably checking off what she'd lost, item by item. Damage control. When she was done, she set the clipboard on the front fender, came over, and stood right in front of Davis. With a big windmill swing, she slapped his face hard.

CHAPTER ELEVEN

Six hours.

That was how long Davis had been in-country, and he already had five confirmed enemies. Three Arab thieves, Schmitthead, and now an overwrought Italian physician. At that rate, by the end of next week—*No*, he decided, *no need to go there.*

The doctor's slap hadn't mitigated anything—she still looked furious. He found himself wondering what she'd look like if she smiled.

He said, "You're welcome."

Way too early for a smile. Just anger. Or, best case, maybe quizzical anger now.

"I will not thank you. You have done me no favors," she said. Her English was decent, albeit laced with a hard accent.

He said, "You were digging a pretty deep hole for yourself. I got you out."

She didn't reply, only stood there. Impassive. Defiant. Pretty. He caught her scent, and she didn't smell like any doctor he'd ever known. No olfactory assault of iodine or antiseptic soap or latex gloves. She smelled sweet, like rain on jasmine.

"Look," he said, "I'm sorry you lost that shipment, but I'm sure there will be others."

"Not for weeks. In that time, do you know how many of my patients will suffer? How many could die?"

Davis took this for a rhetorical question. Still, he had a good reply. "And how many would suffer or die if those thugs had taken you away? I haven't been here long, but I'd bet that losing a good doctor is a lot worse than losing a few crates of supplies."

He thought that might hit home, the idea that she could have been taken away by the South Khartoum Crew. If so, it didn't show. She was still frosty, even in this heat.

"So who were those guys?" he asked.

"I have never seen them, but other aid workers have warned me about them. They have a warehouse and come here occasionally to keep it full."

"Are they really soldiers?"

"Technically, yes. Men like that have been terrorizing this country for years. Lately, however, killing, rape, and mutilation have become unfashionable, so they have turned to more practical endeavors."

"Like stealing shipments of medicine to sell on the black market?"

"Yes. And they will keep doing it until someone stands up to them."

Davis said nothing

"Who are you?" she asked. "You are clearly American, but you are not with the U.N.—I know all the U.N. people here."

"I'm here to investigate an aircraft accident." He gestured to the DC-3 parked nearby. "One of those went down two weeks ago."

She glanced at the airplane and seemed to thaw. "Yes, I heard. It was a terrible tragedy. I knew one of the pilots."

"Really?"

"He helped at our clinic once or twice."

"Tell me, doctor, does FBN Aviation bring in all your shipments?"

"Most of them. But we sometimes use other carriers."

Davis eyed the clipboard sitting on the front fender. He walked over and picked it up. It was interesting, not some standard-issue aid agency request form, but an actual load manifest from the airplane, or at least a copy of it.

Looking over the list, Davis asked, "Would you have had an ohmmeter in that shipment?"

"A what?"

"It says here there was an ohmmeter. You know, for measuring electrical resistance."

"No, that would not have been ours. We receive only part of each shipment. FBN is too lazy to create separate manifests, so they make copies and highlight our portion of each delivery in yellow." She stepped over and pulled a finger down the list. "See? The rest goes elsewhere."

"Really? Like where?" he asked.

"What do you mean?"

"Well, when you unload your cargo and there's a secondary load on these FBN flights, where does it go?"

She shrugged. "I don't know. Sometimes the airplanes stay here when we leave. Other times they are towed away."

Davis could just see the FBN Aviation hangar from where they were standing. "Have you ever seen one of these airplanes towed over there? To that hangar in the distance?"

"Once or twice, perhaps."

"I don't suppose you've ever been over there? Inside?"

"No. Why are you so concerned with this? Has it to do with your investigation?"

"I don't know. Tell me, do you keep these load sheets on file?"

"We keep a permanent record, yes."

"At the clinic?"

She nodded.

"You know," Davis said, "it might help my investigation if I could see them."

Her mouth parted immediately, about to say no, but then she hesitated. "You want my help? After the damage you have done?"

"Maybe I can make it up to you. You told me another pilot helped at your clinic."

"The other pilot was a decent man."

Davis said nothing.

The doctor stared at him, made some kind of survey. "However," she said, "you might be useful."

"I can be very useful."

"If you come, will you come to work?"

Davis considered that. He had an airplane crash to solve, a lost drone to find. "I have a lot on my plate right now," he said, "but I could make some time. Let's call it a trade—I help you at the clinic, and you let me take a look at those records."

"Very well. Tomorrow morning." She gave him directions to the camp.

"Twenty miles," he remarked. "I don't have a car."

"You seem resourceful."

"When I need to be."

For the first time he saw something different in her eyes, a glimmer that wasn't sharp or accusing. There was a crease at the corner of her mouth. Light, even playful. The lady was stunning. Even better, she didn't give a damn. Davis liked that. He watched her climb up to the driver's seat of her empty truck. Watched her sidle into the cab and pull the door shut hard. Harder than she needed to.

He called through the open window. "By the way, my name's Davis. Jammer Davis."

She looked down, paused to make him wait. Like women did.

"Antonelli," she finally said. "Dr. Regina Antonelli."

With that, the truck jerked into gear and was gone. A thin cloud of blue smoke trailed behind, and that soon dissipated into a brilliant red sky as the horizon split the sun.

CHAPTER TWELVE

Davis woke at seven in the morning, sunlight streaming through cracks at the covered window. He heard the same noises you'd hear at any airport hotel in the world. Outside, the dawn patrol taxiing out for takeoff. Inside, bumps and grinds from the plumbing as his neighbors showered and shaved.

He had been right about the elevator on both counts. The shaft was indeed two feet from his pillow. And it hadn't bothered him. He undid the clothespins on the curtains, drew them open to call the morning into his room. Davis shaved over an avocado-green sink before turning on the shower. With the handle full cold, he got lukewarm. He dressed and followed his nose to a coffeepot near the operations desk. Wherever you found pilots, you found coffee. The brew wasn't as good as the fancy stuff he'd had a few days ago in a posh Fredericksburg cafe, but it put a check in his caffeine square.

Antonelli's clinic was twenty miles away, so Davis hit up Schmitt to borrow his Mercedes. Got told to piss off. Investigator-in-charge Davis insisted on something, so the chief pilot scrounged up a key from the bottom of a drawer.

It could have been candy-apple red, deep burgundy, or just brown. The dust was so thick there was no way to tell.

He found the dilapidated Ford pickup parked near a Dumpster at the side of the building. The odometer read 289,000 miles, which, in Davis' experience, was about the limit for a vehicle like that. He'd been told that the truck was used by FBN's mechanics—Johnson and the elusive Jordanian—and also shared with other wrench-turners on the airfield. The cab smelled like grease and glue, and discarded plastic packaging on the floor evidenced everything from spark plugs to potato chips. But the truck started on the first try—score one for the mechanics—and seemed to run smoothly.

Indeed, as Davis picked up the southern road for the half-hour drive, the air conditioner blew like an Arctic wind. Davis had to smile at that. He knew all about mechanics. The original air conditioner had likely given up under the local climatic conditions, so the mechanics, on a slow day, had gone out and requisitioned something a little heavier. Something like the compressor from a Mack truck. They'd have jerry-rigged it into the old Ford's engine compartment, serviced it until coolant was oozing from every seam. What had been a bare bones tool-wagon became a refrigerated break room, even an office where they could do their paperwork.

The road shimmered in the early morning, the sun's angle still low enough to reflect. Not penetrate. Along the margins, scrub-covered terrain materialized out of the dawn, a prickly array of drab color. The truck's undercarriage creaked, and the Mack truck air conditioner spewed chunks of ice. He slowed when he reached the marker Antonelli had given him as a reference, a road sign showing the distance to Wad Rawah as twenty-one. Only somebody had crossed out twenty-one and scrawled thirty-three. It could be that the original version was wrong. Or it could be that somebody felt the need to convert miles to kilometers. Then again, maybe the town had just moved. They were nomads, after all.

Davis looked for a turnoff, but didn't see one. No road, no sign with an arrow, no building in the distance. Nothing but a rocky path on one side that meandered off into the desert. It looked jarring, but Davis decided this had to be the place. He yanked the steering wheel hard right, and a lousy road turned into a raw trail. The truck bounced and groaned, left a rooster tail of dust as it pounded over ruts and loose stone. A minute later he arrived. From a distance it looked like a Boy Scout jamboree, a small city of canvas and wooden poles and rope, all situated in the lee of a large hill. The tents were the open air variety, no sidewalls, some at least fifty feet wide. Military grade, he guessed, probably surplus from a war. Iraq or Afghanistan. Maybe Korea.

Davis parked the truck, and resisted a suburban urge to lock the doors. There was no entrance to the compound, no front or back or reception area. It was just an amoebic outpost of hope in the middle of a godforsaken desert. He searched under the tents—or more accurately, tarps strung tightly over stiff wooden poles—and saw Dr. Regina Antonelli at the side of a bed. Only it wasn't a bed, but rather a blanket on the sand. Around it, fifty other blankets. And in the next tent fifty more. There were a few raised cots, perhaps reserved for the most seriously ill. But only a few.

Antonelli spotted him and waved. Davis maneuvered carefully through what seemed like a human minefield. The condition of the patients was all over the board. Men and women. Young and old. Expectant mothers waiting for their joyous hour. Stricken old men waiting for God. He could discern a few nurses, though no two wore a common uniform. He could tell them apart by the simple fact that they were standing and working. More telling was what was missing. There were no gurneys, beeping monitors, or IV poles. In fact, aside from the patients and blankets, there wasn't much to advance the idea that this was even a clinic.

He watched Antonelli inject something into the arm of her middle-aged patient. His black skin glistened in sweat, and his breathing was shallow and uneven. Davis stood at the foot of the blanket and waited for her to finish.

"Welcome to Al Qudayr Aid Station," she said, beginning to write on a chart. "I will be with you shortly, Mr. Davis." When she finished writing, Antonelli set the chart in the sand near her patient's foot. "We have a great deal of work here."

"I can see that."

"On the best day, we have nine nurses and two doctors to care for our patients."

He surveyed the place. "How many patients are there?"

Antonelli shrugged. "We have no time for such trivia. We simply go from one to the next. Do what we can."

"This place seems pretty remote. Where do they come from?"

"There is a village just over the hill." She pointed toward the high dune. "Some are from there, and occasionally a group will arrive in a vehicle. But most—" she gestured toward the scrubland, "most simply come in from the desert. They walk in, sit down, and wait."

The man in the bed coughed, a weak, wet expulsion. His gums were bleeding and his lips were blue. Antonelli looked at him forlornly, turned away, and began walking. Davis followed. A woman lying in the sand reached out as Antonelli passed, probably more in reflex than hope. The doctor threw out a practiced smile of patience, then dodged her like a soccer player avoiding a tackle. When she was outside the tent, Antonelli paused and stood still.

Her gaze was a faraway blank as she stared at the empty desert. Antonelli clutched her arms to her chest, and he could see anguish in her eyes, weariness in her posture. He was struck by how different she seemed, not the tough-as-nails woman who'd confronted a squad of armed men yesterday.

"You okay?" he asked.

"I'm fine," she replied too quickly. "I did not invite you here to perform counseling. Judging by your performance yesterday, I doubt you would be very good at it."

Davis said nothing.

She clutched some more, twisted her shirt sleeve up to wipe away a tear at the corner of one eye. Antonelli then looked at him more thoughtfully.

"I'm sorry," she said. "I should not burden you with my problems, Mr. Davis."

"It's okay. And call me Jammer."

She looked at him questioningly, then tilted her head in the direction of the patient she'd been tending. "Dengue fever, day six. His circulatory system is shutting down. I don't think he is going to survive."

He looked over his shoulder at the man on the blanket. He didn't look good. Davis had seen death before, but not the kind that came in places like this. Not on this scale. He considered what to say, and only one thing came to mind.

"How can I help?"

The wailing voice beckoned, a tin warble from a cheap speaker outside the hangar. Fadi Jibril eased back on his heels, thankful for the distraction. He had been up all night, taking only one brief respite on the cot near the back wall. The parts from Hamburg had still not arrived, so he'd been slugging through software validation. He was comfortable with the code, getting good results, but there had been little time for integration testing. Jibril was neck deep in a fault injection series when his tired thoughts were mercifully interrupted by the call to prayer.

If there was one constant in his life, one thing that remained steady and true, it was his faith in Allah. He pushed a diagram aside, picked up his Koran from a nearby table, and carefully unwrapped the protective cloth. He made his way to the sink, washed thoroughly, and started off toward the prayer room. The nearest proper mosque was in the main passenger terminal, wholly impractical for those who worked here. As such, the imam had provided a makeshift place of worship in an annex to the hangar. It was an awkward venue, gilt curtains over corrugated metal, fine rugs on cold concrete. To Jibril's thinking, not a fitting place for holy worship. Still, the room was clean, and he could not deny its convenience, so the engineer kept with the old adage: *There is no inappropriate place to pray.*

He was nearing the prayer room entrance when someone shouted his name from behind. Jibril turned and saw a lanky young soldier with a wry smile on his face.

"Special delivery," he said. Three boxes were piled on the concrete at his feet.

Jibril nodded, and the soldier turned away and trotted out the door.

Full of hope, Jibril rushed over. The parts should have arrived yesterday, and indeed probably had, but the local army contingent had a reputation for meddling with shipments. He could lodge a complaint with the imam, but at this point, he reasoned, there was little to gain. At the very least, the ruffians had never lost a shipment. None that he knew of, anyway.

The reinforced boxes were heavy, and Jibril transferred them to his work area one by one. That done, he put the first on a bench, and opened it using the claw end of a hammer. When he saw the telemetry modules inside, Jibril's heart sank. He double-checked the model number, studied the connectors and saw a clear mismatch. He settled heavily onto his work stool and let out a long sigh. Another setback.

Hamburg had sent the wrong parts.

Jibril sat still for a full minute, a cloak of despair casing his thoughts. Then, with all the deliberation he could muster, he picked up his Koran and went to the prayer room.

Davis had never had much of a bedside manner. Fortunately, that didn't matter. He was handy with a wrench, and what the clinic needed more than anything was to have an inoperative generator repaired. The whole tent city was off the larger electrical grid—which according to Antonelli was unreliable anyway—and depended on a pair of old diesel generators. One of these had been broken for weeks, and Davis was tasked to get the thing running.

The clinic had some basic hand tools, and Davis found a few more under the seat of the truck. It took most of the morning, but he finally identified the problem as being in the fuel feed—a severely clogged filter and a faulty shutoff valve. The filter he simply removed. The valve Davis rehabilitated by way of brute force—hammers and wrenches, banging and bending. Neither repair was permanent, but the unit would be serviceable for a few weeks.

It was nearly noon when he finished, and Davis was covered in grease and diesel. He went looking for Regina Antonelli, and found her in the supply tent digging deep into an almost empty box.

"The generator is up and running," Davis said. "But it's only a temporary fix. I'll need a few things to make the job permanent. I made a list of the parts, along with the make and model number of the generator. I'm not sure how long it will take to get spares like that, but maybe I can twist some arms at FBN Aviation, get them to expedite a shipment for us."

Antonelli eyed him, top to bottom. He had to look like he'd been in a grease pit all day. She smiled a half smile, but a smile all the same. It was just like he'd expected. Downright stunning.

"Thank you," she said. "Anything you can do to get replacement parts would be greatly appreciated."

He began cleaning his hands with a rag.

"So how long have you been here?" he asked.

"Since June, but my term is nearly done. Three new physicians arrive tomorrow. I'm hoping they will bring supplies to replace those we lost."

"So you're leaving? Back to Italy?"

"In a few days. I must first oversee the delivery of a shipment to a small village north of here—al-Asmat, on the Red Sea. Even in the north there is need. After two days there, I will continue to Port Sudan and take a passage home."

Davis nodded. "Are you looking forward to it? Going home?"

She shrugged. "In a way. But it is a difficult transition. The people in Milan, they can be rather self-absorbed. Nice food, expensive clothing, exotic cars. It all seems rather trivial when one sees things here. To watch a thirty-year-old pregnant woman die for need of a two dollar dose of medicine—it gives one a certain perspective."

"I'm sure it does," he said.

"But I do not wish to paint myself as a saint. I too have fine clothes, a decent car, and a house twice as large as I need."

"I have all those things too," he said. "Do you think less of me?"

She looked at him thoughtfully. "Sometimes I feel . . ." she hesitated.

"Like you can never do enough?"

She nodded.

"My investigations make me feel that way sometimes. It can be frustrating."

"That reminds me, I have something for you."

Antonelli retrieved a satchel and pulled out a stack of papers that were neatly clipped together.

"These are the load manifests you asked for. They cover the last five months. Please take them if it helps your investigation. I only ask that you return them when you are done. We must keep our records current to avoid funding cuts."

"I'll make sure it all gets back to you. And thanks for digging them out, I know you're busy. I have to get back to the airfield now, but I'll finish with that generator when the parts arrive. I also might be able to get your sterilizer working better if—"

"Dr. Antonelli!" a strident voice interrupted. A nurse came into the tent and rushed to Antonelli's side. Eying Davis with caution, she leaned close and whispered into the doctor's ear.

Antonelli closed her eyes. "Thank you," she said in a soft voice.

The nurse disappeared.

Antonelli seemed to lose her focus, much as she had earlier.

He raised an inquisitive eyebrow. "Bad news?"

"Yes. The man I was treating when you first arrived, the dengue patient. He has died."

"I'm sorry," Davis said. He really was, but he wondered why she seemed so close to this case. Maybe she'd gotten to know the man. Maybe something deeper.

"Was he a friend?" he asked.

"Yes," she replied, her voice shot with anguish.

Davis wanted to help her find strength. He said, "Regina, there are a lot of other patients here depending on you. Being staffed so thin—you are vital to their well-being."

She looked up at him curiously, took a deep breath, and seemed to pull herself together. "Yes, I know. You are right. But perhaps I should have explained. The man who just died—he was the other doctor."

Larry Green was at his desk, ten-mile run complete, by seven in the morning. It had been less than a day since he'd forwarded Davis' requests to Darlene Graham, and answers were already coming in. This told him that the emphasis on finding the lost Blackstar drone hadn't wavered one bit.

The information had again come by courier, and the papers in front of Green ranged in classification from CONFIDENTIAL to TOP SE-CRET. On top were the most recent satellite and radar images of the hangar outside KNIA, Khartoum International Airport. Green had seen a lot of surveillance in his day, and what he saw here didn't add anything new. He leafed through the rest, flicking aside a CIA overview of Sudan's political situation, along with a security assessment on the upcoming Arab League conference in Egypt. He guessed some wonk had thrown that in just to make the file seem a little more substantial. At the bottom of the stack he found a computer disc in a plastic case. A handwritten sticky note was attached:

Larry, Got this from a Navy cruiser that was in Gulf when FBN aircraft went down. Thought you might make something out of it. Still working on aircraft histories for the two tail numbers JD gave you and 121.5 records. DG

Green took the disc, which was dated September 20, the date of the accident, and slid it into the drive on his desktop computer. The screen came alive with a familiar picture, one Green recognized as a slight variation of other displays he'd seen. It was a radar tape, a digital record of what some Navy cruiser had been painting on the night of the crash. Green could see that certain data readouts and information bars at the top of the screen had been sanitized, blacked out electronically to mask sensitive information regarding the range and operational modes of the ship's radar. The Navy might be helping, but turf wars were eternal.

Green oriented himself to the display and saw that north was up. There were no geographic boundaries drawn on the screen, but instead the references used by air traffic controllers—airspace boundaries. Green knew the general area in question, so the layout of the airspace made for a pretty clear picture. Egypt, Israel, Saudi Arabia,

Sudan. For a pilot, these were hard lines you didn't cross, not unless you either A: had the necessary authorizations and a carefully filed flight plan, or B: were in the mood for an armed fighter escort.

As the recording began, Green saw a dozen commercial flights floating across the screen, tiny white airplane symbols with blocked data tags to give their altitude, call sign, and airspeed. There were a handful of other aircraft on the screen, but data on these had been blacked out—once again, the Navy keeping itself to itself.

A time counter at the bottom of the screen told Green he was watching a forty-two-minute show. Ninety seconds in, he saw an airplane take off from Khartoum International. Call sign: Air Sahara 007. Air Sahara was FBN Aviation's corporate call sign. He watched the blip move north and climb. In terms of performance, he was used to watching military fighters and commercial jets, so the whole show looked like it was running in slow motion as the ancient DC-3 clawed for altitude and ambled toward the Red Sea. He also noticed an occasional shadow to the primary return, a second tiny square of light that blinked occasionally into view, then disappeared. Green had seen plenty of echoes like it in his years working with radar, and he was mildly surprised that the Navy's shipboard gear wasn't better. Once the airplane was over what had to be the Red Sea, it started a turn, then another. Soon it was tracking what looked like a nice lazy holding pattern over the water.

Green watched for half an hour as the airplane spun round and round. He waited patiently, expecting the data block to start flashing some kind of warning, expecting the altitude readout to start spinning down like a car odometer getting tripped to zero. But that never happened. The airplane just kept flying, boring a pattern of oval holes in an empty sky. Finally, Air Sahara 007 turned toward Khartoum International, began a slow glide down, and settled to what looked like a pretty nice landing.

"What the hell?" Green muttered.

Had the Navy sent the data for the wrong day? And what had the airplane been doing? If the crew had really been performing some kind of maintenance test flight, there was no need to go out and fly circles over the water. The airplane would have just taken off, done a quick circuit over the home drome, then landed. But it was the pattern that really put Green's thoughts into a spin. It reminded him of missions he'd done himself, a long time ago in an F-15 over the Gulf of Mexico—radar test work with a captive-carry air-to-air missile. That was what it looked like, a test pattern to gather data. Only the DC-3 was a seventy-year-old airplane, and an airplane that old didn't have much left to test.

No, Green thought, none of it made sense. Not one bit.

CHAPTER THIRTEEN

His shirt went into the trash, but the pants were salvageable.

Back in his room, Davis hit the shower. The water was even warmer than this morning, but did the job—a tiny cyclone of brown mud and grit swirled at his feet. He dried himself with two tiny towels and donned fresh clothes before easing down on the bed with the paperwork Antonelli had given him. Davis was not, by nature, a patient man. In a big investigation he would have had help with this part of the inquiry, a small army of experienced people to help weed through records and documents. The only help he was getting here—a seven-thousand-mile phone link to his boss and an Italian doctor with a honey-do list.

The papers were load manifests. Every bit of cargo carried on an airplane had to be weighed and its position noted. This was critical because an airplane's center of gravity had to remain within certain limits, everything added up as if on an apothecary's balance scale. But the manifest had other purposes as well. Customs officers liked to see what was coming into their country. Hazardous materials had to be listed so that first responders knew what they were dealing with in an emergency. Copies of the papers Davis held were on file in lot of different cabinets. The airline. The people who did the loading. The people who did the receiving. Any number of government agencies in between. Chances were, all the copies were the same, but with a company like FBN Aviation you never knew. So Davis took a good close look.

He saw roughly twenty load sheets covering five months of shipments to Antonelli's aid organization. In truth, he would rather have seen the departure manifests—what had gone out. He'd like to find a load sheet originating at Khartoum International that said: CARGO: U.S. BLACKSTAR DRONE (1) SLIGHTLY DAMAGED. DESTINATION: CHINA. That was what Davis needed. Black-and-white proof so he could go home and call it a day.

What he had was a line-by-line inventory of inbound cargo. He found a lot of the things one would expect. Medical supplies, batteries, bulk food, construction materials. But there were also surprises. A Harley-Davidson Softail, a Thoroughbred racehorse, two crystal chandeliers. In one load: a two-thousand-gallon hot tub, nineteen cases of Irish whiskey, and forty thousand condoms. A dictator somewhere was planning a hell of a party.

Davis was halfway through August when he hit pay dirt, four consecutive entries that seemed to jump off the page. One dorsal tracking beacon. Two guidance transponders. One flight control interface module. The kinds of things that Rafiq Khoury was supposedly trying to sell to the highest bidder. Davis was giving these entries some serious thought when his phone rang.

It was Larry Green.

Davis got up and meandered to the window. He spent three rings deciding what he was going to ask for. Then he picked up.

"Hello, Larry."

"Hey, Jammer. How's Africa?"

"Tahiti would have been better."

Davis spent a few minutes discussing Bob Schmitt. Green talked about the unhelpful reconnaissance photos, then got to his real business.

"Darlene Graham sent me some radar data this morning, but it's not making much sense."

"Why's that?" Davis asked.

"Well, on the night in question the Navy had real good coverage of the area where this airplane went down. I went over the recordings twice, and you know what?"

"The airplane didn't go down," Davis said.

There was a long pause on the other end of the line. "How the heck did you know that?"

"Just a guess. Was there anything at all on the tape?"

"Actually, yeah. An airplane with an FBN call sign did take off. It flew out over the water, roughly to where the crash was supposed to have occurred, churned circles in the sky for half an hour, then went straight back to Khartoum International and landed."

Davis said nothing.

"Does this mean anything to you?" Green prodded.

"I don't know. What about the radio traffic—was there anything on guard frequency?"

"One twenty-one point five? I don't have anything on that yet," Green said, "but the DNI's people are working it. What are you looking for? The airplane I saw didn't go down, so why would there have been a distress call?"

"I don't know. Just check it. Something is screwy here. Do you have any history on those two tail numbers?"

"Not yet, but they're working on that too."

"Tell them to work faster." There was an extended silence, until Davis said, "Sorry, Larry."

Green seemed to ignore the apology. "Have you gotten near the hangar?"

"No, not yet." Davis looked at the load manifests in his hand. "But there's something else I want you to check. I need a description of some parts that were shipped here a few months ago."

"Shipped *in*? I thought we were worried about stuff going out."

Davis waited. He and Green had known each other long enough that even silence between them had its meaning. It only took a few seconds.

"All right," Green said, "shoot."

Davis reeled off the parts from the list, along with the shipper of record and some associated letters and numbers.

Green remarked, "AN/DRA, AN/DRW? Jammer, this is all milspec stuff."

Milspec stood for military specifications, hardware that was designed for combat conditions. Green had pegged it just like he had.

"That's what caught my eye," Davis said. "Find out what it is, who makes these parts. And most important—"

"Who in Africa might use stuff like that," Green interrupted.

"Right."

"Okay, the government's open now, so give me thirty minutes."

"Twenty-eight." Davis ended the call.

It took twenty-six minutes. Davis picked up after the first ring.

"I've got some of it, Jammer. These parts are all U.S. manufacture, all milspec."

"And it's drone equipment, right?"

"Yep. Mostly from QF-4 modifications."

Davis knew all about QF-4s. The Air Force had modified hundreds of mothballed fighters, including Vietnam era F-4s, to act as target drones. The Q prefix signified a drone conversion. They flew unmanned from Tyndall Air Force Base in Florida, sortied out over the Gulf of Mexico to act as fodder for live-fire missile shoots. Davis himself had shot down a QF-106, back in the day.

He said, "I doubt there's much need in Sudan to modify old fighters for live missile testing."

"Nope. I'll try to track down the shipper, but that'll take some time. I can tell you that all this stuff is obsolete. These parts have been sitting on shelves for twenty years. I can't figure it, Jammer. If you have the wreckage from a high-tech drone sitting in your hangar, what's the point of ordering a bunch of old-school drone hardware?"

There was a long pause as both men digested it. Davis stared at the window and saw a lizard outside, clinging to the glass. It was big and motionless, no doubt stunned by the scorching heat. He finally said, "You know what I could do with stuff like that, Larry?"

"Yeah," Green said, obviously having reached the same conclusion. "You could take it out of the boxes, throw it away, and use the paperwork and packaging to forward newer stuff anywhere in the world with very little suspicion."

Davis grinned. "If we think so much alike, how come you made two-star and I only made major?"

"Because you—"

"No, no. Don't answer that."

Green asked, "When did these shipments happen?"

"It all came in two loads back in the middle of August."

"So if it worked like we think, we've already missed our chance. The most important parts of Blackstar are already gone. Damn. Darlene Graham isn't going to like this."

"Yeah . . ." Davis hesitated, "but there's still one thing that doesn't make sense."

"What's that?"

"The report that started all this. It said Blackstar is still there in the hangar, right?"

"Yeah?"

"Well," Davis reasoned, "if Khoury turned the place into some kind of chop shop, crated up the bits and pieces and shipped them off months ago—how would there be anything recognizable left? And why is there still activity around the hangar? They should have closed up shop by now."

"I see what you mean," Green said. "Sure would be nice to get a look inside, wouldn't it?"

"I'm working on it. In the meantime, keep checking. I want to know about those tail numbers. Go back a few months and study FBN's international flight plans. If you track those two airplanes, there might be a pattern of shipments. Maybe we can figure out where all those pieces went."

"I'll work on it," Green said, then added, "And Jammer—try to stay out of trouble."

"You know me, Larry."

"Yeah. That's why I said it."

Davis hung up.

He pocketed the phone and considered his options. Everything began to unfold in his head like a big map, paths and destinations and obstructions. As was his custom, Davis selected Route One—the shortest distance.

He headed for the chief pilot's office, but found it locked up tight. There was a security keypad on the wall next to the door, something Davis hadn't noticed on his first visit. It looked pretty serious, a back-lit alphanumeric display that was blank right now, waiting for eight digits in some perfect sequence. Ten to the eighth power. A lot of pos-sibilities, mathematically speaking. The door looked sturdy too, a metal frame with heavy striker plates. All in all, heavy security for the chief pilot's office of a Third World flying circus.

He backtracked to the operations desk and inquired as to Schmitt's whereabouts. Got blank stares and shrugs in return. Davis checked his watch. Four thirty. Too early for a chief pilot to have quit for the day. He sighed in frustration. No matter which way he turned, he was get-ting headwinds. On the crash he had a bogus maintenance write-up and a downed airplane that had turned up in one piece. Larry Green's radar data was just further proof that there had never even been a crash. And on the Blackstar drone he had nothing at all. No Lam-borghini parts getting shipped out. Only Edsel parts getting shipped in. The overall status report on his investigation—sliding backward and accelerating.

Then and there, Davis made his most important decision of the day. He needed a beer. And there was, he suspected, only one place to find one.

Rafiq Khoury's room at the hangar had only one window. It was a modest opening, perhaps an architectural afterthought, and completely covered by a slatted blind that served to keep prying eyes at bay. That the blind might also prevent the illumination of Allah from penetrat-ing his sanctuary had never occurred to Khoury.

He stood at the window now, a finger pulling aside one of the thick slats to watch the Land Rover approach. He had summoned Schmitt to his private office, an unusual request that Khoury expected would instill at least a tremor of foreboding in the overconfident

American. The fact that Khoury had sent Hassan to collect him made the exercise even less nuanced. He watched Schmitt get out of the truck, trundle a few steps across the blazing ramp, then stop to wait for his escort to catch up. Hassan performed well, taking long enough to reinforce who was in charge. Long enough to make the man sweat.

When Hassan finally made his way to Schmitt's side, he dwarfed the squat American. They walked side by side to the door, and Khoury noted the manila files in Schmitt's hand. He let the slat fall, took a seat behind his desk, and waited. The knock came.

"Come," Khoury said.

Schmitt was in the lead, Hassan hovering behind.

"That will be all, Hassan. Wait outside." The giant nodded, then disappeared.

Schmitt was indeed sweating, though it was likely a consequence of the heat, combined with the fact that the man was terribly unfit. Khoury did not bother with his public mask of benevolence—he would never raise a palm of compassion to this man.

"Sit," Khoury commanded, in a tone appropriate for a disobedient mutt.

Schmitt sidled over to a chair and did as instructed. Even so, he sat erect, his posture stiff and his gaze firm. It confounded Khoury that he could not intimidate the man.

"These are the files I asked for?" Khoury inquired, holding out a hand.

Schmitt passed them over. "Yeah. What did you need them for?"

Khoury set the files on his desk and ignored the question completely. "I am told the investigator has arrived."

After a pause, Schmitt said, "He got here yesterday."

"Do you think him competent?"

Schmitt steepled his hands as if measuring an answer. "I imagine he is."

"What is his nationality?"

"He's American."

"*American?*" Khoury spat in surprise. "How can this be? You said the investigation would fall to the Europeans. The French."

"That was what I expected, but apparently the French bureau is a little overextended right now."

Not for the first time, Khoury questioned the decision he'd made that had brought on this entire quandary. When the airplane had gone down unexpectedly, the issue arose as to whether to report it missing. Khoury had imagined any number of difficult scenarios. The crash might have been witnessed, wreckage could have turned up in the busy Red Sea shipping lanes, or the aircraft might somehow have gone unaccounted for. In the end, Khoury had reported the incident hoping to minimize complications. A simple explanation for an ancient, decrepit airplane going down seemed the least-risk channel of action. Now Khoury realized he had made a mistake. An American had taken over the inquiry, and unlike Schmitt and the others, one he had not handpicked.

"What is his name?" Khoury asked.

"Davis. He's a big lug, hard to miss. I gave him a room in the residential compound. Figured we could keep an eye on him that way."

Khoury nodded with approval. He had to admit, his chief pilot had good instincts. Or at least, the instincts of a thief. "That was clever of you. And the man works alone?"

"Yes," Schmitt said.

"Has he already questioned you?"

"We had a chat."

"And you cooperated?"

"I told him there had been some suspect work done on the flight controls, and I gave him a copy of the maintenance write-up from the logbook."

"Did he seem convinced?"

"I don't know. He didn't look at it right away." Schmitt paused before saying, "You know, I've still got my own doubts about what really happened. This story about Anatolii and Shevchenko, that they took the airplane out for a joyride—it just doesn't sound like them."

"I have been told that alcohol was involved."

"Really? Who said that?"

"It is not for you to know!" Khoury snapped. "I only mention it because such a scandal would not reflect well upon our operation. And it is all the more reason for you to keep this investigator off balance. Those two fools destroyed one of my airplanes, and in doing so paid the ultimate price for their recklessness. Otherwise, there is no harm, so this entire investigation is pointless. The sooner the man gives up and goes home, the sooner we can get on with running our airline."

"Davis? He won't give up. He'd love to—" Schmitt cut his answer short.

"What?"

Another pause fueled Khoury's suspicion.

Schmitt picked up, "He'd probably love to string up an ex-Air Force guy like me."

"Why is that?"

"Interservice rivalry. Davis was in the Navy—at least I think that's what he said."

Khoury's mismatched eyes bored into Schmitt, but elicited no reaction. He relented, "Just make sure he works for every scrap."

"I'm already on it. I told him that if he wants to figure out the cause of this crash, he should go out and find the wreckage."

Khoury shuddered within, but his eyes remained fixed. "And will he?"

"He'll try, but without knowing exactly where it went down— Davis could waste weeks. He's looking for a needle in a haystack."

A needle in a haystack. Such a curiously American saying, and one Khoury remembered his mother having used. An American by birth, she had done her best to educate him, including teaching him English. Those lessons had ended abruptly when Khoury was twelve years old, on the day his mother died from a sudden illness. Indeed, the very same day that his downward spiral into a life of misery had begun. But even now her phrases stuck in Khoury's mind. He rather liked this one and committed it to memory. A translated version might sound original to his flock of followers.

He asked, "Where else will he focus his investigative efforts?"

"Who knows. The guy only got here yesterday. Sometimes these things take months, even years." Schmitt looked at him expectantly, as if anticipating some kind of reaction.

Khoury said, "I think this inquiry will not last quite so long."

Bypassing that comment, Schmitt said, "Oh, yeah. And I sent those letters you mentioned."

"Letters?"

"You know, to Ukraine. I am very sorry to inform you, blah, blah, blah. Those letters."

"Yes, of course. And you mentioned compensation?"

"Just like you said. I told both families there was insurance, but that it would take some time to get a payment. I also told them we'd get in touch right away if any remains were recovered."

Khoury nodded, satisfied that this would keep the families quiet long enough.

"To tell you the truth," Schmitt added, "I never knew we had a life insurance policy. I should put that on our list of benefits for our next hiring advertisement."

"Do as you wish," Khoury said dismissively.

"And that reminds me—when can you authorize some hiring? Both those guys we lost were captains. I'm two short right now."

"We will hire replacements soon, but not until this investigation has run its course."

"I can't wait that long to—"

"Enough!" Khoury snapped. He was forced to put up with the moods of Jibril, the engineer, but this man was not so vital. "Do not forget, Captain Schmitt, that you serve in your position at my leisure."

Schmitt settled back into his chair. He fell quiet, yet still looked calm. The man was maddening.

"This investigator, Davis," Khoury asked, "will he expect to speak with me?"

"Sooner or later."

"Let us choose later. Time is what we need. Tomorrow we will send him on a flight."

"One of our flights?"

"Yes. The American captain and Achmed are scheduled to go out.

It would give Davis a chance to see our operation—and perhaps keep him out of the way for another day."

"You *want* him to see how we operate? You sure about that?"

"Do it!"

Schmitt shrugged. "You're the boss."

"Indeed I am," Khoury said, his stare turning hawkish.

With that, Schmitt made his exit.

Rafiq Khoury eyed the door long after Schmitt was gone. He had always been good at reading men, and right now he had the impression that his chief pilot wasn't telling him something. Even more, he didn't like the idea of another American roaming about. Was Davis simply a nuisance? Or an opportunity? In either case, Khoury disliked what the situation demanded.

He would have to tell General Ali.

CHAPTER FOURTEEN

If the operations desk was the nerve center of a flying organization, the bar was its heart—or, in a good unit, its cirrhotic liver. No flying organization could operate without one. It might be situated in a squadron building, outside a main gate, or down the block from corporate headquarters. But there was always a preferred establishment.

At FBN Aviation, it was at the back of the building, as far away from the business end of the operation as possible. Far from the front door where morality police from the Muslim-dominated government might walk in unannounced. Davis heard the bar before he saw it, raucous chatter and bad music. Over the entryway was a sign stenciled in big, colorful block letters: GUNS-R-US. Inside, Davis found a place like a hundred others he'd been in.

The centerpiece was a heavy wooden bar with a scuffed brass foot rail, long enough for ten people to lean on. Different types of flying units had different emphases when it came to décor. A fighter unit would have had an inert missile hanging from the ceiling, maybe an ejection seat all bent to hell that somebody had used, then donated to the squadron as a keepsake. But a trash-hauler outfit was different. Traveling the world was their style, so the bar here had a kind of ramshackle-voyager theme. There were neon beer signs from Japan and Belgium. Native artisan work from Africa and Asia. Pictures were nailed to the wall, poor quality amateur photographs stuffed crookedly into cheap frames. In one, two pilots were sitting on a mountain of ammunition crates, both holding rocket-propelled grenade launchers in mock firing position. Everything in the room had a story, and Davis decided that even if Bob Schmitt was an idiot, he'd at least gotten the bar right.

At the moment, three men were bellied around the bar, two watching closely as the third drew on a cocktail napkin. When he finished, the artist held up his masterpiece and said, "And that, gentlemen, is how a surgeon performs a boob job."

You could learn a lot by hanging out in the bar of a flying unit. You could learn who was a good stick and who wasn't. You could learn about wives and girlfriends, who gambled, and who went to church. And here, apparently, you could learn about boob jobs.

One of the men noticed Davis and stared. Two other sets of eyes followed.

The pilot-cum-plastic surgeon said, "You must be the crash dummy!"

The accent was Deep South. Mississippi or Alabama. He was medium height, thick in the shoulders, and thicker still in the gut. Red hair curled over a chunky, freckled face that was blanketed in a two-day growth of orange stubble. His grin was easy, as wide as the Sahara.

"Yeah," Davis said, "that's me. I'm here to inspect your keg."

"You came to the right place," the man said. He ambled over and held out a hand. "Ed Boudreau, Deville, Louisiana. Damned glad to meet you!"

Boudreau, Davis thought, *from Louisiana.* He remembered the jokes, Boudreau and Thibodeaux. A Cajun with a name like that didn't need a call sign. He shook Boudreau's hand.

"Jammer Davis," he said, "Washington Beltway."

"Well, come on in, Jammer. We heard you was nosing around here somewheres."

Boudreau went straight to a rack on the wall where a dozen steins hung on hooks. They all bore names or call signs, and an emblem that had to be FBN Aviation's unofficial logo—an amateurish, hand-drawn DC-3 encased in some kind of coat of arms, and under that, spelled in block letters formed by bullets, FLY BY NIGHT. Boudreau picked out the mug labeled SCHMITT, a subtle indiscretion that told Davis a lot.

Taking the commander's mug was a serious breach of etiquette. Either Schmitt never drank here, or these guys really hated him. Maybe both. Boudreau filled the mug from a handled tap that was mounted into the door of the refrigerator, then slid the stein across the bar.

"Thanks," Davis said.

Boudreau said, "I'll do the honors. This is my buddy from Warsaw, Henri Podulski."

Podulski. Davis had seen the name on the scheduling board out front, and he'd expected a big, ugly lug. That was exactly what he got. The man was four inches shorter than Davis, but every bit as wide. His face was stony and impervious, pale blue eyes set above Slavic cheeks of polished marble. His massive head was shaved, and at the back were two big wrinkles where his skull and spine merged, like whoever had put him together had ended up a couple of vertebrae short. Davis would have pegged Podulski as former military, but not an airplane driver. More like a tank driver. Davis nodded and got a grunt in return.

"And this," Boudreau said, "is Eduardo."

That was it, just Eduardo. One name, like a Brazilian soccer player or something. It was probably on his pilot's license that way. Eduardo at least shook hands. He was a snappy dresser, nice slacks and a coordinated button-down shirt. He had smooth olive skin and black hair flecked with gray, nicely trimmed. When he smiled Davis was nearly blinded. Eduardo didn't look like a pilot either. More like the guy who'd file a pilot's divorce papers.

"So you'll be looking into this accident?" Boudreau asked.

"I guess somebody has to," said Davis.

"They were good men," Boudreau offered, "we all liked 'em. Have you found out anything yet?"

"About the accident? No, not much. I wanted to ask what you guys knew." Davis said it lightly, but he was dead serious. Without the hard currency of forensic evidence, he was scraping for anything he could get. Every crash got pilots talking in the bar, a lot of brass-footrail experts with theories and rumors and whispers. Davis would listen to every one.

He said, "I understand that this airplane went up for a mainte-nance check flight. Apparently there had been some work done on the ailerons. I was wondering—is there a procedure for that? You know, like a checklist you go through, steps to make sure everything is right?"

Boudreau and Eduardo looked at the Pole, so Davis figured he must be the resident expert.

Podulski said, "Yes."

After a long pause, Davis prodded, "Any chance I could see it?"

The big guy didn't say anything. Not *yes* or *no* or even *go to hell*. He just took a long pull on his mug, got up, and disappeared down the hallway. The guy had the charisma of a cast-iron skillet.

Davis stared at the other two. His expression asked, *Is he always like that?*

Eduardo said, "Henri was close to the Ukrainians. He has lost two friends."

Boudreau agreed, "Yeah, don't mind him. Things have been a little tense around here since the crash. You understand."

Davis took a pull on his beer and nodded. He understood all too well.

CHAPTER FIFTEEN

Podulski came back, sat down behind his mug, and sent a three-ring checklist sliding across the bar.

Davis picked it up. It was the size of a hardcover book, with heavy bond pages that were dog-eared and worn. He flipped to the index, then to a page at the back titled: Aileron and Balance Tab Rigging Certification Procedure. Davis read through it once. It was more straightforward than the convoluted title implied, just a few basic steps. Roll right, check the trim, roll left. Simple stuff.

He asked Podulski, "You ever do one of these checks?"

"Once or twice."

"How long did it take?"

"Five minutes. Perhaps ten."

"So why would these guys have been airborne for half an hour before they crashed? I mean, why would they even fly out over the Red Sea? Seems to me, you'd just take off, climb a few thousand feet over the home drome, do the checklist, and then land. Ten minutes, fifteen tops. When they crashed, those guys should have been right here pulling their second round."

Davis waited. Got silence. Probably because they were all wondering the same thing. When an airplane crashes a lot of questions get asked, but nobody has a more vested interest in finding answers than the other pilots in that flying organization. The guys who had to keep flying the same equipment with the same procedures. With a twist of his wrist, Davis sent the checklist spinning back across the bar toward Podulski.

Boudreau put a hand to his stubbled chin, gave it a rub—Davis could actually hear the coarse grinding noise—and asked, "Is it true you and Schmitt have a history?"

"Yeah," Davis said. "Is that a problem?"

Ed Boudreau from Deville, Louisiana, grinned. He went to the refrigerator, pulled out a tray of cold cuts, cheese, and sliced tomatoes, then a loaf of bread from under the bar.

"Help yourself, Jammer."

Davis didn't hesitate. He built a tall sandwich, a three-layer stack that barely fit into his mouth.

"There's no love lost around here when it comes to Schmitt," Boudreau said. "I was the last one to fly that airplane, had her up the day before the crash. There wasn't anything wrong with those ailerons. And there was no write-up in the logbook about them."

None of the others looked surprised at this revelation. So they *had* been talking.

"That would mean the write-up is bogus," Davis surmised in a serious tone. The tone he would have used if he didn't already know this. "So maybe somebody put that gripe in the logbook to make it *look* like the airplane had been in for maintenance."

"That's what we think," Eduardo said.

"But why?" Davis asked.

Podulski, his voice a stony rumble of consonants, said, "Maybe as reason for this airplane to go up on quick flight."

"It gives a nice tidy cause for you to hang your investigation on, don't it?" Boudreau added.

Eduardo put in his two cents. "It is almost like someone expected this airplane to crash."

"Sabotage?" Davis said. "I don't know, guys. Where's the motive? Those old airframes can't be worth anything. I'll bet they're not even insured. Not to mention the fact that you lose two good pilots. I don't see any upside to that theory."

No answers. Three quiet pilots. Davis had come in not sure how to play this crowd. So far, they'd been willing to help. Even more encouraging, they seemed to be smelling a lot of the same foul odors he was. Davis decided to press further.

"Any of you guys been out to FBN Aviation's hangar?"

"Nobody goes there," Eduardo said. "It is strictly off-limits."

"I delivered an airplane there once," Boudreau said, "about three months ago. They sent me Stateside to pick one up from long-term storage in Mojave. Hopped it back here and left it at the hangar."

"Did you put it inside?" Davis asked.

"No. Just left it on the ramp out front. I ain't never seen them doors open, not even once. But that airplane was gone the next morning, like it had just been swallowed right up."

"Do you remember the tail number?"

"It was an oddball, *X* something. Got the full number in my pilot logbook."

"X-ray Eight Five Bravo Golf?" Davis asked.

"Yeah, I think that was it. Haven't seen her since."

"I saw it on the ramp yesterday," Davis said.

After a silence, Boudreau remarked, "So it's back in service."

"Apparently."

"Doesn't an *X* prefix mean experimental?" Boudreau asked. "That airplane was weird, had all kinds of strange avionics. Flew funny too. Mushy and slow."

Davis figured the "new" X85BG didn't fly that way. He wondered if these guys would notice, if any of them would figure out that the tail numbers had been switched. He decided they would. In such a small company, each airplane was unique, with its own scars and quirks. More than ever, Davis wondered what had happened to the real X85BG. It all made his head spin.

He finished his sandwich and put together a second, two tiers this time. Davis hadn't realized how hungry he was. He was knifing mustard out of a jar when the silence was broken by an authoritative voice.

"Room, ten-*hut!*"

In an instinct bred from four years at a military academy, not to mention a career of service, Davis' spine stiffened. But he didn't stand to attention.

Bob Schmitt laughed as he came into the room.

Schmitt headed for the bar. "If it isn't the great Jammer Davis. You figure everything out yet, cowboy?"

Davis took a bite of his sandwich, and said with a half-full mouth, "Not yet. But I will."

Schmitt went to the rack and looked for his mug, but didn't find it. Because it was in Davis' hand. Schmitt pulled another off the rack, one bearing the name Stan. Drinking from a dead pilot's mug. From the corner of his eye, Davis saw Podulski snarl and flex, like a rottweiler who'd just spotted the UPS guy nearing the front door. Thinking the Pole might go after Schmitt, Davis started a little internal debate about whether to let it happen. It was an interesting conundrum, with lots of pluses and minuses. In the end it wasn't an issue. Podulski grabbed his mug and headed for the door. Eduardo followed.

Davis looked at Schmitt and said, "You really have a way with your men."

"Go to hell."

Boudreau got up to leave.

Schmitt pointed a finger at him. "Hold on, Boudreau!"

The Cajun paused.

"Have you seen your assignment for tomorrow?"

"Not yet. Where am I going?"

"Down range. Central Congo."

"Not another one of them danged jungle airstrips," Boudreau grumbled.

"You'll find it."

"Finding it ain't the trouble."

Davis waited to hear what *was* the trouble, but that never came, because when Schmitt pulled the tap the keg only ponied up half a beer before it started spewing foam. He looked like he might pop an aneurysm.

"Dammit!" he said. "This thing's dry again. Who the hell is snacko?"

"I think it's Achmed," Boudreau replied.

"Well get his ass in here."

Boudreau disappeared down the hall.

Pilots in a small organization always had additional duties. The bottom rung on the ladder was snacko. You kept the bar stocked, emptied an honor box full of quarters and dollar bills, went to the store and bought beer nuts and Twinkies. And most importantly, you kept the keg up to speed. Never fail on that, because if you screwed up, you didn't get fired. You kept the job longer.

"Who's Achmed?" Davis asked.

"One of our local copilots, a miserable kid. When he gets his hands on an airplane it's like a kite in a tornado."

"So what are you hauling down to the Congo?"

Schmitt laughed, and said, "Hell if I know, I never see the contracts. We get tasked to haul God knows what to God knows where. Load, fly, and don't ask questions." Schmitt took a sip of his beer, got an upper lip covered in foam. He wiped it on a sleeve.

"That doesn't bother you?" Davis asked. "What you might be delivering?"

"Screw you, Jammer. It's all legal in my book."

"Guns and ammo? All aboveboard?"

"It can be."

After a long pause, Davis said, "What goes on out at FBN's hangar?"

Schmitt looked at him suspiciously. "That's the second time you've asked about that."

"And that's the second time you haven't answered."

"If I was you, I'd let it go. Khoury's people keep that place under lockdown. Nobody goes near."

"Except one of your mechanics."

Schmitt said nothing, and Davis sensed a dead end. He said, "I watched a squad of soldiers hijack one of your shipments yesterday afternoon."

"Not the first time. They hit us every month or two."

"Are they really soldiers?"

"More or less. It's the airport security contingent, maybe seven or eight guys. They have a little building half a mile up the main road to Khartoum. I guess they get bored, so they heist the occasional shipment."

"Bored?"

"This airport's new, and there's twenty miles of nothing between here and the city. Not much call for police work in the middle of the desert."

Davis recalled his run-in with a band of thieves not ten minutes after he'd arrived in-country. "So nobody complains?" he asked.

"About losing supplies? It's the cost of doing business around here. I think the word they use is 'tax.'"

"Right."

"But they only take aid stuff, never anything of ours."

"So Khoury gets special treatment?" Davis asked.

"Not exactly. The two just keep out of each other's way—like a professional courtesy, I guess."

"Honor amongst thieves?"

"Khoury has connections with the military. That's what it's all about in a place like this. Those soldiers wouldn't do anything to tick off the sheik."

There was a thump at the door, and Davis saw a keg on a handcart. Then came the delivery man, a kid, medium height and rail-thin. He was dressed in a pair of baggy blue trousers and a madras shirt. Or maybe it wasn't madras. Davis had never been sure what the heck that was.

Schmitt said, "It's about time, Achmed. I'm getting thirsty."

The kid said nothing. He looked put out, angry—then again, what nineteen-year-old boy didn't? Davis' mug was empty, but he wasn't going to stay for another. He hung the chief pilot's mug back on the rack without washing it, and was halfway to the door when Schmitt called out.

"Hey, Davis."

He turned.

"Boudreau's going down range tomorrow. You should go along— you said you wanted to see how we fly around here."

Davis thought about it. Schmitt was right, in a way. It would be good to see the operation up close. But he doubted that was the real reason for the invitation. After a long hesitation, he said, "Sure, sounds like fun."

Bob Schmitt smiled.

CHAPTER SIXTEEN

Davis managed three solid hours of sleep and woke at midnight.

He opened the curtains and dressed by the light of a dim half moon. A black pullover, baklava, and desert boots would have been perfect. What he had was a navy blue cotton shirt, brown Dockers, and a scuffed pair of steel-toed work boots. It would have to do. Davis used the stairs to reach the first floor, moved silently down the hallway, and stepped into the night.

The air outside was tormenting. If the desert were blistering hot all the time, one would succumb, not appreciate that there could be anything else. But each night the temperature moderated. Not to the point of being cool or refreshing, but enough to make you dread the next sunrise. That was what Davis felt—the teasing night air.

He walked south on the shoulder of the perimeter road, his boots crunching over stones and sand. Ten minutes out, a vehicle approached, and Davis diverted into the scrub to let a small panel van pass. As soon as it was gone, he went back to his steady pace for another five minutes. Then he turned into the desert.

He began his arc around the FBN Aviation hangar at a distance of half a mile. The moonlight was minimal, but enough for Davis to make his way without stumbling amid the tough-looking stands of brush. In the open desert, the night air seemed more fresh and dry, like the world had taken a deep breath after exhaling the day's heat. Insects that had been heat-struck during the day were active now, chirping and buzzing—happy that the sun was finally gone. Davis was comfortable with the distance he'd chosen. He doubted there would be any patrols out this far, doubted that Khoury's people would have night-vision gear to monitor the perimeter. They were going through the motions of safeguarding whatever was inside. Not expecting an invasion. All the same, he moved carefully. The vegetation was mostly chest high, and as Davis edged closer to the compound he found himself crouching lower. Two hundred yards out, he took a knee and made his first detailed observation.

Set away from the main airfield, the compound stood out like a raft of light on a black sea. It was fenced all the way around, nothing that would keep Davis out—nothing that would keep anybody out—but rather the kind of barrier that showed possession. A line in the sand. The hangar was shut tight, though Davis could see light lining the edges of the big entry doors. A handful of vehicles were parked carelessly near the front entrance. None were big enough to carry a Blackstar drone with a fifty-one-foot wingspan. There was also a pickup truck stationed squarely at the center of the rear fence. Davis figured this for a makeshift guard shack, probably one man inside. He saw three other men at the front of the compound, all watching and moving, weapons hanging at their chests. He saw scaffolding piled in a heap at one side of the building, and next to that was a digging machine, like a small backhoe fitted with a bucket. Davis watched for a full twenty minutes, largely concentrating on the guards. He noted a few casual conversations, but no cell phones or magazines or catnaps. No clear patterns of movement.

Davis decided that they were reasonably competent. Not in his favor. Also against him was the layout. The perimeter fence would be easy enough to breach, but it was surrounded by a fifty-foot clear area all the way around, so any direct approach would necessitate a lot of time in the open. But there were weaknesses. His favorite was the configuration of the lighting. The floodlights belonged on a maximum-security prison, eight tall poles with banks of sodium lights situated at regular intervals along the perimeter fence. But they had been installed to point inward. Good for a working mechanic, which was probably the original intent. Lousy for security. The lights should have been mounted on the hangar itself and pointed outward. As it was, the guards had to stare right into the blaze. Davis didn't. Then there was the matter of dogs—he didn't see any. Tally another in his column.

He began moving again, not getting closer, but circling counter-clockwise. Watching, probing. Davis had never been a Special Forces type in the military, but he'd done his share of foot soldiering, so he knew how to find a position with a good line of sight. As he neared the back, Davis saw a man walk around the hangar and swap out with the guard in the truck. He heard a generator humming, and noted that there were no above-ground power lines running to the compound. He tried to think of a way to get inside. In his favor, he didn't have to extract anything from the building—he just needed one good look. If the Blackstar drone was there, Davis could go back to his room, make a phone call, and that part of his job would be done.

Then a sound made him freeze.

His reaction had nothing to do with military experience, but was rather a caution cued from some deeper, evolutionary part of his brain. A growl, followed by a rabid yelp and a snarl. A dog—no, *dogs*. Not from the hangar complex, but behind him. Davis whipped around and set his legs in a strong crouch. Ready for snapping jaws, a handler with a machine pistol. Ready for anything. He saw commotion behind a tangle of nearby brush, ivory flashes in the drawn moonlight. Then an intense light stabbed in from behind.

Davis fell flat, his lips kissing sand, as a spotlight from the compound scanned the area. He heard shouts from behind the fence a hundred yards away. The words were in Arabic, but the intonation was crystal clear. Alarm. The light kept moving over the brush, searching for the source of the disturbance. It settled on something.

Davis craned his head until he saw them twenty paces away. Dogs, indeed. Three, maybe four. Coats the color of gray brush, wild eyes glinting red, frozen in the stilled white glow. But not guard dogs. Wild, feral beasts. Coyotes or jackals or dingos—whatever the hell passed for canine packs in this part of the world. They were spinning and snapping at one another, a flurry of mangy fur and sharp snarls. Then an even more alarming sound pierced the night. The crack of a rifle shot.

The report was followed by a yelp. Davis hugged the dirt like gravity had reversed, sinking lower and tighter to the sand. Another crack,
and a bullet zinged off a rock not ten feet away. He heard canine
whimpering, sensed the pack scurrying away in a rustle through the
gnarled brush. A stretch of silence was followed by distant laughing
and chattering—the guards in the compound. The searchlight went
back to acquire mode, playing back and forth for thirty seconds, a
minute. Then, as suddenly as it had appeared, the light extinguished.

Davis lay still for what seemed an eternity. He closed his eyes to
focus on sound. Any sound. Would the guards come to the source of
the skirmish to investigate? Or was this their nightly sport? A few pot-
shots at the neighborhood pack to break the monotony? Inch by inch,
Davis rose to his knees and surveyed the compound. Everything
seemed quiet. The lone guard was back in his truck, and Davis didn't
see any posse heading his way. He rose up, haunches on heels and
hands on his knees, and took a deep breath. He hadn't noticed the
spotlight. He *should* have noticed the spotlight. The guards had been
quick to shoot. Reckless, almost. Right then, Davis knew he wasn't
going to get into that hangar tonight. He would need better intel,
more time to prepare.

He took a bearing from his internal compass and began moving
east, away from the hangar. He'd only made twenty paces when he
came upon a tract of beaten ground. It was the place where the dogs
had been working, a small clearing with a distinct mound in the middle. Davis stopped and stared. The dim glow of the moon was aided
by indirect light that spilled out from the distant complex, just enough
for him to see the ghastly sight. The mound of dirt was rectangular and
flat, freshly turned, but one side had been breached, a hole dug by
worn claws and sharp-toothed muzzles.

Hanging out of that opening was a human hand.

Another urge from that deep part of his brain. Check for a threat—
sounds, sights, smells.

There was nothing. No guards, no dogs. Davis edged closer and
recognized an entire arm that looked like it was reaching out from

the grave. The skin was torn, meat ripped away by the marauding an-
imals. He figured the dogs would be back if they were hungry enough,
and in a place like this they probably were. Davis then saw more earth
uncovered on the far side of the flat mound, and in the thin light, a
second body. The upper torso had been uncovered and dragged out
chest high. Again, the corpse had been mauled.

The smell hit Davis next. He'd worked enough crashes to know
the stench of death. Bracing himself, he went closer. Davis was no expert when it came to dead bodies, but he was sure these hadn't been
here long. Probably a week, two at the outside. He saw a faint glint and
recognized a ring on the hand, dangling on a nearly severed finger.
Ring finger, left hand. He crawled to the mound to get a better look
at the second body. This one was worse, meatier sections of the shoulder and chest having been ripped apart in a textbook display of scav-
enger behavior. In the dim light, Davis could make out high Slavic
cheeks and fair hair. He also saw a neat hole in the broad forehead.

Davis took stock of the mound itself, and figured it was just the
right size to hold two bodies. No more than that. A sick feeling rose
in his stomach, a combination of the smell, the visual, and the putrid
thought that was building in his head. Then more trouble.

Growls. Deep and menacing. Not one, but a chorus. He saw
movement in the brush to his left. More on the right. The dogs were
indeed hungry, and they'd come back for more. Davis could fend them
off for a time. He could swing a stick or throw a few rocks. But that
would make noise, and noise might draw more fire from the shooting
gallery. No, he decided. There was nothing more he could do here. It
was time to go.

He scrambled off the mound, sidled a few steps away. But then
Davis stopped. He thought he knew who these two were, but he
needed to be sure. Needed proof. He crawled back to the hand that
was reaching from its grave and saw the ring finger lying in the dirt,
connected by no more than a tendon to the bloodless hand. He
reached down and pulled to complete the disconnect, slid the ring
clear and stuffed it in his pocket. He left the finger there. Davis then
paused for a moment. He wasn't particularly religious, but right now

that didn't matter. These two men might have been. Or maybe someone who cared about them relied on God. Davis did his best with a
silent prayer, a simple, nondenominational request that the souls represented by these two torn bodies were at peace and in a better place.

Just as Davis finished, an engine fired to life near the hangar. Then
another. In a low crouch, he turned east and ran.

Davis moved along the main road, his pace quicker than when he'd
been on the reciprocal track an hour earlier. Approaching the FBN
building, he considered his options. He could report the bodies. But
to whom? He had already seen the military police in action. Any authorities would question why he'd been out hiking the desert in the
middle of the night. If Davis reported what he'd found, it would invite all sorts of questions. Questions he didn't want to answer. It would
introduce an untold number of Sudanese agencies to complicate matters, and likely bring his own investigation to a grinding halt. And the
real bottom line—it wouldn't do a damn thing for the two men who
were half buried out in the desert. Davis decided to keep the discovery to himself. The scavengers would have their day, a macabre but
necessary sacrifice. The most decent thing he could do for the two
men was to find out what had happened.

When he got to his room, Davis went straight to the shower. There
was something about death—touching it gave an irresistible urge to
scrub and cleanse, to wash the scourge away. Yet if the physical grime
could be rinsed, the mental residue was far more persistent. It stained
your thoughts and dreams, and the only agent that would ever wash
it away was the truth. All the same, Davis scrubbed. He spent a full ten
minutes under spray that was hot enough to hang a curtain of fog on
the bathroom mirror. For the first time since arriving in Sudan, he
wanted the heat. Davis bent his head down so the stream could beat
deep into the muscles of his neck and shoulders.

When he was done, he dried and wrapped a towel around his
waist. Davis fished the ring from his pocket and took a seat on the
bed. Turning the ring to get an angle on the best light, he studied it

inside and out. It was a simple enough thing, a plain gold wedding band, maybe wider than most. On the inside was an inscription, the lettering in Cyrillic—just like on the crate he'd seen yesterday. But this time Davis had a head start, knew what it *might* say. He only needed a single word, one he could probably translate given enough common letters. And he did see it, clear as day. ЙРЕНА. He was certain of that translation: IRENA. He remembered the name from Gregor Anotolii's personnel file. Wife: Irena. When Davis looked closer, even the rest of the inscription made sense. ЙРЕНА АНД ГРЕГОР. He knew enough characters, and knew what it might say. IRENA AND GREGOR. No doubt about it.

He eased down on the bed and held the ring between two fingers, turned it back and forth. Davis stared at the ceiling and added this revelation to his other results. A forged maintenance write-up. A downed aircraft that was still flying. Radar data that showed a normal flight profile. And now? Two crewmen dead in a way that had nothing to do with a crashed airplane. More than ever, Davis was investigating a crash where any reasonable investigator would relent and say, *There never was a crash.* But if that was true, then why was somebody going to so much trouble to convince the world otherwise?

Davis closed his eyes and let the fatigue of a long day settle in. His thoughts began to drift as the numbing tendrils of sleep wrapped around him. There, in that limbo of consciousness between dreams and reality, he heard a distant sound. The pitch ebbed and flowed, though not in any lyrical way. Indeed, there was nothing good in how this sound registered. Davis sat up, wide awake again. The sound was definitely there, and he was sure he recognized it. An everyday occurrence, given the right time and the right place. This was neither.

Davis couldn't let it go. He had to know.

Dressing quickly in fresh clothes, he left the ring on the nightstand. The hallway was quiet, the rest of FBN's expatriate staff fast asleep. He went to the stairs and climbed to the roof. Stepping softly across an asphalt-broomed rooftop, Davis made his way to the eastern ledge. He knew exactly where to look, and sure enough he saw it. His second telling discovery of the night.

The roof was bathed in still night air, and so the engine noise was more distinct here, even if the commotion was taking place over a mile away. Davis had good elevation, and there was nothing to block his view. Right at the spot in the desert where he'd encountered the bodies, he saw two security trucks from the compound parked so that their headlights were trained on a single spot in the brush. There, two men with rifles slung casually on their shoulders watched as the backhoe worked the ground. The digging machine's own headlights vibrated as the modest bucket strained and clawed through hardpan earth.

Davis watched for a full ten minutes. What he saw told him nothing about what was in FBN Aviation's hangar. But it told him a lot about Rafiq Khoury. This was no exhumation. They were digging deeper.

CHAPTER SEVENTEEN

Davis woke early the next morning, dressed, and headed for the bar. He found pastries in the refrigerator, took one, and put two U.S. dollars in the honor box. At the front desk he checked the big scheduling board and saw that his flight was set for a 5:15 a.m. departure. Call sign: Air Sahara 12. He didn't see Boudreau, or anyone who looked like a copilot, so Davis headed to the flight line.

The air outside was motionless and cooler than he expected—still teasing—with the sun lost over the horizon. Building and percolating. The flight line was well illuminated, a yellow sodium glare that would carry for another hour, until it was overpowered by nature's heat lamp. Even at this hour the ramp held its familiar scent, the acrid tang of vaporized kerosene hanging on the breeze, cut by the musty aroma of desert sage.

Davis spotted activity at one particular airplane and headed that way. In his Air Force days it would never have been so easy. He'd have found red lines painted on the concrete and armed security keeping a sharp eye—bored two-stripers who lived for the day when some dumbass company-grade officer would screw up and cross without authorization. Here there were no red stripes. The tarmac was barren, save for rows of weeds sprouting at the shoulders and lining up in the expansion cracks.

He spotted Boudreau at the far side of the airplane, pointing a finger and shining a flashlight beam on an engine. Achmed the snacko stood next to him, looking disinterested. They both wore a uniform of sorts, khaki trousers and short-sleeved white shirts with epaulets. Four stripes on Boudreau's shoulders, three for Achmed. Take away the uniforms, though, and they couldn't have looked more different, the Louisianan stout and freckled in cowboy boots, the first officer rail-thin and swarthy, wearing tennis shoes. As Davis closed in, the kid saw him coming and broke away toward the loading stairs.

"Morning," Davis yelled over the clatter of a taxiing turboprop.

"Hey, Jammer! Glad you could make it."

"Wouldn't miss it for the world. But I'm not sure if your first officer feels the same way."

Boudreau shook his head. "I can't figure that kid. I was just trying to show him how the flaps change the shape of the wing to give more lift. He didn't even try to understand. I tell you, that boy's hopeless. I've told him so, but he keeps coming back for more."

"Schmitt won't fire him?"

"We've all asked. He just says we're required to have a Sudanese presence in flight ops. Some part of Khoury's big dream. I've given up that fight."

Davis looked over the airplane. "I won't get many more chances to ride in one of these."

"Yeah, she's a dinosaur all right. This particular airplane has been flying the friendlies since the Roosevelt administration."

"Franklin or Teddy?"

Boudreau chuckled, then banged hard on a panel. "They don't make 'em like this anymore."

Davis had to admit, it sounded solid. But up close the airplane showed its scars. The sun-baked paint, probably once white, was faded and dirty. There were spots where the outer coat had flaked away, and underneath an old green and black camouflage pattern was revealed, like a scar from some sordid, soldier-of-fortune past.

Davis said, "So where are we headed today?"

"Jungle strip, Congo River basin."

"That sounds a little sporty."

"Been to plenty like it." Boudreau bent down by one of the main wheels, took a pen from his pocket and poked it into the air valve. There was a loud hiss of high pressure air. After a few seconds, he stood back up and gave the tire a swift kick, nodded like he was satisfied.

"What was that for?" Davis asked.

"You'll see." Boudreau headed to the boarding stairs. "Come on, Jammer, step into my office."

Davis followed him up the stairs. It was a short climb. Three days ago he'd ridden a massive A-380 across the Atlantic. He felt like he was going from the *Queen Mary* to the *African Queen*. Inside, the DC-3 was all business, sheet metal and stringers and rivets, all seventy years old and counting. There was a chain of floodlights in the ceiling that eked out just enough light to see the rest. A dirty floor blotted with stains from old liquid spills. Battery acid, oil, grapefruit juice—no way to tell. Sawdust and gum wrappers were scattered along the side walls like leaves in a street gutter. Loose pebbles were lodged in the floor joints.

Today's load seemed light, the cargo bay only half full of crates and boxes. The fact that there was volume remaining meant one of two things. Either the receiver was taking a small shipment, or the crates he was looking at were very heavy. Davis noticed that the tie-down straps looked heavy duty, so he guessed the latter. Some of the boxes were stenciled with the U.N. logo and labels that looked fresh and amateurish. SPARE PARTS. CANNED FOOD. MEDICINE. *Yeah*, he thought, *right*. His doubts were confirmed when he recognized the smell. Gun oil. These boxes were indeed heavy, full of things made from nickel and lead and titanium, the part of the periodic table of elements that didn't give way. The part that penetrated softer, carbon-based things.

Davis moved toward the cockpit and found Boudreau in the left seat, the traditional captain's station. Achmed was beside him on the right, slapping switches like they'd done him wrong.

"Easy, son," Boudreau admonished. "You don't treat your girlfriend like that, do you?"

The young man scowled. "Nasira is not my girlfriend. That is not a respectful term."

"Then what the heck do I call her?"

Achmed didn't reply, and Davis saw a glint of mischief in Boudreau's eyes.

The skipper said, "Tell you what, since you're in training to be a

pilot someday, we'll just call her your future ex-wife." Boudreau gave
his signature cackle.

Achmed ignored him.

This could be a long day, Davis thought.

He settled into the jumpseat, a folding bench behind the main
crew positions that was used for observers—third pilots who might
ride along to give checkrides or government inspectors. Which, Davis
figured, was what he was right now. An inspector. So he inspected
Achmed, watched his hands bounce inefficiently over the switch panels, watched him fumble through radio frequencies and confuse the air
traffic controller who issued their flight clearance.

Boudreau was the other end of the spectrum. He moved in me-
thodical flows, well-honed patterns that belied his good-old-boy aura.
Presently, he was building his nest. Even the most experienced pilot
didn't just sit down and fly. There were charts, flight plans, sun visors,
headsets, pens, lucky ball caps, gum, sunglasses. No engine turned until
everything was in the right spot, ready to go, like a ballplayer getting
ready for a big game.

Boudreau tapped the fuel gauge. "Rule number one about flying
into the bush, Jammer—always bring enough dead dinosaurs to get
back out. This is Africa, so we're not talking about a simple flight between two well-maintained airfields. We're on an expedition. Kinda
makes you feel like an Old World explorer, don't it? Just pull up anchor and head toward the edge of the map—you know, where they
always draw those dragons."

"Dragons." Davis sat back and grinned. Boudreau was trying to
wind him up. All the same, he knew there was an element of truth in
it. Fly on a commercial airliner in the West, and your chances of dying
in a crash were about one in a hundred million. In this airplane, on this
continent—not nearly as many zeroes in the denominator.

The two pilots cranked the engines, checked that everything was
in order. Boudreau taxied to the runway and they were cleared for
takeoff. The skipper goosed the throttles full forward, and if the machine had been shaking before, it rattled like a jackhammer now. The
racket from the engines cancelled every other sound, and Davis felt the

familiar push in the back of his seat. The grip of aerodynamic lift took hold, and the main wheels levitated. Everything fell more quiet, more smooth, and, like with all airplanes, just a little more tenuous. Even experienced pilots felt it. There was a tactile certainty to rolling down a runway with rubber on concrete, but once you broke ground everything became just a bit less convincing. Safe, certainly. A sense of freedom, no doubt. But a dash of risk sprinkled in as the vertical dimension was introduced.

The early morning air was smooth, and Boudreau looked right at home, one easy hand on the controls and the other holding a Styrofoam cup full of coffee. Davis' ears popped as the unpressurized airplane climbed. Their initial heading was north, and he could see Khartoum ahead under a hazy blanket of sodium light. The city was split by the dark serpentine shadow of two rivers merging into one, the confluence of the Blue and White Niles.

Once they had some altitude, Boudreau banked the airplane to the right. A minute later they were headed due south for the equator.

Khoury stepped into his office before sunrise, leaving Hassan stationed outside at his usual post. He did not typically rise so early, but today he was keeping the general's schedule. He went into the hangar and found Jibril asleep on his cot. Khoury left him alone, knowing there were limits to how hard he could drive the man. Back in his office, he sat at his desk and waited.

When the call came, he let the first and second warbles run before picking up on the third. Obedient but not kowtowed. "Yes?" Khoury said, as if he might be expecting any number of important calls.

"Give me the report." No salutation, just a command. The baritone from the Ministry of Defense in Khartoum was much in the habit of issuing orders.

"The engineer has nearly completed his tasks," Khoury announced.

"Nearly?" General Ali barked. "The deadline is upon us."

"Everything will be ready," Khoury assured. He then tried to sound casual as he added, "And the crash investigator has arrived."

"How unfortunate," Ali grumbled. "Apparently my request to the Minister of Aviation to arrange a delay has fallen on deaf ears. Another post, I think, that will soon have a vacancy."

Khoury weighed a humorous reply, but decided the most clever reaction was silence.

"Tell me about this investigator," the general prodded.

"His name is Davis. He is American." Knowing this would not sit well, he added quickly, "We were expecting a Frenchman, of course, but perhaps we can make the best of the situation."

"As with the other Americans?"

"Exactly," Khoury said. "He was sent here by their government, and the timing could not be more perfect."

"Yes, I see your point."

Khoury was happy that the general seemed to be taking the news well. He said, "But for now, I will keep the man busy."

"Yes, that *would* be best, dear sheik." Ali went back to issuing orders, "The helicopter will arrive Saturday morning for our final tour. Nine o'clock."

"I will be waiting."

"And bring Hassan this time," the general said with a lighter tone. "I don't think he has ever seen the pyramids."

"Of course," Khoury replied dryly.

There was a deep chuckle from the north before the line went dead.

Khoury set the phone in its cradle, leaned back in his chair, and put his heels up on the hardwood desk. He pulled the kaffiyeh from his head, allowing his shoulder-length black locks to fall free over the collar of his tunic. He considered going out to the hanger again to appraise things, but without Jibril to explain technical matters, Khoury would understand little. It bothered him at times, the degree to which he relied on the engineer, but so far the man had been wholly reliable.

The dawn call to prayer sounded from the speakers in the hangar, spreading with its usual ill fidelity, as if emanating from a soup can. The wailing chant echoed inside the voluminous building, and spilled out across the surrounding desert. Khoury did not move. He imagined his men outside making their way dutifully to the prayer room. Perhaps Hassan would even make an appearance. Khoury, in a custom that would be foreign to most imams, did not join regularly in prayer with his flock. It had been one of his first issuances on arriving here. His office served a dual purpose, one side arranged for work—a desk, a chair, one moderately ornate cabinet—while the other half was committed to worship, a humble space for the imam to conduct the protocols of his faith. None of his followers doubted their imam's reasoning—that his dialogue with Allah was so intense, so personal, that it could only be undertaken in a private arena.

Rafiq Khoury took a deep breath and pulled a key from his pocket, used it to unlock the door of the small cabinet that was an arm's length from his desk. He pulled out a half-empty bottle of Wild Turkey, then inspected three tumblers to judge which was the cleanest. He made his choice, poured three fingers, and leaned back as he took the first sip, making a mental note to keep the ice bucket current. It was so much better over ice. Khoury lit a cigarette and took a long, deep draw, holding the flavor in his lungs before exhaling with the satisfaction of one who truly needed the fix. Soon, lyrical chanting from the nearby prayer room washed in like a distant whisper. Idly, Khoury closed his eyes and swirled the wondrous elixir in his mouth. He felt the familiar burn as the whiskey went down, and when he opened his eyes again Khoury studied the bottle on his desk. He had never been to America, but perhaps someday he would go. If it should ever come to pass, his first stop would be this wondrous place called Kentucky.

Khoury took another long draw on his cigarette, poured a second bracer. He eased back in his chair and closed his eyes. Only a year ago his circumstances had been tenuous. No, his very *existence* had been tenuous. Yet here he was, not only alive, but on the verge of greatness and riches. There were times when he was still stunned by the speed of his advance. By necessity, Khoury had eschewed the traditional path to clerical recognition. To spend years in holy scholarship was an entirely impractical pursuit, though if anyone asked—and they rarely did—Khoury claimed to have run that course. The only ones who could challenge this assertion were other clerics, and he made a marked point of not finding their company. His thoughts drifted, and he wondered what his mother would think of it all. Another of her American metaphors came to mind. *A meteoric rise.*

It fit his situation, Khoury supposed. Still, he had always thought the phrase odd, as meteors did not rise. At least not any he had ever seen. They went the other way, ending, to be sure, quite deep in the earth. Not wanting to dwell on that thought, Khoury tipped back his glass, and again felt the delicious burn.

CHAPTER EIGHTEEN

The sky was as empty as sky could be.

They were cruising at twelve thousand feet, two nautical miles of smooth night air below. The eastern horizon was beginning to glow, but the night had yet to relinquish its grip. The ground below looked like a black hole. The few lights Davis could discern did nothing to define the earth. On the contrary, they created confusion, blurring the separation of up and down by mimicking stars on a matte black sky.

As the airplane droned southward, Davis recognized another amplifier of their isolation. The radios were silent. Most flying was performed under a constant barrage of chatter between air traffic controllers and pilots. But here, the overhead speaker on the cockpit ceiling was ominously silent.

"It's awfully quiet out here," Davis remarked.

Boudreau said, "It's like that sometimes, but you'll get used to it. Right Achmed?"

The ill-tempered Sudanese kid said nothing.

Boudreau shrugged. "Don't make no never mind nohow."

Davis made a brief stab at calculating the negatives in that sentence. He considered writing it down, maybe making Jen diagram it for extra credit in English class. That is, if he ever heard from her again.

"My cup is empty," Boudreau declared. He looked at Davis. "As third-in-command, Jammer, you are hereby designated coffee boy. You ever been checked out on an airplane with a coffeepot?"

"Nope."

"Well, it's easy enough. Just toss in a fresh bag and hit the brew button."

"Okay, but I've got to warn you—my daughter gave me a new coffee machine for Christmas. What came out looked more like it came from La Brea than Starbucks."

Boudreau chuckled. "Well, give it a try anyway, cream and sugar for me. There's a fire extinguisher on the aft bulkhead if you need it."

Davis went to the back and did his best to get things going. While the machine was gurgling, Achmed came back and gave him a gruff look as he edged by toward the lavatory. The kid was surly beyond his years.

When he reached for the lavatory door handle, Davis said, "Hey, Achmed."

The young man paused.

Davis nodded toward the pile of crates in the cargo hold. "I was wondering—how much weight does one of these birds carry? You know, the maximum usable load?"

The kid shrugged immediately, not even considering a reply. "I do not know such things. It is not my job." He reached for the handle again.

"You can flush here," Davis said helpfully.

Achmed looked dumbstruck.

"You know, the toilet. If you flush that thing over a city it can be pretty messy for the people below." Davis pointed down. "But out here over the jungle, a little yellow rain—who's going to know?"

The young Sudanese man looked completely befuddled, like he was picturing some kind of valve in the bottom of the airplane that would open up like a bomb bay door and drop sewage from the sky. The kid didn't have a clue. But there was more in his expression. He seemed edgy, nervous. Davis remembered once getting a briefing on airport security measures. He learned about behavior profiling, and how people who were up to no good tended to highlight themselves. They perspired, fidgeted, didn't make eye contact. That's what Davis was seeing right now. Too many things about this kid didn't add up. He didn't know the basic things any pilot would know. And his base personality was all wrong. Most of the pilots Davis had ever known were like Boudreau, crack full of good humor. Achmed had the bonhomie of an out-of-work funeral director.

He disappeared into the lavatory, and Davis shrugged it all off.

He found the coffee cups and started looking for sugar. As he was rifling through a drawer in the galley, he heard Achmed in the lavatory. He was talking in Arabic, words that meant nothing to Davis. The kid might have been cursing him, or maybe issuing a pox on all pilots. But then he recognized a chanting, almost mechanical meter, and Davis understood.

Achmed was praying.

Davis went back up front with two cups of coffee, and handed one to the skipper. Over Boudreau's shoulder, sunrise was breaking in the east, reds and oranges fusing over a stark landscape, the brilliant rays reaching upward to play on a stratus cloud deck.

Davis said reflectively, "You know, there are times when I hope my daughter will take up flying so she can see sights like this."

Boudreau nodded in agreement. "There's not an office in the world with a better view." He pointed to the right seat, and said, "Want some stick time?"

Achmed was still in the head. "You sure your first officer won't mind?"

"Who cares?"

Davis took the copilot's position. The seat was uncomfortable and had a distinct list to the right. At least he hoped it was the seat, hoped they weren't flying through the air crookedly, say, in a ten degree right bank. Davis knew airplanes got to be like that over time, bent and cantankerous. A lot like people.

"Here," Boudreau offered, "I'll turn off the autopilot." He snapped off a switch. "Get the feel of it. I doubt you'll ever get a chance to fly one of these pterodactyls again."

"Probably not," Davis said. He took the controls and made a few turns, felt the airplane respond.

"How does she handle?" Boudreau asked.

Davis thought, *Like a brick with wings.* He said, "Great."

He hadn't flown much in the last year, and at times Davis felt like an alcoholic deprived of drink. The old beast wasn't nimble like an

F-16, yet there was a directness, an honesty in how it flew. The yoke in his hands was connected directly to the control surfaces without any computer interfaces. He liked that—a basic, no-nonsense airplane that would require basic, no-nonsense flying skills. After a few minutes, Davis was feeling comfortable.

He said, "You know, I can't figure your copilot."

"Me neither," Boudreau agreed.

"And you've got other Sudanese kids at FBN?"

"Yeah, a few, and they're all just like him. Religious, way too serious—definitely not the type to wear you out with idle conversation. But Achmed, he's the least proficient of the bunch. I guess that's why *I* got him."

"He doesn't know squat about how this airplane works."

"I know. I've tried to teach him a few things, but nothing sticks. He could land if I had a heart attack, I suppose, keep the right side up on a clear day. But once he'd learned that much, he seemed to lose interest. The kid just shows up day after day to go along for the ride."

Davis said nothing. He had bad vibes about the kid. Maybe it wasn't just incompetence or lack of interest. Maybe Achmed had been put in Boudreau's right seat for a reason—to keep an eye on things for Khoury.

"All right, Jammer," Boudreau said as he tilted his seat back and closed his eyes, "you've got the con. Fly it like you stole it."

"Right."

"Nudge me in an hour. And don't let me wake up and find you sleeping!"

It was nearly noon when they reached the landing zone.

Outside, Davis saw nothing but jungle, a verdant canopy that carried every imaginable shade of green. It looked thick and impenetrable. There were no section lines on the ground like you saw in the States, no well-surveyed roads or power lines or rail tracks. Even the rivers looked different. In the developed world, nearly all flows of water were manipulated in some way—dams, navigation channels, levees. But here the rivers wandered, looping and arcing in time-honed paths, their very presence defined by no more than subtle variances in the hue of the foliage.

Everyone had returned to their formal stations—Achmed in the right seat, Davis on the jumpseat, and Boudreau flying on the left. Davis was here, ostensibly, to observe FBN's flight operations. Achmed's attitude aside, so far things had looked solid. But that was largely due to Boudreau, whose confidence was no product of FBN's training regimen, but rather sourced in twenty thousand hours of hardscrabble experience. Twenty thousand hours of sweat and storms and profanity. There was simply no substitute.

Boudreau ignored the airplane's indigenous navigation instruments as they neared their destination, relying instead on a handheld GPS receiver. The antenna was stuck to the side window with a suction cup and connected by a cable, a simplistic but effective rigging. A clearing came into view, and Boudreau said confidently, "Yep, this is the spot."

He nosed the airplane over to an altitude of a thousand feet, leveled out, and buzzed the landing strip. On the overflight, Boudreau commented on the surface. "Looks a little muddy down there, but it ought to be okay. That's why I let some pressure out of them tires before we took off. Gives a wider footprint for better traction."

Davis nodded as he looked outside. There was clearly no asphalt below, just a strip of brown dirt pocked with splotches of mud. All along the sides of the runway—if it could be called that—were mounds of rotting timber and brush, probably a full square mile of equatorial rain forest that had been sacrificed for the landing zone.

"It looks a little short," Davis remarked. "How much runway is that?"

"They advertise four thousand feet," Boudreau said.

"Sounds optimistic."

Boudreau laughed. "Hell, gettin' in is easy. It's the takeoff that'll kill you."

If Boudreau was worried, he didn't show it. As if gliding into a short jungle airstrip was no different than gliding into a Baton Rouge bar for a longneck. He banked the airplane steeply to the left to begin his traffic pattern. The airplane slowed, and Achmed put out the landing gear and flaps on the skipper's commands. When Boudreau rolled out on final approach, he set a slightly steeper than usual glidepath.

"Three hundred feet," Achmed said, remembering his callouts. "Two hundred feet."

The strip of brown mud seemed even smaller as a green wall of jungle rose up on either side to swallow them.

"One hundred feet," Achmed mumbled. "Fifty, thirty—"

"Shee-it!" Boudreau shouted. "Go around!" He slammed the throttles forward, and the big engines coughed and rattled, straining for full power.

Then Davis saw it right in front of them, wandering out from the bush. The biggest damn cow he'd seen in his life.

"Pull up!" Achmed yelled.

The thrust took hold, but the DC-3 seemed to hesitate. Boudreau had arrested the descent, but they were hanging in limbo just a few feet above the runway, frozen in the aerodynamic transition from down to up. The huge beast stopped right in the middle of the strip and stared at them stupidly—two thousand pounds of horns and sinew and bovine lethargy. Not what you wanted to hit at a hundred miles an hour.

Davis watched it all unfold in what seemed like slow motion, the massive animal a hundred feet from their nosecone, Boudreau fighting the controls with both hands.

"More flaps!" he shouted.

Achmed froze.

Davis lunged forward and yanked back on what he hoped was the flap lever—the one with the wing-shaped handle. The airplane seemed to levitate, rise as if on a bubble of air. Davis saw the cow's disinterested face slip below, and he braced for impact.

It didn't come. Slowly, the airplane started to climb. Boudreau's hands eased on the controls.

"African forest buffalo," he said. "Biggest damn one I've ever seen."

Davis let out a long, slow breath. "Me too."

Achmed said nothing. He was rigid in his seat, grabbing the arm-rests like he was having a cavity filled.

When they reached a thousand feet, Boudreau circled the airport twice, waiting for the huge beast to wander back into the bush. When it finally did, he made a second approach, this time carrying the in-surance of an extra ten knots. Davis sensed the skipper's hands tight on the controls, ready for another go-around. It wasn't necessary. The big machine touched down, bounced jauntily over ruts in the dirt strip, and came to rest five hundred feet from the departure end. Boudreau tapped the left brake, bumped up the starboard engine to pirouette, and began taxiing toward the spot where he'd touched down.

When Boudreau shut the engines down, everything fell quiet. Fell still. There was no sound at all except the hum of a gyro losing its spin somewhere in the instrument panel, and a faint ticking from the big radial engines as they began to cool. The jungle around them looked impenetrable, thick fronds of jade and emerald, waxen leaves the size of umbrellas. It was calm, almost serene. And that was when it struck Davis.

There was nobody here to meet them.

CHAPTER NINETEEN

Davis was wrong. There were a lot of people.

They came out of nowhere, led by a tall beefy man whose ebony skin glinted in the equatorial sun. A half dozen others followed behind in a formless gaggle, trailing like a prizefighter's entourage. They reminded Davis of the soldiers who had commandeered Dr. Antonelli's aid shipment back in Khartoum, everyone decked out in the latest Third World militia couture. Their fatigues were a mix, some pale green and others a jungle camouflage design, like they'd shopped at different Army–Navy stores. Mismatched berets were all cocked at swashbuckling angles, and everyone sported wraparound sunglasses. Of course, there were also weapons—each man carried either a holstered sidearm or a casually slung rifle.

"Customs?" Davis asked.

Boudreau said, "Don't worry. Nobody shoots the mailman."

"Even after he's delivered?"

Boudreau chuckled, but without his usual gusto. He went to the cargo hold, threw down the stairs, and met the guy in charge. After a short conversation, the cargo door was popped open. More people came out of nowhere, and before long the place was crawling with activity. Men in uniform snapped orders to skinny boys wearing laceless Nike sneakers and faded T-shirts with sports logos. They unstrapped deck tie-downs like they'd done it before, and moved the load outside in a human chain. Davis stood under a wing and watched it all unfold. A truck appeared out of the jungle, some kind of bastardized troop carrier. It had iron rails welded to the sides of the rear bed, and tires that looked like they belonged on a 747. The bigger crates were put on the truck, the smaller ones simply muled down a dirt path on strong, sweaty backs.

At the tailgate of the truck two crates were cracked open, and a soldier—the acting quartermaster, no doubt—began issuing ammunition to a line of Kalashnikov-toting kids. Davis watched them jam magazines into empty weapons like they knew what they were doing, watched them stuff extra mags away until their pockets were bulging. Everybody was sweating, sweltering. The heat here was every bit as oppressive as Sudan, only thicker and heavier, weighed down by a sky that was darkening as thick clouds percolated in the midday blaze. Any calendar would tell you it was autumn, but this close to the equator the seasons became meaningless. It was like this every day of the year. It was like this for Christmas and Ramadan, for every birthday and funeral. Always hot, always wet.

Davis hoped the urgency being shown was a function of proficiency and not nerves—there was a reason these guys needed weapons. The uniformed men had formed a perimeter of sorts, all eyes locked on the encircling curtain of vegetation. They looked tense, the way soldiers did when they expected action. Somewhere in this malarial jungle, there was an enemy. Maybe two or three enemies. A neighboring army, a rival tribe, some opposing force that had their own weapons, their own kid soldiers in Air Jordan T-shirts, pockets crammed full of 7.62-mm projectiles. It was a sad story, but one that had been playing out here for generations.

Davis spotted Boudreau at a small alcove in the mesh of green. He was standing next to a hut that Davis hadn't even noticed before, an almost comical administrative center. It had a thatched roof and walls, and was sided by a water buffalo—not the kind that wandered onto runways, but the kind that had wheels and a big metal cylinder that held four hundred gallons of potable water. Davis walked over.

"These guys work fast," he said.

Boudreau was eyeing the clouds overhead. "They'd better, this weather is building."

Davis did his own meteorological survey and saw stacks of cumulus clouds growing, bubbling vertically like a pot on boil.

"You seen Achmed?" Boudreau asked. "He's got some work to do before we go."

"No, I don't know where he went."

"I can't imagine he just ran off into the woods. Even he's not that stupid."

Davis shrugged.

"Well, he'd better show soon," Boudreau said, "because as soon as these guys are done with the unload, we're outta here."

Fadi Jibril's eyes were locked to the wing in front of him as he worked a joystick furiously. The control surface should be moving, but nothing was happening.

He cursed under his breath.

The engineer shut everything down, removed power from the computers, and disconnected the battery in the aircraft. He let it all sit for a full minute—perhaps not as much for the electronics as to keep his own fuse from blowing—then powered everything back up. One minute later, he tried again. Still dead, no motion at all.

"Dirty whore!" He threw a screwdriver at the dull black craft and it pinged off, leaving a noticeable dent in the radar absorbent coating. Jibril cupped his head in his hands.

The new modules from Hamburg were his best chance. They were definitely the wrong model, but Jibril had hoped he could still make them work. He'd been forced to rewire the output cable and power supply, and then reconfigure a number of circuits and relays. The work was time consuming and tedious, but without these modifications the units were no more use than the shoddy Chinese devices they'd replaced.

Jibril forced his eyes to a wiring diagram on the bench in front of him. He tried to remember which connections he had already altered. His mind was getting fuzzy, a blur of schematics and diodes and wiring. He was tracing a current flow with a pencil when he sensed shuffling behind him. Jibril turned and saw Muhammed the mechanic.

"I need a three-eighths-inch spanner," the Jordanian said.

Jibril pointed to a rack of wrenches, and Muhammed took the one he needed.

"Are you progressing?" asked the unsmiling mechanic. It was nearer an accusation than a question.

Jibril knew his technical troubles had become common knowledge. When he'd arrived last spring, the others here treated him with respect, knowing, he supposed, the importance of his work. All summer they had offered notes and prayers of encouragement, sent small pieces of cake and *gashaato*. Jibril had been a hero to the imam's followers, even if few had the education, the technical knowhow to appreciate his genius. Now, however, the mood had changed. The *gashaato* no longer came, and Jibril often felt eyes on his back as he came and went.

"We will be ready, if Allah wills it," Jibril replied.

Muhammed frowned. "The sheik is concerned."

"The sheik is always concerned. Everything will be ready."

The mechanic slapped the wrench idly in his palm, then turned and went back to the other airplane.

Jibril stood and stretched. He wandered to the entrance of his work space and watched Muhammed fight the wrench. It took him three minutes to pull the drain plug on the underside of the left engine of the DC-3. When it popped free, oil gushed out in a torrent, thick and black, and the first gallon splashed over the concrete floor and his shoe before Muhammed slid a bucket underneath to catch it. *Typical,* Jibril thought. The man had certainly not been brought here for his skills as a mechanic. Jibril even suspected that Muhammed's credentials might not be completely legitimate. Come Monday, he would take a look at the old airplane himself to ensure it was ready. *More to do,* he thought.

Jibril turned away. He retreated to his working area, drawing the curtain closed behind him. The curtain was designed to allow no one a glimpse of his work, but at this moment served better to screen his tattered psyche. Jibril's unease went deeper than technical issues or run-ins with Muhammed. As he closed in on success, he was kept awake at night by that last overriding question. What was the target? For weeks now he had been asking the imam, yet Khoury put forward no more than a rough geographic path to the final launching point. Security, Jibril supposed. *But if I cannot be trusted, who can?*

He sat heavily on his work stool, and forced his eyes to the wiring diagrams on the bench. With a pencil, he began to trace the flow of current. The imam had been firm. Only seventy-two hours remained. This implied a deadline that was out of his control. A public meeting? A clandestine rendezvous? A private tryst? Not knowing who or what was being targeted, Jibril could only guess. But guess he did. And the most logical answer—*who* they were targeting—made his pencil run over the diagram that much faster.

It took twenty minutes to complete the unload. The man with the entourage started walking away, and the load crew bailed out and followed. Soon they would all disappear, Davis reckoned, vaporizing back into the jungle.

"Looks like they're done," Boudreau said, checking his watch. "Not bad, only thirty minutes on the ground. I'm gonna go look for Achmed. Why don't you start the preflight, Jammer."

"Sure."

A preflight was a walk-around inspection undertaken before every flight. All airplanes had peculiarities, but most of the things you looked for were standard. Leaky hydraulic lines, bald tires, birdstrikes from the previous flight. *Or maybe the horn of a forest buffalo gored into the belly,* Davis mused. He went to the nose of the airplane and started a clockwise inspection. At the right main landing gear he heard thunder. At the tail he felt the first raindrop.

He was on the port side, running a hand over the propeller, when something whizzed by his ear and smacked into the wing.

An instant later the sound of the shot caught up with the bullet. Davis hit the dirt.

The nearest cover was the left main landing gear assembly, and he crawled behind it on knees and elbows. There was shouting in the distance, and he saw soldiers scrambling. Those with weapons were poised for action, sweeping muzzles left and right across the jungle in search of targets. A short burst spewed from a machine pistol, then another, and soon a battalion of light weapons on full automatic were sweeping the foliage at hip height. Palm fronds and giant leaves shredded in a vapor of green.

Davis spotted Boudreau running for the boarding ladder. "Come on, Jammer! We're gettin' the hell out of here!"

Davis kicked to his feet and ran for the stairs. Another shot smacked in and ricocheted off steel. He went to ground again, jamming his left wrist as he hit. He sensed direction from this shot and looked toward the hut. He saw a man crouched near the water tank with a rifle pointed at him. No, not a man—Achmed. The gun at his shoulder kicked, and a puddle of mud exploded to Davis' right.

Davis jumped up, vaulted onto the steps, and dove inside the airplane. He flopped into the cargo hold like a fish falling into a boat. Pulling up the stairs behind him, Davis caught a glimpse of Achmed lining up another shot. Water was pouring down from holes in the big storage tank, spraying Achmed like some kind of crazy fountain at a waterpark. All around him, soldiers were peppering the jungle with lead.

In two big steps, Davis was at the opposite side of the cabin securing the cargo door. An engine coughed to life as another bullet smacked into the cabin. The old aluminum skin was no match for high-velocity rounds. When Davis reached the flight deck, Boudreau was cranking the starboard engine, running the port side up to power. His hands were flying over the levers.

"I found Achmed," Davis shouted.

"Where?"

"I'll tell you later! Go!"

The airplane was positioned well at one end of the strip, pointed straight down the open runway. Score one for Boudreau's forethought. Davis felt a surge as both engines roared to full power, but the sound wasn't loud enough to overcome the crackle of small-arms fire. Rain began smacking the windshield, big fat drops that sounded like stones as they hammered the Plexiglas. The picture outside was madness, a dozen child soldiers wasting ammunition, officers shouting and waving directions as they tried to keep order. Davis caught a glimpse of Achmed, still crouched next to the hut. He was banging on the breech of his weapon like it had jammed.

"I hope you got that cargo door closed," Boudreau shouted. "She don't fly too good with it hanging."

"I got it," Davis said, falling into the right seat as the airplane bottomed out on a pothole.

They were gaining speed, bouncing over water-filled ruts. The tree line at the end of the clearing was tall and coming on fast.

"Flaps to twenty," Boudreau ordered.

Davis found the lever and yanked it into the right notch. He watched the gauge as the flaps drove slowly to the commanded position, and hoped it would provide enough lift. The trees were getting closer, seeming to grow taller every second. The visibility was increasingly obscured as thickening sheets of rain pelted the windshield. Davis checked the airspeed indicator and saw eighty knots, barely accelerating. They were committed to a takeoff, no room to stop. The airplane was going to go over the trees or into them.

Boudreau pushed forward on the control column, and the nose of the airplane fell ever so slightly. Then he pulled back and Davis felt the nose inch upward, but the trend was mushy and unconvincing. He sensed the landing gear lift up from the dirt, but then drop again and bounce. The gunfire was no longer an issue—that was behind them— but the trees out front would kill them just as surely. He looked over and saw Boudreau fighting the controls. He wished the skipper would give an order, come up with some long-forgotten trick to save the day. He didn't say a thing.

A hundred yards from the treeline, the main gear lifted again, but it wasn't going to be enough. The forest canopy filled the windscreen. It looked almost black now in the thickening downpour, a massive shadow a hundred feet high. The angle of escape was impossible. Maybe you could do it in an F-16, stand on your tail in full afterburner. But never in a vintage DC-3. Davis looked for a soft patch in the green-black wall, ready to grab the controls and steer toward it. He saw nothing but jungle, thick and impenetrable.

Then, seconds from crashing into the forest, the airplane was struck by something else.

CHAPTER TWENTY

Thunderstorms, for all their apparent chaos, are quite predictable i
design. In the downpour stage, air and water rush down from a cen
tral column, hit the earth, and flow uniformly outward in a shape re
sembling an inverted mushroom. At the base are horizontal wind flow
known as microbursts, sudden gusts that can reach hurricane forc￼
Davis knew all about the phenomenon because it had caused an
number of spectacular aviation disasters. A gust of wind, though, irre
spective of severity, is a relative event. One that comes from behin￼
your airplane causes a loss of airspeed, never a good thing when clos
to the ground. The gust that struck at that moment, fortunately, wa
quite the opposite.

Davis watched the airspeed indicator jump from ninety knots t￼
a hundred and fifty in a matter of seconds. This increase in airflov
gave the airplane all the aerodynamic purchase it needed, and i
seemed to levitate as if riding on some invisible elevator. Davis felt
mild impact as they clipped something, and then the world disap
peared in a gray curtain of swirling cloud and rain.

Boudreau reverted to the instruments, flying blind, and Davis di￼
the same. He paid particular attention to the altimeter. Two hundre￼
feet above the ground and steady. Then a torturously slow climb. Thre
minutes later they had a thousand feet between their wheels and th
jungle.

An ashen Boudreau looked over, and said, "Landing gear up."

Davis reached for the gear handle, but paused.

"Did it sound to you like we hit something?"

"Yeah," Boudreau said, "I heard it."

"There might be a tree branch hanging from one of the gear assemblies. If we retract it now we might damage something, maybe break a hydraulic line."

Boudreau pointed to the fuel gauge. "Yeah. But if we don't lift it, then we leave all that drag hanging. She'll run out of gas before the next station." He grinned and repeated, "Landing gear up."

The captain was right. Davis pulled up the landing gear handle and held his breath. Everything seemed to work.

"There, see?" Boudreau said. "They don't build 'em like this anymore."

Davis said nothing.

The flight to Kampala, Uganda, took two hours. Boudreau parked the airplane at a fixed base operator, or FBO, that was already hosting a handful of private jets. A guy holding two orange batons directed them to a parking spot and shoved chocks under their wheels, and within seconds of shutting down a fuel truck pulled up.

Once everything had been secured, Boudreau threw down the boarding stairs, had a short conversation with the fueler, then motioned for Davis to join him. They'd flown the last hop at eight thousand feet—down in the dirt by modern standards—yet even at that altitude the air in the cargo bay had gotten cooler and dryer. So when Davis stepped out onto the ramp, the humidity wrapped around him like a wet blanket.

"Time for a BDA," Boudreau said.

BDA was Air Force for "battle damage assessment." In the fighter world it was an inspection you performed after you departed a combat zone. You'd join up close and look over your wingman's airplane for damage. But in a big airplane you didn't have a wingman, so the BDA had to wait until you landed.

Boudreau pointed up, and Davis saw two bullet holes high on the fuselage. "I don't think we'll be anywhere near the record," the skipper said in mock disappointment.

"What's the record?" Davis asked.

"Ninety-one."

"Ninety-one bullet holes?"

"Well, not all of 'em was from bullets. There was some shrapnel damage too, a rocket propelled grenade, we think."

Davis thought, *What the hell am I doing here?* He said, "Terrific."

After a full circle around the airplane, Boudreau announced, "Seventeen."

"Not even close. Should we go back and try again?"

Boudreau grinned.

As he looked over the airplane, Davis was struck by what *wasn't* going to happen. There would be no corporate incident report or diplomatic complaint. No police investigation or insurance claim. Not even a safety inquiry. He and Boudreau would top off with fuel, then fly back to Khartoum. Tonight a mechanic would put some aluminum speed tape over the bullet holes, and tomorrow the airplane would be back in service.

Boudreau leaned into the right main landing gear well. He came out with a handful of vines that had been tangled around the strut. "There's a service door missing," he said. "Ripped right off the damned hinges."

"So we clipped a tree after all," Davis said.

"Yeah, but the damage is cosmetic. She'll fly. Come on, let's go get some lunch."

Boudreau led the way to an administration building, a relatively new structure that was nicely air-conditioned. Inside, they found free coffee and pastries. Put eight hundred gallons of 100-octane fuel on a company credit card, and the crew got all the sugar and caffeine they could stand. Everybody was happy.

They sat in a lounge that was as comfortable as any Davis had seen in the States, big leather lounge chairs parked in front of a wide-screen TV that was presently showing a cricket match. He was beginning to see why Boudreau had chosen the place. When the skipper excused himself to the head, Davis figured he'd have a few private minutes.

He pulled out his phone, confirmed he had decent reception, and made a call.

Larry Green answered right away, and after a few pleasantries dove into his briefing.

"I got a few things on those tail numbers you asked about, Jammer."

"I'm listening."

"X85BG was purchased by FBN three months ago. It was built in 1952 and had at least ten owners over the years."

Davis thought, *It's way older than I am.* He said, "Who was the most recent?"

"FBN bought it from long-term storage, one of the boneyards out in California."

Davis remembered Boudreau telling him that he'd picked up an airplane in Mojave. "But who bothers to put an airplane that old in storage?" he pondered aloud. "It should have gone straight to the scrap heap—couldn't possibly have had any value."

"Actually, this one might have. It was a special airplane, one of a kind. The previous owner was a flight test company called Flightspan. They're based in Utah, do a lot of contract work for the government and big aerospace contractors."

"Doing what?"

"Flight testing software. This airplane was a flying testbed. It had two complete sets of flight controls—the normal one, and a secondary set that was used to check out developmental flight software and electronic suites. It could be programmed to simulate any kind of airplane. Manufacturers would rent it out, install their software, and iron out kinks in the flight control code before risking it in an expensive new airplane."

"So FBN bought a testbed airplane?"

"Not quite. This thing had been in the boneyard for a long time, over ten years. It's old school, as things like that go. Most of the fancy electronics had been removed."

Davis decided to chew on that for a while. He asked, "What about the accident airplane, N2012L? Do you have anything on that one yet?"

"It was purchased by FBN last May from a broker in Ecuador. Nothing remarkable in its history. The last operator was a cargo outfit in Antigua. FBN only paid twenty thousand U.S. for it."

"I spent more on my last car."

"Me too," Green said.

"So it was just your basic airplane."

"As far as I can tell. What do you make of it?"

Davis thought long and hard. "I don't know, but I'll tell you why I asked about these tail numbers. The accident airplane, N2012L—I found it."

"How the heck did you manage that?"

"Easy. It was sitting on the ramp outside FBN Aviation. The registration had been altered to X85BG, including the tail number—you could see where it had been painted over on both sides."

Davis heard a whistle from across the ocean. Green said, "So if that's the real N2012L, then where's X85BG? You think maybe that testbed airframe is the one in the drink?"

"I have no idea. I don't know if *any* airplane went down. But N2012L was right there in front of me. I'm sure of it."

"But this doesn't compute," Green said. "Why go to all the trouble?"

"The usual reasons don't fit, do they? It's not an insurance scam, because neither airplane is worth anything. Same with a resale angle. If you had an airframe that was due for an expensive maintenance check, and another that wasn't, you might switch them out before a sale. But here there's no incentive, no value in either airframe."

Davis asked, "What about flight plans? Did you track those down?" He heard papers shuffling over the phone.

Green replied, "N2012L was pretty active before the crash, flew all over Africa and the Middle East. One trip to Bulgaria. Pretty much the same routes all their equipment flies."

"Nothing out of the ordinary," Davis surmised.

"Nope. Nothing at all."

Boudreau came back from the latrine with things on his mind.

"So you really think Achmed started that whole thing?" he asked.

"I'm sure of it," Davis said. "I saw him with a rifle. He was shooting from a position near the hut."

"I guess it wouldn't have been hard to get a gun. Hell, they were everywhere."

"He was acting pretty strange on the flight downrange this morning."

Boudreau shook his head. "But I just don't get it. I've flown with him a bunch of times. The kid never says much, but I'd never have figured him for the violent type."

"There *was* one thing different about today's mission."

"You?"

Davis nodded. "I spent some time in the military as a ground-pounder, long enough to recognize when I'm being used for target practice."

"You think you were set up?"

"I can't see it any other way."

"Schmitt?"

Davis shook his head doubtfully. "He and I have a history, but not the kind of thing you'd kill a guy over. I think I'm hitting a nerve somewhere else."

"Your investigation?" Boudreau asked.

"That'd be my guess."

Davis reached for a pastry from a cardboard platter. He had to pull hard, the sugary drizzle having glued it in place. He took a bite and the sugar hit right away.

Davis said, "But we did have one thing on our side today when Achmed was shooting at us."

"What's that?"

"He's no better an assassin than he is a pilot."

Larry Green had never been to the White House. To be precise, he wasn't there now, but the West Wing annex was close enough that he'd consider the square filled.

He was escorted to Darlene Graham's office by a Marine, a square-jawed young man who addressed him as "General," a title he hadn't heard much since retiring from the Air Force. Graham was at her desk, and rose to meet him. Her handshake was warm, but Green thought she looked stressed.

"Good morning, Larry."

"Hello, Darlene."

Green looked around the room appreciatively. It wasn't overdone in a wasteful way, but definitely first class. Freshly painted walls, a few high-end knickknacks and paintings. Everything was clean and well lit, but there wasn't much to put Graham's signature on the room. It had an air of anonymity—which, if you were chief of the nation's combined intelligence services, was probably the way to go.

She said, "I just got back from giving the president his daily intelligence briefing. It was hell."

"What's up?"

"This Arab League conference in Cairo next Tuesday has got everyone in a tizzy. The Arab world has been in a state of flux since all the uprisings, but now that things have settled there's a lot of optimism. We see this as a rare opportunity, a chance to lay a long-term foundation for peace in the region. Israel has been dropping hints that they might ease up on the West Bank settlements, and maybe even talk about Jerusalem. Egypt has long been the heart of the Arab world, and they're trying to convince the more hard-line players to fall in step. The potential exists for a real agreement. That being the case, the president is pushing hard. He wants us to keep track of everything that's going on in the area." Graham went to her desk. "Which leads us to Davis—have you heard from him?"

"He called this morning. No luck getting into that hangar yet, but he did run across some documents you might find interesting." Green explained about the inbound shipments of old drone hardware. Graham listened intently, particularly when he explained the theory that it was done to disguise Blackstar parts going out.

"And this took place two months ago?" she asked.

"Roughly. It's a little circumstantial, but Khoury was definitely up to something."

"So we might be too late."

"Possibly."

"Our most recent surveillance shows that there's still a lot of activity around the hangar," Graham argued. "If Blackstar is long gone, then what are they working on?"

"Jammer and I were wondering the same thing. What about your source, the one who told you about Blackstar originally? Have you gotten any updates?"

That question hung in the air like an overfilled blimp before the DNI said, "No, we haven't heard from our source in some time."

She left it at that, and Green didn't press.

The DNI sat behind her desk and began working her computer. "I have some of the information Davis was asking for," she said. "First is the emergency frequency record. There's one part you might find interesting." She swiveled the computer's monitor sideways so they could both see it. Graham dragged the cursor back and forth over a progress bar until the reference read 1923:50Z. She hit play. For thirty seconds there was nothing, then on Channel 16, the marine VHF emergency frequency:

"This is the Ocean Venture transmitting on emergency frequency. Is there any craft in distress? Our lookout reports seeing a large splash and explosion in the vicinity of Alam Rocks."

A pause, then thirty seconds later: *"This is Ocean Venture, is there any craft in need of assistance?"*

Again, silence.

Graham stopped the recording. "That's all we could find," she said. "No more mention of the incident. I checked on the *Ocean Venture*. She's at sea right now, supposed to make port in Stockholm in two days. We could interview the crew, I suppose, maybe check the ship's log when they arrive."

Green cocked his head. "I don't know if that's going to tell us much. The most relevant part is right there—her crew saw something hit the water." He thought back to the radar data he'd seen yesterday. "The time is right," he said. "But like I told you, I watched that radar tape over and over. The airplane I saw did not go down. It went right back to Khartoum International and landed."

Graham said, "When I heard this VHF data, I called the National Reconnaissance Office and had them dig up one more thing." She switched to another file on her computer, and a sequence of ten photos came to the screen. She enlarged one. "As I'm sure you know, we have a considerable array of satellite assets covering this part of the world. These are composite images, radar and infrared, for the area in question right before the ship made that radio call."

Green looked closely as the DNI stepped through the series. The images were virtually blank—cold, featureless ocean—except for one where there was a clear disturbance, a spray of white near the center.

"What's that?" Green asked, pointing to the blob of white.

Graham pointed to the central five photos in sequence. "Nothing, nothing, splash, nothing, nothing."

"So something did go into the water," Green said.

"Something big," Graham confirmed.

"But I still can't get past those radar tapes. That airplane landed back in Khartoum shortly after this picture was taken."

Graham shrugged. "Doesn't make sense, does it?"

"I'll need to tell Jammer about this right away."

The DNI gave him a circumspect look. "Larry, listen. I appreciate all that Jammer is doing, but you both need to remember one thing— he is there to find Blackstar, or at the very least figure out where it went. This DC–3 crash is only a license for him to go poking around. Nothing more."

Green shook his head. "You've got to understand him, Darlene. If I tell Jammer to blow off this crash, he'll dig in his heels. Just how he is. I've always trusted his instincts in situations like this, and he hasn't disappointed me yet."

Graham didn't reply, and in the ensuing silence Green began to ponder. There had been something nagging him, ever since he'd seen it on his own screen.

He said, "That radar stuff you gave me—do you think it was good data?"

"You mean as far as quality?"

Green nodded.

"Our best stuff is in the Middle East. If two ducks have a midair collision, we know about it."

Green gestured to the computer, and said, "Do you have a copy of it here?"

"Larry, are you not listening? I told you to forget about this crash!"

Green said nothing, only stared at the DNI.

She sighed and began typing. Soon the radar sequence began playing out on the screen. On Green's prompt, she advanced to a point midway in the flight. The airplane symbol turned circles over the Red Sea, and both watched closely when it reached the point in time when the radio call and satellite data indicated that something had hit the water. Nothing happened.

Green felt as if he was missing something. Watching Air Sahara 007 turn south and head for home, he realized what was different. Realized what *wasn't* there.

"Go back," Green said, "ten minutes."

Larry Green had a lot of flying time under his belt, so he had a lot of experience with radar. The equipment could be temperamental, prone to spurious strobes and false returns. That was what he had initially thought he'd seen on this tape—a false echo. The second white square that had come and gone, like an intermittent shadow on a partly cloudy day. Green had figured it for a nuisance reflection or a software glitch. But as Graham ran the loop, he could see it was real, consistently in and out. Until, as now confirmed by the other data, the moment of impact. Afterward, on the way back to Khartoum, no more ghost. Which meant that the secondary reflection wasn't a ghost at all.

"Well, I'll be damned," he said.

CHAPTER TWENTY-ONE

They took off from Kampala an hour later, at three in the afternoon. Davis watched the city fade away beneath them. It looked like an urban lesion on the jade-green jungle, a handful of roads creeping into the treeline like some kind of concrete kudzu. Just over his shoulder, on the starboard side, Davis could make out Kilimanjaro in the distance, sans Hemingway's snows.

Dead ahead was a big thunderstorm, classic in its anvil shape. To the left and right, cumulus formations were building in the late afternoon heat, huge vapor dirigibles climbing into the stratosphere. Soon they'd all shoulder up to one another, bond and mix to saturate huge chunks of sky.

Boudreau was working the weather radar. The storms ahead showed up as coded colors. Green meant rain, yellow meant heavy rain, and red was a place you just didn't go. Presently, Boudreau was navigating through a broken maze of green and yellow splotches, turning left and right to find the path of least resistance. *A lot like me*, Davis thought.

His thoughts settled on what had happened in the jungle. Davis was pretty sure he'd been set up. Somebody had given Achmed an assassin's mission, with him as the target. But who? Schmitt was a possibility. But Rafiq Khoury, cleric gone wild, was a much more likely suspect. If that was the case, it meant that something Davis had done, or might do, was making Khoury nervous. It could have to do with his reconnaissance mission last night. Maybe Khoury had discovered that it was the American investigator, not just a pack of wild dogs, who'd stumbled across the bodies of the two missing pilots. Or maybe

Davis had asked about FBN Aviation's hangar once too often. Whatever the case, he was getting close to something. There was a time when that would have given Davis a sense of satisfaction. But right now he didn't feel satisfied. He felt restless, uneasy.

He had almost crashed twice today in a fifty-year-old airplane, near misses with a forest buffalo and then an equatorial jungle. In the last twenty-four hours he'd been shot at twice, one more statistic he had no desire to extrapolate forward. He was riding a tailwind of good luck, one that could end as abruptly as the wind gust that had saved him and Boudreau a few hours ago. He knew what Larry Green would say if he knew all this. *Chuck everything and go home, Jammer. You should be sitting at the kitchen table having a quiet chat with Jen.*

But that wasn't going to happen, and for the most discomforting of reasons. Davis was looking forward to that next shot across his bow. The next surge of adrenaline. It was like flying a jet through a canyon, approaching a turn at five hundred knots without knowing what was around the next bend. Another canyon? A fork in the path? A sheer wall of rock? You never knew unless you kept going.

His thoughts were derailed by what sounded like a thousand tiny hammers hitting the windshield. The din increased until it became a constant static, like they were flying through gravel.

"Hail," Boudreau said in a calm voice. The voice any normal person would use if, say, a sun shower had started to sprinkle on their Buick. "Shouldn't last long," he said, fiddling with the radar. "We'll be through it in a couple of minutes."

"Best news I've heard all day."

"I've got the power up," Boudreau said. "We should reach Khartoum in about four hours. There's a cot and a pillow in the rear cabin, near the galley. Why don't you get some rest, then come back up to the wheelhouse in an hour and spell me."

Davis thought it sounded like a good plan. He had no idea what might be waiting for them in Khartoum. Chances were, Rafiq Khoury wasn't expecting to see this airplane again. Certainly not expecting to see him. So when they taxied up and parked, there might be raised eyebrows. Or, for all he knew, another gunman to finish what Achmed had started. Things were getting ugly fast, so Davis would have his guard up from here on out.

Ready for the next curve in the canyon.

Air Sahara 12 landed in Khartoum an hour before sunset. Davis got the landing, and while it wasn't his smoothest, he didn't do any damage. Boudreau taxied in, eschewing the painted yellow taxiway lines for a direct route to the parking apron. They worked together to put the airplane to bed, powering down radios and instruments, running a simple shutdown checklist for a simple airplane.

"I guess I've got a few logbook write-ups to make," Boudreau said. "Bullet holes in the fuselage, hail damage on the radome, an access door ripped off. Johnson won't be happy."

"Mechanics rarely are," Davis replied. "They figure pilots for gorillas whose only job is to go out and tear their airplanes apart."

"What about Schmitt? Who's gonna tell him about Achmed's lousy marksmanship?"

"I think I should," Davis said. "He and I have a few things to talk about anyway."

"Okay. But if you need backup, let me know. Once I finish here, I'm heading to the bar. A day like this, a man's gotta replace his electrolytes."

"Right."

Davis dropped the boarding stairs and was struck by the heat, another blistering day taking its time to fade into night. He smelled the desert again, sweet and musky, a replacement for the heavy, organic jungle air they'd imported from the equator. That was one of the things about flying—every time you opened the door you got a new smell, a new temperature, a new sky and horizon. It made you realize how diverse the world was. And how small.

He walked across the hot concrete to FBN Aviation. The front door rotated open, breaking its rubbery seal, and Davis stepped into the chill. Schmitt's door was ajar, and when Davis turned the corner he found the chief pilot elbow deep in his filing cabinet. When he turned, Schmitt seemed surprised to see Davis, although not in the sense that he was looking at a ghost. So maybe he hadn't known about Achmed's ambush.

"Well, look who's back!" Schmitt shoved the drawer closed and pulled a security bar into place, snapping on a combination padlock.

"Surprised?" Davis replied.

"Nothing about you ever surprises me." Schmitt went to his desk and sat. "So how did it go? Did you get a good look at the operation?" The question came with a smile, almost like a stab at humor.

"Yeah, I got a real good look. But things didn't go quite as planned. Your boy Achmed had a particularly bad day."

"That idiot? He's having a bad life. Just don't tell me he botched a landing and bent another one of my airplanes."

Davis looked hard, but still saw nothing. Schmitt was good at certain things. Acting wasn't one of them. He was a guy who put every thought, no matter how ugly, right out there for you to see. And so, even though Schmitt had sent him on this flight, Davis was reasonably sure he knew nothing about Achmed's assassination plot. Reasonably sure.

"We left him down in Congo," Davis said.

Schmitt's expression turned serious. He said nothing.

"We ended up in the middle of a major firefight. I'm not sure Achmed survived. He's still down there, and your airplane is full of holes—new ones, I mean."

"What about Boudreau? Is he okay?"

Davis didn't have to feign the surprise that came over his face. He'd never known Bob Schmitt to care about another human being. Best guess—the chief pilot was afraid of losing his best captain.

"Boudreau's fine."

"And the delivery?"

"The delivery was made. You can tell that to your boss."

Schmitt frowned. "What happened? Was it a rebel attack?"

"I don't know," Davis said. "I'm not sure I could tell the difference between the rebels and the good guys—if there are any good guys. The whole situation was pretty chaotic. We'd just finished the offload when people started shooting. Boudreau and I figured it was time to leave."

"I want to see the airplane," Schmitt said, bolting up. "You wait here." He strode out of his office to the operations desk.

While he was busy, Davis took stock of the room. He noticed a computer situated on an L-shaped extension to Schmitt's desk—as far as he could remember, the only computer he'd seen since arriving in Sudan. He noticed that the mouse was on the left side of the keyboard, and wondered, *How can anybody do that?* The guy really was weird. His attention went to Schmitt's filing cabinet, and he noted that the locking bar on front didn't look particularly solid. He then studied the stout hallway door, top to bottom. It looked solid. There was no keypad on the inside, but then Davis saw why—a motion detector above the inner doorframe. Keypad to get in when the door was locked, motion detector to get out. A common arrangement. He went to the entrance and paused right under the doorframe. Schmitt was still engaged at the front desk. Davis put his arms up on the top frame like he was leaning into it for support. There were certain advantages to being six foot four.

Schmitt finished at the desk and pointed to him. "Come with me. I want this story from both you and Boudreau."

Davis stepped out into the hallway.

Schmitt reached by him and pulled the heavy office door closed. A red "locked" light on the keypad illuminated. "Let's go," he ordered.

"Sure."

They were nearly to the door when Davis felt the phone in his pocket buzz.

"I'll catch up," he said.

Schmitt turned around and gave him a pained look, but that didn't mean much—it was how the man went through life. Forty-something years ago he'd come out of the womb and gotten slapped by an obstetrician, and Bob Schmitt had been slapping the world back ever since. But right now he was a man on a mission, so he disappeared out the door.

Davis saw a message to call Larry Green. He dialed, and Green picked up halfway through the first ring. Like he'd been waiting with his hand poised on the receiver.

"Jammer, I'm glad you called. How's everything going?"

At the moment, Davis figured he could answer that in a very negative way, but Jen had been telling him he needed to become a more positive person. He said, "There are indications I'm making progress."

"Good. I saw Darlene Graham today, and we figured a few things out."

"I'm glad somebody has."

"We've been going down the wrong path. An airplane *did* go down that night. We have radio traffic and satellite photos to confirm it. Right time, right place."

"Wait a minute. You told me an FBN airplane took off, flew some circles, then went right back and landed."

"It did, but there's more to it. The radar returns I saw for that night showed a shadow. It came and went, so I originally figured it was just a glitch in the processing. You've done enough radar work to know how common queertrons like that are."

"Sure. But now you don't think it was a spurious return?"

"Nope. I think it was a two-ship formation."

Davis took a few moments to think about that. "You know, if you put it together with the rest—a lost drone, some telemetry hardware—do you realize what we could be looking at?"

"I know what you're going to say, Jammer. Exactly what came to my mind. I suggested to Darlene Graham that they might have tried to fly Blackstar, maybe with the other airplane as some kind of mother ship to control it."

"Is that feasible?"

"The engineers back here say there's absolutely no way. Two reasons. First, Blackstar has some very advanced flight control software, all fly-by-wire stuff. The inputs come over a secure satellite link from halfway around the world, and there's no way anybody could duplicate that feed—everything is strictly encrypted and the frequency hops around constantly."

"Okay," Davis said. "And the other reason?"

"That's the slam dunk. This is our latest stealth platform. According to Director Graham, Blackstar would have been invisible to the type of radar that took the pictures I saw. You wouldn't get the slightest blip."

"Okay, good point. But if it wasn't Blackstar, then what kind of two-ship formation was out flying around in the middle of the night?"

"Beats me," Green said. "I guess the important thing is that *something* went down in the water."

Davis added, "And we know it wasn't N2012L, which is what somebody wants us to believe."

"That somebody being Rafiq Khoury?"

"Most likely."

There was a prolonged silence before Green said, "Jammer, I don't like how this whole thing is going down. Darlene won't be happy, but I'm pulling you out. Get on the next plane home, we'll have a beer tomorrow night. The CIA can fix this mess on their own."

Davis didn't say anything right away. He'd always known his old boss as a bundle of energy, a guy who could never sit still, so right now Davis had a mental picture of Green circling his desk as if he were training for some kind of office marathon.

"Larry, do you have good coordinates on this crash site?"

"Did you not hear me? I said get out now—that's an order, mister!"

Davis said, "You know what I did last night, Larry? I went for a walk in the desert, over by that hangar. And do you know what I found?"

No reply.

"Two bodies. They were buried out there in the sand, only not very deep. Some dogs had started digging them up. After I left, a few of Khoury's people went out with a backhoe and dug a little deeper. Later, I identified one of the bodies. Can you guess?"

Green responded, "The two Ukrainians?"

"Yep." Davis let that sit for a few seconds, then said, "I don't like

how this is going down either. But two pilots are dead and Bob
Schmitt is running a flying unit. Fire me if you want, but I've got
things to do. Now, I want those coordinates."

"You really are a dumbass, Jammer."

Davis said nothing. Green relented and read off the latitude-
longitude set. Davis searched the operations counter, found a pen and
a scrap of paper, and scribbled the numbers down.

"Where do you take it from here?" Green asked.

Davis knew the answer to that question. But he didn't say it, because his attention was now riveted outside. A big SUV was heading
right for Boudreau's bullet-ridden airplane. Davis suspected he knew
who was inside.

"Larry, I gotta go."

CHAPTER TWENTY-TWO

Davis walked out into the heat.

He made it to the airplane just ahead of the advancing Land Rover. The truck rolled to a stop in front of the bullet-riddled DC-3. The driver's door opened, and an immense man got out. He was taller than Davis by a good two inches, outweighed him by fifty pounds. His arms and legs belonged on an oak. He was dark skinned, with close-cropped black hair on a head the size of a basketball. His cheeks were dark, the kind of five o'clock shadow that didn't care what time it was. As he walked around the front of the Rover, Davis was sure he felt the guy's footsteps transmit through the ground—like a Tyrannosaurus rex out for a stroll.

T. rex opened the passenger door, and Rafiq Khoury stepped out. Dark glasses, bird's nest beard, slender limbs. Just like the photo Davis had seen. The cleric walked toward them—no, he flowed toward them, an apparition of white cotton fluttering in the torrid breeze.

"What has happened?" Khoury asked, addressing Schmitt.

Davis wondered how Khoury knew that *anything* had happened.

Schmitt looked cautious—like any American who worked for a fundamentalist Muslim cleric would. He said, "There was trouble on our delivery to Congo today. Some gunfire broke out while the airplane was on the ground, right as they were finishing the unload. The airplane took a few hits."

Khoury looked over the aircraft—even a nonflier couldn't miss the damage—and then swiped a fleeting glance at Davis who was standing away from the rest.

"And the crew?" the imam asked.

Boudreau said, "Achmed is still down there. We don't know what happened to him."

Ever so slightly, Khoury's head cocked to one side. Davis would have given anything to see the expression hidden behind his knock-off Serengetis. As if to accommodate, Khoury walked toward him. He stopped right in front of Davis and very slowly pulled his glasses away from his eyes. Davis was taken aback, struck by the intense, mismatched gaze. That hadn't been in the file, hadn't been in the lone photo in which Khoury's eyes were masked behind dark glasses. Davis almost felt as if he was looking at two different souls. Yet it struck him, aside from the eyes, that there was nothing special about the rest of the man. Take those away, put Khoury in a suit and tie, add a decent haircut and a shave, and he might have been a fastener salesman at a convention. Which somehow put even more emphasis on his gaze.

"I am Imam Rafiq Khoury. I manage FBN Aviation. You are the investigator who has come to help us?" The cleric's English was good, if a little deliberate.

Davis considered a number of smart-ass replies, but said, "I am. The name's Jammer Davis."

"I understand that you were also on this flight today, Mr. Davis. May I ask why?"

Davis thought, *Because you and Schmitt sent me.* He said, "Because I wanted to check out your operation."

Khoury nodded. It was a good answer, convenient for everyone. He asked, "And what did you think?"

"I think your captain did a first-rate job." Davis nodded toward the airplane. "The rest speaks for itself."

"We must all pray for Achmed's safety. He is a strong young man, and Allah will be with him."

"Yeah," Davis said, "he seemed like a great kid. The kind of kid who always did what he was told."

Khoury stared at Davis with his incongruous green-and-brown gaze. With far less deliberation than he had used to remove them, Khoury put his glasses back on. He reminded Davis of an actor, every movement and word calculated for effect. But Davis didn't allow himself to be distracted. Didn't lose his SA. While he and Khoury had been staring each other down, the big guy had slowly arced around behind Davis, almost as if he was stalking. Like T. rex's probably did millions of years ago. Yet if there was a scent of trouble on the air, it dissipated when Rafiq Khoury took a step back.

"Tell me, Mr. Davis, how does your investigation progress? We have been operating our airline for nearly a year, and this tragic crash is our only case of misfortune."

Davis looked over the bullet-riddled airplane behind them. "If we don't count today's misfortune."

"I am sure our mechanics can repair the damage."

"And I'm sure you can recruit a new kid to fill the hole in the right seat."

Khoury stiffened, but said nothing. Davis figured the imam wasn't used to being challenged. Around here, arguing with Khoury was tantamount to arguing with God. But even if Davis had been a man with strong religious leanings—even if he was a Muslim—he couldn't imagine turning to this man for anything spiritual. Khoury struck him as a manipulator and nothing more.

Loudly enough for everyone to hear, Davis said, "Since you're here, Mr. Khoury, maybe I could ask you about the airplane that went down."

The imam hesitated, and Davis imagined his eyes moving fast behind the dark glasses. Searching for help.

Schmitt tried to give it. "What could the sheik know that would help your investigation?"

Davis kept his gaze locked on Khoury. "You seem to have connections."

"I have many followers."

"Do any of them work in the government?"

No response.

Davis continued, "You see, I was wondering if any wreckage might have been discovered along the coast. When an airplane goes down in the water there's always debris, so something should have been found by now. Seat cushions, plastic fittings, maybe a wing floating on an empty fuel tank. It might have been picked up by a fisherman, or maybe washed ashore. There's even a chance that the body of a crewmember might have been found, but we just haven't heard about it." Davis paused for effect. "Could you do that for me, Mr. Khoury? Ask around and see if any bodies have, you know, turned up?"

Davis let his gaze drift obviously to the T. rex who was still rooted a few steps behind him. He locked eyes with the brute. Everyone knew the storm flag had been raised. Knew it was snapping stiff in a force five gale of bullshit. Davis watched as Khoury considered how to respond. It wasn't a short-term, tactical deliberation, but the longer strategic variety, like a chess player thinking five moves ahead. Only Davis doubted the imam was a good chess player. He figured Khoury for the type who would analyze things in a linear fashion. *My move, my move, my move, check.* Davis had played a little himself, and he knew that you had to consider your opponent's countermoves. When you did, the mathematical possibilities got real big, real fast. And Davis had always been good at math.

"I have heard nothing," Khoury said. "But I will see to it that the authorities are notified. It should be simple enough to have the police agencies along the coast report on the matter."

"Great," Davis said, beaming a huge smile. "My investigations always go faster when I get that kind of cooperation."

Khoury turned to address Schmitt. "I must go now. If Mr. Davis needs anything else to aid his inquiries, see to it."

"My pleasure," the chief pilot said.

The imam walked briskly to the Land Rover. His T. rex stomped ahead to beat him there, and pulled open the door with forced delicacy, as if he didn't want to rip it off its hinges by accident. A minute later, Rafiq Khoury's British-made SUV swerved away.

Davis was the first to speak. "So who was the Sasquatch?" he asked.

Boudreau answered. "His name's Hassan. Sort of a bodyguard, I guess. You never see Khoury without him."

Schmitt added nothing.

With Khoury gone, the tension was sucked right out of the air.

Davis' eyes skipped past the chief pilot and landed squarely on Boudreau. "Buy you a beer?"

The Louisianan smiled. "Captain always buys the first round."

Boudreau bought the first round, and the second. By the fifth he was all alone.

It wasn't an uncommon situation. No pilot ended up in a place like this—a makeshift watering hole in the African desert—without a sad story. As a career, aviation could be both rewarding and costly, both enlightening and depressing. Broken marriages were common. Stress-related illness—ulcers and high blood pressure—a fact of life. And some turned to drink. Boudreau was coming in for a landing after a tough day, and this was his way of keeping the right side up. Davis thought no less of the man. He'd faced his own demons when Diane had died, and might have hit the bottle hard had it not been for Jen. His daughter had needed him more than ever, and Davis made sure he was there for her with no complications or distractions. Over time, their bond had become more of a two-way street. Jen was *his* foundation now, a stabilizer for the top-heavy monument that was his aviator's ego.

Davis was enduring Boudreau's sorrowful account of former wives and airlines. It was a saga of scandal and disrepute that, in the hands of the right screenwriter, might have made a smashing miniseries. He was on wife three and airline five when Johnson came into the room. Like any good mechanic, he was covered in sweat and grease. He sidled up next to Davis and put two thick, hairy forearms on the bar.

"Buy you a beer?" Davis asked.

A downtrodden Johnson shook his head. "I've been looking for you, Jammer. We need to talk."

"About what?"

"Things are getting weird around here."

"Like they haven't always been?"

Johnson ignored that, and said, "A few weeks ago we stopped getting our usual shipments of expendables. You know—tires, hydraulic fluid, oil. Stuff like that."

"Have you run out?"

"No, not yet. We've got enough to keep operating for two weeks, maybe three. That is, if we keep flying."

Boudreau sensed a hot rumor, and asked, "What do you mean, 'If we keep flying?'"

Worry was etched into Johnson's meaty face. "I've been in this industry a long time, over twenty years. It hasn't always been pretty. I've been furloughed twice and seen three former employers go out of business."

"And you think that's going to happen here?" Davis asked. "Just because you're running low on oil?"

"There's more. Three of our airplanes have been grounded for maintenance problems. One in Rwanda and two in Qatar."

"Airplanes break," Davis said. "Especially airplanes that are seventy years old."

"I tried to track down what's wrong with them. I talked to the local contract mechanics in each place, and they don't know anything about it. I've worked with the guy in Rwanda before. He says our airplane is just parked. Nobody even called to ask him to look at it. He snuck aboard and looked at the logbook for me. That airplane is clean, no write-ups at all."

Johnson pulled a paper from his pocket and handed it over. "And check this. It's the schedule for the next two weeks. They always give it to me ahead of time to plan out the required service checks. After Sunday, there's not a single flight scheduled."

Davis looked it over. Today was Friday. After the weekend, no flights. Not a single one.

"Did you look into this?" Davis asked.

"Yeah, I went to Schmitt. He said he'd been given some cock-and-bull story about next week's flights getting moved around for a big job. He said the schedule wouldn't come out until the last minute."

"Has that ever happened before?"

"Never. And Schmitt told me something else. He said Podulski and Eduardo have been deported."

Boudreau jumped in. *"Deported?"*

"Some kind of problem with their work visas," said Johnson.

Davis studied the two FBN employees. "Okay," he said, "so what do you guys think is happening? Is FBN Aviation in financial trouble? Is management going to pull the plug?"

"I've seen it happen before," said a grim Boudreau.

Johnson kept silent, and Davis tried to read him. Ever since arriving in Sudan he had wondered who Darlene Graham's "reliable human source" could be. He figured it was likely an American, and there were only three here—Johnson, Boudreau, and Schmitt. The mechanic standing in front of him didn't strike Davis as the secret agent type. He was blue collar all the way, a guy who'd spent a long career in a tumultuous industry. A guy who was worried right now that another job, another line of paychecks, was about to come to an end. Davis would put Boudreau in the same equation, a long-suffering vagabond in a very unsteady line of work. Aside from that, Davis was pretty sure that if Boudreau was the source he would already have come out and told him as much. There was, however, one big problem with all that division—it left Bob Schmitt as the very odd remainder.

Johnson said to Davis, "If management has decided to wrap up the company, it might have to do with this crash you're investigating."

It almost sounded like an accusation. "Possible, I guess," Davis said. He then put some directness in his voice. "Tell me something, Johnson. Were you the one who repainted the tail number on N2012L?"

The mechanic hesitated and looked at Boudreau, then shook his head vigorously. "No. I noticed that, but I had nothing to do with changing it. If Schmitt or Khoury wanted something sketchy like that done, they'd have asked Muhammed."

Davis said, "Okay, I'll buy that. But what do you think is behind it?"

Johnson shook his head. "I've thought about it long and hard, but it makes no sense. Maybe it has to do with this shutdown."

Davis remembered what Schmitt had said on their first meeting in his office. *If the Sudanese government steps in and shuts down FBN Aviation, it'll be up and flying again inside a week. Same airplanes, same pilots, new name.* Fly By Night Aviation was a company with no board of directors, no stockholders. But the company had backing somewhere.

Davis said, "So they might be resetting all the tail numbers and paperwork, shuffling the company like a big deck of cards. Khoury puts it all in some magical filing cabinet to make FBN Aviation disappear, and in a week or a month the airline comes out fresh and shiny under a new name."

"It makes sense," Boudreau agreed.

"You've got some clout, Jammer," Johnson suggested. "Can you ask around? Find out what's happening?"

Davis shrugged. "I don't know. If Khoury really *is* shutting FBN down, I'd probably be the last one he'd tell."

Johnson looked crestfallen.

Davis put a hand on his shoulder. "Look, if I hear anything I'll let you know."

The mechanic turned to leave, but then paused. "Oh, and Jammer. There's one other thing you should know."

"What's that?"

"That doctor, the one whose shipment was ripped off the other day."

"What about her?"

"It happened again."

Davis' eyes locked on Johnson. He fell completely still, like ice had been injected into his veins.

Johnson said, "There was a shipment to replace the last one, arrived from Naples this afternoon. The same bunch came and took it. Only this time it got a little rough."

The ice hit his spine. *The same bunch.* Not soldiers or police. More like thugs with a precinct. Davis kept a low, even voice. "Rough? What happened?"

"I didn't see exactly. The soldiers were driving away when I got there. But the doctor and that kid who helps her—they were pretty beat up."

"How bad?"

Johnson told him.

Davis said, "You got a key to the pickup?"

Johnson nodded.

"Give it to me!"

Khoury walked into Jibril's work area to find the engineer busy, as he always was. When Jibril looked up and saw him, he seemed to tense.

"Good evening, sheik," Jibril said.

"Good evening, Fadi. I don't wish to take you from your work, but time grows short for our lesson."

"Lesson?" Jibril asked haltingly. "Oh, yes. Of course."

Without another word, without even issuing his usual status report, the engineer turned away and led toward the old DC-3.

Khoury definitely sensed something awry. He fell in behind Jibril and followed him to the aircraft, climbing up the short set of steps and ducking inside. Jibril took the lone chair at the workstation he had designed, a desk-like setup with one main screen that was surrounded by electrical equipment. A tangle of wires sprouted underneath, as if some creature had made a nest using loops of electrical conduit, power packs, and surge suppressors.

Jibril began to work the keyboard silently.

Khoury could take no more. "What is it, my son?"

The young man said nothing for a moment, and Khoury sensed him gnashing through a decision. He hoped it was not technical in nature, as there was no time for further setbacks. Khoury moved to one side until he drew Jibril's gaze, locking eyes with the engineer to demand the truth.

"I am concerned about the final targeting sequence," Jibril said.

"What about it?"

"Should we not preprogram the final coordinates?"

Khoury heaved an inner sigh of relief. He had long expected this to come up. "You have already loaded the initial course to the holding pattern. That will be our staging point."

"But why can we not program the entire route?"

"Because," Khoury explained, "we do not know it. Our target will be moving. We can anticipate a general location, but precise coordinates will not be available until the final minutes. Which is why you must teach me how to enter the final numbers."

"But I will be there to do it," Jibril countered.

"Of course, but as an engineer you understand the importance of backing things up. Have you ever written one of your computer programs without making a copy?"

"No, of course not."

"There you are. Allah's will is never done absent challenges, Fadi. We must seize every chance to bring Him glory."

The engineer thought about this, and seemed to relent. He began his lecture. Jibril demonstrated how to alternate between screens and how to monitor the performance and signal strength. He then showed Khoury how to send the terminal pairing of navigation coordinates. Jibril gave up his seat and made Khoury run through the entire targeting sequence once, then again.

"There is nothing more to it," Jibril said. "You need only the coordinates and a precise time. With that, the rest is fully programmed. Simplicity itself. But know that once the final command is sent, we will have no control. Everything is autonomous at that point."

Khoury nodded, satisfied.

"Still . . . there is one thing I don't understand," Jibril said hesitantly.

Khoury remained silent, inviting him to continue.

"If our target is in Israel, why is the initial point so far to the south?"

Khoury stood and backed away from the workstation. He clasped his hands behind his back and began a tight pattern of pacing. "It is time for you to know our target, Fadi. Indeed, it is only thanks to your work that we have this opportunity." He looked intently at the engineer. "We have a chance to strike a blow as never before."

Jibril looked fittingly humble.

Khoury lowered his voice. "We are going right to the top, Fadi. Our target is the Prime Minister of Israel."

Jibril nodded slowly, as if this only confirmed what he had long suspected.

"If it is the will of Allah," the imam added.

Minutes later Jibril was alone, working on the guidance console in the DC-3. As he typed on the keyboard, he wished he had a connection to the Internet. This morning he had seen a newspaper, a local rant that was nothing more than a twenty-page editorial affair put together and issued by the government. There were, however, occasional reprints of articles from other papers in the region, straight blurbs of factual material that were permitted either by virtue of being innocuous, or because they supported the local view of world events. Jibril had read an article relating to the upcoming Arab summit in Egypt. At the end of the article was a single paragraph mentioning Israel. The government there was seeking to keep a low profile, apparently not wishing to overshadow their Arab neighbors' attempt at peace. To that end, the Israeli prime minister was scheduled to leave tomorrow for talks in Washington, D.C., and later continue on a goodwill mission to the Far East.

He would, according to the report, be abroad for the next ten days.

Davis covered the twenty miles to the Al Qudayr Aid Station in fifteen minutes. The broiling sun was falling low, almost resting on the western horizon. When he arrived at the barren turnoff, the engine of the truck-slash-breakroom sounded like it had thrown a rod. He skidded to a stop outside the little city of tents, white smoke spewing from under the hood. Davis threw open the door, left it that way, and ran to the tents. He spotted a gathering in one corner, a half dozen people in mismatched scrubs circled around a cot. Davis slowed as he closed in.

He recognized Antonelli, standing in the group with her back to him. He also recognized the patient on the cot. It was the kid who had been with Antonelli the first time he'd seen her. He was beaten to hell, the right side of his face a meaty mess, his hair matted with blood.

There was a wicked slash near one temple with fresh stitches. His right arm was in a sling and his eyes were closed, but he seemed to be breathing well enough as a nurse held a wet cloth to his forehead.

When Davis approached, everyone turned to look. Antonelli was the last, and when she turned he got a look at her face. There was a big welt on one cheek and blood under her nose. Her hair was bunched in a tangle on one side, like somebody had taken a handful to get a better grip.

Antonelli didn't need to say anything.

Davis looked at the young man on the bed. "Will he be okay?" he asked.

She cocked her head. "By the grace of God, yes. I think so."

He looked her in the eyes and saw a resolute sadness, deep and permeating. But there was also determination, the same tenacity that had been there yesterday. The same tenacity that would be there to-morrow and the next day and fifty years from now.

Davis knew all too well what was brewing inside him, sensations derived from a distinct physiological response. Adrenaline, increased pulse rate, liberation of nutrients—all the things that kicked in as the body prepared itself for battle. When flight was no longer an option. It was a surge Davis usually controlled. When somebody gave him a cheap shot on the rugby pitch or cut him off on the freeway. Those things he could manage. But right now the impulse was something Davis didn't want to suppress. He wanted only one thing. One shred of information.

He looked straight at the doctor, and asked. "Was it the same guys?"

She gave him a tentative look, knowing the answer but not sure whether to give it. She looked at the medical professionals around the bed, one by one, as if taking some kind of secret ballot. Finally, Antonelli nodded.

"Yes, the very same."

"You said they had a warehouse?"

She nodded. "A mile north of the airport on the main road."

That was all he needed. Davis turned on a heel and headed for his smoking truck.

By the time he hit the main road, the engine was running rough. But it was running. Davis turned off the Mack truck air conditioner to ease the load on the V-8, made five miles, then ten. The airport slid by his right window. Davis kept going, the truck's headlights drilling into a new black night. One kilometer north, just as Antonelli had said, he found what he was looking for. Davis pulled over to the shoulder, left the engine running. Darkness had arrived in full, so he watched through a cloud of steam, the truck's high beams playing the mist to create a surreal scene.

Jammer Davis was nobody's savior, no keeper of right or honor. But certain things crossed his line. Things like hitting women and beating up kids. It might have been because Davis had a daughter of his own. Somewhere, Regina Antonelli had a father, and Davis understood how he'd feel right know if he knew what had happened. So there was no quandary. No internal strife or gnashing through moral dilemmas. Davis knew what had to be done. The only question was how, the cold execution of a tactical decision matrix like he'd done a hundred times in his military career.

Rage is not necessarily a bad thing. The blind variety can get you killed, but properly focused and trained with precision, it can be quite effective. Right now, Jammer Davis was focused. His breathing was slow and rhythmic, his muscles relaxed as he stared through the windshield and counted.

There were five.

CHAPTER TWENTY-THREE

Davis looked up and down the road to Khartoum. He could see for miles in either direction, and there wasn't another set of headlights in sight. The road was probably never busy. A surge of traffic now and again, an hour before and thirty minutes after any of the ten or twelve daily flights was processed. But at this hour on a Friday evening, he was completely alone. As were the men he was watching.

Davis had parked next to a guard station, a shack with twin rail-road-type crossing gates that were both pointed straight up. The gates looked like they hadn't moved in years. The barriers were here, Davis supposed, so the military could govern access to the airport in the event of a crisis. But today the control point was unmanned because there was no crisis. Hadn't been one yesterday. Doubtful there would be one tomorrow. Which led to the larger problem—a contingent of armed men with nothing to do. In a disciplined fighting force, not an issue. Here it was trouble.

Their modest compound was two hundred yards off the main road, central on a patch of desert where the scrub had been bulldozed away to leave a bare scar on the earth. The main structure was well lit, an office no bigger than a double-wide trailer. This was fronted by a heavy canvas awning that formed a makeshift patio, thirty feet of shade for lounging and recreating—where the soldiers were now. Next to this headquarters complex was a rectangular building with corrugated metal sides and a flat roof. A warehouse, apparently, because parked in front was a mid-size truck, the same vehicle he'd seen drive away from the airport two days ago with a load of Regina Antonelli's supplies.

Presently, the cargo bed was covered by a tarp, and underneath a load jutted up at points along the length like so many lumps in a python.

Davis counted one last time, got the same answer. Still five men under the awning. He looked close, but saw no evidence of soldiers in any of the other buildings. At this time of night, any more than five would be overkill for a remote outpost like this. One man was leaning against a pole that held up the awning. The other four soldiers— if you could call them that—sat playing cards. Having served in the military, Davis knew all about guard duty. He knew that playing cards was a good way to cut the boredom. Just like personal phone calls or watching a game on TV. All soldiers did that. But never the entire detail at the same time. That was dumb, even dangerous. It told Davis that this unit wasn't expecting enemy action any time soon. Told him there was no chance of a snap inspection from headquarters.

He watched the loner stab a needle into his arm and shoot up— something. The man went limp, to the point that Davis thought somebody ought to lash him to the pole. His buddies didn't seem to notice. They were the other extreme, raucous and lively.

He hadn't drawn their attention yet, so Davis kept studying. The men at the table were sitting on plastic chairs, white and cheap, the kind you bought at Wal-Mart for $4.99 and could stack in a nest on your porch when you weren't using them. He spotted four guns, probably AKs, all leaning on one another, barrels up and butts in the sand. They made a neat little tree, all right there in one place. If there were any other weapons, Davis didn't see them. Everything else under the tarp fell in the category of junk. A jerry can marked PETROL, a bicycle leaning on a crate, its front wheel removed and lying on the ground. To one side, some construction equipment—a shovel, a few bags of cement, a small pneumatic jackhammer. A bath towel and a Sudanese flag were strung side by side on a support wire, flapping in the breeze with equal indifference.

There was a moment of truth at the table. A smiling winner raked in the pot while the investors sulked and wrist-flicked their cards spinning to the middle of the table. From where he was, Davis couldn't see anybody's rank. It didn't matter. If you watched a group of soldiers long enough—even a feral group like this—you could figure out who was in charge. Dominant mannerisms, command presence. And Davis didn't even need that, because he noticed the way one man held his head at an angle. Scarface. The long pole in a flimsy organizational tent.

From the highway checkpoint, a dirt path led to the little outpost. Davis put the truck into gear and crawled forward at idle. They still hadn't noticed him, so he flicked on his high beams. Like anybody would to navigate a raw desert trail at night. He'd covered half the ground when one of the soldiers pointed and said something. Scarface turned and stared.

The old truck's twin white beams jarred up and down, strobing everything in their path. Vapor belched from under the hood, a steady white cloud spewing into the hot evening air. The engine was running rough, coughing and sputtering, and Davis thought, *Good*. The men rose from their chairs but didn't look alarmed. Curious was more like it.

Davis estimated the tree of rifles to be twelve, maybe fifteen steps from the card table. He remembered that Scarface had carried a sidearm, a Heckler & Koch 9-mm, if he wasn't mistaken. He searched and found it, a belted holster hanging on a hook near the gun stack. So there was a good chance that all the firepower was right there in one place. Three or four seconds from anybody's hands. Six or seven seconds from being used. That was a lot of time when you counted it out, which was exactly what Davis rehearsed in his mind. One . . . *strike*. Two, three . . . *strike*. All the way to seven. He worked everything out, a nice tight blueprint in his head. Of course, plans like that had a way of going wrong—seven seconds left a lot of room for error—but you had to start somewhere. Davis figured he was solid until about three. After that, he'd go with the flow—or against it, actually.

With fifty feet to go, Davis spotted a bottle of whiskey on the table, along with three tiny glasses. Three glasses, four men. So one of them might be sober, maybe a devout Muslim. Or perhaps they were playing by frat-house rules, losers having to drink after each hand.

Whatever. He was dealing with five men, most of whom had been drinking. And with his target set full, Jammer Davis began to sort.

In air-to-air combat, before merging with an opposing force, you always perform a radar sort with your wingman. This short-term tactical plan dictates which of the bad guys you will each take out—right shoots right, lead shoots high, a preplanned sequence of death that is as cold and clinical as it is optimistic. Right now, Davis didn't have a wingman or Sidewinders on his rails. But going in he at least wanted a plan.

He decided that the man on the left, a small guy with a beret, would be first. He was closest to the weapons. The addict leaning on the pole was last—no doubt about that—which meant that his gray area involved the three in the middle. Scarface was the boss, so he was high on the list. A tall, rangy man looked like a pushover. The one Davis didn't like was in the middle. He was short and burly, with a flattened nose on a squashed face. There was a toughness about him. On looks alone the guy could get work tossing steamer trunks on a wharf. Yet what bothered Davis most about the man was right there in front of him on the table. The largest chip stack.

Davis pulled the truck to an easy stop twenty feet from the awning. Steam swirled from under the hood and spread in a mist of white. He got out of the truck slowly and muttered a few expletives, like anybody would after blowing a radiator on the edge of the Sahara Desert.

By virtue of physical size, Davis was not a man easily forgotten, so he was sure that some of these soldiers—the ones who'd been at the airport two days ago—would recognize him. Scarface certainly. Davis gave a subtle wave, as if he recognized them too.

"Hi," he said, adding in his best helpless-foreigner shrug.

Scarface gave an almost imperceptible nod. Not one of the men under the tent looked worried. Their initial curiosity had graduated to amusement. They were completely confident, an outlook derived by some equation involving their superior numbers and the whiskey on the table.

Davis went to the hood, opened it very, very slowly, and then stood with his hands on his hips. He turned to the soldiers, and said, "You guys got any water?"

It was the man on the right, the rangy one, who came forward. Not Davis' first pick, but at times like this you didn't get to choose. The guy covered most of the twenty-foot gap in six lanky strides, stopping a couple of paces shy to peer hesitantly into the steaming engine compartment. He opened his mouth but didn't say anything, probably because he didn't speak any English. Or maybe because the mechanical issue involved was obvious enough—a cracked hose near the top of the radiator spewed superheated water like a miniature volcano. Davis could smell alcohol on the man's breath, something cheap and harsh. Even in a fundamentalist Muslim country, soldiers found their rotgut.

The rangy soldier was roughly four feet away from the open hood, a reasonably safe distance. About where Davis would have stopped. He figured that soldiers in Sudan knew all about overheated engines. There was probably a whole course on it in basic training. Davis took one last look at the others. He saw Scarface glance away momentarily at his drug-addled fifth.

Right then, Davis began to count.

The windmill is an underrated strike.

Davis rotated his right arm up and then arced down, his fist falling like a wrecking ball. The blow struck between the man's neck and collarbone, and his head snapped forward. Before his knees could even buckle, Davis grabbed him by the collar and drove the soldier head-first into the engine compartment, slamming his face squarely onto the steaming radiator hose. His screams were cut short when Davis slammed the hood down on the back of his head. The long, rangy limbs went soft like slack rope.

One down. His internal clock was running.

Three . . .

After a stunned moment, the others at the poker table started shouting. Davis didn't understand a word, but he didn't need to. The cadence was enough, explosive and breathless. A plan of action, maybe some profanity mixed in. *Let's kick his ass, Hussein!* Something like that.

The man with the beret lunged in from the left, and took a wild swing with the whiskey bottle in his hand. He was the smallest of the lot, a full foot shorter than Davis, built out of matchsticks. His impulse to grab the bottle wasn't bad. His execution was. Davis raised an arm to deflect the blow, rotated his opposite elbow to the guy's jaw. The strike didn't put him down, but stunned him to immobility. Davis' next swing was big and full, a roundhouse that caught the man squarely in the solar plexus, a good target because it has nerve bundles and vital arterial junctions. Even more importantly, the solar plexus lies very close to an opponent's center of gravity. If the guy had been any smaller, the blow would have sent him into orbit. As it was, he went airborne in the direction of Davis' follow-through, sailed five feet through the air, and hit the dirt like a sack of wet gravel. Two down.

Six . . .

The odds were improving, but the first two had taken three blows, six seconds. Davis was over budget. And so, just like he'd figured, things started to go to hell. The squashed-faced guy was moving for the guns, which was what he should have done. Scarface was going the other way, which was what he should have done.

There was no choice. Davis lunged for the gun stack, got there just as the squat soldier was swinging a Kalashnikov in his direction. Flying through the air, Davis hit the man shoulder first and everything went flying—the soldier, his rifle, the whole tree of rifles. The squat guy was quick to his feet, and the fighter's nature Davis had expected took over. He started swinging, a storm of short, compact punches that caught Davis in the body and face as he was rising. Davis, however, became a bigger storm, a category five maelstrom of fists and elbows, blocking and striking, backed by over two hundred pounds of follow-through. In close quarters combat, you hit hard and often, overwhelm your opponent. That's what Davis did. The squat guy doubled over after a knee to the gut, then crumpled like his bones had disconnected after a hammer fist to the back of the neck. Three down.

Davis turned to find Scarface, but didn't see him right away. *Ten? Twelve?* He had no idea. His clock was pointless.

Davis spotted him, ten paces away and half hidden behind the hanging beach towel. He had a knife in his hand, a combat blade. The ten-inch Rambo special would look pretty impressive in a bar or at a poker game. Even useful in a fight if you knew how to use it. Scarface didn't. He was holding the thing all wrong, jabbing and pointing like it was a fencing foil. Right then, Davis realized that this commander had not been promoted for his fighting skill. Davis walked straight at him, remembering the cut on the kid who'd been with Antonelli.

Scarface started swinging wildly, scything the blade in big defensive arcs. Davis grabbed what was at hand—the loose bicycle wheel. He wound up backhanded, and threw it like a ten-pound Frisbee. It hit Scarface in the head and knocked him back two steps. Davis grabbed an overturned plastic chair and kept going, no hesitation in his advance. The commander recovered and started swinging the knife again. Davis held out the chair and fended him off like a lion tamer, didn't stop until he'd backed him up against the wall of the building. Davis ripped the Sudanese flag off the support line. With Scarface cornered, he used the chair to keep separation, then the flag to snag the knife on its last pass. He locked down on the man's wrist, wrestled the knife away and tossed it far into the brush. Scarface should have stopped right there. Instead, his tactical disaster was made complete when he threw what could charitably be described as a punch.

A village somewhere had lost its idiot.

With a vision of Antonelli's bruised face in his head, Davis pulled back his right hand and unloaded. It was just one blow, a compact delivery, but he rotated all his weight behind the strike, augmented with more than a little anger. The palm heel to the base of the nose, properly delivered, is among the most incapacitating of blows. The force of the strike lifted Scarface off his feet and slammed his head back into the corrugated aluminum wall. In that instant, his head stopped its rearward movement. Davis' hand did not. Something had to give, and predictably it was the target's nasal cartilage and vasculature. Maybe to

FLY BY NIGHT 179

a lesser degree the wall, where a round indentation came pressed into the aluminum.

Scarface collapsed to the dirt. He didn't move.

Davis took the intermission to check on the others. He saw three men right where he'd left them, barely moving. No threat. The addict was still leaning on the pole in glassy-eyed oblivion. Definitely no threat. Scarface moaned and his eyes flickered. A hand went instinctively to his shattered face. He blinked repeatedly, an involuntary act to wash the blood out of his eyes. When he finally focused, it was on Davis. Six feet up.

"Who . . . who are you?" he croaked in English.

"I'm with the United Nations—Enforcement Division."

Scarface spit out a mouthful of blood and asked a slow, gurgling question, "What do you want?"

Davis walked over to the pile of construction equipment, grabbed the dusty jackhammer and hauled it over. He poised it over Scarface's chest, watched his eyes go wide.

Davis said, "I want you to stop pilfering." He pointed to the other men strewn about under the awning. "I don't care about any of them. You are the commander, and from this point forward your unit mission has changed. You will no longer raid. Instead, you are assigned to protect every aid shipment that comes into this territory. If any load of cargo to any aid organization is interrupted, by your people or anybody else, I will come back for the one person in the Sudanese Army who is responsible." Davis lowered the blade of the jackhammer. "I will find you and use this, and I don't mean on a sidewalk. I will bend you over and use it on you. Get the picture?"

Scarface nodded to suggest he did.

"Good." Davis tossed the jackhammer aside, and it crushed the rickety card table in a colorful spray of chips and playing cards.

He walked to his pickup truck. Steam was still coming from under the hood, but less now. There was a chance it might still run for another mile or two, until vital parts of the engine melted and seized. Davis decided it was time for a trade-in, and there was only one other vehicle on this dealer's lot. He reached into the pickup and took the keys from the ignition, threw them far into the desert. From behind the front seat he grabbed a handful of a mechanic's most useful tools—plastic zip ties. They were long and thick gauge, probably used for keeping cargo bay panels in place or tying down instruments with broken mounts. A thousand uses really, which was why mechanics loved them. Cops loved them too, but had a different name. They called them flex cuffs.

Ignoring the addict, who had passed out right where he'd been standing, Davis dragged the rest of the squad together in pairs. Moaning and bloody, nobody resisted. Davis sat them down, one by one, and bound their wrists behind their backs, looping the ties through their belt loops. Then he connected them in pairs, bound their wrists so that it looked like they were playing patty-cake back-to-back. He doubted they could drive like that, even if they had a vehicle. He was sure they couldn't ride a one-wheeled bicycle. But they could probably walk, so Davis considered making it a three-legged race, only to find he was running short on zip ties. Also on time.

He went to the three-ton truck parked in front of the storage building. The keys were in the ignition—that was how it worked in any army. Davis cranked the big diesel, shifted with a grinding of gears, and rumbled off toward the main road. Asphalt was soon humming under the truck's knobby tires, a steady reverberation that brought Davis down from his adrenaline high. The headlights cast an easy white glow, and Davis took deep breaths. He began to feel the edge from his scrum—a badly scraped knee, a sore shoulder, nerve pain in one wrist. There would be more when he woke up tomorrow morning. Davis then felt something sharp stabbing his upper right thigh. He reached into his pocket and pulled out the source—half of a tiny circuit board. He reached deeper into his pocket and pulled out the rest of his phone. A crushed plastic shell and shattered display.

That was when it hit Davis. He had screwed up. And he was now truly on his own.

CHAPTER TWENTY-FOUR

When he arrived at the aid station, Antonelli was the first one out of the tent. She watched Davis step out of a stolen army truck. Then she looked at what the truck was carrying.

"Idiot!" she yelled.

Davis had hoped for a little more gratitude. But he didn't argue because she was right.

"What have you done? They will come straight here, you know that. Take it away right now!"

"No," he said, "we've got some time."

She stepped closer, until she was an arm's length away. Her hand came up, and Davis half expected another slap. Instead, two fingers went to his chin, and Antonelli turned his head slightly to catch the light. "Are you all right?" she asked.

"Right as rain."

Her tone softened considerably as she shifted into doctor mode. "You need a cold compress."

"I'd rather have a beer."

The doctor ignored that. Davis saw a question rise to her lips, then dissipate like a receding wave on a beach. She was wondering about the soldiers.

"They're a little worse off," he assured her, "but they'll be fine."

It was pure conjecture. Davis had no idea what damage he'd done. Whatever it was, he figured they deserved it. But the soldiers would be talking by now, at least the ones who were coherent. Eventually, they'd extricate themselves from their predicament, at the very latest when the next shift came on duty. Davis was sure he'd put some fear into Scarface, which might buy a little time. But it wouldn't stop the inevitable. Sometime tonight Davis' raid would become public knowledge, and everyone would start looking for a big American. Questions would be asked at the aid agencies, and it wouldn't take long to firm up a connection to the ICAO investigator from Washington. From that point, Davis would be a fugitive, which wasn't going to do his investigation any good. He really had screwed up.

Acting on impulse had gotten him into trouble before, but this time he'd done it behind enemy lines. By midday tomorrow he was going to have a lot of new adversaries. Davis didn't know how many because he didn't know how many men were in the Sudanese Army. It had to be a lot.

"I think we're safe until morning," he said. "I'll make sure the truck is gone before then."

She led him to the tent and made him sit in a plastic chair that looked a lot like the one he'd just used to fend off a knife attack. Antonelli produced some gauze and antiseptic.

"Sit still," she ordered.

She began dabbing over his right eye. The antiseptic stung. He watched her work, felt her practiced hands smooth over what would soon be the newest scar in his portfolio. He could see thoughts turning in her head.

She said, "My replacements have arrived—three new doctors. As I mentioned before, I am traveling to the coast tomorrow." She gestured to the truck Davis had brought. "We should unload a few things for this station, things we are in desperate need of, and the rest we can transfer to the vehicle I am taking to the coast."

Davis said nothing.

"As soon as this stolen truck has been unloaded, you must take it away. Somewhere far from here."

"Okay."

Antonelli finished with his eyebrow. She stood back and they looked at one another squarely. He at her bruised face and she, in turn, at his.

"What you did, I cannot condone," she said. "However, I think your intentions were good. So thank you."

"Anytime." He gave her a half smile. "But I do have to ask a favor in return."

She raised an inquisitive eyebrow, inviting him to continue.

"I may be persona non grata around here tomorrow. I'd like to come with you to the coast."

Davis wasn't being completely honest. With a few phone calls and some diplomatic arm twisting, there was a chance he could get out of the hole he'd dug for himself. But he had another reason for going to the Red Sea.

Antonelli nodded thoughtfully, and said, "Yes, you've been helpful—in your very unique way. I suppose it is the least we can do in return."

Davis smiled again, all the way this time.

It took thirty minutes to unload the stolen truck. Ten minutes after that he was at the wheel again, this time rumbling back to Khartoum International. Davis was getting tired, but he had one more chore for the night.

Schmitt's parking place was empty, and Davis pulled the big army diesel into his spot, not stopping until the front bumper had struck the CHIEF PILOT sign and bent it to a forty-five-degree angle. Like an artist putting his signature on a painting.

In another ten minutes, Antonelli would arrive in one of the aid agency vehicles to collect him. But Davis needed the ten. He walked quickly to the hangar and found the forklift. The crowbar was still underneath the seat. He took it and walked back to FBN Aviation's front door, holding the bar hard against his leg with his right hand. The front desk was manned twenty-four-seven, but at this hour there was no more than a skeleton crew. Two men eyed him as he came through the door, the same two Davis had met when he'd first arrived, one small guy and the other a tall English speaker. He ignored them both, and they seemed to ignore him. He turned the corner and disappeared down the hall like he was heading for his quarters. Just out of sight from the front desk, Davis stopped at Bob Schmitt's office door.

Ever since arriving, he had wanted a look at Bob Schmitt's files. In truth, he'd like a whole day in that cabinet, and in a proper investigation he would have had it. But this wasn't a proper investigation, so instead of filing a subpoena or an official request for records, Davis was relegated to doing things the old-fashioned way—breaking and entering.

The crowbar was still at his side, but he didn't need it yet. Truth was, he doubted it would even work here given the door's heavy steel frame. The red light on the security panel was glowing steady. He raised a leg and gave the door a tap with the toe of his boot. Still red. He kicked again, a little harder this time, and was rewarded with a green light and a mechanical *click*. Davis smiled and nudged the door open. Before leaving Schmitt's office that afternoon, he had adjusted the interior motion detector, tilting it down and inward so that the sensor was pointed at the door itself. All it took was a firm kick to rattle things, and the electric eye sensed enough motion to command the unlock. Simple enough.

Davis snapped on a light switch, shut the door quietly, and went to the cabinet with the crowbar ready. He slid it through the exterior locking bar, just below the combination padlock, and was about to heave when he paused. This way would work, but it would make a lot of noise. He wondered if there might be an alternate method. Bob Schmitt was an idiot, but he was also a pilot, and Davis knew how pilots viewed things like information security. He started looking. The edge of the file cabinet, the nearby wall trim, the underside of the wooden picture frame around the Sudanese president. Nothing. On top of the cabinet was a pile of office supplies—copier paper and file folders and staples. He found it on the underside of a stack of Post-it notes, scribbled in pencil. 30–12–28. Davis shook his head.

He spun the tumblers, gave a solid pull, and the lock snapped open. Davis disengaged the bar as quietly as he could, set the crowbar aside, and opened the bottom drawer. He saw personnel files, just like the ones Schmitt had already given him. He saw gaps between the manila sleeves that implied a few were missing. As they were arranged alphabetically, it was easy enough to figure out which ones: Boudreau, Johnson, and Schmitt. The three Americans.

Davis moved to the middle drawer, rifled through maintenance requirements and flight plans. He found records for each aircraft in FBN's fleet, but noted two missing. Schmitt had given him the file for N2012L, so that was in his room. But there was nothing at all on X85BG. Scanning the records of the remaining aircraft, Davis was struck by a certain symmetry. FBN's airplanes had been purchased from tiny operators all over the world, yet they had one thing in common—U.S. registration. Every single one. He moved to the top drawer and found Schmitt's personal gear. A headset, some charts with notes, a pilot's flight logbook.

Davis picked up the logbook. Pilots were required to track their flight time. There were currencies to keep up, things like night landings and instrument approaches. And if you ever switched jobs, you needed a written record of your fight experience. Davis went to the back of Schmitt's logbook and found the most recent entry. He'd flown ten days ago, Qatar and back. Davis flipped though a few pages until he found the day of the accident, maybe hoping for an entry to tell him that Bob Schmitt had been flying N2012L on the night of September 20th. There was nothing. Schmitt hadn't flown the entire week of the crash. At least that's what it said in his logbook.

Davis was putting everything back where he'd found it when he heard a noise from the hallway. He took one last look in the top drawer and spotted a cell phone on the bottom. One that looked a lot like the one he'd been issued. The one he'd annihilated. He thought, *They really do hand them out like candy.* Davis pulled it out and hit the power button. Nothing happened. A dead battery perhaps. Or it might be broken. Then again, Schmitt could have confiscated the handset from someone else and disabled it. A lot of possibilities.

Davis put the phone back where he'd found it, and once again pondered the chances of Bob Schmitt being a CIA source. It was no minor coincidence to find a CIA-issued phone in the man's three-drawer file, but there were any number of scenarios that might have put it there. Davis wasn't ready to trust Schmitt. Not yet.

"What are you doing here?"

Davis wheeled around and saw part of the skeleton crew from the front desk, the taller set of bones.

Davis said, "I'm investigating."

"You should not be in here!" the man said.

Wanting to keep him off balance, Davis said, "Never despair of God's mercy." It was a quote from the Koran, the only one he knew.

"You are not Muslim."

"Me? No, I'm a pugilist agnostic."

The guy stared at him blankly.

Davis explained, "I believe in hitting people—I just don't know who." He took a step toward the man.

Bones looked over his shoulder for help, but didn't find any. He said, "Abu is calling the security forces!"

"I've already met the security forces," Davis replied. "They're not coming." He kept advancing.

The skeleton took one step back, followed by another. And then he was gone.

Seconds later, so was Davis.

CHAPTER TWENTY-FIVE

The arriving helicopter was late, but Rafiq Khoury was in no position to complain.

It was half past eight in the morning, and he was standing on the tarmac next to Hassan, trying to stand straight as the settling chopper's downwash raked across them. The sound was penetrating, a thumping pulse that carried right through Khoury's body, rattling his bones and his brain. The aircraft was a twin to the one General Ali had brought last time, a heavy Russian gunship bristling with antenna and armament. Khoury was sure there were other helicopters in Sudan—he had seen government ministers riding in civilian models that were far sleeker and quieter—but he supposed the general preferred this type for that very reason. It rattled people.

The machine crouched onto the concrete, and a crewman wearing a helmet beckoned them with a wave. For once, Hassan did not let Khoury lead. He strode ahead and climbed aboard, leaving the imam to follow. Khoury struggled to get a leg up into the cabin and, after three failed attempts, felt himself being pulled up by the elbows and directed none too delicately to a webbed seat. The crewman buckled Khoury's lap belt, slid the access door closed, and the symphony of racket began—churning gears and vibrating rotors.

Khoury held fast to the frame of his seat as the big machine began to levitate. Hassan had taken the seat across, shoulder to shoulder with General Ali. The minister of defense was decked out in his finest regalia. Together the two men made an imposing pair. Ali was not as tall as Hassan, yet his thick chest and heavy gut would sum to a balance on any scale. The general's pockmarked face held a twinge of amusement as Hassan whispered into his ear. Or maybe he wasn't whispering—the ambient noise was deafening.

"Is everything ready?" Ali barked across the divide.

"Yes," Khoury said. "Jibril is still working, but he says all will be ready."

"And the rest?"

"I have formally dismissed all employees except the Americans."

"What about Achmed?" the general asked.

"I received his call this morning. He expects to return tomorrow, or perhaps the next day. Flights out of the Congo do not always run as scheduled."

"Let us hope he returns in time. We will need him come Tuesday. What about the hangar?"

"Everything is being prepared for Monday's transformation. I particularly liked your idea about the flag."

Khoury saw it again, crinkles of cruel amusement at the margins of the general's expression. He was impressed, in a way, that the man could still find humor given the stakes. Come Tuesday's upheaval, there would certainly be moments of indecision and panic, a degree of unpredictability that could put them all at risk. The general had the benefit of foresight, but his light mood spoke a confidence that Khoury did not wholly share. He looked out the small window and saw the hangar in the distance. The general had picked them up on the opposite side of the airport—as had long been the case, he kept his distance from FBN Aviation, lest anyone make an association.

General Ali said, "There was an unattractive incident last night involving some of my men at a checkpoint outside the airfield."

"I heard nothing of it," Khoury replied.

Hassan leaned in again to whisper. The general nodded and said, "It may involve your American investigator."

"Davis?" Khoury asked.

"Yes. I want your help in dealing with him."

Khoury had seen the general "deal" with people before. It was not a pretty sight. "What can I do?" Khoury asked.

"Since he lives in your compound," Ali said sarcastically, "perhaps you could *find* him. He has committed crimes."

"Will you arrest him? Would that be wise? It could draw attention to our work, and since he is here as the official representative of—"

"He has committed crimes!" Ali interrupted, leaning his massive bulk forward. "My soldiers have begun to look for him. When we return today you will do your part." He raised a blunt finger. "We cannot afford to have him interfering at this critical moment. Find him and give him to me!"

Khoury held steady. He knew the general relied on intimidation for his livelihood. It was his stock in trade. Yet Khoury was a master of opportunism. He said, "But Davis *is* an American. If your men should take him into custody, what would they do? Throw him in prison? I suggest we put him to far better use."

The general calmed as he considered this. "Yes, perhaps you are right. But first we must find him. When we return from our tour today, that is your priority."

"Rest easy, General. A man like him in our country? He has nowhere to hide."

Davis woke with his shoulder slumped against the passenger door of the truck cab. Antonelli had offered to drive the first shift, knowing he'd had a long night, and she was there next to him, concentrating on the road, dark eyes sharp with two hands hugging the steering wheel in a wide bus driver's grip. The highway was better than most, so Davis reckoned they had been making good time. Yet the miles covered had done nothing to change the scenery outside. Still parched vegetation, brittle and sun-yellowed, clinging to life on loose rocks and sand. Still God's xeriscape.

The cab of the truck was cramped for such a large vehicle, and even with the seat all the way back Davis' knees were wedged against the glove compartment. It was also hot. If there was an air conditioner, it wasn't keeping up. Davis wondered briefly if this was where FBN's mechanics had gotten the big compressor for their own truck. If so, then the behemoth was spinning a unit from a Ford F-150 under its massive hood. It certainly felt like it.

Davis looked over his shoulder and saw a young man riding in the open bed, the kid he'd last seen in a cot in the clinic. He was crammed into a shady spot amid the cargo, leaning on a wooden crate. His arm was in a sling and his face was heavily bandaged. Otherwise, he'd been cleaned up and looked much improved. Eighteen-year-old bodies had a way of healing fast. Antonelli looked better too, the only marks from her assault being a few scrapes on one hand and a bruised cheek. She looked over and caught his gaze.

"Good morning," she said.

Davis shifted higher in his seat. "Morning."

"Did you sleep well?"

"I always sleep well." Davis noted the sun brooding high overhead. "What time is it?"

"Ten o'clock, perhaps ten thirty."

Under present circumstances, he figured that was close enough. He said, "I left my watch in my room. Actually, I left everything in my room."

"When we arrive at al-Asmat, we can stop at the shopping mall and put you in some new clothes."

Davis looked over and saw a slight grin. He gave one back.

Antonelli shifted her eyes to the road and steered around a tumbleweed that was rolling into their path. Davis took that moment of distraction to check her ring finger. He didn't see a wedding band, although there was a faint tan line where one might have been. Which made for a lot of possibilities. It could be that she wasn't married. Or maybe she was, but didn't want to flash bling in such an impoverished country. Davis *could* just ask. He didn't.

He said, "How far to the coast?"

"Our drive will take most of the day. We should arrive early this evening."

Antonelli started to wrestle with a road map, turning it back and forth with her free hand. After a few tries she handed it to Davis.

"You can be our navigator. I think there is a turn soon, but I can't find it."

"A paper map? Don't see these much anymore." He took it and saw the problem right away. Davis began straightening the factory folds, and once he had it fully open, put the origin at the bottom and their destination on top, then made the creases he wanted.

"There's an art to this," he said. "Spend a few years in the cockpit of a small jet, and you learn how to tame a chart. You have to fold so that only the part you want shows—the rest is superfluous." He finished and showed her a nice neat rectangle that covered their entire route. "See? Jammer's map origami. I'm a master."

She looked mildly impressed. "Are you an equally good investigator?"

"Not really. I'm more of a nuisance than a detective. But I get results."

"How is your work progressing on this crash? Do you have a solution yet?"

"Somebody suggested one to me when I got here. But everything I've turned up so far has proved that theory wrong. I actually found the airplane that was supposed to have crashed sitting on the tarmac over at the airport."

She gave him an incredulous look. "You cannot be serious."

Davis nodded. "And then I found the crew." He left it at that, not wanting to expand on the specifics of that revelation.

"So you are saying there was no crash?"

"I don't know, I'm still working on it. I thought I might ask around when we get to al-Asmat. If something did go down it was close to there, about twenty miles north."

"You'll need my help. I speak Arabic and few in the village speak English."

Antonelli began telling him about al-Asmat. As she did, she drove like all Italians—one hand steering, the other talking. The village sounded like a simple place, and right now that appealed to Davis. He needed a little time to slow down and think things through.

"About what you did last evening," she said. "I want to thank you again. It was very noble."

"Actually, it was very stupid. But I've done dumber things. Practically made a career of it."

"Yes, I imagine you have."

He gave her the grin that deserved, then asked, "How many times have you come to Sudan?"

"This is my third tour."

She said this like it was some kind of combat duty. From what he'd seen, it nearly was.

She added, "I would like to come back again next year and—"

Antonelli's thought was cut short, and Davis followed her eyes. A vehicle was coming in the opposite direction. At least Davis thought it was a vehicle—at the moment it was no more than a cloud of dust. He watched closely to see what materialized out of the brown mist, and it wasn't good. A small military convoy, three vehicles. Or to be exact, three EQ-2050s, China's knock-off clone of the U.S. Humvee. In his previous life, Davis had been required to memorize the silhouettes and capabilities of ground combat vehicles, both the good and bad guy versions. Air-to-ground pilots had to know things like that before they started bombing and strafing.

"Will they stop us?" he asked.

"Not without reason." Antonelli banged on the rear window and pointed ahead. The young man in the cargo bed nodded, acknowledging the warning.

She said, "We have our aid agency markings displayed prominently."

"Those soldiers back at the airport didn't seem to care."

She didn't have an answer for that. He saw her hands go tight on the steering wheel. The little convoy closed in, then passed and kept going. No hesitation at all. The cloud of dust behind them began to recede. Davis watched until it disappeared completely.

Antonelli heaved a sigh of relief. "They seemed in a hurry," she said. "Do you think—"

"No," he said quickly. "What I did last night was nothing in a place like this. They'll send out the police to ask a few questions, maybe add a squad of soldiers at the checkpoint. But nobody's going to bother with a country-wide manhunt."

The cab went quiet and Davis looked ahead, watching for anything else coming their way. All he saw was heat shimmering on an empty road, mirage-like waves that disassembled the horizon.

"You want me to drive for a while?" he asked.

She smiled appreciatively. "Yes, perhaps soon."

The smile captured Davis. He studied her features and decided that she could never be anything but Italian. Straight nose and olive skin. Roman eyes, dark and lively. There was a regalness about her.

"Contessa," he said.

"I beg your pardon?"

"You look like a contessa."

"Have you ever seen one before?"

"Not that I know of. But if I did, she'd look like you. I'm sure of it."

She nodded. "I suppose that is a compliment."

"I suppose. I'm starting to like you more and more, Contessa, in spite of the fact that the first time we met you took a swing at me."

Another smile, this one starting slowly at one corner of her mouth, then spreading until lines came creased at the corners of her eyes. Antonelli's olive gaze came alight as she said, "And I am starting to dislike you less and less."

Rafiq Khoury had never been to Egypt, so as the helicopter made its final approach he was glued to the window. The landscape looked no different from Sudan, flat and brown and arid. The only landscape he had ever known. He could see the city of Giza in the distance, low earthen buildings arranged in no particular scheme. Khoury heard lively chatter from the two pilots, and shifted his gaze forward. In the front windscreen, framed by their shoulders, he saw a view that took his breath away.

It was a vision of legends, of pharaohs and ancient civilizations. The impression of size was heightened by the motion of the helicopter—the pyramid of Giza seemed to rise as their aircraft descended, the massive tomb reaching up to almost touch the blue sky. It was the same impression people had likely been having for thousands of years, but for Rafiq Khoury the effect was doubly inspiring. This was not only an ancient treasure to behold. This was their objective. After six months of hard work, Khoury had arrived at the site where his metamorphosis would be finalized—from wretched prisoner to member of the ruling elite.

The helicopter touched down, and Khoury saw a contingent of Egyptian soldiers outside turn their heads aside to avoid the wave of dust. They were not enlisted men, but rather officers in dress uniform. There was even a red carpet laid out across the sand. As this was an official government visit, the Egyptians had dispensed with any kind of customs inspection. Khoury imagined he could get used to such conveniences. No, he *would* get used to them.

A crewman opened the side door of the helicopter. Being nearest the opening, Khoury started to move, but was immediately pulled back and driven into his seat by what felt like giant hook. The long arm of Hassan.

General Ali pushed by him and whispered harshly, "Say nothing!"

Their first half hour was spent enduring a tour of the pyramids, no doubt the same trivia that impaled millions of tourists every year. Khoury thought General Ali looked impatient. But then, he always did. Khoury and Hassan kept to the rear, and if the Egyptian colonel leading the way had any reservations about General Ali's unusual entourage—a lone civilian bodyguard and an imam—he made no mention of it. Sudan was, after all, a fundamentalist Muslim state. Khoury toyed with that thought—a cleric with full diplomatic standing. The established imams of Sudan, those who had earned their religious reputations the old-fashioned way, might not approve. But Khoury would answer to none of them. He decided to bring it up with General Ali in the near future. *Imam of State*. Khoury rather liked the sound of it.

After what seemed an eternity, the colonel led them outside to the stage where the ceremony would take place. Finally, he began to address security matters.

"The crowd will be small," he said, "and very thoroughly screened. No fewer than six hundred soldiers and police will be committed to the immediate area."

General Ali said, "That puts a great many weapons within reach of the stage."

The colonel bristled at this naked reference to the assassination of Anwar Sadat, when a group of rogue soldiers in a parade had opened fire. "We have learned our lesson," their guide said acidly. "Those with critical access have been carefully screened. The rest are here for intimidation, and will have no ammunition." The colonel quickly launched into a detailed description of security measures, things like transportation to and from the event, and coordination among the various state security details. It was the same briefing he had likely given yesterday to generals from Jordan and Algeria.

When he seemed done, General Ali asked, "How long will our president be exposed?"

The colonel handed over a timetable. "The heads of state are to arrive at the preparatory area behind the stage no later than nine forty-five that morning. They will be in place on stage at precisely ten, and the ceremony will be complete by ten thirty-five."

Khoury thought, *A thirty-five minute window. More than enough.*

"What about other contingencies?" General Ali asked.

"Such as?"

"Such as air defenses."

The colonel grinned smugly. "If you refer to an Israeli air strike, I doubt the Zionists would be so bold. Even so, our Air Force will have twelve fighters airborne. All of our air defense radar and missile systems will be active."

Every one of them looking north, toward Israel, Khoury thought but didn't say.

General Ali nodded approvingly. He asked a few more questions, and everyone turned almost jovial as they headed back to the helicopter. The colonel saw them off, and as the Sudanese chopper began its ascent, the Egyptian saluted smartly. General Ali snapped a hand to his visor in return.

Khoury remained in character. He issued his most pious wave. As he did, he regarded the scene, an odd mix of the ancient and contemporary that seemed delicate, almost precarious. On this morning, all was serene. In three days' time, however, the mood would be different.

Very different indeed.

CHAPTER TWENTY-SIX

Nearing al-Asmat, they left the main road. The path that led to the village was narrow and rutted, winding carelessly across the region known as the Red Sea Hills. If there were any hills, Davis didn't see them. Perhaps some mild bumps on the far horizon, but otherwise just a gradual flat plain that sloped down to the sea. The vegetation had almost completely disappeared, giving way to rutted soil that was crusty and cratered. If there was a road to the moon, this was what it would look like.

Davis was driving now, Antonelli navigating. The kid was still in back, using his good arm to hold steady against the pitching truck. They could have squeezed him in the cab, and Davis had offered when they'd stopped to switch drivers, but the kid insisted on staying where he was. Davis figured it for some kind of self-deprivation thing, a Bedouin gene that insisted he suffer the desert in the same manner as his ancestors.

The village came into view, but there was no marquees with WEL-COME TO AL-ASMAT on one side and THANK YOU FOR VISITING on the other. Probably because they didn't have visitors. The place was nothing more than a few dozen buildings, squares and rectangles that looked as if they were growing out of the hardpan earth. Most were clearly homes, smooth-sided mud-brick dwellings cooked to impervious perfection, the sweat of artisan masons baked in for centuries.

Antonelli guided through a series of turns while Davis manhandled the moody truck, grinding through gears and fighting the heavy steering wheel. The road disappeared completely, and they began to crunch over a path of dirt and stone. At the edge of the village was a small souk where a dozen men and women were engaged in buying and selling. It was a market that had probably been here since the pharaohs. Merchants and smugglers and pirates, arriving by camel and sailing dhow.

She pointed to one of the village's biggest structures, and said, "Turn right, stop there."

Davis did both.

The big machine settled and seemed to groan with relief when he set the parking brake and killed the engine. When Davis opened the door and clambered down, the Red Sea was thirty steps in front of him. But there was no trade wind or refreshing ocean breeze. The heat was still suffocating, perhaps heavier now, and the smell of fish hung on the viscous, saline air.

A group of people came out of the big building to greet Antonelli. The young man who'd been suffering in the truck's bed began to shout wildly. He climbed down and got the kind of hugs you only got from family. Now Davis understood. Arriving with battle scars, riding shotgun on a tall pile of goodwill—the kid must look like a conquering hero. In a way, he was.

Antonelli took a few hearty embraces as well. She had indeed been here before. After all the happiness ran its course, she walked over to Davis.

"I explained that you've come to help. I'll introduce you later."

"Okay."

No time was wasted. A group of men and boys began to pull boxes from the truck. Davis jumped in and lent a hand, because it was the kind of job that didn't need a common language. Twenty minutes later, everything was on the ground and the sorting began.

Antonelli came over, and said, "They will take care of the rest. To show the village's appreciation, a meal is being prepared for us."

"Great," he said. "This being a fugitive has given me a heck of an appetite."

He followed Antonelli into a courtyard. There was a perimeter wall draped in fishing nets, and big conch shells were lined up on the rim getting bleached by the sun. At the base of the wall was a tall stack of wooden traps—crab or lobster, he guessed—and rows of filleted fish had been hung out to dry on a rack near the house.

An old woman with deeply wrinkled skin was sweeping the steps at the home's entrance. She exchanged a greeting with Antonelli and stepped aside to let them pass. Davis gave her a polite nod, and she responded with the kind of wry, knowing smile that only seventy-year-old women can get away with. There was no door, only a pulled back curtain, and the first room they entered was a kitchen. Pots and utensils were hanging on hooks, the kind of thing you saw back home as a decorative accent. These specimens, however, were well used, dented and worn. Davis could see heat coming from an oven built into the wall, and next to it a stolid matron, gray hair and an outdoor face, was standing at a wooden counter doing something to a fish. They passed right through the house and ended up in another courtyard, this one looking out over the sea. There were two potted palm trees and a canvas tarp for shade. A table for two was being set by a young woman. When she saw them coming she held out an arm elegantly. She could have been the maître d' at the Savoy.

Antonelli hesitated, and it took Davis a moment to shift gears. He'd spent the last four days cracking heads and looking for charred metal, so the shift in deportment put him off balance. Finally catching the hint, he swept past Antonelli and pulled a chair back for her. She slid in.

Davis took the opposing seat, and said, "Does this mean we get the rest of the night off?"

"I think we have earned it."

The maître d' became a waitress and asked something of Antonelli, who nodded vigorously. The woman moved at a languid pace. She'd never have kept a job at a diner in the States, never have made it serving milkshakes on roller skates. But here, in what was probably the closest thing to a restaurant in al-Asmat, she was perfect.

"I hope you asked for something to drink," he said. "I'm pretty thirsty."

"The desert has its way."

"Is there a menu?" he asked.

"No, there is only the chef's special, but I have never been disappointed."

"So how long are you planning to stay here?" he asked.

"I leave for Port Sudan in three days. Until then, my work is here. There are people who have been waiting months for primary-care issues."

"And I raise a stink when I have to wait thirty minutes for an office visit."

Antonelli smiled. "Yes, we do take these things for granted."

Davis surveyed the beach. What he saw wasn't a powder-white strand from a tourist brochure, but rather tan desert that disappeared in a scalloped profile at the water's edge. Gentle waves collapsed on themselves submissively a few feet from shore. Davis knew a little about the Red Sea. It was a narrow body of water, so there was no reach for the wind to build and carry swells. Today there was no wind to begin with. He also knew that the Red Sea was unusually saline, narrow openings at either end, and hot desert air sucking out moisture like an invisible sponge. He was surprised there was any water at all.

"And you?" she asked. "Will you come to Port Sudan with me?"

"No. I still have an investigation to complete."

"In al-Asmat?"

"Maybe. If an airplane did go down, it was close to here." He pointed on a diagonal across the coastline. "Twenty miles that way."

"You can find this airplane in the sea?"

He shrugged. "I don't know. I can try. Actually, you might be able to help with that."

"How?"

"You speak Arabic. I'd like you to ask around, see if anything strange has washed ashore or been picked up at sea. When an airplane goes down in the water, something always floats."

"All right, I will ask."

The maître'd-slash-waitress came back with a bottle of wine, a corkscrew, and two mismatched glasses on an old, corroded steel tray. She set it down, and Antonelli went to work on the cork.

"Alcohol?" he remarked. "Isn't this a fundamentalist Muslim country?"

"I'm Italian," she said.

Davis could have thought for a hundred years and not come up with a better reply.

Antonelli made quick work of the cork and poured two generous servings. She said, "To the people of Sudan. May they be happy and well." She raised her glass.

"To the people of Sudan," he repeated.

They both took the required sip, and when her glass came down Davis found himself looking at her lips. They were broad and full, with a tendency to stay just slightly apart. Like an invitation.

"So, Contessa, I really don't know much about you. Is there a count?"

"If there was, you would be calling me Countess."

He grinned, said nothing.

"But yes, there is. Only, not for much longer. He left me."

Davis thought, *What an idiot.* He said, "I'm sorry," because that was the polite thing to say. Even if he wasn't.

"He is a brilliant surgeon, cardio-thoracic," she said. "Handsome, wealthy, charismatic. Line up a hundred men and ask any woman which they would marry, my husband would always be the first pick."

Davis waited for the punch line. Waited for the he-left-me-for-that-bitch howitzer round. It never came.

"He is perfect in his own eyes as well. He . . ." her words drifted off.

Davis let the silence build.

"The divorce has been coming for years," she said. "We both saw it. I have found my calling here in Sudan, although I still live and work in Milan for a portion of each year. We have taken different roads in our lives."

"No second thoughts?" he asked.

"No." One word, but delivered with unwavering decisiveness.

"Children?"

"No," she said. "But someday. I am hopeful."

"I highly recommend it."

"It is the best one can do for the world," she asserted, "to raise a person who will be good and kind."

He nodded.

"So, Mr. Davis—"

He held up an admonishing finger.

"Sorry—Jammer." She said it just like he knew she would. *Zh* for the *J*. Accent on the second syllable. *Zhammér*. He liked the way it sounded. "Enough about me," she continued, "I would like to hear about you."

After a pause, he said, "My wife died. It's been almost three years."

Her turn to say it. "I'm so sorry."

"Diane and I were happy. Very happy. I had just retired from the Air Force and taken a job with the NTSB as an accident investigator. Things were going great. We had a terrific daughter, and our future was playing out nicely. Diane was killed in an automobile accident."

"How awful. And your daughter?"

"She struggles with it. So do I. But time helps with things like that. Jen is in Norway right now, staying with friends and spending a semester in school. That's the only reason I can be here now."

"You would be a good father, I can see it."

"I don't feel like I am."

"Why do you say that?"

"Right now, for example. I haven't talked to her in over a week. My phone was my only link, and it's out of commission."

Antonelli reached into her purse, pulled out a heavy satellite phone, and slid it across the table. "The agency tells me I should not use it for personal calls. I ignore them."

"Thanks."

He picked it up and dialed Jen's number. Six rings later he got her recording.

It's me. You know the deal.

He waited for the tone. "Call me at this number or I'm putting you in a convent." He gave Antonelli's number, then hung up.

Across the table, the doctor had her knuckles to her mouth as she stifled a snicker.

The meal that came was fish—grouper, if Davis wasn't mistaken—served with rice and some kind of local vegetable. It was damned good, one of the best meals he'd had in months.

Antonelli seemed to enjoy it as well, though at times she fell distracted. He'd noticed it before, on the long drive from Khartoum. Briefly, he thought she might be pining over her soon-to-be-ex-husband. But Davis discarded that idea. He was beginning to understand her, and suspected he knew what was really preoccupying her thoughts. Treatment plans, shipment dates, patients who needed specialists. Antonelli was the kind of doctor who took her work home. Davis recognized it because he was the same way.

To one side of the patio, the low sun was playing the hills in the distance. On the other side, the sea fell to a deep shade of purple, its choppy texture driven by a gathering breeze.

"Tell me, Jammer, how do you find an airplane that has crashed into the sea?"

Davis again looked toward the water, this time eyeing the shoreline where a small fleet of fishing boats was beached above the high-tide line.

"Actually, I need your help with that. I need to hire a guide."

"A guide?"

"A fisherman, somebody who knows the local waters. And he has to have a boat."

She looked at him curiously. Almost mischievously. Her mind had to be working out wild scenarios, some probably pretty amusing. *If she only knew*, he thought.

"Let me go make an inquiry," she said. Antonelli got up and headed into the house.

By the time they finished dinner, the sun had set. They walked out to a beach that was pockmarked with footprints, the thin divide where al-Asmat met the sea. Somewhere behind them a generator was humming, providing power for pole-mounted bulbs that gushed blotches of yellow light over the waterfront.

Davis and Antonelli found their man pulling his boat onto the beach for the night. He looked like a fisherman, a North African version of Hemingway's old man. He might have been fifty years old, might have been a hundred. His skin was wrinkled leather, somewhere between black and brown, cured by a lifetime of saltwater and sun. The close-cropped gray hair was thin, and his black eyes were set deep behind clouded sclera, as if they had their very own measure of protection against the elements. His hands were scarred like any fisherman's, having been pierced by hooks and fish spines, calloused from casting hand lines, hauling anchor ropes, pulling oars.

When Davis and Antonelli walked up, the man stopped his shoving and stared at them. There wasn't any anticipation or annoyance. Maybe curiosity. Two westerners walking onto his spit of beach, clearly with something on their minds. That couldn't happen often in al-Asmat. Probably hadn't happened to this guy in all his years. Fifty or a hundred. Davis considered helping him pull his boat a few feet higher onto the beach, but decided against it. A guy who spent his life alone on the sea might take that the wrong way.

Antonelli looked at Davis and said, "What do you want me to ask him?"

"Just tell him I'd like to hire him."

"He'll think you want to go fishing."

"Tell him I need to find something in the water."

Antonelli said it in Arabic. The old man listened, replied with one word.

"He wants to know what you're looking for."

"Okay, tell him."

Antonelli did, and the old man looked at him quizzically, probably trying to wrap his mind around the idea of using a boat to find a sunken airplane.

Davis said, "I want to hire him and his boat for a day. Ask him how much."

She did, and got two words from the old man this time. It was probably the longest conversation he'd had in a month.

Antonelli relayed his answer. "How much do you have?"

Davis took out his wallet and turned it upside down over the weathered wooden seat in the boat. A small pile of twenties and some other odd denominations fell out. Two hundred bucks, maybe a little more.

The old man nodded, then spoke again. He was chewing something now, and Davis recognized it as khat, the herb that was wildly popular in this part of the world as a mild stimulant.

"He wants to know how you will find this airplane in the ocean," Antonelli relayed.

Davis took out the scribbled coordinates he'd taken from Larry Green and showed them to the old man.

The old man shook his head. Spoke again.

"He says the ocean is very big, very deep. How will you *find* it?"

It was a valid question. Davis had done marine investigations before. He was practically an expert. To find submerged wreckage you wanted magnetometers and side scan sonar. You used ships that had navigation computers coupled to autopilots so that search patterns got corrected for wind and drift. Everything tight and precise. Davis had none of that. He told Antonelli his plan.

She told the old man.

He, in turn, looked quizzically at Davis. A smile creased his mahogany face and his clouded eyes sparkled. Sometimes you didn't need to know a person's language to understand exactly what was on their mind. Certain expressions were universal.

This I gotta see. That's what the old man was thinking.

Which, Davis decided, meant that his answer was yes.

It was fully dark when Antonelli and Davis made their way to the house where he'd be staying. He looked up and saw a matte-black sky that was impossibly full of stars, what you saw when you got away from the places where most people lived. There was no moon, and Davis realized he should have known this already—the precise phase, whether it was waxing or waning. He should have worked that cycle in reverse to discover what had existed on the night of the accident. An investigator had to have all possible information, and that was a freebie. Right there in the *Farmer's Almanac*. But Davis hadn't, because he'd been distracted by other things. Right now he was distracted by the very attractive woman who was leading him into a sandstone building.

She stopped at the front entrance to address him. "This is the home of one of the village elders, but he is away right now. He keeps a room for guests in back. Don't expect much, it's rather small."

"I'm sure it'll be fine."

Davis followed her inside. It really was small, just enough space for a bed and a nightstand. Right now the bed was only a naked mattress, but at the foot was a stack of sheets and a blanket—a blanket for God's sake—resting on top of a pillow.

"You can make the bed?" she queried.

"As long as you promise not to check my square corners."

She laughed. "There is indeed something I am beginning to like about you, Jammer."

"My rapier wit?"

She shook her head. "More, I think, your directness. I feel as if I always know what you are thinking."

"No. You don't."

Antonelli's smile turned coy and she went to the door. "Perhaps for the better. I'll be staying in the home to the right. It's a good thing we stopped drinking when we did because I must wake early to open the clinic."

Davis was feeling the wine, but not so sure they should have stopped. "I'm afraid I won't be much help in your clinic tomorrow."

"I understand. Pay the old man a good wage, and the money will make its way around town. Everyone will approve."

"That's a good way to look at it. Oh, and I was wondering—any idea where a guy could get a pair of shorts around here?"

"Shorts?"

"I may get wet tomorrow, and all I have is what's on my back."

Antonelli stood there thinking about shorts. He stood there thinking about her. She was positively stunning. Stunning in a pair of loose khaki work pants and a stained shirt, her long dark hair tied back in a big knot.

She said, "It might be difficult to find something in your size, but I'll see what I can do."

"Thanks."

She turned to go, and called over her shoulder, "Good luck tomorrow, Jammer."

"Thanks." He hesitated, then said, "Hey, Contessa."

She stopped and turned.

"Are you free for dinner tomorrow?"

She made him wait. Pretended to think about it. "Perhaps."

And then she was gone.

CHAPTER TWENTY-SEVEN

It was a chamber of commerce morning, or would have been if al-Asmat had a chamber of commerce. He found breakfast—a chunk of bread, some dates, and a small pot of coffee—on a tray near the door. There was also a pair of old shorts, folded once, and a tattered old T-shirt, XXL. On top of it all was a note written in a loopy cursive:

Same restaurant, same time. See you there. Contessa.

Davis held up the shorts. They were full of holes. Moths, bullets. No way to tell. They looked like a tight fit, but for what he had in mind that might be a good thing. He went to work on breakfast. The bread was stale, the dates fresh. He ate it all. The coffee was magnificent, not because it was any kind of fancy brew, but because he hadn't expected any at all.

When he stepped outside the sun was already up. Seven o'clock, maybe seven thirty. He doubted precision timekeeping was a priority here. The air was still and dry, which seemed at odds with being adjacent to the sea. The temperature differential between the two should have manufactured some kind of air movement. There should have been alternating onshore and offshore breezes, cycling with day and night. There was nothing.

Davis looked for a path that led to the water, and quickly discovered that all paths led to the water. He supposed that was how it worked in a fishing village. He found the old man at his boat, coiling a line, and when he saw Davis coming he smiled a smile that put two rows of yellow, broken teeth on display.

Davis stopped right in front of him, and said, "Good morning."

The old man nodded blankly.

It struck Davis right then how hard this was going to be. He didn't speak a word of Arabic. His skipper probably knew "fish" and "dollar." Maybe, "Down with America" or, "I am not a pirate." That was the best he could hope for. So they'd have to do everything by pantomime. Pointing and nodding and waving off mistakes.

The old man finished coiling his rope. It was at least a hundred feet long, and he held up one end to show Davis the modification he'd been working on. The old guy had clearly put some thought into their mission, and Davis recognized it as just what he needed. He nodded approvingly, and thought, *Okay, maybe this little expedition will work out after all.*

The boat was beached amid an outcropping of rock that was etched with tide pools. Around the freeform ponds, smooth shelves of stone were covered by gray lichens and green algae, and barnacle-like shells clung for their lives as an easy morning surf sputtered over everything again and again. Davis looked over the boat for the first time in the light of day. It was no more than twenty feet long, but the short waterline was compensated for with thick, tall gunnels. At the back, screwed onto the blunt transom, was a Yamaha outboard so small it seemed comical. Davis eyed the gas tanks. There were two, both pretty good size. Davis pointed to the gas supply and stretched out his arms to suggest measurement, adding an inquisitive face. *Do we have a lot?*

The old man pointed to the sun, then arced his arm all the way across the sky until it landed on the western horizon. *That will last all day.*

Okay, Davis thought, so far so good. He saw a chart on the seat, an old nautical print that covered the local waters, everything within fifty miles of the village. That was probably the old man's limit, as far as he would take the little boat, which was fine with Davis because the area he wanted to search was well inside. The chart had two dozen *X*s scribbled randomly across the reefs, which made it look like a pirate's treasure map. More likely his hot fishing holes. Or maybe his father's— the chart was dated in one corner, 1954. *Is anything in this country new?* Davis wondered. The depths on the chart were listed in fathoms, and

Davis decided that at least those measurements couldn't have changed much in the last sixty years.

The old man watched Davis use a finger to roughly sketch the area they'd need to search. It was near something called Shark Reef. Davis sighed. The depth went from two fathoms—twelve feet—to over a hundred, the outer reef giving way to a blue-water abyss. That being the case, they were going to need some luck to find anything. If the wreckage had gone over the precipice, it would never see the light of day again.

Davis reached for the mask and snorkel. He'd seen it last night, tucked under the wooden bench. He put the mask to his face, and it seemed to fit. The snorkel was like any other—not much could go wrong there.

The old man was clearly done with the preliminaries, because he went to the bow and started pushing the boat out to sea. An official crew member now, Davis went alongside, got a good grip, and things went faster. The boat looked smaller once it was in the water. It began moving on waves that barely registered to the eye. The old man held out a hand, inviting him to climb aboard.

Davis stepped off of Africa and onto the boat. The old man gave one last push seaward, and flipped himself over the rail with a lot more grace than Davis had managed. There was no Coast Guard safety briefing about life jackets or fire extinguishers or emergency whistles. The skipper just went to the motor and squeezed a bulb in the fuel line. He grabbed a pull cord at the top of the little Yamaha and gave a good tug. Nothing happened.

Davis didn't say a word. Wouldn't have even if he could speak the skipper's language. After five unproductive pulls, the old man pulled off the cowling and started fidgeting with a wire. Davis was not instilled with confidence. He looked at the other fishing boats along the beach. There were seven, and of those, only three even had motors, the rest relying on canvas and wind. None looked more promising. The old man kept busy, but his hands were never impatient or agitated. They were careful, almost respectful. Davis realized that this motorized contraption, made in a factory ten thousand miles away, was to the old man what a camel had been to his grandfather—a temperamental thing that had to be coaxed into the right behavior. A vital part of his livelihood. With the cowling off, he gave another pull and the motor coughed. Two tries later it began to run. The old man dropped the cowling back into place and secured it, then pointed the boat north.

The seas were gentle, lapping at the bow in a soft rhythm. Davis watched the old man look up at the sky, then back at the village. He was probably taking bearings from landmarks, Davis reckoned, using a process of navigation that had been handed down by his father and grandfather. He half expected the skipper to pull out a sextant or a compass.

Davis reached down and offered up the chart, stuck his finger on Shark Reef. "Map?" he suggested.

The old man wagged a finger at him. "Gamun," he said confidently.

"Gamun?" Davis repeated, wondering if he was about to be guided to sea by the whims of some mythical nautical god.

The skipper reached into his pocket and pulled out a handheld GPS receiver. Made by Garmin. He smiled broadly. "Gamun."

The old man gave the throttle a turn, and the little boat pushed quicker through the sea.

They reached the search area two hours later. The old man pointed to Gamun, and then down into the water.

Davis could still see the coastline to the southwest, a strip of brown to split the variant blues of water and sky. In the distance a big freighter was plowing west toward the Suez Canal. It seemed motionless, a great rust-red slab, the only indication of headway a crease of white spray at one end. Davis pulled off his T-shirt. The sun was hammering down, already searing into his back and neck. He hadn't brought any sunscreen, hadn't thought to ask for any in the village. He was sure the old man had never heard the term SPF in his life.

"Listen," he said to get the old man's attention. "We need a search pattern." Davis made chopping motions on the bench seat at even intervals, then traced an interlacing pattern with his index finger.

The old man said it again. "Gamun." He showed Davis the receiver, showed him a base waypoint, and then hit a button labeled: OFFSET.

Davis raised his palms. "Okay, okay."

He should have known better. You couldn't live your life on the sea and not, at some point, drop something valuable overboard. A good lobster pot, a fishing pole, a valuable anchor. Sooner or later something went over and you had to get it back. So the old man would know all about marking a point and running a search a pattern around it. Essential stuff, with or without Mr. Gamun. The old man took the long rope and secured one end to the transom, then showed the other end to Davis. He had fashioned a grip out of what looked like a broom handle. Now it looked like a rope for water skiing. Only Davis didn't have any skis.

The seas were still light and the tiny boat rocked gently. Back on the beach it had almost seemed like a reprieve; a day on the water where he wouldn't have to face jungle ambushes or break up well-armed poker games. But now this little cruise seemed less appealing. Davis was about to get dragged through the sea for hours on end. He was going to have waves slapping him in the face, saltwater pouring down his snorkel, the sun beating hard on his back. Altogether, it put a serious damper on his yo-ho-ho.

Davis turned back to business. He touched the outboard's throttle, then gave a big thumbs-up. "Up means faster." He made a big zooming noise and pointed to the engine. "Thumbs-down, slower."

The old man nodded like he got it.

Davis considered more signals, but thought, *Screw it. It's time to get wet.* The old man heaved the rope overboard and put the idling motor into gear. Davis sat on the gunnel, and the boat tilted to starboard. He back-rolled into gin-clear water, swam to the rope and let it feed through his hand until the handle came to him. Davis grabbed on and waited for the slack to play out. When it did, he raised one hand out of the water and gave a thumbs-up.

With a jerk on the handle, they started moving.

Fadi Jibril had finally succeeded.

He'd spent two hours checking and double-checking the main

flight control channels, measuring deflections and response times. Everything worked flawlessly. There were still constraints, of course. The mother ship on the other side of the partition would have to remain within range of the receiver—they had learned that the hard way on the test flight. *But that is why we perform test flights,* Jibril thought.

He had not left the hangar for two days. The pressure to succeed, catalyzed by his concern regarding the ultimate target, had distracted and confused Jibril. He'd hit a low point yesterday, a frustrating afternoon of self-doubt and marginal progress. Then Jibril had gone to pray. He had opened his heart and mind, and in doing so Allah had rescued him once again, brought him back with a renewed sense of faith. And as Fadi Jibril trusted Allah, he would trust the imam. Khoury's words still echoed in his mind. *You will be to Sudan what A. Q. Khan was to Pakistan. The father of a nation's technical might.* The imam had become his foundation once again, and Jibril threw himself into his work with renewed vigor. Now, with the systems engineering complete, all that remained was a very different type of work.

He had undertaken his research and planning some months ago, and the components Khoury had procured for the undertaking were all here. It was now only a matter of putting everything together. Not difficult work, but certainly delicate, even dangerous. Which was why he had left it as the final task.

Jibril had never realized the level of science involved in constructing bombs. At first, he had been awestruck, marveling at the twisted innovation of so many brilliant engineers. It seemed at odds, somehow, for a scientist to spend years learning how to build and create, only to then apply that knowledge in the design of devices that destroyed. At base level, bombs were simple enough—a high-explosive mass, some compounds more potent than others, the destructive yield of which was largely a function of weight. There were certain variances, primarily matters of shaping and directing the destructive force, multipliers for effectiveness based on the nature of an assumed target—hardened armor or soft flesh. Still, a primary explosive charge involved little more than brute force, not much of a challenge from a technical standpoint. It was the fusing that Jibril found truly fascinating.

A projectile could be designed to detonate before it had even struck a target, as was the case with aircraft missiles. An engineer somewhere had thought to create a radar fuse to trigger the warhead milliseconds before physical intercept. The result, an expanding ring of shrapnel traveling at Mach. From an engineering standpoint, elegant lethality. Then there were bunker buster bombs, essentially high-explosive telephone poles that were dropped from great height and speed to multiply the kinetic result. Here, detonation was delayed, milliseconds added after the initial strike to allow the explosive package to penetrate earth and concrete. Impact sensors and timers. The arcane science of annihilation.

In comparison, Jibril's task was not so difficult. He was happy with a simple contact fuse, little more than a plunger at the forward edge of his projectile to register impact. As a backup, he included an accelerometer. Any sudden, extreme deceleration would bring detonation of the main package. Either fuse could work independently, and Jibril elected to add no delay as he was attacking a soft target, no bothersome walls or armor to penetrate. Deliver the unit to the right place at the right time, and obliteration, as brought by six hundred pounds of U.S.-manufactured Tritonal high explosive, was a fait accompli.

Jibril worked the contact fuse into place at the front of the aircraft, securing it in the machine-drilled hole he had completed earlier. The wiring was redundant, two sets, either independently capable of initiating the main charge. He would not make the final connections until the hour before launch. A stray current here would do more than fry a circuit board—it would level the hangar. When his work was done, Jibril studied everything with a critical eye. He saw no concerns. All was ready.

If he were an engineer in the West, now would be the time for celebration, perhaps a bottle of champagne cracked across the bow of his creation with his team. But there could be no libations with the team assembled here. Jibril sat alone on his work stool and again thought about his "soft target," the prime minister of Israel. He wondered how the imam could be so sure of his targeting information. How could he know the man would be unprotected, out in the open? How would they receive the last minute update? The aircraft's VHF radio? Doubts niggled again. Jibril had double-checked, and every news article he saw confirmed that the Israeli prime minister was indeed scheduled to be out of the country. But then, who believed anything the Zionist government put out? Such reports could well be a cloud of disinformation. And the rest? Imam Khoury must have some very good spies, he reasoned.

Jibril heard a noise, and turned to see Muhammed. At the top of a tall ladder, he was monkeying sideways along the scaffold-like framework of the hangar. He kept moving across the wall until he reached the large photograph of the Sudanese president. With both hands, Muhammed began working the picture free of its mounts. Jibril wanted to shout up and ask what on earth he was doing, but the urge was overridden by his baseline dislike of the man. He watched Muhammed toss the picture to the floor where it crashed onto the cement, the frame splintering into a dozen pieces. Even more incredible was what went in its place. Muhammed drove a series of tacks into a wooden support plank. He affixed one edge, then kicked left and right with a filthy boot to unfurl the rest. Fadi Jibril could only stare in disbelief.

Displayed in all its glory was a large American flag.

Jammer Davis had been in the Red Sea before, on a scuba diving jaunt after the first Gulf War. It looked a lot like he remembered, one of the most vibrant coral ecosystems on earth. Individually, the specimens of corals, fish, and invertebrates found here were unique. Collectively they were awe inspiring. At least they would have been had Davis been of the mind to notice. But he wasn't here to tour the seascape. He was looking for a downed aircraft, either the wrecked hulk of a DC-3 or a state-of-the-art drone. Which, he didn't even know.

Davis had a reasonable amount of faith in the coordinates provided by Darlene Graham and the United States Navy. He had a reasonable amount of faith in the old man and Mr. Gamun a hundred feet in front of him. But none of that matched his faith in Mother Nature's unpredictability. He'd seen a lot of things happen to airplanes that hit the water. If the vector is straight down, the hull will hit hard and typically break into a thousand pieces, virtually all of which sink instantly. With a low-angle impact, the fuselage might stay in one piece and get carried for miles by currents before hitting the bottom. Or, being a pressure vessel to begin with, an airplane might stay afloat and drift for hours, even days. USAir 1549 had proved that in the Hudson River.

Once, Davis had watched an entire navy search two years for the wreckage of a three-hundred-ton wide-body airliner. They'd come up with nothing. Right now, Davis didn't have a navy to work with. He didn't have locator beacons from black boxes or state-of-the-art sonar equipment. What he had was a rough starting point, a hundred feet of rope, and an old man with a twenty foot canoe to pull him through the sea like some kind of massive trolling lure.

But there were factors in his favor. His biggest break involved the depth of the water. The average ocean depth is over twelve thousand feet, but Davis' Mark-1 eyeball told him he was in no more than fifty feet of water. And he had visibility on his side. In the Baltic or Gulf of Mexico, you'd be lucky to see your hand if you held it at arm's length. But here, in the crystalline Red Sea, Davis could see the bottom a hundred feet in any direction.

The towline cut hard into his hands, and Davis was seized with the unhappy realization that this might take time. All day or all week. They could go faster to cover more sea floor, but his arms would only give out that much sooner. Fifty feet below, the visible light washed out so that only greens and blues remained, which meant Davis had to concentrate on shape. Man-made things tended to stand out in a natural environment—straight lines, perfect circles, angular geometry. He could be looking for an entire aircraft, or he could be looking for something smaller, jagged metal and smashed hardware as a minimum. Davis wasn't sure what type of aircraft he was looking for, but a DC-3 or a drone were his best bets, and both were low-speed designs. Even under the most extreme circumstances, neither would have struck the ocean at a pulverizing speed. So Davis was pretty confident he was looking for something at least the size of a small car.

But all he saw through the old mask was an endless expanse of coral shelves and outcroppings, white sand in the canyons between. The waves that had been tolerable when he was in the boat now acted with more fortitude. They slapped his face, alternately drawing the towline slack and then snapping it taut. Davis gave a thumbs-down. *Slower.* He felt the tension ease. Every ten minutes or so, he saw the marine world under him begin a slow rotation as the old man turned to a reciprocal heading. Back and forth. He kept count for the first ten passes. Then he stopped, not wanting to overanalyze or second-guess the skipper's seamanship. Davis stopped calculating and just looked.

He saw nothing.

CHAPTER TWENTY-EIGHT

At noon he took a break, spent thirty minutes in the boat drinking fresh water and massaging his aching arms. His hands were blistered, so the old man wrapped a fish-scented rag around the handle, securing it with string as only a seaman could.

Davis got back in the water.

Two hours later he spotted something, but it turned out to be an old sunken boat, thirty feet of metal and wood that had probably hit bottom back in World War Two. What remained of the hull was encrusted in sea life, a sarcophagus of soft coral and gorgonians that muted its shape. Even so, Davis had spotted the symmetrical outline. Spotted it by shape alone, just as he'd hoped.

Hours later—he had no idea how many—Davis needed another break. He gave the old man the cut signal and the little outboard went silent. As he swam to the boat, his arms were stiff and sore, but it at least felt good to use them in a new motion. Davis clung to the side of the boat like a huge limpet. There was no boarding ladder, but the old man had fashioned a rope with knots, and he hung it over the side. Davis waited to synchronize with the swells, then heaved himself up, happy to take the old man's helping arm. He collapsed on the seat, and stripped the mask and snorkel from his head.

Davis sat with his elbow on his knees, exhausted and sore. The old man handed him a bottle of water. He imagined what the old guy must be thinking. *Looking for airplanes in the ocean.* The old salt would have been well within his rights to be laughing his ass off right now. But he wasn't. His expression was dead serious, his eyes sharp behind a lifetime of cataracts. It was the same look that would be there when he needed a school of mackerel to feed his family. Briefly, Davis considered trading places with him. The fisherman was probably half Davis' weight, and they'd get far better gas mileage. But that didn't make sense. Davis knew what to look for, and the old man knew how to run the boat and the GPS, how to keep a tight search pattern. No, Davis was stuck, resigned to being dragged around for the rest of the day like a two hundred and forty pound baitfish.

He got back in the water reluctantly, going over the side like a man headed to some kind of aquatic chain gang. He vowed no more breaks. Davis didn't know the time, but it had to be late afternoon. There were two hours of daylight left, maybe three. He decided he'd hang on as long as he could, until his arms and hands gave way, or until the sun set. When they began moving, he realized he was getting hungry. Below, he'd seen any number of nice hogfish and grouper, enough to make him consider the spear and sling he'd seen in the old man's boat. They could stop long enough for Davis to hunt down a nice dinner. But there was a serious downside to that idea. Being dragged behind a boat in the open ocean, Davis decided the last thing he needed was blood in the water.

Churning through the waves, he began to have doubts. Had the Navy's data been good? Was the search pattern tight enough to account for the visibility? Was the old man keeping a good track? It all weighed on him, even more than the salty ocean he was battering through.

An hour later Davis' arms were like mush, his huge shoulders cramping. An hour after that—or was it two?—he could barely focus on the sandy bottom. His fingers began to slip. The sun was getting lower, and the bottom fifty feet below had begun to fade to green-gray obscurity. He gave it ten more minutes. His body was giving out. Then he gave it ten more. And that was when he saw it.

A DC-3 that looked like it was flying across the ocean floor.

There was no mistaking the shape. The still shadow of an almost fully intact DC-3 came out of the gloom like a ghost. Davis raised his arm and waved a frantic cut signal. He felt the line go slack, then looked up at the boat and gave the old man two thumbs-up. He was trying to think of a signal that would tell him to mark the spot with Mr. Gamun, but then he saw the skipper already fiddling with the device. The old guy really knew his stuff—a few waves or some current, lose the light, and their hard-won find could be lost in seconds.

Davis took a deep breath, piked his legs up, and free-dove down. For the first time today he could have used fins. Fifty feet was a long way to free-dive, beyond him for sure with bare feet. But even if he could only get halfway there, Davis wanted a closer look. The airplane was lying on its belly, the port wing fractured at midpoint but still attached, probably held in place by control cables and fuel lines. The starboard wing was missing entirely outboard of the engine mount. The fuselage was in good shape, only a few accordion-like wrinkles just forward of the tail and a misshapen cockpit that had clearly taken the brunt of the impact. All in all, a wreck in good shape, better than a lot Davis had seen. A wreck that had to be chock-full of clues as to what had happened.

He pulled himself down, kicking and stroking until his lungs strained. He got close enough to see what he really wanted—the tail number. It was there in big black lettering, no mistake. X85BG. They really had found it.

Davis turned upward, heaved an explosion of air at the surface like a whale after sounding. He floated for a few seconds and took in the wreckage, mentally mapping the layout. He used his internal compass to determine that the airplane was pointed east. Final orientation wasn't necessarily a good indicator of heading at the time of a crash, but right now Davis would take any scrap of evidence he could get.

Bobbing in the Red Sea, he stared at the wreckage through the thick faceplate of his mask, wondering how he was going to get closer. He gave particular attention to the cockpit. Davis knew who *hadn't* been flying that night—the two Ukrainians. According to Boudreau, no other company pilots were missing. *So who the hell was down there?* he wondered. A pair of FBN's homegrown Sudanese pilots? It was just one more thing that didn't make sense. He paddled back to the boat and clung to the side. The old man looked at him eagerly, expectantly, then put his arms out like wings and pantomimed a zooming airplane.

"Yeah," Davis said with a nod. "Airplane."

The old man smiled his broken toothed smile.

The weather gods were still smiling as the boat approached the village, the evening breeze driving tranquil, rolling swells of blue. The outline of the coast was fading, little more than disjointed groups of lights that resembled an arrangement of golden gems strung on some unseen necklace. The sun had faded, but for Davis its effects lingered like a thermal hangover—his back was sunburned, and his body encrusted in salt residue from evaporated seawater.

Nearing the beach, he spotted Antonelli. She was standing there in hospital scrubs and tennis shoes, waving like you would at an arriving cruise ship. Davis gave a truncated wave in return, his shoulder and arm muscles having locked up on the return to port. The old man motored straight onto the beach and two young boys came to put round logs under the wooden hull, a poor man's roller system. Davis and the old man got out, and they all pulled the boat above the high-tide line. Antonelli gave a hand, as she was prone to do.

She said, "You look exhausted."

"Rough day at the office."

She held out a small canvas bag. Davis took it and found four water bottles inside.

"Thanks."

He passed one to the old man who took it and smiled appreciatively. Davis twisted the cap off another, sucked down half the bottle in one draw. It was cool and fresh. He squirted some on his face and wiped away accretions of sweat and seaweed and Red Sea salt. He held out the bag and offered one to Antonelli.

"No" she said. "I never drink from any bottle that doesn't have a cork."

"Right."

"Did you have any luck?" she asked.

"It took all day, but yeah—we found her."

"That's wonderful!"

"It's a start."

"What will you do next?"

Davis eyed the old man who was busy securing the engine. "I'll need to hire him again tomorrow. And ask him if anybody around here has scuba gear."

Antonelli did. The old man stared at Davis with his weathered grin, then started talking. He went back and forth with Antonelli for a full minute before she gave Davis his answer.

"There is another fisherman who has some gear. He charges a lot when the others lose nets or traps in deep water."

Davis jerked a thumb toward the old man. "I already gave him all my money."

"I told him I would cover your debts with a loan, but only if the gear can be had at a reasonable price—all, of course, at very unreasonable rate of interest to you."

"Thanks again."

"Not at all," she said. "And by the way—the medicine you retrieved for us has already saved one life today."

"Glad to hear it. So are we still on for dinner?"

"Of course," she said, coming closer.

Davis had always had a lousy sense of smell—not a bad way to go through life in his opinion—but right now it was working, registering a curiously inspiring mix of perfume and iodine.

Antonelli tugged on the ragged old T-shirt she'd found for him. Davis had put it back on for the ride to shore, but it was nearly shredded after a day at sea on a frame two sizes too large. She said, "The dress standards here are casual, however I will insist on something better."

"Half an hour?" he asked.

"Done."

She walked away, and Davis watched her go. The sway of her hips, the flow of her hair in the breeze. The old man caught him looking, and smiled like old guys did anywhere.

Davis grinned back and made two gestures. He pointed to his own eyes, and then a rounded movement with his hands toward the east. *See you in the morning.*

The old man nodded enthusiastically. Davis had the distinct feeling he was beginning to enjoy this little sideshow.

CHAPTER TWENTY-NINE

There are nine hundred thousand words in the English language. Jammer Davis couldn't think of a single one.

She was standing by the same table on the same patio where they'd dined yesterday. Only the doctor was not the same. She was wearing a pair of blue shorts and a tiny white shirt knotted above the belly. Even with flat shoes, her long legs seemed to go on forever, lithe and brown. The shorts and shirt accentuated her curves and exposed a stomach that belonged on a late-night infomercial for blasting abs. If Davis was built for rugby, Antonelli was a pole vaulter, all long limbs and sinew and muscle. Her flawless skin was dark, though not so much a tan as the native bronze of her Mediterranean heritage. Davis had never seen the doctor in anything other than work clothes and hospital scrubs, so now he knew what he'd been missing. His only concern was that her new fashion statement would raise eyebrows in the village—they *were* still in a Muslim country. But then, Antonelli knew the local sensibilities better than he did.

"Hi," she said for a second time.

He finally spit it out. "Hi."

Davis pried his eyes away from Antonelli, and they landed on a bottle of Pinot Noir on the table. It was open, and situated nicely between a pair of mismatched glasses, probably the same two they'd used yesterday.

He said, "I see you were serious about only drinking from bottles with corks."

Antonelli poured. "Wine is very serious."

They took their regular seats and toasted a successful day, his in the ocean and hers in the clinic. The wine was quite good. As far as Davis could tell.

She said, "You must tell me about what you found in the sea."

"I found what I was looking for. The wreckage is lying in about fifty feet of water. But I need a closer look."

"What will that tell you?"

"A lot, I'm hoping. Chances are this wreck will never be brought to the surface. Sudan doesn't have the resources for that kind of salvage. But I can learn a lot from a closer look. I'll see if there was any cargo. I'll check the position of switches and levers in the cockpit to verify the configuration when the airplane hit, things like landing gear and flight controls."

"And that can give you a solution?"

"It's a start. But there might be more to it."

"Such as?"

"FBN Aviation is a shady operation. Aside from delivering supplies to people like you, they deliver a lot of things that are . . . well, less helpful to the world."

"Weapons?" she suggested.

"I'm sure you've seen them. For my investigation that brings a lot of possible causes into play. This crash might not even have been an accident. At least not in the usual sense."

Antonelli pulled her glass from her lips in mid-sip. "Are you saying FBN might have sabotaged the airplane?"

Davis shrugged to say it was a possibility.

"What about the pilots? I knew one man fairly well, the one who helped at our clinic."

Davis studied her for a moment, wondering how far to go. He relented. "I probably should have leveled with you earlier about that. I told you that I found the crew, the two Ukranians."

She looked perplexed. "Yes?"

"Actually, I found their bodies in the desert a few days ago. They had been executed."

Antonelli gasped. "Executed?"

"I'm sure of it."

"But who would do such a thing?"

"My guess is FBN Aviation. Imam Khoury has his own private army. And I suspect it goes higher than that. In a place like this, Khoury would never be able to operate without support from someone in the government."

She said nothing for a long time. The same woman who had served them last night arrived with food and a smile.

When she was gone, Antonelli said, "The world can be a cruel place."

"Yes it can," he agreed. "But it can also be a good place."

She raised her glass. "To the good."

He tapped his against it. "To the good."

The meal was fish, well seasoned, accompanied by couscous. It was even better than the previous evening. Or maybe Davis had only worked up a greater hunger by getting dragged through the Red Sea all day.

Midcourse through dinner, Antonelli offered up her phone for another call to Jen. Davis had also been contemplating a call to Larry Green. The general might have new information, although more likely he'd just order Davis home again. In the end, neither idea got off the ground for the most basic of reasons—her handset was low on power and wouldn't hold a connection. Davis was disappointed, because he really wanted to talk to his daughter. He had fewer regrets about the call to D.C. After his dive tomorrow, he'd find a way to get back to Khartoum. Then he'd find a phone and check in. *What difference could a day make?* he reasoned.

Davis made Antonelli tell him about her day at the clinic, and that subject lifted the mood considerably. Or perhaps it was the wine. They pulled a second cork before finishing, and still had half a bottle left when the server took away their plates. Both agreed that a walk on the beach was in order. She grabbed the glasses. He grabbed the bottle.

On reaching the water, they turned left, and meandered toward the dim orange glow. The sun was finally gone, resting after another twelve-hour shift spent beating the earth into submission. Waves slapped gently onto shore, and above the tideline a warm offshore breeze rustled through a thin stand of palms. With the village behind them, they followed a strand of sand that curved out toward sea, then disappeared at a point miles in the distance. They strolled side by side, their steps irregular, arms swinging carelessly. It might have been the wine or it might have been the mood, but for the first time in days Davis found he wasn't thinking about crashes or drones or thieving soldiers. It felt good.

Antonelli looked skyward, and said, "It's such a clear evening. We should look for shooting stars."

"You can't. They only come when you're not looking for them."

She frowned in mock disappointment.

"But I'll watch just the same."

She said, "Tell me, Jammer, will you go back to Washington as soon as you have solved the mystery of this crash?"

"Yes."

"Are you looking forward it?"

"Washington? Not really. But home—yes. When Jen gets back, I'll be there for her. I promised her that a long time ago."

"When your wife died?"

"Yes. And I meant it. What about you? Are you looking forward to going home?"

"Milan? No, not really."

Davis didn't reply.

"Does that sound strange?" she asked.

"I guess not."

"Here I work hard, but the rest of my life is simple. In Milan it is somewhat the reverse."

"I know what you mean. E-mails and meetings."

"Divorce lawyers," she said.

Davis stopped.

Antonelli began to laugh. "There is probably not a lawyer within a hundred miles of this place."

"Probably not."

She held out her empty glass and ordered him to fill it. He pulled out the cork and did as instructed. When her glass was half full, the bottle ran dry. Davis held up the empty, and said, "Too bad we don't have something to write with. We could send a message."

"And what would this message say?"

"I don't know. I'm not much of a poet."

"Most of us aren't." Antonelli took a long draw on her wine before looking contemplatively out to sea. She said, "You know, Jammer, I have three wonderful bathing suits back in Milan."

"I'll bet you do."

"But none here." She finished her wine, wound up, and threw the empty glass out to sea. "Sad, is it not?"

"Very," he said. It truly was.

Antonelli took the empty bottle from his hand and launched herself running into the Red Sea, ending in a headlong dive. When she surfaced, she started wriggling, and seconds later threw her wet shirt at him. It hit Davis on the shoulder and stuck there. Her shorts came next, flying past his head and splattering into the sand.

Davis said nothing. He just stood there, hoping she'd see him as the strong silent type. Not the befuddled speechless type. She began twirling a pair of wet red panties on her finger. He was debating the merits of ducking when she stuffed them into the bottle and shoved the cork in place.

"We have nothing to write with, but perhaps this will make our message clear, no?"

"Crystal," he replied.

She giggled before tossing the bottle over her shoulder and out to sea.

"Come in," she said, "the water is wonderful."

"I don't have a bathing suit either," he reasoned weakly.

"*Precisamente!*"

Davis thought, *What happens in Sudan stays in Sudan.*

He stripped off his shirt, and was reaching for the button on his trousers when a voice called from down the beach.

"Doctor Antonelli!"

It was a young girl Davis had never seen. She was running and waving her arms frantically. She blurted something to Antonelli in Arabic. The doctor issued what sounded like instructions, and the girl did a quick about-face and began running back to the village.

Antonelli looked at Davis forlornly.

"Bad news?" he queried.

"Actually, good news. A young woman has gone into labor."

"Now?"

"These things do not wait." She pointed to her clothes lying in the sand. Davis retrieved them, rolled up the legs of his pants to the knee and walked out to sea to hand them over. There was more wriggling as Antonelli reapplied her top and bottom.

"But . . ." he hesitated, "are you okay to deliver a baby?"

"After a few glasses of wine, you mean? I would never do it if there was a choice. But here, and at this moment, there is not. I am the only physician they will find." Antonelli stood up, her clothes dripping with saltwater and clinging to her body in amazing ways. "Besides," she said, "such things have a way of sobering one up."

"Yeah. I'll bet they do."

They waded ashore, and Antonelli started back to the village on a brisk jog. He let her go ahead, and called out, "Is this what it's like being married to a doctor?"

"Yes," she shouted over her shoulder.

Standing ankle deep in the Red Sea, half naked, Davis looked up to the sky. He saw a shooting star streak overhead.

CHAPTER THIRTY

"Where the hell is he?" Darlene Graham shouted.

Larry Green had been summoned to the West Wing Annex for a second time, only this meeting was distinctly less enjoyable. He'd never seen the DNI rattled before, so he was sure she was getting pressure from above. For her that meant only one person.

"I don't know," Green said. "My last two calls to Davis went unanswered."

"Well let me give you an idea of what he's been up to. We got a complaint from the Sudanese embassy. Apparently there was a fight at a security checkpoint outside the airport two nights ago. A big American beat the hell out of a squad of soldiers. Two are still in the hospital. The Sudanese ambassador is not happy. He insists it was the air crash investigator we sent over."

Green said, "Jammer would never do something stupid like that." He thought, *Damn it, Jammer. Why do you always do something stupid like that?*

"He was supposed to keep a low profile," Graham continued. "How will he get anything done if they throw him in jail?"

"Darlene, Jammer doesn't see the world like we do. You have to understand how he works."

The director only stared.

"Let me tell you a story. A long time ago, he and I were scheduled to fly out to the range to drop some practice bombs. In the briefing, he told me he could hit a target without even using his heads-up display. I said bullshit, so we bet a beer. We went out and flew, and sure enough on his first pass, shack. He hits the truck. Then the second and the third. I didn't believe it, so in the debriefing afterward I looked at his gun camera film. No heads-up display data, no death dot or dive scale. No calculation of any kind. All he used was a visual sight picture and intuition. Somehow the man flew over a target at four hundred knots and dropped his bombs at precisely the right millisecond. Three bull's-eyes."

"And you're telling me that's how he's going to operate here? Intuition?"

Green spread his arms, palms up. "My point is, I don't understand how he works. All I know is that he gets results."

Her tone softened, "Okay, listen. We haven't heard from our source in two weeks. Our communications link seems to have failed."

"Could the source have been compromised?"

"It's a possibility. But it means that right now Davis is our only set of eyes in that country, and in less than two days the most important meeting in a generation is going to take place in Egypt. If there's something in that hangar, something that could throw a wrench in the works in any way, I have to know what it is. The *president* has to know."

"I understand. I'll do everything I can to get in touch with Jammer. But let me make a suggestion."

"Go."

"Even if we get in touch with Jammer, I don't know how much he can do. We should defend against the worst-case scenario."

"Which is what?" Graham queried.

"Let's assume FBN Aviation is a front for some kind of attack. We know they've acquired airplanes, telemetry equipment, and flight control hardware. It's not out of the question that they're trying to turn a DC-3 into some kind of flying bomb. Or there could be suicide pilots involved—Davis told me FBN has been training Sudanese kids from scratch. We've been worried about that kind of thing for a long time."

There was a long pause before Graham said, "What do you think the target would be?"

"In that part of the world it seems obvious enough—something in Israel. And since terrorists love symbolism, they'll probably hit on the very day that the Arab countries are meeting to discuss a wider peace. It would steal the headlines, trash the whole process."

"You're right about that."

Green realized his thinking had reverted—he was talking less as a crash investigator and more as a general. "We need to put the Israelis on alert so they can establish strict air cover. They're good at it—no sixty-year-old airplane would ever get through one of their defensive counter-air screens. Not even if FBN launches their whole fleet."

"All right," the DNI said. "I'll put that forward to the Joint Chiefs. If they agree, well pass it across."

"And we can help out," Green said. "We need a carrier nearby."

"Two already in the neighborhood."

"So there you are. With all that surveillance, there's no way anything could get into Israeli airspace without being seen. Not a chance."

"Where the hell is he?" General Ali's voice cannoned over the speakerphone.

Khoury was in his office, Hassan hovering at his side. Khoury was exhausted, having been up most of the night. A few fitful naps had done nothing to refresh his outlook. Now, at six in the morning, the general was sounding reveille.

Khoury answered, "We have not found him yet."

A stream of obscenities assailed the air. Khoury waited for the tirade to pass, then said, "But we have discovered that a truck he has been using was seen a number of times at an aid clinic outside town. It is the same clinic from which your soldiers were . . ." he paused, "acquiring supplies."

"So get over there and track him down, you fool! This is no time to have an American spy running free!"

The line went dead.

Khoury took a long, tired breath. One word clattered in his head—spy. Could it be true? Having met Davis, Khoury had trouble envisioning the American as any kind of secret agent. A soldier, perhaps. Even a killer like Hassan. Certainly nothing more. Still, the general was in a dangerous mood, the pressure clearly getting to him.

There was no choice. All it took was a nod, and the huge Nubian turned on a heel and strode purposefully outside.

As soon as he was gone, Khoury began to think more positively. If Hassan could learn where Davis was, Khoury would simply forward this information to General Ali. The army was best suited for that kind of hunt. If Davis was found, they would have one more American to parade in front of the world. And if not? Nothing changed, as far as Rafiq Khoury could see. No one could stop events now.

Hassan arrived at the Al Qudayr Aid Station in a flurry of dust and noise. He jumped out of the Land Rover and was immediately flanked by two Kalashnikov-toting young men. Hassan led to the biggest tent, where an old woman in nurse's clothing came forward to challenge him. She was rail thin but had steel in her eyes, the kind of confidence often displayed by matrons who thought they'd seen every trouble life had to present.

"What do you want here?" she said, her tone confrontational.

A sea of less confident eyes watched from around the tent.

"Are you in charge here?" Hassan asked.

"No."

Hassan reached out with his massive hands and grabbed the woman by the neck. He began to squeeze and her eyes bulged, looking like they might come out of her head. She turned red, then purple. She slapped helplessly at Hassan's massive forearms. He lifted her off the ground and looked around the tents, waiting for someone to come forward.

"Stop!" a voice shouted. A young man in doctor's scrubs crossed over from an adjacent tent. He walked with authority, but stopped a good ten paces away.

Hassan eased his grip ever so slightly. Gurgling noises leaked from the nurse's gullet, like an animal in its death throes.

"An American named Davis was here two days ago. Where is he now?"

The doctor hesitated, so Hassan cut off the gurgling. His victim began to lose all color.

"He went to the coast with one of our staff doctors."

"Where?"

"The village of al-Asmat. Now let her go, please!"

Hassan seemed to consider the request. He released the nurse's neck, shifted his hands down to her waist and raised her over his head like a human barbell. Hassan sent her flying toward the doctor who, to his credit, tried to catch the poor woman. The two tumbled to the dirt in a rolling heap of hospital attire and stethoscopes.

Hassan kicked over an empty cot and strode away.

When Davis rose the next morning, his waking thoughts were the same as when he'd faded off. Regina Antonelli. He hoped the delivery of the child had gone well. Even more, he hoped she was free again for dinner tonight. She'd been in his mind increasingly each day, but last night had reached a new plateau. It was a nice reboot for his outlook on life, a nice diversion from his troubled investigation. Now, however, the stark reality of another day's light was pouring into his window, and Davis was forced back to less pleasurable concerns.

He sat up quickly, a minor mistake as his lower back clenched into a hard cramp. His head remembered the wine as well. Davis had no idea what time it was, but a look outside made it clear he'd already overslept his agreement with the old man—*Meet me at the boat at sunrise.*

Davis washed in a stone basin and donned his loaner shorts. Having dried overnight, they were stiff enough to stand on their own, but that would change as soon as he jumped back in the sea. Outside he found a breezeless morning, the sea air seeming even heavier than yesterday. Davis plodded over the hot sand with bare feet, something that wouldn't be an option in another hour. The old man was waiting, sitting on the gunnel of his boat and whittling a gnarled piece of wood with a pocketknife. Whatever he was making, it was nothing artful. Rounded and with a handle, his project had the distinct appearance of utility, perhaps a reel for hand-line fishing. The old man wasn't the sort to waste time, something Davis appreciated.

When he looked up and saw Davis, there was no recognizable expression, no annoyance at having had to wait. The old man simply put down his work, hopped off the boat, and went to a heavy canvas bag that was sitting on the hot sand.

Davis stopped right in front of him, and for the second day in a row said, "Good morning."

The old man nodded without looking, then began extracting scuba gear from the bag. At least Davis thought it was scuba gear. There was a regulator with two accordion hoses, the kind that wrapped around both sides of your head and met in a mouthpiece. It looked like something Jacques-Yves Cousteau would have put in his garage sale fifty years ago. There was no backup octopus rig, no depth gauge or buoyancy compensator. The lone air tank, gray and corroded, didn't even have a plastic boot on the bottom to keep it upright. *Beggars can't be choosers,* Davis thought. He hooked up the regulator to the tank, opened the air valve, and heard a brief hiss as the system charged with pressure. Then he heard another hiss, this one softer. One that didn't stop. He found the leak in the right-hand air hose, just under a stencil that warned of something in Cyrillic.

The old man was looking at him.

Davis lifted a foot, and used a flat hand to imitate a swimming fin. "Any fins?"

The old man shrugged. Not a chance. There was a slight gleam of anticipation in his gaze. Davis supposed the old guy had a great time last night telling his buddies how they'd spent their day on Shark Reef. And he probably couldn't wait to see what lunacy the big American was going to come up with today.

Davis shut off the air and put his hands on his hips. When he'd asked for scuba gear this wasn't what he'd had in mind. It was probably something the Soviets had left behind back in the Cold War days. Khrushchev's Cold War days. There was no pressure gauge, so Davis didn't know much air he had. There might be enough for an hour on the bottom, or he might have five minutes. In the end there was really no choice. This was likely the only diving gear in a hundred mile radius. For sure, the only gear he was going to find today. So Davis was committed, because even one minute with the wreckage might give him his answer, might explain why X85BG had made its last touchdown fifty feet beneath the Red Sea.

"I thought you could use this."

Davis turned and saw an angel carrying a big cup of coffee.

He took it with reverence. "Bless you."

"Sleep well?" Antonelli asked.

"Always." He took a long hearty sip. "So did the village population go up by one last night?"

"Two."

"Twins? Good thing you were there."

"There are midwives. That's how it's been done for a long time. But yes, a little training always helps."

He sipped again while he looked over the scuba gear. "So how much did I pay to rent this stuff?"

"One hundred U.S."

Davis shook his head. "I guess the pirate culture is alive and well in the Horn of Africa."

The old man said something to Antonelli.

She relayed to Davis, "He says you must go soon. The air is heavy today, and rain may come in the afternoon."

"Rain? It does that here?"

"On occasion."

"Tell him I need a few things before we go. Half a dozen plastic jugs, empty, the bigger the better. A screwdriver, a hacksaw, and maybe a claw hammer."

Antonelli stared at him quizzically.

"Hand tools work just as well underwater. The jugs act as salvage buoys. If I find something I want to bring up, I can tie them on and fill them with air."

As Antonelli passed on the request, Davis picked up two fist-sized lumps of coral from the beach and dropped them into the boat. The old man didn't bat an eye as he walked off. He was probably having great mental fun picturing what Davis was going to do fifty feet underwater with saws and hammers and rocks.

"So are you free for dinner tonight?" he asked.

"Yes," she said. "Barring any new arrivals. But there is one bit of sad news."

"What's that?"

"There will be no wine. Apparently we drank all they had in the village."

"Wow. I've never single-handedly drunk a town dry before."

"You had my help."

"Right."

"Will you be long?" she asked.

"Five hours, maybe six. It depends on how much air is in this tank."

Antonelli studied the equipment. "It looks quite old."

"It belongs in a museum."

"Is it safe?"

"About as safe as the airplanes I've been flying lately."

She gave him a rueful glare.

Twenty minutes later Davis was seated backward in the boat, the old man steering by Mr. Gamun's instructions. Back on the beach, he saw Antonelli give a subdued wave. Davis returned it. He liked the doctor. Liked her a lot. In some strange corollary, he even found himself wondering if Jen would like her. But that was a question for another day. Right now Davis had to plan.

Not knowing how long he would have on the bottom of the sea, it was important that he prioritize his inspection of the wreckage, consider which parts of the airplane to study first. The cockpit was high on the list because he needed to know who'd been flying X85BG. He suspected it was a pair of Sheik Khoury's Sudanese contingent, although according to Boudreau and the others no crewmembers other than the Ukrainians had gone AWOL. Still, somebody had flown the airplane from Khartoum to its watery grave. Hopefully somebody with a wallet or a passport, something to explain who they were and what they'd been doing. Davis also had to look at the configuration of the airplane. Were the gear and flaps extended? Had the engines been shut down? He'd look for obvious signs of distress, like a damage pattern from a missile strike, or soot from a fire. Anything to tell him what tragedy had befallen the last flight of X85BG.

More importantly, anything that would tell him what the hell Rafiq Khoury was up to.

CHAPTER THIRTY-ONE

When they arrived at the crash site, the old man tossed over an anchor—actually a concrete block on a rope—and Davis dove in with only the mask. He spotted the wreckage instantly. Mr. Gamun had them right on the spot. Davis clambered back into the boat and began to don the scuba gear. The harness consisted of a collection of straps and a metal ring to hold the tank in place. Sized medium at best, the rig fit over Davis' shoulders like a dog bridle on a horse. Even with the straps fully extended, he had to leave two buckles unlatched, flapping by his hips. He decided it was secure enough to keep everything in place for one dive.

Davis grabbed the hammer and got the old man's attention. He leaned toward the transom and banged the hammer three times on the engine's lower housing. He handed over the hammer, held up three fingers, and jabbed his thumb in an upward motion. *Three bangs, I come up.*

The skipper nodded like he got it.

Davis put on his mask and stood in the gear, his legs bending in rhythm with the rocking boat. He reached down and picked up the coral he'd taken from the beach and wedged the rocks into his pockets. This would act as his weight belt, to be discarded in the event of negative buoyancy. He put the screwdriver in a back pocket, but decided to leave the hacksaw and bottles here. He'd come back later if he needed them. That was it. Davis was breaking pretty much every rule in the dive book. He didn't have fins or decompression tables or a wrist computer. His divemaster was a hundred-year-old Sudanese fisherman who didn't speak the same language. Davis didn't even have a diver's most critical safety instrument—a buddy.

He nodded toward the old man.

The old man nodded back and leaned to the port side of the boat to act as a counterweight. He was smiling again.

Davis turned to starboard. One giant step later, he splashed into the crystalline blue water.

"Have you seen Davis today?" Khoury asked, already knowing the answer. His chief pilot was on the other end of the phone.

"No," Schmitt said, "the last time I saw him was Friday, when he got back from the Congo."

"Very well," said Khoury. "But if you should see him, tell him to contact me. I wish to speak to him."

Schmitt remained silent, not inquiring about the subject. Khoury's doubts about the man were fed once again.

"Tell me about tomorrow's flight," he continued. "Are you prepared?"

There was a long pause. "Yeah, I'll be ready. But I don't like it. It'd be nice to know what the hell is going on. First all my pilots are either deported or disappear, and now we're flying again?"

"I have told you, the flight tomorrow involves a joint military project between Sudan and Egypt. You will be delivering a specially instrumented airplane to an airfield near Cairo."

"The airfield you showed me on the map?" Schmitt asked.

"Yes. After arriving, transportation has been arranged to take you to Cairo. All your exit papers are in order."

"And the rest of my money?"

"Did you not receive the first installment?"

"I called the bank. It's there."

"Good. And once you have completed your contract, the rest of your severance will follow."

"Three days ago you told me we'd be hiring soon. Now FBN is shutting down?"

"Enough!" Khoury barked. "I do not answer to you. We have been more than generous. If you would rather, I can send Hassan right now. He has matchless talents when it comes to escorting malcontents to the door."

"All right," Schmitt said. "I'll be there bright and early. What am I going to do for a copilot?"

"Achmed has returned, praise be to Allah."

"Achmed?" Another long silence, then, "Yeah, what a blessing."

Khoury hung up and sighed deeply. He wished he did not have to rely on Schmitt, but there was simply no other way. None of his more loyal pilots were up to the task. Achmed would at least take the copilot's seat to monitor Schmitt and make sure he did nothing destructive.

A knock from the inner hangar door startled Khoury. Muhammad had gone home for the day, so it could only be one person.

"Come, Fadi."

The engineer entered. Khoury thought he looked tired and haggard, even more so than usual. He felt a pang of concern.

"I have finished, sheik. All is ready."

Khoury rose and embraced the young man, a gesture of goodwill that was truly heartfelt. "One day to spare. You have done well, Fadi. Allah smiles upon us."

"Yes, sheik."

Khoury kept an arm around Jibril's shoulder and led him to a chair.

"There is something I must ask you," Jibril said, taking a seat.

"Anything."

"My part here will soon be done."

"Yes, and you have performed brilliantly."

"Afterward . . ." Jibril hesitated, "Yasmin worries where I will find work."

"Fadi, a man of you talents will never be wasted."

"But you see, my wife wishes to return to the West. I know I can find work there, yet—"

"You worry that what happens tomorrow will be tied to us," Khoury suggested. "Do not be concerned, my son. We know how unforgiving the Israelis can be, so we have gone to great lengths to ensure that this strike can never be brought back to us. The Mossad may buzz with anger, but nothing can ever be proven. That is the beauty of using American hardware, don't you see?"

"Yes, of course. I understand that."

There was more than a trace of guilt in Jibril's tone, the kind of emotion Khoury was expert at recognizing. "So what more could there be?" Khoury asked. "You will be able to find work anywhere."

Jibril shook his head. "My concern is not for my work, sheik. You see, Yasmin and I are expecting our first child soon. How will I . . . how will I raise him to be a good Muslim in America or England?"

A relieved Khoury said, "Fadi, Fadi. I am acquainted with many other imams. Indeed, you were recommended to me by the imam in Virginia, were you not?"

Jibril nodded.

"Then trust that I can put you in contact with followers of the faith wherever you go. They will guide you, make your path to a new life smooth. Allah has no limitations, Fadi. He does not exist only in certain corners of the world. He is everywhere. Even those in America can be His children."

Khoury saw his words hit home. This was what Jibril wanted to hear. He looked truly relieved, and his tiredness was gone in an instant.

"Yes, you are right. I must go tell Yasmin." He jumped up from his chair, but Khoury put a firm hand to his shoulder and eased him back down.

"You cannot go to your apartment, Fadi. Not today."

"But I have not seen Yasmin in three days."

"Fadi! You know the importance of what we are doing. For everyone's sake, it is better that you sleep here tonight. There can be no distractions whatsoever."

Jibril sighed aloud.

"Tomorrow we will celebrate a great victory. Then you can go to Yasmin, tell her of our success. The two of you will plan a great future for your child, and I promise to do everything in my power to help."

"Yes, sheik. Thank you." Jibril retreated to the work area.

When he was gone, Khoury took a deep breath. He eyed the cabinet that held his stash of whiskey, but for once ignored it. Instead he crossed the room and pulled back one slat on the window blind. Hassan's shoulder was there by the door. Khoury felt a strange coldness, and he let the slat fall.

In the beginning, General Ali's man had been a comfort. Now Khoury was less sure. Yesterday he'd seen Hassan's work. The two Americans, Johnson and Boudreau, had been rounded up and brought in. Hassan had taken charge and beaten the men severely before handing them over to General Ali's men.

Schmitt and Jibril, the other links to America, still had parts to play for another day. Four Americans, altogether—two pilots, a mechanic, and an engineer. Soon, the general's men might round up Davis as a fifth. Then all would be situated for the photographers, posthumously if necessary, amid the remnants of FBN Aviation—a hangar and the wrecked shell of an airplane. The standard of proof, as presented by the new Sudanese government, would be incontrovertible. Everything was going as planned for the big show. Indeed, that was how Khoury viewed it—as if it were a major Hollywood production.

He eyed his cabinet again, and this time succumbed. Opening the bottle, Khoury poured a generous bracer to quell his nerves. He took a liberal sip, allowing the drink to swirl in his mouth, and closed his eyes. Unfortunately, the vision that came to mind did nothing to soothe his frayed edges—Hassan looming ominously at his threshold. Khoury had always thought himself a shrewd man, one who retained command of situations. But he now feared that he had lost a degree of control. For all the potential ahead, he remained at General Ali's mercy. The man had made a great many promises. He had supported the concept of an "Imam of State," a position that, leveraged properly, would enhance Khoury's following overnight by a factor of a hundred. Alternately, Khoury had been offered the ministry of his choice. But for all the general's assurances, there was one outstanding dilemma, one quirk of fate that left Khoury hanging on a precipice. It involved his mother.

By her blood, Rafiq Khoury, director and CEO of FBN Aviation, was himself half American.

Davis decided the reef was aptly named, because as soon as the bub-
bles cleared away the first thing he saw was a shark. And not just any
shark, but a full-grown tiger with its blunt body and lateral stripes.
Cruising twenty feet below, the fish was bigger than Davis by a factor
of two. It swam with an undulating side-to-side motion, slow and ar-
rogant, as creatures at the top of the food chain tended to move.

Davis had been fascinated by sharks as a young boy, and had read
every book he could get his hands on to learn about them. He knew
that sharks possessed excellent receptors for motion, able to detect the
slightest thrash or vibration from a wounded fish. Davis wondered if
the big beast could sense his elevated heart rate and respiration right
now. If so, it wasn't making an impression. Sharks preparing to feed ex-
hibit a distinct, agitated swimming motion—hunched spine, pectoral
fins down, sharp spasms in the stroke. The huge fish lumbering by
showed none of that. He—Davis could only think of it as a he—simply looked on with disinterest at the puny six-and-a-half-foot creature
that had just fallen into its reef. The tiger glided by no more than ten
feet away, its dead starboard eye both uninterested and unafraid. Even
so, Davis watched closely as the big fish moved away, watched until it
faded to nothing in the hazy submarine horizon.

He turned his attention to the wreckage and started down. His
regulator had a minor leak, and so with each breath he sucked in a
trace of salt water. As he descended, Davis couldn't help but be mes-
merized by the reef's beauty, an endless array of color and movement.
Schools of brightly colored fish swirled over coral heads while sea fans
swayed back and forth in rhythm with the currents. The reef also had
its sounds, a constant chatter of clicks and grunts, backed at the moment by the far-off pulse of a big engine, probably a freighter miles in
the distance.

Davis approached the wreckage from behind, where the relatively
unblemished tail section loomed up with its inverted T shape. The aircraft skin was clean, only a slight dusting of algae and silt. In a year's
time, barring any salvage, the transformation would be well under way.

The ship's metal skin would become encrusted with coral polyps and sponges. Crabs would nestle in the throttle quadrant, worms would take up residence in the pitot tubes, and a dizzying array of fish would find refuge in the hull. In ten years, Neptune's claim would be complete—X85BG would be no more than substrate, an unrecognizable base for a new section of reef.

His regulator was still leaking as he neared the bottom. Without a depth gauge Davis couldn't be exact, but he reckoned that his earlier estimate of fifty feet was accurate. He stopped at the tail section for a closer look. There was no obvious damage to the elevator or rudder surfaces, no popped rivets or warping that would indicate stress failure due to an aerodynamic overload. Davis saw a sizable dent on the starboard leading edge of the horizontal stabilizer, but this was most likely impact damage. When an aircraft hit the ocean at a hundred and fifty miles an hour, things got bent. He glided forward along the hull of the airplane, and detoured to the port side to inspect the engine. The propeller tips were uniformly bent back, which meant the engine was likely running on impact. There was no damage to the exhaust manifold to indicate an infrared missile strike. No apparent fire damage. The flight controls on the trailing edge of the wing—the subject of the bogus logbook write-up—showed no overt evidence of failure. Davis floated over the spine of the airplane to the starboard side, and looked it over with equal diligence, found all the same things. No smoking gun.

He moved forward toward the cockpit, gliding above what looked like a perfectly good airplane that had just flown into the sea. It did happen. Pilots could get disoriented by visual illusions. They could get distracted. Davis had once studied a case in which a perfectly airworthy wide-body airliner had flown into a swamp because the crew had gotten preoccupied by a failed twenty-cent lightbulb. Unfortunately, things like that were difficult to prove without flight data and voice recorders. Even then there was no guarantee. If Davis was going to find the cause of this crash with one brief inspection, it would have to be a slam dunk, something that stuck out like a full moon in a night sky.

Ten feet ahead of the wing joint, the airplane's fuselage had buckled, another probable result of impact forces. At the top of the spine he saw a failure in the skin, a meter-long tear that allowed a clear look into the cargo bay. The light was sufficient to confirm that there had been no cargo, but Davis did notice a rack of electronic gear that was unlike anything he'd seen on the other FBN airplanes. He figured it might have to do with this particular airplane's past life as an avionics testbed. But even that didn't make complete sense. Normally any deadweight was stripped from airplanes, and old, unused avionics would certainly fall into that category.

A large moray eel had taken up residence in a crevice where an antenna had been ripped out, and Davis gave the creature a wide berth as he moved forward. A look at the cockpit was his best chance to nail down a cause, so the investigator in him was eager to keep moving. The human in him, however, wasn't in such a hurry. In a crash like this, relatively gentle and intact, he might well find two pilots still strapped into their seats. The sea is never kind to flesh, human or otherwise. Over the last weeks, bacteria and scavengers had likely made substantial headway, so whatever he was about to see would be gruesome.

Then, five feet from the cockpit, he heard it.

Clang, clang, clang.

The signal from the boat. Davis had arranged it with the old man as a precaution, not imagining what it could really be used for. He looked fifty feet over his head and saw the bottom side of the old wooden boat. It wasn't capsized or sinking or listing on a tsunami. Davis listened closely, but didn't hear an approaching engine from a Sudanese naval patrol boat. If there even was a Sudanese navy.

Clang, clang, clang.

Davis took a deep breath, and that highlighted his second problem. His lungs had been working harder in the last few minutes, and he realized he was pulling air from the tank, sucking in the last hundred pounds of pressure. His air supply was down to a matter of minutes—three, maybe five. He would be heading up to the boat very soon, but Davis had to get one look at the flight deck before he surfaced.

Clang, clang, clang. Quicker and more insistent. Not good. The old man wasn't the excitable type.

Davis approached the starboard side of the cockpit, which had taken the brunt of the impact. The copilot's window was ripped away, leaving a hole large enough to swim through. But he didn't have to swim through. The scene inside couldn't have been more clear. Davis stopped breathing as he tried to comprehend what he was looking at. When he finally inhaled, the old regulator stole his breath in a decidedly more literal fashion.

In one gulp, his flow of air stopped, and the Red Sea came flooding into Davis' lungs.

CHAPTER THIRTY-TWO

He was flying an F-16 at 31,000 feet, an easy cross-country leg dodging cotton ball clouds and sightseeing. It was the annual deployment to an excercise called Red Flag, at Nellis Air Force Base in Las Vegas, and Davis was enjoying the day at five hundred knots. Fat, dumb, and happy.

He was the number four airplane in a flight of four, bringing up the rear as tail-end Charlie. That being the case, nobody was watching him very closely. Not that they would have noticed anything had they been looking. The malfunction in his oxygen diluter had likely been there a long time, a tiny valve that had failed and wasn't metering enough pure aviator-grade oxygen to the pilot's mask. On your typical day, on a typical mission, not a big deal. Unnoticeable, really. But the second malfunction was another story, a fatal catalyst for the first. That was how most aircraft accidents happened. Not a single catastrophe, but a chain of small misfortunes that turn into something bigger. The pressurization leak in Davis' cockpit that day was slow and insidious. If he had looked at the cabin pressure gauge at just the right time, he'd have seen it clear as day. But nobody looks at a cabin pressure gauge. Not without a reason. So, on that day so many years ago, Jammer Davis had become hypoxic.

For a victim, hypoxia is a hard thing to recognize because your brain gets fuzzy. You might notice tingling in your fingers, or get lightheaded. But more often than not, you just fall asleep. In a single-seat fighter, five miles in the air, you snooze like a baby for the last two minutes of your life while your jet dives to the hard desert floor below. Your last landing, and not your best.

On that day so many years ago, it had all happened before anybody even knew there was a problem. Least of all Jammer Davis. But he hadn't ended up as a hole in the caliche, hadn't ended up as a statistic, because just as he was fading, just as his brain was shutting down, he'd heard a faint voice. It wasn't the volume that had gotten his attention, or even the familiarity of Larry Green's tone. What registered was the urgency.

"Jammer, go emergency oxygen! Emergency now, Corvet 4! Jammer, oxygen! Do it now, God dammit!"

A four-alarm bell in his brain.

On that beautiful summer day, a long time ago, Jammer Davis had learned about the deprivation of oxygen. He had snapped out of the deadly haze just long enough to slap the three levers on his oxygen controller to the emergency position: 100 percent O_2 under positive pressure. When he did that, the world came back. But in the next seconds there was a moment he would never forget, a brief interlude of fear, of helplessness. He was hanging in limbo, coherent enough to know he was on the edge of death, yet knowing he might not be able to do anything about it.

That's where Davis was right now. Only this time he didn't have a panel of levers to slap and start a fresh flow of air. This time it was all in reverse. Deep in the Red Sea, coherent to begin, but knowing he would fade fast. The regulator in his mouth was useless, which meant the only air available was fifty feet over his head. His lungs were already heaving, pushing the wrong way to rid themselves of the quart of sea water he'd just sucked in.

Control was everything. He kicked toward the surface, wishing to hell he had fins.

Not fast enough.

Reaching down, Davis dumped the two lumps of coral he'd been using as ballast.

Not fast enough.

Control.

The tank and harness were slowing him down, dragging through the water like a giant sea anchor. He unsnapped one buckle, then a second, and the rig sank to the bottom. Free of the drag, Davis kicked for all he was worth. He was wearing only the mask now, and he looked up to find the surface. It looked like it was a mile away. His old scuba training kicked in. *Exhale as you rise in an emergency ascent.* Easy for the instructor to say in class. Even easy to practice in a swimming pool. Not so easy to do in open ocean when you hadn't taken a breath in over a minute. When you were burning through oxygen as every muscle in your body strained for speed.

The surface was getting closer. The surface was fading to gray. He kept trying to exhale, but there was nothing left. Gray turned to black.

Then, finally, light.

Davis broke the surface, gasping and coughing up water. Sweet air filled his chest, hot and dry and wonderful. His vision came back and he fell still. Davis looked up and saw nothing but sky. Then the boat twenty yards away. He didn't start swimming right away, only stayed where he was, treading water and breathing. Just breathing. The old man was standing in the boat and gesticulating wildly. The hammer was still in his hand. Davis remembered. *Clang, clang, clang.* What had that been all about? He looked out to sea, expecting to see a freighter or a battleship bearing down. He didn't see anything.

The old man yelled something, but Davis couldn't make it out. Not that he would understand anyway. He swam closer and soon had a hand hanging over the starboard gunnel.

"Haboob!" The skipper yelled, clearly concerned.

"What?"

"Haboob!"

He started gesturing for Davis to get in the boat. When he didn't right away, the old guy pointed up at the sky and made wild motions, spinning and twirling. Like a whirling dervish. Davis wondered if a tornado was about to hit, but when looked up he saw a perfect dome of blue above, liquid and aqueous in its own right.

He tossed his mask into the boat and heaved himself aboard. That was when he saw it. To the south, a wall of brown that blocked out the horizon. Blocked out everything. It had to go up five thousand feet, maybe ten, the top edge boiling and churning like some massive oncoming wave. Davis had experienced desert storms before, north of here on the Saudi peninsula. He knew they were mostly wind, occasionally a trace of rain thrown in to torment the woeful, arid world below. He also knew that such storms could cover half a continent and last for days or even weeks.

The old man was already cranking the motor.

"Yeah," Davis said, "maybe we should head home."

Seconds later, their concrete block anchor had been hoisted aboard and they were doing exactly that.

The old man kept his eyes locked on the sky as the boat plowed through waves. There was concern in his eyes, so Davis was concerned too—men who spent their lives on the sea weren't prone to idle worry. The wind had definitely picked up, maybe twenty knots, and three-foot seas slapped the bow, casting rhythmic sheets of salt spray over everything. The mountain of roiling brown was getting closer, almost blotting out the coastline.

Davis hadn't made any gesture like he'd wanted to go back down and retrieve the scuba gear, and the old man didn't seemed concerned about the loss. By leaving it there, Davis figured he was saving the owner a terrible death by drowning. And for his own purposes, Davis had no need to go back down on Shark Reef. The wreckage had told him all he needed to know. He knew why the airplane had crashed. And he had a pretty good idea of what was now sitting in FBN Aviation's hangar. One look in the cockpit had made everything clear.

As he eyed the storm, Davis noticed the old man chewing khat again. When the skipper saw Davis looking, he held out a small plastic bag full of the dried leaves, a gesture not unlike a good ol' boy from South Carolina offering up a pinch of chewing tobacco. *What the heck?* he thought. He took a small pinch, but the old man made a *bigger* gesture with his hands. Davis took some more. He put it in his mouth and started chewing. It was slightly on the bitter side, but not bad.

Davis looked at the sky again and wished there wasn't a storm on the horizon. He was already fighting enough heavy weather. Rafiq Khoury's dubious corporation. Bob Schmitt's suspect airplanes. A squad of Sudanese soldiers. For all he knew, the whole Sudanese army. Davis needed help. But what were the chances of that? Even if he could get in touch with Larry Green, what could the general do? Send in the Marines? Special Forces? Order an air strike on FBN Aviation's hangar? Davis knew, in a general sense, what Rafiq Khoury was up to. And there wasn't much time to stop it, not given what Johnson had told him about the flight schedule. Yet the scenario Davis had was no more than a hunch, and nobody in Washington, D.C., was going to authorize an attack on foreign soil based on Jammer Davis' best guess. Certainly not in time to make a difference.

So Davis was flying solo—again. And there was only one way he could stop whatever was happening. He had to pay another visit to Rafiq Khoury's hangar.

The little boat struggled for headway. The seas were serious now, bigger waves that came spilling over the side. The old man handed Davis a bucket, something that didn't need any translation, and he started to bail. The wind was coming from onshore as the storm pushed air forward to announce its arrival. The huge wall of brown seemed to hover right over them, clouds at the leading edge rolling and curling in a wild transfer of energy.

Davis could just see the beach as the gust front rolled over the village. They were two hundred yards from shore, but his exposed skin was already getting sandblasted by wind-driven particles. Davis squinted against the dust and watched the world turn shades of khaki as clouds blocked the sun.

The old man said something. Probably, "Look," because he was pointing toward shore.

When Davis saw it, his heart skipped a beat. Soldiers.

The old man eased off the throttle, and they both watched two uniformed men walking across the beach, their heads bowed into the wind, their uniforms pressed to their bodies by blasts of molten air. One of them stopped and pointed, noticing the little boat offshore. The whole world seemed to pause as they all stared at one another. Everyone wondering what to do. Wondering what the other guys would do. One of the soldiers broke the impasse. He pulled the rifle from his shoulder and trained it on the boat.

The old man said something else. Probably, *"Shit!"*

"Yeah! Go!" Davis responded, waving toward open water.

With the wind blowing toward them, Davis easily heard the first shot over the whine of the little outboard. He had no idea where the round hit, but wasn't waiting for the next. He ducked down behind the stout hull of the boat. The old man had the same idea, his hand the only part of him exposed as he kept a grip on the motor's steering arm. It wouldn't take long to get out of range, particularly since the visibility was going down fast. A minute, maybe two, and they'd be safe. But then what? Davis wondered.

He had one big problem. If the army had found him here, they'd probably tracked him through the clinic in Khartoum. So if he was at the top of their post office wall, Antonelli's picture was likely right underneath. It wouldn't matter that she'd done nothing but get slapped around by some thugs. She would be guilty by association. And Antonelli was in the village right now. She could already be in custody, something Davis didn't want to think about. He made his decision.

Davis shuffled aft. He pointed down at the boat, then north toward Saudi Arabia. He made a shooing motion to the old man. *Take the boat out to sea.*

The old man nodded.

Then Davis made more gestures. *Slow down,* followed by, *Me into the ocean.* Not for the first time, the old guy looked at him like he was crazy. Davis stole a look toward shore, squinting against the wind-driven mist of quartz and mica. He couldn't see a thing, and so neither could the soldiers on shore. He reached for the diving mask, and as he did Davis felt a strange sensation. He was lightheaded, even a little euphoric. Perfect. He realized he was still chewing absentmindedly on the khat. Davis spit it into the sea. He put on the mask, straddled the seaward rail, and gave the skipper a little wave.

The old man waved right back. As if it was the most normal thing in the world.

Davis vaulted into the sea.

CHAPTER THIRTY-THREE

Spend a career flying jets, and you learn how to make decisions fast. In combat that was how you survived. New lieutenants learned rule number one right away when they got their asses waxed in mock dog-fights—he who hesitates dies. It was like a chunk of your brain got overdeveloped, bathed in some sort of neural steroid. Of course, fast decisions weren't always the right ones. You acted first, then lived with your choices. As time went by, your choices got better, an almost evolutionary process. Which was why you trained. A good system, all in all, but the bottom line never wavered. If things look overwhelming, never dither. Do something. Anything.

So Jammer Davis had thrown himself into the sea.

He'd done it with the fuzziness of a man drugged. *How stupid had that been?* Now he had to live with it.

It took twenty minutes to swim to shore. Davis could have covered it more quickly, but once he was close he eased his pace, allowing time for reconnaissance. The storm had arrived at strength, a meteorological buzz saw with winds whipping over the village at fifty, maybe sixty miles an hour. Davis didn't see any activity, but the visibility was marginal. He decided the soldiers had hunkered down in one of the houses to wait out the storm. They might still be looking out a window, waiting for a small fishing boat to come out of the churning sea and seek refuge. But nobody would notice a diving mask-encased head bobbing in the surf. Davis briefly wondered where the villagers would throw their allegiance. He remembered seeing a Sudanese flag on a pole in the middle of the settlement, but he hadn't seen a single photo of the president. He decided the people here would be loyal to the same things they'd always been loyal to—family, tribe, God. In that order. They'd been fishing and living and praying here for a million years. Soldiers with rifles going from house to house wouldn't be thought of as highly as their regular doctor, or even the big American who was hiring people for bizarre fishing expeditions.

The entire coastline had disappeared, everything overtaken by a massive, Sahara-sized wall of dust. The sea was in pitched battle with itself, hip-high waves slamming ashore with venom. In a maelstrom like that, the soldiers would never see Davis as long as he stayed in the water. But as long as he stayed in the water, he wasn't going to do Regina Antonelli any good. None at all.

As he crept ashore, Davis could see one jeep and one truck, both Chinese. Both parked at the edge of the village. The truck was green and bulky, with a bed for carrying troops. Together, he guessed they had brought eight, possibly ten men to al-Asmat for the search. Plenty to take one big guy into custody. Unfortunately, these troops were likely more competent that the ones he'd already met. They wouldn't be drunk or casual, because they were here on a mission. And because they already knew what Davis was capable of.

He crawled from the surf and instantly appreciated the protection it had afforded. He was still wearing tattered shorts and a short-sleeved shirt, so his arms and legs got peppered by granules of high-speed sand. He left his diving mask on, which must have looked ridiculous. Many years ago, on Davis' first deployment to the desert, the Air Force had issued him a pair of sand goggles. He'd thought that was ridiculous too—until the first sand storm.

Davis kept low and used all the available cover. A fishing boat, a stack of lobster traps. He made it to the courtyard wall of the first house, the place Antonelli had been staying. He stopped and listened, heard nothing but storm-driven sand lashing over buildings and whipping through fishing nets. He spotted two soldiers in the doorway of a house a hundred feet away. The door was lee to the wind, and they were staring outside indifferently—more to marvel at the haboob than to look for him. Davis was hoping they were all in the same place, mingling and bantering as they waited for the storm to pass.

He moved closer to the courtyard entrance of the house where he hoped to find Antonelli. He crouched behind a potted palm that was getting thrashed by the wind, and tried to see if anyone was inside. Unable to tell, Davis waited. When a particularly nasty gust stirred up a cloud of brown, he took his chance. He ran fast across the stone surface, tiny dust explosions marking each step. When he burst inside, he saw the same old woman who'd been working the kitchen counter when he'd arrived. She stared at him oddly. Davis took off the diving mask and a look of relief washed across her face. She tapped twice on what looked like the door to a pantry, and it swung open. Antonelli emerged.

She walked hurriedly to Davis and went straight into his arms.

"You've seen the soldiers?" she asked.

"Yeah. How long have they been here?"

"Not long. They were just beginning to search when the storm hit."

"All right. We need to get you out of here."

Antonelli didn't ask why, so she'd already come to the same troubling conclusion he had. By helping him, she had put herself at risk.

"Did you complete your dive?" she asked.

Davis thought, *All except the last two minutes when I almost drowned.* He said, "Yes, and I figured out who was flying that airplane when it crashed."

"Who?"

"Nobody."

She looked at him quizzically.

"At least not anybody on board. The whole flight deck had been modified—the pilot's seats were gone, part of the instrument panel ripped out. There was a big box mounted directly over the spot where the captain's control column used to be. I'm sure it was hooked into the flight controls."

"I don't understand," she said. "How can an airplane fly without pilots?"

"Happens all the time these days. This particular airplane used to be an experimental model, a flying testbed. A long time ago it was modified to be controlled by computers. I think somebody working for Rafiq Khoury modified it further. I think they put in new flight control servos, a little telemetry, and turned it into a full-scale remote controlled airplane."

"You mean it was flown by radio commands?"

"Exactly. There was another airplane out flying that night, right alongside the one that crashed. A ship to control the one they modified. They both took off from Khartoum and flew all the way to the Red Sea before something went wrong."

"But why would Rafiq Khoury do this?"

"I don't know." Davis hesitated, then added, "But that other airplane, the control ship, is probably sitting in Khoury's magic hangar right now. And I think there might be something else parked next to it—a CIA drone that crashed last winter."

"An American drone? You mean like the ones that are always in the news?"

Davis nodded. "I think Khoury is trying to get it into the air. I think this old DC-3 I found in the sea was put together as a test airframe to make sure everything worked."

"This sounds so complicated. Why would anyone go to such trouble?"

"That's the big question. It doesn't make sense, does it? If Khoury only wanted to crash an airplane into something valuable, he could do that with a suicide bomber. A cleric like him must have plenty of loyal followers who'd be willing. In fact, I've already met one of them. But whatever the end game is, it's got to be big to justify so much planning and expense. Looking back, I'll bet FBN Aviation was established from the beginning for no other reason than to fly this drone. The timing is too much of a coincidence—FBN was set up right after the CIA lost its drone. The rest of their business, shipping cargo and gunrunning to the subcontinent, that was only eyewash. This is a well funded, well thought out operation that's leading to something serious. And it's going to happen soon."

Davis heard noise outside, men laughing. They weren't close, but the mere fact that he could hear them meant the wind was howling less. The storm was losing its punch. Antonelli noticed too, and they exchanged a cautious glance.

"Do you think the government is part of it?" she asked. "These soldiers here now?"

"I don't know."

"But what can we do?" she wondered aloud.

"Right now, two things. I need to get you safe. And I have to get back to Khartoum."

"How? Our truck is not even here."

"Where is it?"

"Raheem took it to another village east of here. He won't be back until tomorrow."

"Great. Are there any other vehicles in town?"

"Only the two the soldiers brought."

Davis smiled.

He'd assumed that the squad looking for him now would be sharper than Scarface's bunch. He was wrong. The two vehicles parked at the perimeter of the village had been left unguarded.

His first job had been to get Antonelli safe. She was hunkered near a storage shed just outside the village, ready for a rendezvous that he hoped would come sooner rather than later. On returning to the village, Davis watched the soldiers long enough to establish that they were indeed together in one building near the center. He gave the circumstances some thought, the enemy's position and objectives and capabilities. Then he considered his relative standing, and a plan came together. The hornet's nest was right there in front of him. All Davis had to do was kick it at the right time.

The storm was ebbing, and a few drops of rain began to fall in the gusty aftermath. Big globules splattered to the ground and disappeared immediately into parched, dust-laden earth. Like they'd landed on a sponge. Davis had the diving mask strung on an arm now as he skirted the edge of the village—he could get by with just squinting, and didn't want to sacrifice any peripheral vision. He had to work fast, because soon the soldiers would be coming out to pick up their search.

The big truck was a three-and-a-half-ton Dong Feng, a People's Republic of China knock-off troop carrier. It looked heavy and slow. The jeep was an ancient BJ-212, the kind of thing China had been selling on the cheap to Third World countries for decades. It looked by far the more nimble of the two, and carried two jerry cans for gas, hopefully full. The jeep also had the only radio, so it was the obvious choice. Davis moved fast, angling first toward the big truck. He found what he wanted in the troop bed, a lug wrench secured to one side-wall with a wingnut. He removed it and went to work on the truck.

When he was done, Davis kept the wrench and climbed into the jeep. He hit the start button and the engine churned, but didn't start.

"Damn it!"

Davis checked the hornet's nest, just in view around a mud-brick wall. No response. He cranked the engine again, and this time it caught. He put the jeep in gear and turned south toward the desert. He paused when he had a hundred yards of separation, waiting for the swarm. Nothing happened. He revved the engine. Still nothing.

Christ these guys are stupid.

He leaned on the horn, and finally three men stumbled outside. The wind was still strong enough to flatten their uniforms against their bodies. Davis was about to wave when one man shouldered a rifle. Davis revved the engine and the jeep lunged forward—as much as a Chinese jeep could.

He was steering toward the open desert when the first bullet pinged off the frame of his windshield.

CHAPTER THIRTY-FOUR

He was high on khat, driving a Chinese jeep as fast as he could through a sandstorm in the world's largest desert. People were shooting at him. But at least he was wearing his diving mask.

How do I get into this shit?

Davis decided the khat had dulled his decision making. He went for max speed just to see what the jeep could do, and at sixty-five miles an hour had the accelerator pegged to the floorboard. Not great, but maybe good enough. The steering was exactly what you'd expect from a mass-produced Communist military vehicle—the wheel seemed to float in his hands as he careened over the semi-improved road.

Davis looked over his shoulder and saw the truck behind him. Right now, given the visibility, he figured he had to keep his adversary within half a mile—any more and they'd lose him. But he didn't want much less either, because they had the artillery. He estimated there were four, maybe five soldiers in the truck, which meant that his plan, drug-addled as it certainly was, seemed to be working. Davis had known he was going to need a good head start to get clear of al-Asmat, yet the tactical impediment had been obvious. The soldiers had brought two vehicles. There was no way to steal both without getting Antonelli involved. Taking one and disabling the other was an option, but that carried consequences. At that point, whoever was in charge would have no choice but to call for backup—a fresh vehicle or even a whole new squad. Replacements would arrive in an hour if they came by chopper, two if it was by land or sea. In that time window, Davis might get fifty miles of separation, a hundred if he was lucky. He wanted more.

Thus his plan to split the force. Right now he was leading half the soldiers deep into the desert. The other half were back in the village, out of the fight. The group back in al-Asmat might well have access to a satellite phone or a handheld radio. If not, they might confiscate one in the village. But they wouldn't send for backup—not yet. That call, Davis knew, was one no field commander would make except as a last resort. It was admitting defeat, and defeat never looked good on a performance report. As long as there was a chance they could wrap Davis up on their own, nobody in this unit would call for help. So with the guys behind him engaged in hot pursuit, the soldiers back in the village would sit patiently, wait for their buddies to return with their trophy. That was Davis' logic, anyway.

Having successfully divided the enemy, it was time to conquer.

With the chase established, Davis kept his speed up. Soon, however, he saw a problem. The truck was gaining. Worst case, he had figured the two vehicles for equals on performance. He'd been wrong. What do to about it? Davis had decades of military training under his belt. He knew how to fight with jets and fists and guns. Fighting with Chinese four-wheel-drive utility vehicles—not a clue. So he did what any rugby player would do. He mashed his big foot harder on the accelerator.

With the truck closing fast, his clever plan was looking less clever every second. Davis got a picture in his mind, the right front wheel of the truck. He had loosened all five lug nuts, thrown three away, and left the final two half a turn from falling free. The big wheel had to be close to separating, wobbling as the truck spun and crashed over the rutted road. That was his theory. But reality was arguing otherwise. The troop carrier was only a hundred yards back now. Davis took off the mask to get a better look and promptly fumbled it out the door. Storm-driven sand was still swirling, and his eyes began to sting. The driver behind him had an enclosed cab.

He never heard the sound of the second shot—only a metallic crunch as the round exploded into the UHF radio on the dashboard. Davis began to think his plan was faulty. Could one of the two re-maining lugs have bent under the uneven pressure and jammed in place? If so, the wheel might never fall off. He figured he was five miles from the village, just what he'd had in mind. But until the wheel fell off, the rest of his scenario was out the window. He glanced over his shoulder. Eighty yards.

He who hesitates dies.

Davis yanked the wheel hard left and turned off the road, immediately hit a dune at the shoulder and flew airborne. The jeep landed hard, skewed onto the driver's-side wheels, then righted itself in a sideways slide. Davis corrected, and loose stones peppered the wheel wells before everything straightened out. The off-road surface was punishing, and Davis had to slow down. The truck was bearing down, even closer now, but its driver faced the same dilemma and had to slow. Davis saw the men in the truck's bed bouncing airborne and hanging on for dear life—nobody could shoot from a platform like that and expect to hit anything. Better yet, it had to be beating the hell out of the wheel lugs.

Davis yelled over the roar of the engine, "Come on, dammit! Fall off already!"

The truck wasn't gaining anymore. Stalemate. Then the ride began to smooth as the desert settled into waves of soft sand dunes. The truck began gaining again, and another shot smacked in. Too close. Plan B was dead. Davis reverted to physics. The forces on the lug nuts had to be at their highest in a hard turn, and a left turn would pull the right wheel away from the truck. Which begged the next question—how to put the truck chasing him into a hard left turn?

Only one method came to mind.

He spun the wheel and the jeep slid through a turn, a spray of sand arcing to the outside like a skier rounding a turn. Davis got low, using the dash as a shield, and steered straight for the truck. The closure turned extreme as the speed of the two vehicles became additive. Davis kept his head down, stealing occasional glances. Two more bullets ricocheted off metal. He favored his left just slightly in the game of chicken. Fifty feet apart, Davis took one last look, then ducked down and held tight. It was up to the other driver now to lose his nerve.

He did.

In a flash, the big truck flew by on the right. Davis watched it happen over his shoulder. The truck began to slide, spraying a massive plume of sand into the air. Then it disappeared completely, lost in its own private dust storm. Davis kept his eyes padlocked on the swirl of brown, and seconds later a single wheel came bouncing out of the cloud. It rolled a hundred feet, hesitated upright for a moment, then fell on its side.

Davis eased off the accelerator and began breathing again.

He picked up Antonelli as arranged, and drove southeast along the coast road. The storm had passed, replaced by a sudden calm that was totally at odds with the maelstrom of the last hour. The haboob had left its calling card, a thick residue of dust that covered the road like brown snow.

"Did you see any more soldiers?" he asked.

"I heard shouting, but I was not close enough to the village to see what was happening."

"That's good."

"What became of the others, the ones who followed you?"

It sounded like an accusation, and he noticed her grim expression. "Look, Contessa, I'm no assassin. Their truck had an accident."

"How convenient."

"Very."

"We are safe then?" she asked.

"For the moment. They'll be confused. The guys out in the desert will spend some time trying to put their truck back together, but they don't have the right tools. I made sure of it. Eventually, they'll walk back to the village. That'll take some time too."

"And the soldiers in the village?"

"They know I'm not there," he said, "so hopefully they'll give up the search."

"But they have associated the two of us," she said. "They will look for me as well."

"Possibly. But they won't find you."

Antonelli said nothing.

"Listen, I'm sorry. Sorry to have dragged you into this mess. I have to get you away from al-Asmat. You can't stay here any more than I can."

"It's not your fault. I—"

"No," he broke in, "it *is* my fault. If I'd been thinking more clearly two nights ago you'd be back in the village working right now and not speeding around in this stupid contraption."

"True. But if you had not come here, you would never have discovered the truth about the crash. I am no expert in such things, but it is clear that Imam Khoury is planning something awful. So I am glad to be here. Glad that I could help you."

Davis didn't respond.

He knew he ought to say something deep and philosophical, but his mind-set was purely tactical.

"We have two overriding concerns. First, we have to get you safe, and the only way to do that is to go back to Khartoum and hand you over to the Italian Embassy."

She seemed to ignore that, and said, "What is the second concern?"

"Whether or not those goons back in the village have communications." He pointed to the bullet hole in the dash. "I think that was their only hard-wired radio, but they might have a satellite phone. If not, they'll try to find one in the village."

"They could find mine," she said.

He shot her a pained look.

"You pulled me away in such a hurry—I didn't have time to retrieve anything."

"I know," he admitted, "my mistake. We could use it right now, but there's no going back."

She nodded.

With a jolt, the jeep bounded up off the primitive road onto a strip of asphalt. The ride improved considerably. Antonelli eased the death grip she'd had on the dash and settled back into her seat. She fell silent and seemed to relax. Davis didn't. He drove hard and fast, pushing the rickety jeep for all it was worth. It was late afternoon, and the approach of night seemed to have accelerated under the red, dust-laden sky. It had been a tumultuous day, but the night wasn't going to be serene or restful. Khartoum was four hundred miles south, and Davis calculated that if they drove straight through they'd arrive just before sunrise. And they *would* drive straight through.

Davis was feeling it again, the same compelling impulse he'd had three nights ago. People had been shooting at him. People were hunting Antonelli. They had an excuse for coming after him, of course. He had banged up some thieves at a poker game, thieves who happened to be soldiers. But Davis suspected the real reason for putting a target on his back involved something more troubling. More substantial. He saw it now like he had seen it so many times before. He was getting close, nearing a solution, and people were getting nervous. Rafiq Khoury, or whoever controlled that hangar, had killed the two Ukrainians. That was for sure. Buried them twice, deeper the second time. Two good guys, by all accounts, executed and stuffed into the hot earth.

Somebody was going to a lot of trouble. They'd guarded a secret hangar for months. Started an entire airline from scratch. Turned an ancient airplane into a drone. Performed a test flight and crashed it.

A hell of a lot of trouble.

Jammer Davis didn't know the end game, didn't know what they were aiming at. But he did have one advantage. They didn't know he was aiming at them.

CHAPTER THIRTY-FIVE

There are reasons armies attack at four in the morning. It has to do with sleep cycles and circadian rhythms. Jammer Davis wasn't quite so calculating—that was when he arrived.

He was dog tired after the eight-hour drive. He and Antonelli had taken turns at the wheel, and Davis had used the time to plan. His first idea was to go to the terminal or the FBN building and find a phone, but if he did that they might be seen. And even if he could get through to Larry Green, any help would be a long time in coming. In the end, Davis decided his best weapon was invisibility. They hadn't run across any patrols during the night. Four hundred miles north, the authorities would be scouring the coast for a man and a woman in a Chinese jeep. Nobody would expect them here.

Davis was at the wheel now, and he turned off the airport perimeter road a mile from FBN Aviation's hangar. He guided the jeep into the brush and covered a quarter mile before a wheel got hung up in a dry gulch. They dismounted and surveyed the problem.

"We can get it out," she said. "A little digging, then you can push and I'll drive."

"No. It's not worth the time or the noise. We leave it here."

The jeep still had a quarter tank of fuel—they'd gone through both the jerry cans—and Antonelli watched Davis drop the key in his pocket.

"Never discard a possible asset," he said. "An old Marine gunny told me that once."

It dawned on Davis that a weapon might be useful. Two days ago he'd had access to a whole tree of rifles and a semiautomatic handgun. Unfortunately, at the time there had been other things on his mind—retaliating against a band of thugs and retrieving what they'd stolen. *Just one more screwup,* he thought. Davis searched the jeep, expecting to find a Beretta or a Glock. Hoping for a hand grenade or two. All he found was an old pair of field glasses under the seat. Undaunted, he picked them up and trained them on the hangar a mile away.

"I don't see much," he said.

"We'll have to get closer," she replied.

"No. This is where we split."

"But I can—"

"No," he broke in. "I should have gotten you safe already."

"I'm perfectly capable of taking care of myself."

"Yes," he agreed, "you are. And right now I need you to do just that. Walk to the passenger terminal and find a taxi, take it to the embassy."

"I don't have any money."

"The driver won't know that. Somebody at the embassy can take care of it."

Antonelli looked anxious, but in a way that had nothing to do with paying for cabs. Davis walked closer and put a hand on her cheek. "I need you safe, Contessa."

"I'm safe right now."

He shook his head. "No, everything I've done has been wrong."

Her lips parted to argue, but he put his index finger to them. "We'll talk about it some other day."

She leaned in and kissed him. He pulled her closer and held tight. As soon as their lips parted, Davis said, "You know—those twins had terrible timing."

"Yes, they did. Perhaps another time we—"

The dawn silence was suddenly broken by the whine of a turbine engine. Davis pulled away.

"I've got to go," he said, already backpedaling. "Be careful."

"You too."

Davis turned and began jogging toward the hangar. "And by the way," he called over his shoulder, "when you get a cab, make sure you take one from the stand."

Antonelli stood still until Davis disappeared. She turned toward the distant terminal, but paused after only a few strides. For a very long time she stood stockstill, poised on the balls of her feet. To anyone watching she would have looked like a climber wavering at the crest of a perilous summit. Then she tipped off the mountain.

She went after Davis.

A thin glow was just showing in the east as he closed in on the hangar. Davis slowed his approach, much as he had four days ago. The compound's floodlights were bright, their intensity washing out the breaking dawn. Davis' angle of approach was such that the main hangar doors weren't in view, but the backside of the building looked exactly as it had before. The sound of the turbine was still there. It was nothing big, and certainly not throttled to full power, but now that he was closer Davis could pinpoint the source. A jet was idling in the hangar.

He had been moving slowly out of caution—and if he was honest, weariness—but the implications of a jet engine in FBN's hangar shifted his stride to a higher gear. He began jogging, weaving though gullies and around vegetation. When he finally achieved line of sight to the front of the hangar, the first thing he saw was an antenna-encrusted DC-3. The tail number was N55US, a number that meant nothing to him. A number that wasn't even in the files in Schmitt's cabinet. From an official, regulatory point of view, the "US" at the end meant nothing. As a matter of symbolism, it gave Davis yet another mental chill.

A man Davis had never seen before, dressed in mechanic's coveralls, was closing the DC-3's side entry door. He secured the latches and gave them a slap. There were only two reasons a ground crewman buttoned up an airplane—it was either going to bed or being prepped for flight. That fifty-fifty was answered when the port propeller began to turn. The big radial coughed, spit black smoke, and chugged into a rhythm. As Davis kept moving his angles changed, and moments later he got a glimpse of what else was in the hangar. It brought him skidding to a stop on the hardpan earth.

The interior of the hangar was lit up like a museum display, and parked under the bright fluorescents was the exact thing Davis had hoped not to see. The Blackstar drone with its engine running.

Sitting motionless on the concrete, Blackstar resembled a massive ebony arrowhead, lethal and sharp. One landing gear strut didn't look quite symmetrical, and even at this distance Davis could see rough patches on Blackstar's radar-absorbent skin. Rudimentary repairs, probably no more than aluminum tape, or if they were really creative, fiberglass from a bucket, slapped and wrapped. Simple adaptations. Simple like roadside bombs made from fertilizer, triggered by garage door openers. That was how war was conducted in this part of the world. Indeed, Davis realized this was exactly what he was looking at. A machine of war about to be deployed. Blackstar had crashed and been damaged, but now it was reconstituted. Rebuilt with obsolete parts from old QF-4 drones. The CIA's wreck had been claimed, taken from Africa's junkyard, and restored.

Davis threw stealth out the window. On a dead run, he aimed for the clear area that bordered the connecting taxiway a quarter mile ahead. Through breaks in the vegetation, he studied the DC-3. The airplane was covered with antennae, a bristling array of fittings and appendages. If he were an engineer who specialized in electronic signals, he might have been able to guess the purpose of each accessory by its size and shape and location on the airframe. But Davis didn't need any of that. All he needed was situational awareness, the big picture right in front of him. Two aircraft—a drone and a control ship. Rafiq Khoury had no capability to bounce signals through satellites, as was Blackstar's original design, so he had gone old school—a line of sight radio channel, probably VHF. *Simple adaptations.*

The DC-3's starboard engine began to crank. Davis watched the ground crewman pull chocks from under the wheels, then scurry over and stand next to Blackstar. But he didn't touch those chocks. Black-star stayed where it was as the DC-3 began to move, taxiing to one side of the concrete apron.

Davis kept running, his feet pounding sand while his brain cranked logistics. How would it work? How could they get both aircraft aloft? Which would take off first? He didn't see how Blackstar could even reach the active runway—the machine would have to negotiate over a mile of connecting taxiways. A normal airplane was guided to the runway by pilots. Getting a drone into the air was different. You had to tow it to the end of the runway with a utility tug, point it in the right direction, and then light the fuse like you would a rocket, maybe a few gentle directional inputs once the airflow was sufficient over the flight controls. So a drone parked in a hangar with its engine running made no sense at all.

Yet Davis was sure of one thing—if he could get close enough to Blackstar, he could stop it. He could throw something under the lop-sided landing gear while it was moving. No, toss a wrench or a rock into the engine inlet. Something big and dense to get sucked in and act like a bomb, turbine blades chewing themselves to bits, the engine trashed in a matter of seconds. He could make that happen.

But he had to get closer.

With two hundred meters to go, he tripped over a bush and went sprawling through the scrub. Davis scrambled to his feet and kept moving, faster now, his eyes locked on the black dart at the mouth of the hangar. He saw the ground crewman pull the chocks from under Blackstar's wheels, heard the engine wind up to a higher power set-ting. Much higher.

The machine began to shriek. It jumped out of the hangar and began rolling down the long taxiway. Davis saw the flight controls flexing at the trailing edge, moving up and down as the aircraft picked up speed. Right then, he realized his mistake. Blackstar wasn't going to use the primary runway for takeoff. A mile-long stretch of rein-forced taxiway would do just as well.

Davis watched helplessly as the drone accelerated, watched it pass by on the taxiway at eighty knots, then a hundred. The nosewheel rotated slowly upward, and the craft began to fly. The landing gear retracted, including the wheel that was crooked, and the drone began a smooth climb. Soon Blackstar faded from sight, just as it was designed to do.

A black weapon disappearing into a black sky.

Rafiq Khoury's heart had nearly jumped out of his chest when the DC-3's big engines exploded to life, popping and backfiring. The noise and vibration were much greater than he'd expected, although not as worrisome as General Ali's cursed helicopter. It was peculiar, Khoury imagined, that he had never before flown in one of these craft—he *was* the de facto owner of the airline. But then, this would be a day of many firsts.

He was standing next to Jibril, who was focused intently on the computer screen at his workstation. A map display was selected, and Khoury could see Blackstar drifting slowly to the north, represented by a capital letter *C*. In a rare idle moment, Jibril had earlier explained that he'd chosen this symbol as an insult to Cal Tech, an American university that had denied him admission. An academic's sense of humor, Khoury supposed.

"We have good signal strength," Jibril announced. "All channels are active."

Khoury assumed this was good news. "What distance can we allow?" he asked.

"With our aircraft on the ground, and the drone at ten thousand feet, we should stay within twenty miles. Once we are airborne, this distance increases."

Khoury felt the big airplane begin to move under his feet. He looked to the rear of the cabin and saw his two guards situated on fold-down seats. They were his best men, fully committed, armed, and very capable. Khoury doubted they would be necessary, but he could not deny the comfort of their presence. In the other direction, he saw two familiar shoulders at the threshold of the flight deck—Schmitt in the captain's seat and Achmed to the right. The American was the weakest link in the chain, Khoury knew, but there was simply no other way. Achmed was not enough of an aviator to make the plan work—he had admitted as much—and so Schmitt was a necessary evil. But as Schmitt watched the airplane, Achmed would watch him. Khoury had promised the American a substantial payday for this last mission, along with safe passage after their landing in Egypt. But he had also offered no alternatives to the arrangement, an omission that certainly spoke volumes. The imam was an expert at sizing men up, and he was sure that his chief pilot was no more than an opportunist. Bob Schmitt would do what was best for Bob Schmitt. The other two, Boudreau and Johnson, Khoury would never have trusted on a mere bribe. They were now in the custody of General Ali's men, and in a matter of hours all would rendezvous at the abandoned airfield in northern Sudan. There, the last act would be staged, this very airplane set ablaze. A fiery finale, meticulously documented for the world.

"How fast is it going?" Khoury asked, eyeing Blackstar on the screen.

Jibril pointed to numbers at the bottom of his display. "One hundred knots."

"That seems rather slow."

"Unmanned aircraft are not designed for speed. They are meant to stay aloft for long periods of time. Anyway, our own aircraft will struggle to keep that pace. The flight to the staging point in Egypt will take a full three hours."

Khoury checked his watch. So far, all was on schedule. The engines roared to a crescendo, and as the DC-3 began to accelerate Khoury felt a surge of confidence.

Davis sprinted toward the taxiway, his lungs straining. He had miscalculated and missed his chance with Blackstar. All that was left now was the DC-3. But what could he do? Rocks and wrenches? He could throw them all day and not stop the old tank. *They don't build 'em like this anymore.* Davis imagined someone inside the airplane's cabin hunched over a workstation, watching a rudimentary instrument display. They'd be pushing and pulling a joystick like a teenager at a gaming console. Flying Blackstar. But the DC-3 had to get airborne because Blackstar was moving. If the drone got out of range and lost its controlling signals, it would cease to be a drone. It would become a ballistic projectile—exactly what had happened eight months ago when Blackstar crashed into the African desert.

He was running hard, harder than he ever had in the Rugby Union Over-30s. The taxiway was still a hundred meters in front of him. An Olympic sprinter on a good track could get there in ten seconds. An oversized prop forward stumbling through the desert in the dark? A lot more. The DC-3's massive radial engines were rumbling at full power. He guessed the airplane would use the same procedure Blackstar had—a takeoff run on the taxiway. At this hour there wouldn't be air traffic to avoid on the other runways. Chances were, the control tower wasn't even manned. So in a matter of seconds the airplane would barrel past on the strip of asphalt ahead.

Davis' chest was heaving, pulling massive gulps of air. He tripped again, but didn't go down. Breaking out of the brush, he slid to a stop on the taxiway's dirt and rock shoulder. The DC-3 was approaching fast, gaining speed. The fuselage was a shadow now, no longer washed in the bright lights of the compound. Davis saw a white glow from the cockpit, reflections from the flight instruments and perhaps a dome light. Enough to see a familiar silhouette. A thick round face topped by a mop of black Brillo.

Right then, Bob Schmitt looked out his side window and spotted Davis. His eyes bulged wide.

CHAPTER THIRTY-SIX

A lot might have gone through Davis' mind if he'd had the time. Phones in cabinets. Less than honorable discharges. Dead Ukrainians. Walt Deemer. Some of that might have made Davis believe that Schmitt could be on his side. Some of it would shut the door on the idea. But there was no time to think. Not even a second. Davis had only one option—he had to trust the man.

With Schmitt staring at him, Davis stood straight, almost as if at attention. Very deliberately, he tapped a closed fist to the side of his head and gave signals in rapid succession: one finger up, two fingers up, two fingers sideways, five fingers up. He did it again, faster, hoping Schmitt could see in the early light. Or hoping he could guess what Davis wanted. 1–2–7–5. Their old squadron VHF frequency, 127.5 MHz. He thought he saw a quick wave in reply. The airplane passed, and Schmitt glanced over his shoulder as the airplane thundered away. Davis tapped two fingers to his wrist, where a watch would be, and added a one and a closed fist for a zero. Ten minutes.

Seconds later, Schmitt and the airplane were gone in a churning rumble, rising into the waking sky.

Davis needed a radio, needed it now. The hangar seemed the most likely place to find one.

Ever since Larry Green confirmed that something had indeed crashed into the Red Sea, Davis had asked himself one question. As improbable as it seemed, could Khoury's people be trying to get Blackstar back in the air? The technicians in D.C. would have said no. They'd have said that the craft's guidance signals came by way of en-

crypted satellite commands, and as such, no one in a backwater like
Sudan could have a technical prayer of making it work. But when
Davis had seen the modified cockpit at the bottom of the sea, he'd
suspected they were very wrong. Now he knew it. And he understood
why FBN Aviation had shipped in so much old-school hardware—
telemetry interfaces, actuators, guidance modules. Somebody had
taken out the original, high-tech parts, and replaced them with relics.
Then they'd made it all work. But that left one unanswered question,
the one Antonelli had nailed. *Why?*

Davis closed in on the hangar. There was no one in sight. The man
he'd seen pulling the chocks had to be nearby. Davis stopped at the big
entry doors and saw a void in the middle of the place where the two
aircraft had been, tools and stands and work benches all around. He
then looked up and froze at the sight—a huge American flag hanging
from the rafters on the far wall. Davis stood dumbfounded, stunned by
the incredible image. The Stars and Stripes fluttering softly in a hangar
owned by a mad Sudanese cleric. He forced his feet to move, realizing there was no time to figure out what it meant. His universe was
shrinking rapidly. He *had* to find a radio.

Davis sprinted to the side of the building where a door led to what
looked like an administration area. He burst through, and once again
came to a sliding stop. The man with the mechanic's coveralls was in
the middle of an office. Only the mechanic wasn't working with a
wrench. Instead, he had a camcorder held up to one eye and was pan-
ning across the room. When he sensed Davis' presence, the camera
came down. The man backed away cautiously, his eyes locked to Davis,
and then bolted through a door on the opposite side of the room.

Davis heard him yell, "Hassan! Hassan!"

He stood still and tried to decipher yet another incredible scene.
The office was torn apart. Chairs upside down, file cabinets tipped
over with drawers agape. Loose papers carpeted the floor like some
mini-haboob had rolled through the room. But the thing that really
drew Davis' attention was resting on the hardwood surface of the desk.
Bob Schmitt's Korean-made nameplate. And behind it, nailed to the
wall, a photograph of the president of the United States. A Klaxon

rang in his head, a five-alarm bell that blotted out the world. At that moment, everything made sense. Terrible, logical sense.

Davis heard more shouts from outside. Urgent Arabic. Closing in.

His universe was down to one word. Radio. He didn't see one here, hadn't seen one in the hangar. But Davis knew where to look. Knew where to find half a dozen. Turning back the way he'd come, he started running again.

His boots hammered over concrete, strides eating up ground. With three DC-3s to choose from, Davis headed for the nearest one.

As he ran, a terrible picture brewed in his head. The American flag, Schmitt's nameplate, a ransacked office. And a man, probably the Jordanian mechanic, making a video record of it all. Taken together, it answered the "why" question. Blame. The Blackstar drone was going to strike, and when it did, the evidence would be insurmountable. Wreckage that was certifiably MADE IN USA. As an accident investigator, Davis knew how clear that would be. The rest was window dressing, visual sweetener for a media campaign. A hangar rented by a shady corporation that flew U.S. registered aircraft. Worst of all, plenty of unwitting, verifiable Americans on display—Boudreau, Johnson. Schmitt was the question mark. Davis hated the man, but he couldn't believe he'd be party to this. More likely, he was being used at the moment for his flying skills, and later would be lined up as a third American scapegoat. Two pilots and a mechanic paraded for a sensational trial. Headlines as bold as they came. With such overwhelming evidence, could Washington deny it? Who would listen? Certainly no Arab nation.

The only question remaining was the target. In this part of the world there were a lot of options. Jerusalem? Mecca? Either devastating in its own way. Davis could think of only one way to get that answer. Ask Bob Schmitt. Schmitt could tell him because he was flying toward the target right now, even if he didn't know it.

Davis reached the first DC-3 and pulled open the entry stairs. He climbed inside and rushed to the cockpit, tried to remember where the battery switch was. He found it, powered up the airplane, and tuned the primary radio to 127.5 MHz.

Davis picked up the hand microphone and switched on the overhead speaker. "Schmitthead! Are you there?"

"We are nearly eighteen miles behind," Jibril admonished. "We should be closer."

Khoury stood behind Jibril and watched the engineer manage his creation. "But you said we could control the craft at twenty miles," he argued.

"By my calculations, that is the nominal performance. But we have never tested control beyond that range. There could be nulls in either the sending or receiving antennae. Here in safe airspace, we should err on the side of caution and stay close."

Jibril's jargon meant nothing to Khoury, but his caution carried weight. "Schmitt!" he barked.

Khoury saw the American fiddling with something on the central instrument column. Schmitt peered back from the flight deck.

"We must go faster!" Khoury ordered.

Schmitt looked at his instruments. "I'm dead on time," he argued, "right where you told me to be on the route."

Khoury glared. "Do it!"

The pilot shrugged and pushed on a pair of levers. The engine noise rose to a higher pitch. Khoury then heard a less agreeable sound—an argument from the flight deck. Schmitt was pointing to a gauge, and soon Achmed came back from the copilot's seat, his perpetual scowl in place.

"What are you doing?" Khoury asked.

"The infidel says there is low oil pressure on one of the engines. He wants me to check for a leak."

Achmed went to a window on the left side of the cabin and studied the engine.

Khoury studied Schmitt.

"Well it's about damned time!" Schmitt's voice came in a hushed growl over the radio.

"Are we comm secure?" Davis asked.

"You've got about a minute. I sent my copilot back to the cabin to check on a bogus oil leak. I'm flying with your buddy, Achmed."

That name struck Davis hard. The last time he'd seem Achmed, the kid's eye had been behind the reticle of a gun sight.

Davis said, "Do you realize what's going on here?"

There was a long pause. "This is my fini-flight with FBN," Schmitt said, using the old Air Force slang for the last flight with a unit. "After this, I get a nice severance check and a good letter of recommendation."

"Is that what Khoury promised?" Davis said sarcastically. "You must realize that the airplane you're flying is the control ship for a drone."

"Yeah, so what? These idiots in this part of the world have spent the last two thousand years poking each other in the eye. I'm just going to make a few bucks out of it this time." The transmission crackled as the signal began to degrade. Schmitt was getting too far away.

"This is a lot more than some regional skirmish, Schmitt. That drone is going to strike something big."

"Like what?" Schmitt asked.

"I don't know, but you can expect them to hang it on you, Boudreau, and Johnson. Get it? Three Americans. They hoisted the Stars and Stripes in the hangar you just left, and there's a guy inside taking video of a desk with your old nameplate on it."

No reply.

"Are you still there?"

"Yeah," came a crackling reply, "I saw the flag."

"Listen, dammit! I don't expect you to sing 'God Bless America' here. I'll just appeal to your more basic instinct. They're setting you up. You're not going to get any fat bonus, you're going to get a life term in a Third World jail cell. Maybe worse."

Again silence.

Davis threw his last pitch. "I found a phone in your filing cabinet that looked a lot like one I had. Did you pass some information to the CIA a few weeks ago?"

"Could be. A guy I met on a layover in Riyadh gave me the phone, said there could be a little money in good information. I'd seen the drone once, so I made a call. After that, the handset died on me. Nothing more I could do."

Davis could argue that point. Now wasn't the time. "Who's on the airplane with you?"

"The engineer, Khoury, Achmed, and two of Khoury's thugs."

"We need to figure a way to stop this."

"What do you expect me to—" Schmitt cut off his transmission.

There was silence for a moment, then Schmitt and a voice Davis recognized as Achmed began arguing about an oil pressure gauge. The transmission was continuous, so Schmitt had jammed the radio's transmit switch on. Davis sat there and listened to the "hot microphone," eavesdropping on the flight deck of the control ship. He thought he heard Khoury's voice in the background, but the words were indistinguishable. Soon everything was indistinguishable as the transmission faded. Schmitt's airplane was too far away.

"Dammit!" Davis muttered. Without the radio link he was helpless.

Then he heard Schmitt's voice again, a briefly coherent transmission. His words were clear—not because the microphone was near his lips, but because he was shouting. "Dammit Achmed, I'm the captain, and that's that! Take the airplane while I go back and check. Heading three-five-zero, and keep the speed up!"

The transmission faded again, this time to nothing. But Schmitt had just told him a lot. They were indeed following Blackstar, controlling it. They were heading north. And most important of all was the fact that he'd keyed a hot microphone. Bob Schmitt had made up his mind. He was on Davis' side.

And he was asking for help.

Davis waited five minutes, hoping for something more. The speaker over his head was stone silent. Even if Bob Schmitt had seen the light, he was flying away at over a hundred miles an hour. Probably ten miles in the last five minutes. Davis turned to the larger problem—the attack that seemed imminent. Was the drone carrying a weapon? Or was Blackstar itself the weapon, every cavity from nose to tail packed with high explosives? The latter smacked of simplicity, so that got Davis' vote. The northerly heading would take them to Egypt, then Israel, so the target had to be in that direction. A lot of possibilities.

But what to do about it?

Davis had no way to contact Larry Green, or for that matter anybody who could help. And even if he could get through, what would he say? "There's a DC-3 and a drone heading north out of Sudan. Jammer Davis says shoot them both down." What were the chances of that? Davis knew all too well how the alphabet soup of intelligence and military organizations in Washington operated. Collectively, they were like some massive bureaucratic train, full of momentum, full of confidence that brute size would be enough to overcome any obstacle. Never mind that the bridge ahead was out. That's where Larry Green and Darlene Graham and all the rest were heading at this very moment—to the bottom of Confidence Gulch. But sitting where he was, Davis was in no position to help either. No help to Schmitt or anyone on the other side of the Atlantic.

Davis stared at the instrument panel in front of him. *He who hesitates dies.*

He started flipping switches, trying to remember the right sequence. Davis was about to start the port engine when he remembered the chocks. He bounded outside and scrambled beneath the airplane. The big wooden wedges under each main wheel were connected in pairs by a short length of heavy rope. They were as big as concrete blocks, and nearly as heavy. Davis kicked away the front chock on each side, and didn't worry about the rear. On the way back to the entry door he spotted another problem—the forklift was parked just behind the cargo door, too close to the horizontal tail for the airplane to move.

"It's always something," he muttered in frustration.

Davis started the forklift, and after some trial and error with the levers and foot pedals, soon had it backed up and clear. He set the parking brake, jumped off, and had one hand to the entry stairs when he heard tires squeal and saw the glare of headlights wash over the fuselage. Davis turned to see Rafiq Khoury's Land Rover settle in front of his left wing. Hassan the giant stepped out.

It's always something.

CHAPTER THIRTY-SEVEN

There is a reason boxing matches are classified by weight. Owing to the laws of physics, a larger man has a significant advantage. Davis had been in plenty of fights in his time—some with referees and official sanction, others decidedly less formal—yet aside from a few child-hood scraps with older boys, he had held the size card probably 98 percent of the time. This was the other 2 percent.

Hassan seemed in no hurry as he strolled closer. Chances were, he was a 100 percenter. Fortunately, size wasn't the entire issue. Training and experience also came into play. Unfortunately, the T. rex had something there too. Davis saw it in his movement and balance, the way his eyes registered everything. He had parked the Rover to block the airplane's forward path. So he was big *and* trained. But Davis wouldn't give him the trifecta of the last variable.

Davis stood calmly as Hassan approached, hoping like hell the guy spoke English. He said, "Did you lose your master?"

Hassan didn't respond, so he either didn't speak English or wasn't going to let Davis distract him. As he ducked under the left wing, Has-san grabbed a set of wheel chocks. When he cleared the wing and stood tall, he raised one of the wooden blocks with a bent vertical arm, leaving its mate dangling by the short rope that connected the pair. It looked like he was holding a massive pair of nunchucks. Davis searched left and right, figuring that he wanted something too. He stepped sideways toward a toolbox that was resting on the back of the forklift. Davis looked into the tray of assorted tools and grabbed the biggest thing he saw, a foot-and-a-half-long crescent wrench that looked better suited to an ocean liner than an airplane.

Hassan quickened his pace, and when he was five steps away he pulled the chocks back and took a big roundhouse swing. Davis realized late that he'd let Hassan get too close. Maybe he'd underestimated his reach or the length of the connecting rope. Whatever the case, when the big blocks came his way in a sweeping arc, there was only one way out. Davis ducked low. But Hassan had anticipated the move. He kept the swing low so that Davis couldn't get completely under it.

Maybe he does have the trifecta. That was Davis' last thought before a twenty-pound block of oak ricocheted off his head. He went down hard, his knees crashing to the concrete. The world seemed to spin around him.

"I have no master," Hassan said.

Davis tried to move, tried to focus. His head was vibrating like a well-thumped tuning fork. When his vision cleared, he was looking at Hassan's knees. Davis shifted his eyes up and saw the big Arab lifting one of the massive yellow chocks high for a coup de grâce. But then Hassan finally made a mistake. He was taking too long, savoring one extra moment. Davis clenched his right hand and felt the wrench still there. He swung, twisting his entire body to get weight behind the blow, and connected with Hassan's knee.

The big Arab screamed and fell back, hit the ground clutching his leg. Davis tried to shake off the cobwebs and get to his feet. They'd each gotten in one blow. Both were on the ground. Hassan was first up, but he looked unsteady on a bad leg. He came like a limping bull, shoulders down and arms outstretched. He reminded Davis of a rugby player heading into a tackle. *That's good*, he thought. *That's my ground.*

Hassan was tall, his center of gravity riding high over an injured base. Davis set himself lower, planted his feet, and put a shoulder into Hassan's gut. The collision was massive, but Davis had better balance. He began moving, pumping his legs, and the two men went down again, this time together. He felt Hassan grappling, trying to keep him close. Davis pried away, knowing mobility was his advantage. Nearly out of the Arab's grasp, Davis slipped on an oily spot on the ramp and fell back, landing against the side of the forklift. Hassan was on top of him instantly, pushing Davis into the forklift and pinning his head to the driver's seat. The massive Arab was lying on him, a forearm jammed across Davis' neck. Both men grappled and swung, but the close proximity stunted any force behind either man's blows.

Davis tried to use his legs to sweep Hassan's away, but the bigger man had a good set. Hassan stopped punching, transferred all his effort to the arm across Davis' throat. He didn't have to do anything else—keep that, and it was just a matter of time.

For the second time in two days, Jammer Davis struggled to breathe. He had the same feeling, the same sense of foreboding he'd had yesterday when his scuba gear had malfunctioned—the body's natural reaction to a lack of oxygen. His punches were ineffective, and he swept his free hand under the seat searching for the crowbar he'd used two days ago in Schmitt's office. Not there. His vision began to fail, but Davis kept clawing, searching for anything to help. His hand found a lever, and he realized the forklift was still running. He jammed the lever forward, and the machine jerked into gear.

Hassan's balance was upset, and he tried to pull himself up onto the moving tug. Tried to keep his advantage. Davis got a breath, found the accelerator with his hand, and pushed it to the floorboard. The machine jumped forward.

Hassan tried to hang on, his legs dragging alongside. Neither man saw the airplane coming. The forklift's twin iron bars, raised to mid-height on the lifting mechanism, speared the fuselage of the DC-3. Initially, the aircraft's thin metal skin was no match, but then the forklift slammed to a stop as more integral parts of the airplane came into play. Davis was thrown forward against the steering wheel and levers, and that was where he stopped. Hassan went airborne. His massive body flew ahead, smashing into the fuselage and then down to the concrete.

Davis righted himself quickly and shifted the forklift into reverse. He pulled back, and the forks came out of the airplane like two knives out of a soda can. He saw Hassan under the airplane, rising unsteadily to his feet. His other leg looked damaged now. The man was nearly immobilized, but his eyes were more fearsome than ever. His massive arms flexed, ready to swing and claw. Davis wouldn't get close enough for that. Not again.

Hassan stumbled toward him, and Davis jumped down off the machine and backed two steps away. Then he saw what he needed. He hefted the entire toolbox from the back of the forklift. Filled with all the tools it took to keep an airliner running, the big red box had to weigh two hundred pounds. With Hassan only steps away, Davis lifted the box over his head, one hand in front and one in back, and threw it like a harpoon. It flew straight at Hassan, who did the natural thing. The wrong thing. He tried to catch it. It was like trying to catch a ship's anchor. The blunt metal side of the box struck Hassan squarely in the chest, lifted his feet, and planted him flat on his back. He didn't move.

Davis did. He climbed back onto the forklift, put it in gear and spun a quick half circle until the twin loading forks were directly over the groggy Arab. Davis lowered the forks.

Hassan saw the twin metal tongues coming down, one across his legs and another over his chest. He pushed out with his huge arms, caught one of the forks and tried to straight-arm it. He succeeded to a degree—the bar stopped moving, but the front wheels of the loader began to rise off the ground. Davis stopped the lift mechanism. He got out of the driver's seat, walked over, and stood by the struggling Arab.

"That's not bad," he said. "I've never seen anybody bench-press a forklift before."

The man said nothing as he strained under the weight.

"Where is that drone going?" Davis asked.

Hassan's eyes flicked away from the tremendous machine that was hovering over him. He looked at Davis with seething hatred and spit in his direction.

"Yeah, I figured as much." Davis leaned closer, and put a casual arm on the lifting blade to add a little extra weight. "About those two pilots, the Ukrainians. That was your work, wasn't it?"

Hassan's face was crimson, the veins in his arms popping out as rivers of blood flowed to his muscles. Muscles that were beginning to quiver from exhaustion. "You," Hassan grunted, "will be next."

"No," Davis said. "I don't think so." He took his arm off the bar, exchanged a glare with the hating eyes, then vaulted up astride the forks, one under each leg.

Hassan's eyes went wide. The extra two hundred forty pounds did the job. The Arab's arms began to shake violently. They wobbled. And then they folded. The twin forks fell hard. Laying supine, Hassan's chest was the thickest part of him, and that was where the damage was done, nearly a ton of weight crushing vital organs in his torso. There was a massive letting of air as the big man's chest caved in, expiring like a Thanksgiving Day parade balloon with a pulled plug.

Davis didn't say a prayer. Wouldn't have if he'd had the time.

He looked at the DC-3 in front of him and saw two gaping holes in the fuselage. An out-of-service airplane if he'd ever seen one. Fortunately, there were two spares. He began trotting toward the nearest one, but as Davis approached the abandoned Land Rover he slowed. Hassan had left the door ajar. It almost looked like an invitation.

A quick detour put Davis in the driver's seat. He scoured the floorboard and consoles, hoping for a cell phone or a radio. Maybe a master plan in an envelope labeled TOP SECRET. That was what he needed. What he got was discarded food wrappers, broken sunglasses, pencils with broken points, and empty water bottles. He was about to give up when something in the backseat caught his eye—a stack of heavy bond paper, at least a thousand sheets face down in a neat, rectangular brick. Like it had just come from a printer's press. And with that idea in his head, Davis correlated the smell. The acrid chemical vapor of freshly run ink.

He reached back, took a page off the top of the stack, and turned it over. He saw a full bust photo of an officer in service dress, wheel cap over brass stars and a forest of ribbons. The wide ebony face was set in a stony, no-nonsense stare. There was something familiar about the photo, although Davis was sure he'd never seen the man before. Then he noticed a name and a title printed at the bottom. The name was a match—same as the soldier's acetate nametag in the picture. But the title was wrong. Very wrong. It didn't say General or Commander or Chief of the Armed Forces. The title Davis saw made no sense at all.

PRESIDENT ALI

OUR GLORIOUS LEADER.

CHAPTER THIRTY-EIGHT

The fuel tanks in the next DC-3 were nearly empty, so Davis ran to his last chance. It wasn't much better. Three hours of fuel, no more. He didn't know how far he was going to have to fly. All he knew for sure was that each minute he wasted took the two-ship formation of Blackstar and Schmitt's DC-3 farther away. If he could get up in the air, the radios would have a much greater range, and he reckoned he could contact Schmitt again.

His head ached, and when he rubbed it Davis felt a warm patch of blood on his scalp where the oak block had connected. Another ding for his collection. He slapped switches and levers into position, then took a quick look at the laminated preflight checklist to see if he'd forgotten anything. Davis cranked the engines, and the big radials spit to life. Just as the starboard motor caught an idle, however, he saw another problem—Regina Antonelli running across the ramp. She passed the damaged airplane, and Davis saw her eyes go to Hassan's body under the forklift. Antonelli didn't even slow. She kept coming straight at him. Straight at the churning propellers.

"Christ!" he spat.

He tried to wave her away through the window. She looked right at him, but ignored the warning and kept coming. Then Davis saw why. A truck in the distance, a small pickup with a gun mounted in the bed. It didn't look military, so it was probably one of Khoury's. Not that it mattered. Davis set the parking brake, went to the cabin, and threw open the boarding door. Antonelli was there waiting.

"I had to come back because—"

"Get in!" he barked.

When she didn't move instantly, Davis reached down, grabbed a fistful of shirt, and hauled her up into the cabin. Antonelli went sprawling, but Davis made no attempt to help her up. He slammed the door shut, raced back to the cockpit, and slapped the throttles forward. The big machine lurched ahead and Davis began a right turn. Over his shoulder, he saw the truck bearing down. A man was standing at the gun station, holding his balance with one hand as the other worked to feed an ammo belt. The truck changed its vector, swerving around a wheel chock, and the gunner fell on his ass.

Finally a break, Davis thought.

Having learned from Schmitt, he steered for the longest taxiway in sight. The big machine accelerated. At sixty knots the truck started to drop back. At eighty it disappeared. At ninety they were airborne and climbing into the light of a new dawn.

Antonelli edged her head into the cockpit. After an awkward silence, she said, "I went to the hangar first, but couldn't find you."

"Why the hell did you even come back?" he snapped.

The doctor just stood there and stared. Didn't answer. They both already knew.

As Fadi Jibril was watching his computer monitor, he felt Khoury's presence over his shoulder.

"Are we on schedule?" the imam asked.

"Yes, no more than a minute behind," Jibril answered. "We will reach the staging point in two hours. When can we expect to receive the final targeting information?"

"Soon, Fadi. Achmed is handling it. He will take the coordinates over the radio from our man on the ground in Israel."

Jibril moved the cursor back and forth on the computer screen. As if his mind was on his work. In truth, he found himself analyzing the imam's words. He had left this one unresolved task to Khoury— the receipt of the final coordinates. *Over the radio . . . from our man on the ground in Israel.* How could this be? Jibril wondered. This airplane had four radios, two he'd specially designed and installed. Jibril had positioned and checked every antenna, analyzed the configuration for interference, susceptibility to icing, and power requirements. He knew, by precise calculation, the range of each component. Israel was seven hundred miles away, over two hundred from the staging point. That was the closest they would ever get. The range of the best VHF radio on the airplane was less than one hundred sixty miles, even under the most favorable atmospheric conditions. They could never receive a signal from Israel. Did the imam not know this? Then Jibril recalled the other thing that had been bothering him—the Israeli prime minster was supposedly in Washington today. Jibril had not followed his instinct to verify this—it would have been simple enough. Instead, he had trusted Khoury blindly.

"Sheik . . ." Jibril hesitated, "are you sure we can receive this report?"

"Of course," Khoury said, a comforting hand falling to Jibril's shoulder. "Achmed is in contact with our operative as we speak. All is on schedule." The hand stayed on Jibril's shoulder for some time before Khoury said, "I must go and check with him now." The imam went to the cockpit.

Jibril's hand fumbled over the controls, and his stomach churned. He manipulated his computer to show a new readout. He had thought it useful to create a program to monitor the VHF radios, giving him the ability to track the frequencies tuned by each component. Presently, two were controlling the drone as expected. One of the airplane radios was tuned to an air-traffic-control frequency. Jibril studied the last radio, the auxiliary VHF on the flight deck. It was tuned to 127.5 MHz, a frequency that meant nothing to Jibril. Was this the frequency that would be used to receive the targeting coordinates? It had to be. But how at this range? He saw the imam engaging one of the two security men. Again Jibril felt uneasy, and for the first time asked himself why Khoury had even seen a need to bring these men.

Jibril had also programmed the ability to listen to the radios, and so he clicked a symbol on his screen to send the audio from 127.5 MHz to his headset.

Fadi Jibril heard nothing.

The airplane was steady on a heading of three five zero. Almost due north.

Antonelli had taken the copilot's station—not for any duties, but simply because that was the only other seat on the aircraft. Davis watched her scanning the sky, watched the early light play through her raven hair. She was beautiful. She was maddening. He had tried to be angry with her for not going to the embassy, for not extracting herself from the danger he'd put her in. It was all but impossible. Antonelli had done exactly what he would have done.

As the airplane climbed, he explained what he'd found at the hangar. He told her that Blackstar was on its way to an attack, and that the United States was being set up to take the blame. "The only thing I can't figure out," he said with one hand on the control column, "is what they're targeting."

"We are heading north. Could it be something in Israel?"

"That was my first guess, but now I'm not so sure."

"Why?"

In truth, Davis couldn't peg where his reservations had come from. He said, "I took a look through Khoury's Land Rover, the one that was near the—" his voice trailed off.

"Body? I have seen bodies before, Jammer. I also see the wound on your head, so I won't pass judgment."

"Fair enough." He had taken one of the posters from the Rover, folded it up and stuffed it in a pocket. He pulled it out and showed Antonelli. "Any idea who this guy is?"

She looked closely. "I may have seen his picture before. But I definitely recognize the name. General Ali is the Sudanese minister of defense."

"Okay," he said. "Now look closer, at the bottom. Check the title."

Antonelli did, and the revelation clearly hit her. "What could this mean?"

Davis studied the picture again, and had the same odd feeling he'd had earlier—that he'd seen it before. Then it dawned on him. He hadn't recognized the *picture*. It was the pose. *Eyes cast downward slightly. Watching.* Just like the propaganda photos of the president that were hung in every office of every building in Sudan. There were a thousand copies of General Ali's photo back in the Land Rover, all cut to fit in the very same picture frames. Davis stared at the poster.

"Contessa . . ." he hesitated.

"What is it?"

"I haven't seen much news lately, but that Arab League conference is taking place today, right?"

He could see her run a quick calendar in her head. "Yes, it is scheduled for this morning."

"And who will be there?"

"The leaders of virtually every Arab country," she said.

"What about the Sudanese president?"

"Of course, it has been in the local papers for weeks."

That's it, Davis thought. It all made perfect, wicked sense. He stared at Antonelli and waited. She was a smart lady, so it didn't take long.

"A coup d'état?" she exclaimed.

"Disguised as an attack by the United States. Ten or twenty heads of state killed, including the Sudanese president. If it happens, there will be power struggles all across the region tonight, just like after the uprisings that got rid of Mubarak and the rest. The Arab world will be so shocked and incensed by the idea of a U.S. attack that nobody will give a second thought to the minister of defense taking charge in Khartoum."

Antonelli stared out the front window. "What can we do?" she asked.

Davis checked the manifold pressure on the engines and bumped up the throttles, pushing the old radials as hard as he dared.

"We can fly faster."

CHAPTER THIRTY-NINE

The clock moved with glacial speed.

Davis tried the radio every five minutes. Twelve times in the first hour. The second hour he called every three minutes. Not a word came in reply. He was in a familiar arena, indeed his area of expertise—one airplane hunting another. Only he didn't have radar for guidance, and wasn't talking to anyone who did. He was fighting blind, just lumbering along as fast as the big machine would go, hoping like hell they were flying in the right direction. He figured the geometry of the intercept for a classic tail chase. His only chance was speed, but in that respect Davis was on unfamiliar ground. If he were flying an F–16 in full afterburner, he'd be somewhere over Europe right now, albeit out of gas. As it was, he might be gaining ten miles an hour on the pair of aircraft in front. Assuming they *were* in front.

He knew he couldn't rely on radio contact alone. Schmitt might not be in a position to reply. Truth was, he might already have a bullet in his head like the two poor Ukrainian bastards. So Davis kept a keen eye out the window, looking for a slow-moving dot. Or better yet, two. It was like playing hide-and-seek, only the playground was the size of a country, a hundred thousand square miles of empty sky.

"I need to look at that," Antonelli said, interrupting his thoughts. She was staring at the side of his head, the place where an oak log had slammed into his skull.

Davis didn't argue.

Her hands held his head gently, and after a brief appraisal the doctor disappeared for a time into the aft cabin. She came back with a first-aid kit.

"Is that really necessary?" he asked.

Antonelli didn't bother to reply. She cleaned and dressed the wound, and at the end wrapped a long bandage around his head three times. Davis saw his reflection in the side window.

"I look like a pirate."

"Good, because you often act like one."

He grinned. "Anyway, thanks."

"You're welcome. Now can you tell me where we are?"

"Egypt, I think." Davis left it at that because there were no positives in an expanded answer. He was sure they'd crossed the border, and that was a problem. He hadn't talked to an air traffic controller all morning. Not that he was concerned about air traffic—running into another airplane over the middle of the Sahara Desert was one chance in a billion. But he was very worried about an Egyptian fighter draped in missiles swooping up on his wing. Not by choice, Davis had reverted to bygone days. He was flying this old crate like pilots had flown her when she was fresh out of the factory. Maneuvering a slow airplane in a big sky, keeping out a sharp eye.

He tried to raise Schmitt again on the radio. Still nothing. Davis checked his fuel state and saw another worry. In thirty minutes, maybe forty, things would get very quiet. Antonelli had her eyes glued to the sky now, helping him look. She was clearly anxious, and Davis decided she could use a distraction. He handed over the microphone.

"Here," he said, "keep calling. Electrons are free."

"What do I do?"

"Just press the button and talk. The captain's name is Schmitt. No wait—his call sign is Schmitthead."

With a questioning look, Antonelli put the microphone to her lips.

Fadi Jibril heard the woman's voice. He pressed his headset to his ears and listened more closely.

"*I repeat, are you there?*"

Jibril wanted desperately to say something, yet he had not designed the workstation with any capability to transmit. From his seat, he could monitor the frequencies but not talk. Jibril was trying to think of a way around this when a familiar hand grasped his shoulder. The gesture that had once comforted now felt like the hand of death.

"Is the drone in position?" Khoury asked.

Jibril pointed to the screen. "Yes, here. It is established in a holding pattern at the initial point, very near our own position but at a lower altitude. If you go forward and look out the window, slightly to the right, you should see it."

Khoury didn't move. "It is time to finish our work, Fadi. Achmed has received the final coordinates."

For Jibril, these were the words that brought the truth crashing down. It was a lie, pure and absolute. He had been listening to the auxiliary frequency for the last two hours. There had been no instructions from any contact in Israel. The only thing Jibril had heard was the desperate voice of an unknown woman. He suddenly realized that Rafiq Khoury was not alone behind him. One of the guards was standing at his side.

"Yes, of course, sheik."

Khoury placed a handwritten set of coordinates on the work table in front of Jibril. N29°58'50.95" E31°09'0.10".

"Now!" Khoury commanded.

Jibril's hands went slowly to the keyboard. The coordinates were not in Israel—he knew this instantly—but without a map he could only estimate. Jibril tried to mentally plot the lat-long pairing using the map on his display. Somewhere north of their present position. Near Cairo perhaps? He thought about questioning the numbers, but Khoury would only grow suspicious.

The hand of death left his shoulder.

Jibril decided that identifying the target was not important. All that mattered was the evil around him. Deftly, he brushed a finger on the caps lock key and began typing the sequence. The coordinate field on the screen became populated with an indecipherable mash of symbols.

"What are you doing?" Khoury objected.

"I don't know what is wrong, sheik. The—"

Two arms wrapped around Jibril's chest, restraining him like a straightjacket. Khoury leaned in and entered the final coordinates, just as Jibril had taught him. The same scramble of symbols.

"What have you done?" Khoury hissed.

Fixed to his chair, Jibril watched as the imam figured out the problem. He released the caps lock key, and his second attempt succeeded. The message FINAL POSITION UPDATE CONFIRMED flashed for three seconds, followed by a lone word in surreal green letters at the center of the screen. AUTONOMOUS. In a matter of minutes, Blackstar would turn north on its final course, guided in the terminal phase by onboard systems that would hold to an accuracy of less than ten meters. Precise enough, Jibril supposed, for whatever Khoury had in mind. Worst of all, there was no way to change the command or abort. Blackstar was now irretrievable.

Jibril began to struggle against the arms that anchored him to his chair. Struggled until something blunt crashed into his head. Dazed, Jibril went limp and felt warmth oozing down one cheek.

Khoury leaned forward to be in his field of vision. "In the end you have failed me, Fadi. Fortunately, your American conscience is too late."

"My . . . my what?"

Khoury started to speak again, but was interrupted by shouts from the cockpit. The words were indistinguishable to Jibril—his headset still covered one ear, and the other was ringing from the blow he'd taken. But his eyes were sharp enough. He saw Achmed coming aft again. He began jabbering to Khoury, gesticulating wildly. Only when he got closer did the words register for Jibril.

"Again he sends me here!" Achmed complained. "There is nothing wrong, I tell you. He is a madman!"

Khoury stared at the cockpit, suspicion in his mismatched gaze. He murmured into Achmed's ear.

From the headset, Jibril heard the woman's voice crackle across the airwaves again. It was maddening. If he spoke only once again in his life, it would be to warn whoever it was, hope that they could forestall the terror about to rain. But Jibril had no voice. The only way to transmit was to use the microphones in the cockpit.

Moments later, his headset buzzed as someone did exactly that.

Davis heard Schmitt growl over the radio, "Who the hell is this?"

He took the microphone from Antonelli. "Say position!"

After modest pause, Schmitt said, "We're thirty south of Giza, near our IP."

IP was the military abbreviation for "initial point," the spot you used as a beginning reference for a final attack run. Davis checked his instruments and estimated that Schmitt was twenty miles ahead.

Schmitt again. "Jammer, I don't have much time. Khoury and Achmed are getting suspicious. Can somebody tell me what the hell this is all about?"

"Yeah, I'll tell you," Davis said. "That drone you're controlling is about to obliterate the Arab League conference in Giza."

Another pause, this one much longer. Davis imagined Schmitt deciphering the ramifications of that. He wasn't stupid—just self-centered. He'd been concentrating on a nice payday, and probably assuming that anything involving Rafiq Khoury and Fly by Night Aviation had to be minor league. Now he was thinking differently, understanding the damage about to be done.

"So what can we do?" Schmitt finally replied.

Davis had no answer. He'd come this far just to establish contact, but now what? If he were sitting in the cockpit next to Schmitt, they could put aside their miserable past and come up with a plan. Davis could swing a fist or a crash ax while Schmitt flew. From where he was, Davis was helpless.

"How much time is left?" he asked. "Do you have any idea when this strike is going to happen?"

Schmitt said, "I can see the drone now. It's in a holding pattern a thousand feet below me."

"Okay, so it hasn't launched yet. If there's enough time we could—"

"Ten o'clock!" Antonelli shouted from across the cockpit.

The way she blurted it out, Davis' first instinct was to turn his head sixty degrees to the left—the ten o'clock position to any pilot—and look for an incoming missile. Then he put it in her layman's terms, lowered the microphone, and looked at her. "Ten o'clock?" he repeated.

"That's when it will happen."

"How the hell could you know that?" Davis asked.

"It has been in the news for weeks. The Arab League conference begins at ten o'clock. All the heads of state will be gathered."

Davis wasn't wearing a watch, so he cross-checked the clock on the old airplane. Twenty-three minutes. He fumbled over the chart he'd been working with and estimated the position of Blackstar relative to Giza. Twenty minutes was just about right—if Blackstar left right now.

He keyed the microphone. "Schmitt, I think the drone is going to depart the IP any minute. We've got to do something now. What if you powered down all the electrical busses on your airplane? Could that interrupt the control? Maybe screw something up?"

"I could try, but it wouldn't work for long. I've got two of Khoury's goons over my right shoulder. They have guns and aren't going to let—hang on, Jammer. I'm watching the drone right now, and it just took a turn to the north. Maybe if I—crap!"

Schmitt's microphone went hot again, and Davis heard shouting. Schmitt was clearly struggling. More shouts in Arabic, loud and clear. Close to the microphone. Close to Bob Schmitt. He was under attack. The transmission cut off.

Davis tried to imagine what he would do in that situation. Outnumbered, outgunned. Only one idea came to mind.

"Defensive maneuvering! Push over, negative Gs! You're strapped in but they're not! Do it now!" Davis hoped Schmitt could still hear the radio. He repeated it all, then kept repeating it because that was all he could do. Davis saw a tiny dot ahead and thought it might be Schmitt's DC-3, but soon he realized it was the other aircraft—the ominous arrowhead that was Blackstar. It was heading north, just like

Schmitt had said, so the DC-3 had to be to its left. Davis scanned, and did see a second dot, perhaps ten miles ahead. He watched closely, and for the first few seconds the airplane was cruising straight and true.

Then it looked like a roller coaster in a typhoon.

Rafiq Khoury had been keeping an eye on the stunned engineer while his men—Achmed and the two guards—dealt with Schmitt. Khoury was a satisfied man. His work was done, and all that remained was to rendezvous at the abandoned airstrip with General Ali's helicopter—or rather, President Ali's helicopter. There, they would kill Jibril and the Americans, and as a final touch make this aircraft their funeral pyre. He wondered briefly if the general had captured the last American, Davis. Khoury decided it didn't matter. They had succeeded in every way. Khoury was staring at Jibril's computer screen, idly imagining the possibilities his new life would present, when he suddenly began to fly.

He rose effortlessly into the air, as if the world around him was tumbling. There was no up or down, only spinning references and objects soaring past like gravity had taken leave. He hit the ceiling hard, and his eyes shut reflexively. When he opened them again, Khoury saw madness. Bodies and crates and equipment, hanging suspended like so many flakes in a snow globe.

Then, all at once, gravity returned with a vengeance.

From the ceiling, Khoury crashed down like a brick to the metal floor. He heard snapping noises that could only be his bones shattering. He felt indescribable pain in his lower leg. Screams filled the air, cries of both desperation and agony. Khoury tried to move. He got one elbow to the deck and raised his head from the cold metal.

Then it all happened again.

Schmitt's DC-3 was careening through the sky, oscillating and tumbling.

"What is happening?" asked a horrified Antonelli.

"Negative Gs, then positive. Schmitt is pushing and pulling from stop to stop on his control column. It's a last ditch maneuver. He's buckled into his seat, so he'll stay put, but anybody who isn't strapped down in that airplane is getting thrown around like beads in a maraca. I just hope that seventy-year-old airframe stays in one piece."

They both watched Schmitt's DC-3 swirl up and down through two more violent cycles, actually flipping inverted on the second. Then it seemed to settle, like a floating leaf that had cleared a section of rapids to end in a calm pool.

The two airplanes were only three miles apart now, nose to nose. Davis had to look out the right-hand window, past Antonelli, to still see Blackstar. The drone was getting smaller, a dot nearly lost in the dusty haze. Davis banked the airplane to change the relative geometry, and the closure to Schmitt's airplane slowed. He picked up the microphone, and said, "Schmitt, are you there?"

There was no reply.

CHAPTER FORTY

Jibril opened his eyes, or rather tried to. Oddly, the world that spread before him put the word "entropy" in his mind. It was a term he had learned long ago in some undergraduate chemistry class. The measure of a state of disorder. That was what he was looking at—bodies strewn about the cabin amid wiring and paper and equipment. One of Khoury's guards was nearby, his neck folded impossibly against a shoulder, blank eyes staring into space. Fadi Jibril had never seen death before, but he was seeing it now. Near the flight deck he saw three more bodies, two piled in a heap—the second guard on top of Rafiq Khoury, and Achmed crushed under a pile of equipment that had broken free. He could also see Schmitt at the controls, or at least his shoulder. His shirt was covered in blood, as was the hand Jibril could see on the control column. But the hand was steady.

Jibril performed a self-assessment. His head throbbed where he'd been struck with the butt of a gun, and his right shoulder felt like it was on fire. He saw blood on the console in front of him and, in a strangely detached thought, wondered if it was his. When Jibril tried to move, his right leg shot with pain. He called out to Schmitt, but the pilot didn't seem to hear.

He reached down and unbuckled his lap belt, the thing that had saved him. Jibril tried to stand, but his right leg buckled immediately, and he tumbled to the steel deck. Grimacing, he pushed onto his side. Jibril looked up, and when he did, his eyes registered something different. It took a moment to realize what it was. Rafiq Khoury had moved. He was closer to Schmitt now.

Jibril tried to yell, tried to raise an alarm, but only managed a hoarse grunt. He began to crawl, watching in horror as Khoury, his body bloodied and distorted, lunged forward and attacked Schmitt. The two men grappled, falling sideways onto the instruments and levers between the cockpit seats. There was a tangle of bloody arms and whipping fists, howls of pain and rage. He watched the two men fall back into the cabin, leaving the craft to fly itself. The imam was utterly insane, Jibril thought, attacking the only person who could fly the airplane. Soon Khoury was on top with something big and heavy in his hand. He was hammering at Schmitt, striking again and again. The burly American tried to fend off the blows but was clearly weakening under the onslaught.

Jibril tried to crawl closer, but his shattered leg was useless. He spotted one of the guard's weapons nearby, a machine pistol. Jibril had never used such a thing in his life, but he would learn right now. He stretched out and touched the barrel with his fingertips, dragged it closer until he had a good grip. He pointed the steel barrel at Rafiq Khoury and tried to pull the trigger. Nothing happened. The trigger seemed jammed.

More screams from the front, Khoury still pounding away.

Jibril brought the gun closer. Weapons had safety levers, and the engineer tried to deduce where it would be. He found it near the trigger, a tiny black lever. Jibril flicked it forward, pointed the barrel as best he could and fired. The weapon kicked in his hands, and a deafening noise reverberated through the cabin.

Khoury seemed to freeze, his arm poised overhead for a final strike. Schmitt managed to roll clear, and Jibril fired again, this time holding the trigger down. The gun kicked three more times, and he saw the imam shudder, saw his white robe blossom with splotches of red. Then, finally, he collapsed.

Schmitt pushed clear of Khoury's body and rose unsteadily. There was agony in his battered face, but he caught Jibril's eyes and the two exchanged a look. Schmitt gave a subtle nod before stumbling back to the flight deck.

Jibril tried to move again, but the pain in his leg was excruciating. He eased back and tried to take pressure off the limb. Resting on the cold steel deck, he closed his eyes. Jibril cursed inwardly. How could he have been so blind to the imam? He had only seen what he'd wanted to see. Heard what he'd wanted to hear. *You will be to Sudan what A. Q. Khan was to Pakistan. The father of a nation's technical might.*

With his head vibrating against the steel floor, he let his mind drift. His free thoughts went, quite naturally, to his wife and unborn child. Precisely where they always should have been. Jibril hated how he had been used and manipulated. Hated the damage about to be wrought. So he began to pray. He begged forgiveness and threw himself openly onto whatever reckoning he deserved. The pleas were very different from those he had been issuing for the last six months. Indeed, they were the inverse. Fadi Jibril prayed that his diligent work would some-how fail.

"Schmitt, are you there?"

Davis had been calling frantically for the last three minutes, but gotten no answer. He looked outside and found a bare speck in the distance—Blackstar heading for its target. It was decision time. If he lost sight of the drone, got too far behind, he might never see it again.

"What is happening?" Antonelli asked, her eyes locked to the nearby DC-3.

"I don't know," Davis said.

Schmitt had clearly taken his advice and put the airplane through a series of violent maneuvers. Then the craft had settled to a more straight and level trajectory. But as Davis watched now, he had the distinct impression the airplane was unguided, meandering up and down, drifting through shallow turns. As if nobody at all was flying.

Finally, a shaky voice rumbled over the speaker. "Davis?"

It was Schmitt, but he sounded tentative and unsettled in a way Davis had never heard before.

"You okay?" he answered.

A long pause. "Yeah, we're under control."

"We?"

"The engineer and me. We're the only ones left. He's banged up, but alive. He's on our side now."

"So you're secure?" Davis asked, wanting to be sure.

"Secure—sure. Khoury and his bunch are done. You had a good idea."

"I never thought I'd hear that from you."

"And you won't ever again."

Yeah, Davis thought, *Schmitt's just fine.*

"But we're not out of the woods yet," Schmitt added. "I think I bent this old airplane. She's flying crooked and the ailerons are binding."

Davis looked past Antonelli. He didn't see Blackstar. "Dammit!" he muttered. He banked the airplane hard and pushed the throttles all the way up. Davis put the microphone to his lips, "Do what you have to, just get that bucket on the ground. And ask the engineer if there's any way to stop Blackstar."

Davis watched the airspeed inch upward. He needed knots, so he pushed the nose down to help the old bird accelerate.

After a minute, Schmitt came back. "Jibril says no, he can't control it. Blackstar is on its own now. But you've got the target right. It's heading for the conference in Giza."

"All right," Davis replied, "I'm going after it."

"Going after it?" Schmitt spat. "What will you do if you catch up?"

"Hell if I know."

The Great Pyramid of Giza has been casting a shadow for over four thousand years, but never before had it fallen over such a luminous array of dignitaries. Twenty-two leaders of the new, emerging Arab world were mingling in the staging area, a sheltered enclosure behind the main stage. This alone might have given any right-minded security chief pause, but up to this point everyone was behaving, save for the occasional incoherent rant by the madman of Libya.

The usual throngs of tourists had been turned away today, leaving countless vacations bruised and tour guides wagging excuses. It *was* the only way. Presently, a single person stood on the stage, the conference's beleaguered director of security. He was an Egyptian, a senior man in the new president's Office of State Security. Nearing the end of his career, the director was known for his steady demeanor under pressure—something he relied upon now.

He stood on the stage and looked out at the crowd, which was actually not that large, and then at the media corral where a veritable army of reporters stood in wait. The journalists were geared for battle—cameras, microphones, smartphones. If all went as planned today, a positive tilt toward peace in the region was anticipated, even if the ceremony itself would quickly be forgotten. *And any problems?* the director mused. Any problems would be splattered across the world in a matter of seconds, and from a hundred different angles. That was the problem in his line of work. The better you performed your job, the less it was noticed. But if you screwed up—

The director put a hand in his pocket and keyed the microphone that was wired to his collar. "Report."

The reply came to his earpiece immediately, "Still Condition One. No threats, sir."

The director did not respond. *Thirty more minutes of that,* he reasoned, *and I'll soon be in a soft chair by the sea.*

His earpiece crackled to life. "One moment, sir. Our Air Force command center has received a warning from their U.S. liaison officer. One of their aircraft carriers is tracking an unauthorized aircraft thirty miles to the south. It's heading this way."

"What are they doing about it?" the director asked, not bothering to inquire why it took the Americans to bring the matter to everyone's attention.

An interminable pause. "Our own Air Force is sending a pair of fighters to investigate. The colonel insists on leaving the bulk of his force in sector three to watch the northern border. He says the reported target is moving very slowly and not a possible threat."

There was nothing the director of security could say to that. The Air Force was the Air Force, and if something slipped through it would be their heads rolling in the gutters of Abdeen Palace. All the same, he turned to his right and scanned the southern sky.

CHAPTER FORTY-ONE

Davis was captain of a seventy-year-old airplane, one in which he had logged no more than four hours of flight time. He was nearly out of fuel, violating Egyptian airspace, and heading for a high-profile political event without clearance. His copilot was a general practice physician with zero hours of flight time. *But at least I'm not high on khat*, he mused.

He scanned the northern sky, looking high and low, not sure what kind of profile Blackstar had been programmed to fly. Stay high and rely on stealth? Or go low and mask behind the terrain? The landscape was relatively flat, no mountains or canyons in which to hide, so Davis' gut told him to look high. That would also give Blackstar more kinetic energy in its terminal dive—more bang for the buck. He figured he was twenty-five miles from Giza. Blackstar had to be close, no more than five miles ahead. Unless it had been programmed to fly a circuitous route. Swing wide and come in from the east? Davis had no way to tell.

"There!" Antonelli shouted.

Davis saw her pointing to the four o'clock position, back over her shoulder.

"Christ, we passed it up."

The doctor had good eyes—Davis banked right and saw it, the arrow-like Blackstar daggering ahead like some kind of remote controlled demon. Which was exactly what it was. He picked up an intercept track. They'd be right beside the drone in a matter of minutes. Whatever good that would do.

"Where the hell are the fighters?" he asked.

"The what?" Antonelli replied.

"The Egyptians must have air cover, fighters watching out for trouble. They can't see Blackstar—that's why Khoury used it, because it's stealthy. But now we're here. This old trashwagon must have a radar cross section the size of a building. *Somebody* has to be tracking us. I figured that if we followed along and tied ourselves to Blackstar, we'd draw some support. Somebody who can take it out."

They both swept their eyes over the sky but saw nothing. Then an F-16 flying at supersonic speed flashed a hundred yards in front of them.

Antonelli jumped back in her seat, and a second later they hit the jet's wake vortices, two sharp bounces that made the old airplane groan.

"What was that?" she exclaimed.

"Egyptian Air Force," Davis answered. "Just like I was hoping."

"What are they going to do?"

"Good question."

Davis had a lot of air combat training, much of it flying against F-16s like the one that had just screamed past. He was, however, used to having a little more performance at his disposal.

"I'm hoping these guys will be on our side."

"So am I," Antonelli agreed.

Davis watched the fighter that had just dusted them go high, a big whifferdill to reposition. *That's what I'd do.* He looked left and right, searching for the other jet. Fighters always came in pairs. You might not see the second, but it was there somewhere. If Davis were to guess, he'd have it camped out at their six o'clock right now, flying S-turns, because F-16s weren't meant to be driven at a hundred and twenty knots. The pilot probably had an AIM-9 heat-seeker locked and loaded, giving a nice solid "ready" tone on one of their big radial engines. That idea didn't sit well with Davis, but there wasn't much he could do. He had asked for fighters, now he had them. But they clearly hadn't seen the drone. Their radars had guided them to a big, ponderous DC-3, so that's what their eyes had locked onto.

Davis searched for Blackstar but didn't see it. In all the commotion he'd lost his visual.

"Dammit!" he said. "Do you see the drone?"

Antonelli craned her neck left and right, searching the sky. "No, not anymore."

"Great. Just when we get help."

"What can we do?" she asked.

Davis saw the high F-16 dropping to his altitude, probably getting ready to introduce himself with a few visual signals.

"There's only one option right now. We surrender."

Davis held the control column firmly and rocked his wings, big side-to-side rolls that were unmistakable. It was a signal any fighter jock in the world would understand. *Knock it off.* A pilot's white flag.

The lead F-16 pulled up on his left, no more than a hundred feet away, trying for a visual to the captain's window. Davis tuned his primary radio to 121.5 MHz, the international distress frequency, and tried to make contact. The fighter didn't reply. He was watching the lead airplane edge closer when Antonelli blurted, "There!"

He looked where she was pointing and saw Blackstar. It was five, maybe seven miles away, still heading north. Closing in on its target.

"I see it," Davis said, "but they don't. These guys intercepted a blip on their radar, and found an old DC-3. If we keep this heading, we're going to lose sight of the drone. All we're doing is pulling them away from the real threat." He tried the radios again. Still no reply.

"Why don't they answer?" she asked.

"I don't know. Maybe they haven't tuned the frequency yet, or maybe they've got people on other radios yakking in their headsets—a command center or air traffic control. It can get pretty busy at a time like this. In a minute or two or ten, we'll be talking to them. Unfortunately, we don't have that kind of time."

Antonelli looked out her window at the sleek jet. "But if we cannot talk to them, how will they find the other craft?"

"There is one way," Davis said. "If I break away toward Blackstar, they'll follow. The problem is, there's a guy parked behind us right now. If we make a threatening move, he's going to fire a missile—but I don't know how long he'll wait to do it. Could be five minutes, could be five seconds. For us, it's a risky maneuver."

Antonelli didn't waver. "We've come this far."

Davis looked at the doctor in his copilot's seat. She had sharp eyes and a cool head, so she was already a better copilot than Achmed. And she was still damned nice to look at. He smiled at her. "You know, by the time you're done with me—those divorce lawyers back in Milan are going to look pretty tame."

"No. They are still far more trouble." She added a grin.

The light moment was interrupted by an orange light flickering on the forward panel. FUEL LOW. Davis checked the gas gauge and saw the needles bouncing on the big *E*. At this point, he figured bouncing was good. That meant there were still a few gallons of 100-octane sloshing in the tanks. When that stopped, when the needles didn't move at all—that was trouble.

"Well," he reasoned, "if we crash, we won't burn."

Antonelli's smile faded.

Davis looked at the lead fighter to make sure the pilot was paying close attention. He then yanked the control wheel all the way to the left. The big airplane rolled into a steep bank, heading right for the F-16. The Egyptian pilot pulled up hard to avoid the collision and disappeared over their heads.

When Davis rolled out of the turn, they were heading straight for Blackstar. He realized he was holding his breath, waiting for the heater to smack into an engine any second. Left or right? he wondered. Davis waited, watched the engine gauges and the fire warning lights. His hands might have crushed the control wheel. But no explosion came. A minute passed, then another. Davis couldn't see either fighter, but Blackstar was getting bigger in his windscreen.

Davis spotted it first this time. "There!" he said, pointing straight up. They both watched as one of the F-16s raked down from high on Blackstar.

"They see it!" Antonelli said, joy in her voice.

Davis didn't feel the same joy, not when he saw what they were doing. "No, no! They see it but they've got it all wrong. They're trying to shoot from a forward aspect, nose to nose. They're trying to use radar missiles, or maybe a face shot with a heat-seeker. That'll never work against a stealthy target."

Right then Davis glanced ahead and spotted something else in the distance. Three pyramids no more than fifteen miles away.

"Guns, guns!" he shouted over the radio.

Davis wasn't sure if the fighters were even tuned to the emergency frequency. Using old-fashioned bullets was the only way they were going to stop Blackstar in time, and that had to be a visual shot, no radar-computed, death-dot gun solution from a heads-up display. The two fighter pilots had to forego all their training, all their gadgets, and go back to basics. In the age of computer-guided smart weapons, their only chance was to throw stones.

Davis had the DC-3 almost next to Blackstar, a half-mile abeam and easing out front. He could see the pyramids clearly, ten miles and closing fast. They were surrounded by what looked like ancient ruins, and beyond that the city of Giza baked in the mid-morning haze. He saw a small airfield in the middle of the city, and thought with a strange calmness, *Maybe I can glide there when I run out of gas.* At the base of the right-most pyramid Davis saw a collection of tents and vehicles. A collection of people. At this speed, he figured they had four minutes. Then he noticed Blackstar nosing down toward its target, accelerating. Three, he corrected.

The fighters were high, their pilots clearly stumped as they shuffled through modes on their radars, thinking and coordinating with time they didn't have. The DC-3 was a mile in front of Blackstar now, but Davis didn't pull back on the power. He didn't have armament of any kind. But there was a way. There was also one big complication.

"What are they doing?" Antonelli asked, her head craning to watch.

"They're failing," Davis said. "They're not used to dealing with stealthy targets, so they don't know how to bring this thing down. But we can."

When her eyes came inside the cockpit they were full of surprise. "What could we do?"

Davis told her. Then he told her the risk involved. He said, "I can't make a call like that. It's up to you."

Antonelli paused briefly. Davis couldn't imagine what was going through her mind. She looked at him confidently, almost serenely, and nodded.

"You're sure?" he asked.

"Yes, do it!"

"Okay, here goes." Davis shoved the throttles all the way to the forward stops, and the old radials gave a beastly howl.

CHAPTER FORTY-TWO

The director of security watched the chaos. He'd been getting regular updates over his radio, and had heard the Air Force commander's assuring confirmation that everything was indeed under control. Yet he could see the fighters off to the south. They were high, flying in circles, and the small black speck beneath them was getting larger, not careening to the ground in a ball of flames as it should.

"What are they doing?" he murmured under his breath.

On the stage, the president of Algeria was wrapping up his keynote speech, and behind him, oblivious to the madness, twenty leaders of the Arab world were listening respectfully. The journalists were focused entirely on the podium, feeding the event across the world and unaware of the aerial bedlam a few miles to their left. Suddenly, the director saw a fourth airplane in the distance coming into view from one side. It was big and slow, and looked like it was heading straight for the black dot.

More radio chatter—confusion and accusations. Whatever was happening in the sky, the consequences were no more than a minute away if nothing changed. And nothing *was* changing. He could take no more. The director keyed his microphone and gave the command. He hit the panic button.

Seconds later, fifty armed men rushed the stage to form a perimeter. The principles were shoved unceremoniously toward exits. People fell and chairs went flying. One of the security men on stage pointed toward the southern sky, and a sea of heads followed the gesture, including many of those in the media section. In the next moments, no fewer than a hundred cameras were redirected.

All fell squarely on Jammer Davis.

In the art of aerial combat there are three geometries to intercept a target. Lag pursuit puts you behind another aircraft. Pure pursuit is a constant turn in which the nose is kept fixed on a target moving in your windscreen. Davis was flying the third version—lead pursuit. He was aiming for a point in front of Blackstar, keeping the drone stationary in his windscreen. Watching as it got bigger and bigger.

He looked over his shoulder and saw the pyramids only a few miles away. He was close enough to see people scrambling in all directions. Davis estimated he was no more than a mile from Blackstar, and closing fast. The DC-3's big radials were straining, every needle on the engine gauges up against a red line. Some beyond. The F-16s were still up high—watching, thinking. Not getting the job done. Davis would only have time for one pass. He glanced at the gas gauges and saw them still bouncing. Then he glanced at his copilot.

"Shoulder straps!" he ordered, then started working his own into place. "Get strapped in, pull everything as tight as you can!"

Antonelli fumbled, not knowing how the harness arrangement worked. He reached over and helped her, pulling nylon straps with one hand and flying with the other. Half a mile to go.

"Fold your hands over your chest!" he ordered.

Antonelli did her best to curl protectively in the old seat.

Four hundred yards. He had nearly two hundred knots of closure and a high angle. Davis went into a zone.

Just like in the heat of an aerial dogfight, he threw out the rest of the world. Closed all unnecessary sensory inputs. There were only two things in his universe. Two airplanes—the one he was connected to, and the one he was aiming at. Davis didn't consider how to do it because there was really only one way. One way that he could ram Blackstar and come out alive. His airplane was bigger and, he hoped, sturdier. Use a wingtip, then hope to hell Boudreau was right. *They don't make 'em like this anymore.* At that moment it occurred to Davis that Blackstar was probably packed with high explosives. One more thing to worry about if he had the time.

In the final seconds, Davis' hands eased on the control wheel, not so much moving as caressing the airplane. The strike had to be perfect. Too close and the DC-3 would cartwheel down and make a smoking hole in the desert. Not close enough and he would miss Blackstar completely.

One hundred yards.

What had been a black dot now filled his windscreen. Davis was using only his fingertips on the controls. Coaxing. The windshield went completely black and Blackstar flashed by his left side.

Impact.

There was an incredible bang as the aircraft met, and the old DC-3 shuddered. Davis' grip on the wheel hardened—any more and he'd pull it right out of the mount. He was ready to react, but nothing happened for a moment. Davis had four or five heartbeats to be happy. Happy that he hadn't misjudged by a fraction and guided the cockpit straight into twenty thousand pounds of opposite-direction steel. Happy he wasn't falling to the ground in a propagating fireball. Jammer Davis thought he might damn well have done it. He looked over his shoulder for Blackstar.

He didn't see the drone. He also didn't see the outboard ten feet of his left wing.

The nose of the DC-3 began to fall, rolling uncontrollably to the left. Davis countered on the controls. Nothing happened because the aileron, at least the one on the left, was a mile behind them and free-falling to the Sahara Desert. The airplane was out of control, rolling and nearly upside down. Davis heard a scream from his right. He tuned it out. He pushed forward on the controls and found that the elevator still worked.

I still have a tail, he thought.

Davis stepped on the rudder, and the airplane stopped rolling. They were upside down, falling closer to the desert, but Davis had marginal control. He tried to roll level with the rudder, but the rate was too slow—the airplane would hit the ground before he could get right-side up and pull. There was only one thing left. Davis pushed the control wheel forward.

Everything that had been on the floor went to the ceiling—dirt and charts and a long-lost pencil. At negative one G they were flying inverted. Davis was hanging in his harness, glad he'd strapped in tight. The airplane was no longer descending, but skimming three hundred feet above the flat desert—crooked, uncoordinated flight with a broken wing and big control inputs to the tail that were all cancelling out. The old boat was hanging on a knife's edge of aerodynamic equilibrium.

Then the port engine began to sputter.

Davis checked the instruments, and saw both motors spiking and bouncing in alternating death throes. For the last thirty seconds he hadn't even been sure they were running, hadn't had time to check. He might already have been flying a glider for all he knew. But upside down, any remaining fuel had gone to the top of the tanks. Since the fuel pumps were at the bottom, starvation was a given. Nothing he could do. But they were still flying, and that was all that mattered. He just had to put the airplane down right now. Right here.

Davis looked out the front windscreen, and right away wished he hadn't. It was filling fast with a massive image that took his breath away. The giant Pyramid of Giza loomed like a mountain hanging from an upside down sky. Davis was close enough to see the massive blocks of earthen stone and the thick joints, see the pointed tip that was situated squarely in their path. He tried to roll again, but when he did the nose fell and the pyramid got bigger. He only had seconds. An engine stopped dead. He sensed drag on the left side as the dead propeller caught the airstream like a barn door catching a hurricane. Davis rolled toward the drag with rudder, and the crippled beast responded.

With the tip of the pyramid directly in front of them, Davis mashed his foot all the way to the floor hoping for a vector that would take them over it. The pointed crest seemed inches from his head as they flew by sideways, the stunted left wing pointed at the ground.

This time, no impact.

The nose began to fall and Davis looked out ahead. They were going down now. The question was where. He saw open desert to his left and with the airplane right-side up, Davis began pushing and pulling, willing the machine in that direction. A busy road skimmed underneath their windshield, close enough that he could see the wide eyes of a taxi driver. Past the road, a boy and his herd of goats were running for their lives. The airplane glided over them, and from that point there was nothing but sand.

The airplane hit hard, making contact on the belly because there hadn't been time for anything fancy like landing gear. Davis heard another scream before he was thrown violently against the straps, twisting and shaking for what seemed an eternity. The noise was incredible, a metallic crunch like two train cars crashing at speed. It kept going and going, aluminum tearing and glass shattering. The world disappeared in a cloud of dust.

His head hit something. Everything went deathly still.

CHAPTER FORTY-THREE

The prisons of Egypt are notoriously famous. Over the last generation many of the world's most renowned terrorists, including Ayman al-Zawahri, Osama Bin-Laden's right hand man, have gotten a start there. They are squalid places where beatings and torture approach the level of artistry. They also tend to overcrowding, guests of the state crammed by the dozen into cells designed for two. So, as Jammer Davis stirred on a strangely cool concrete floor in a private cell, physically battered but intact, he was not an unhappy man.

He had arrived roughly twenty-four hours ago, though it was only an estimate since the décor in his efficiency suite did not include a clock. Davis had slept practically the entire time, another tally mark for his list of challenging venues where he'd been able to get rest. With considerable effort, he sat up. His right arm and shoulder still hurt—something from the crash. He looked down and saw blood on the shoulder of his shirt, and reaching up felt a crust on the side of his head—the bandage Antonelli had so carefully wrapped was gone. To the positive, his ankle injury from last week's rugby match seemed much improved.

Davis looked around the cell and saw that nothing had changed. A ten-by-ten confine, one door with a slot at the bottom, no window, one lightbulb hanging from a wire twelve feet over his head. That was all, aside from an unhealthy accumulation of dirt and grime, and the occasional visiting rodent. Much could be realized, however, by what was not here. There was no bucket or blanket, which made Davis think that he was not registered for an extended stay. He had not been stripped naked or sprayed with water, so interrogation was likely not imminent. Indeed, there had been no human interaction whatsoever. No military interrogator with a rubber hose, no good cop-bad cop routine with the police. There hadn't even been an air accident investigator to take his statement. He *had* just crashed an airplane.

Davis remembered climbing out of the wrecked DC-3, remembered pulling Antonelli out with him. She had seemed to come through the landing—if it could be called that—with no significant injuries. But there hadn't been time to ask. No more than thirty seconds after they were clear, a squad of soldiers had come in a truck and rounded them up. They'd been separated immediately. A bag was slipped over Davis' head, and he was driven directly here. Once in the cell, they'd pulled off his hood, removed a pair of metal cuffs, and shut the door. Left him sitting on the concrete floor. So he'd slept. Slept because he was dead tired. Slept because it was a good way to not feel the pain in his shoulder and his arm and his head. Slept because it was a good way to kill time until whatever happened next happened.

Davis was sitting on the floor, ruminating on it all, when he heard a rustling noise outside his cell. The slot at the base of the door opened and someone slid a tray of food inside.

"Hey!" he shouted. "I want to see somebody from the U.S. Embassy!"

No reply. Not that he really expected one.

The food looked exactly like what it was—daily fare from an Egyptian prison kitchen. A chunk of hard bread, something glutinous in a bowl, a bottle of water. It was the best meal Davis had seen in two days, and made him realize how hungry he was. He stood up slowly, which introduced a few new aches, and retrieved the tray. He began to eat and drink, and as he did, Davis listened at the door. The only sound from outside was a whisper of distant Arabic chanting, no doubt from other cells. So he wasn't completely alone.

The bread was like a rock. He ate every bit. The gruel in the bowl was awful, but he scraped it clean with two fingers. Davis was pondering the merits of shoving the tray back through the slot when he heard voices. One—gloriously—that he recognized.

The lock rattled on the cell door, and Larry Green walked in. The door shut immediately behind him.

Green stood still for a moment studying him. He finally said, "I send you here to investigate an airplane crash, and what do you do? You crash another one."

"Good to see you too, Larry."

"Then you get thrown in prison."

Davis said nothing.

"And to top it off, you nearly annihilate one of the Seven Ancient Wonders of the World."

"Are you enjoying this?"

Green clearly was, but when he came closer his grin faded. He put a hand to the side of Davis' head. "Anybody look at that yet?"

"My private physician."

"Are you hurt anywhere else?"

"Nothing dire."

Green stood back. "Well you look like hell."

"Thanks. Now can you tell me what happened—did I take it out?"

"The Great Pyramid of Giza?" Green was smiling again.

Davis was silent again.

"You got Blackstar, Jammer. It hit a half mile south of the event. Went straight in and made a heck of a crater. CIA has some people digging it out right now."

"You said they didn't do crash work."

"In this case I think we all know the cause. It's just a matter of sweeping things up."

"So how is it all playing out?" Davis asked.

"Well, you boosted everyone's news ratings. There are pictures of your aerobatic prowess in every newspaper in the world, and the videos have gone viral. Bad news is—you won't get any credit. The Egyptian authorities are giving out another pilot's name as the pilot-in-command."

"Who?"

Green's eyes went to the stone ceiling. "Achmed somebody or other. He was another casualty of this whole fiasco."

Davis thought, *How perfect.* He said, "Is this whole plot out in the open?"

"Bits and pieces. There's some manipulation going on, but blame for the whole fiasco is getting put right where it should be. On the late Rafiq Khoury and the guy who employed him."

"General Ali?"

Green nodded. "You even had that part figured out, huh? The coup attempt?"

"Yeah."

"It's a good thing you were on top of it. If this attack had gone down as planned, we'd be in a damned fine mess right now." Green then added in a matter-of-fact tone, "Those were the president's exact words, Jammer. I saw him right before I left Andrews."

"We're still going to catch some blame. That was our drone any way you look at it."

"Yeah, we'll have a black eye, I suppose. But nothing like it could have been. Darlene Graham's people are working quietly with the Egyptians to show this for what it was—a crazy plot by a handful of crazy people. General Ali was arrested in Sudan and probably doesn't have a real bright future."

"And Khoury?" Davis asked.

"He's dead, but I think you knew that. We did find out a little more about him. Apparently the NSA tapped into a database in Sudan. It seems that eight months ago "Imam Khoury" was six years into a twenty-year stint at Kober Prison."

"He was in prison?"

"Yep. As far as we can tell, the guy was never any kind of cleric. He acquired a modest following while he was locked up, a sort of jail-house preacher. Khoury had been in and out of lockups pretty much his whole adult life. Petty stuff—thieving, smuggling, fraud. He was a con man who got offered the gig of a lifetime. General Ali decided he needed an imam to make things work, and he must have made Khoury an offer he couldn't refuse. There's a strange coincidence, though. Rafiq Khoury was actually born to an American mother."

"Maybe that's why he was chosen," Davis suggested. "That would have given pretty much everybody at FBN Aviation ties to the U.S."

"Yep. One more American to shoulder the blame. I don't know what General Ali promised Khoury, but I can't imagine he was going to get anything short of a bullet in his head in the end."

Davis nodded, and asked, "What about Regina Antonelli?"

Green eyed him. "Your copilot?"

"A darned good one too."

"The Italians have already arranged her release. She's on her way to Rome right now. I met her briefly at the airport—quite a looker. How did she end up in your right seat?"

"Long story," Davis said. "What about Schmitt and the engineer?"

"Schmitt crash landed his airplane about twenty miles south of here at a military airstrip. The Egyptians have him locked up there while everything gets sorted out—but you know Schmitt."

"You think he'll land on his feet again?"

"Probably," Green said. "The engineer's case is a little trickier. His name's Fadi Jibril, practically a kid. He went to university in the States, then came here and created this monster. The DNI's techs back in D.C. say he must be a brilliant engineer to have pulled it off. According to Schmitt, Jibril was the one who shot Khoury in the end. That might mitigate his crimes. The Egyptians have Jibril in custody, too, so they'll be the ones who figure out what to do with him."

Davis nodded. "So when can I get out of here?"

Green stepped back and knocked twice on the cell's thick steel door. It opened right away, and a half dozen men were standing outside, a mix of what could only be U.S. Embassy staff and prison officials.

"How about right now?" Green said.

Five minutes later, Davis was in the backseat of an armored Mercedes limo, the driver whisking them expertly through heavy traffic.

"You can get cleaned up and issued some fresh clothes at the embassy," Green said. "We'll be on a Gulfstream headed home in two hours."

Davis didn't reply. Home sounded good. But Norway sounded

better. Maybe he could talk Green into it. With a stop in Italy along the way to pick up another passenger. They owed him something.

He said, "Can I borrow your phone, Larry?"

Green handed over his mobile.

Davis dialed Jen's number. In the biggest surprise he'd had all week, she picked up immediately. He wanted to launch on her right there, scold her for being out of touch for a week and not returning his calls. But he just couldn't do it. Right now, he only wanted to hear her voice.

"Hey, sweetheart, it's me."

"Hi, Dad!"

"How are you?"

"Great. I'm watching this crazy thing on YouTube right now. It's been all over the news. Some guy down in Egypt almost crashed his airplane into the Pyramid of Giza. Have you seen it?"

"Uh . . . yeah. I did see it, actually."

"Isn't that insane? The guy must be the worst pilot ever!"

Jammer Davis grinned. "Yeah, sweetheart, the worst pilot ever. No doubt about it. So tell me about school—"

Author's Note

I have made every effort to keep my research for this book both timely
and accurate, however two locales are fictional. The new Khartoum
International Airport has been in the planning stages for many years,
yet remains little more than a blueprint. I have accelerated the construction for reasons of dramatic convenience. The village of al-Asmat
is also fictional, though any number of such fishing villages dot the
Red Sea coast.

Other faults and inaccuracies are unintentional, and attributable
only to me.

Acknowledgments

As always, I must recognize my coconspirators. Thanks to Bob and Patricia Gussin for their enduring support and encouragement. To Frank Troncale, David Ivester, and Kylie Fritz at Oceanview Publishing for making things happen. Susan Hayes, your ever-sharp copyediting skills save me endless embarrassment. To my agent, Susan Gleason, whose experienced eye is invaluable. And to Maryglenn McCombs, magnificent publicist and better friend. Thank you.

And of course, a heartfelt thanks to my family for their unwavering support.

CPSIA information can be obtained
at www.ICGtesting.com
Printed in the USA
BVOW08s0002240217
477018BV00001B/3/P